STORY RIVER BOOKS

Pat Conroy, Editor at Large

All the Governor's Men

∼ A MOUNTAIN BROOK NOVEL ∼

KATHERINE CLARK

Foreword by Pat Conroy

The University of South Carolina Press

© 2016 Katherine Clark

Published by the University of South Carolina Press
Columbia, South Carolina 29208

www.sc.edu/uscpress

Manufactured in the United States of America

25 24 23 22 21 20 19 18 17 16
10 9 8 7 6 5 4 3 2 1

Library of Congress Cataloging-in-Publication Data

Clark, Katherine, 1962 November 11–
All the governor's men : a mountain brook novel / Katherine Clark ;
Foreword by Pat Conroy.
pages ; cm. — (Story River Books)
ISBN 978-1-61117-628-5 (hardbound : alk. paper) —
ISBN 978-1-61117-629-2 (ebook) I. Title.
PS3603.L36485A79 2016
813'.6—dc23
2015022535

This book was printed on recycled paper with
30 percent postconsumer waste content.

FOREWORD

Katherine Clark published her first novel *The Headmaster's Darlings* to wide acclaim in 2015, and it is certain to become a classic American novel about the transformational power of great teachers. Katherine also introduced her readers to the paradisiacal charms ensconced in the site of her childhood, the dreamy hill town of Mountain Brook, Alabama, sitting as it does like a queen's jewel box above the roiled city of Birmingham in the valley below.

All the Governor's Men is the second in her series of Mountain Brook novels, published by Story River Books as the most ambitious literary project our young press has yet undertaken. Through Katherine's novels, we glimpse the entire history of Mountain Brook, and in this second novel, we peer into the political world of Alabama and the slow, tortuous death rattle of the Jim Crow South. *All the Governor's Men* tells the intimate story of one Alabama election that seems so authentic and universal it could stand as a case study in the ruinous underworld of politics everywhere. In the South, as in the rest of the world, politics is a blood sport that attracts its own special breed of gladiators and hangers-on. Katherine's novel illustrates how fools can disguise themselves as idealists, and even as heroes, until the mask of idealism falls away to reveal a grotesque—or, worse yet—an all-too-human visage beneath.

In this book, Clark does for Alabama politics what Robert Penn Warren does in *All the King's Men* for the Louisiana of Huey Long. Both novels let us know that Southern politics contain all the seeds of malice and corruption, with the music of stump speeches and good intentions played on instruments slightly out of tune. The disorder of politics is simply a magnified reflection of the egregious flaws in the family of man.

In *All the Governor's Men,* South Alabama boy Daniel Dobbs returns to his home state after graduating from Harvard, filled with a revolutionary zeal to bring Alabama into mainstream American society. He enters the political fray on the side of the gubernatorial campaign against that stalwart bastion of Old South populism, George Wallace, now wheelchair-bound after surviving an assassination attempt while running for president of the United States.

Daniel's parents were raised on farms and are newly broken in to their uncertain position on the lower rungs of the middle class. They have made only a modest advance up the social and economic ladder from their hardscrabble origins. Daniel, meanwhile, aims to ascend fully. He has chosen his girlfriend, the Harvard-educated Mountain Brook native Caroline Elmore, with exquisite care and a cunning eye fixed on the future.

But when Daniel brings his aspirations to the palatial Elmore residence in Mountain Brook, we come to know the clash of cultures and values that will plague the courtship of the small town boy and the Mountain Brook girl. No one understands better than Katherine Clark the immense power that social class still exerts in the South, in all its complexity and nuance. Her eye is unerring and her conclusions can be ruthless, but she writes with grace, subtlety, and a satirical voice that renders her set pieces hilarious.

Because I was born with the state of Alabama in my bloodstream, this novel holds particular fascination for me. My mother's family hails from Piedmont, Alabama, a backwater town at the foot of the Appalachians. It was the home place of my grandparents, and it loomed large in my upbringing as a geography to flee. It was a suffering place in my mother's haunted imagination, and it's why I identify so strongly with Daniel Dobbs's dreams of escape from his own origins.

I also got my own personal education in the glorious cesspool of Alabama politics when a producer wanted me to write a screenplay about the career of George Wallace. This script was eventually written by someone else, and starred the excellent Gary Sinise in the title role, but in the late 1980s, I traveled to Birmingham to discuss this project. I was met at the hotel by Gerald Wallace, the former governor's infamous brother. Because I have a particular fondness for scoundrels, I liked the open-faced sleaziness of Gerald the moment I met him. Our first conversation was memorable.

"Do you want to go to the dog races with me tonight, Conroy?"

"No, thanks, Gerald, but you have a good time without me," I said.

"Do you want me to send a whore up to your room?" he asked.

"No, thanks, Gerald," I said. "But thanks for thinking of me."

"You a faggot? I could send a faggot up just as easily."

"You go on to the races," I said.

"You like little boys? That could be arranged."

"Your generosity knows no bounds, Gerald," I said.

"You know that writer from Georgia? The one who wrote that book about my brother?"

"I know him well," I said. "That was a brilliant book he wrote."

"I got him a blow job every night he was here."

"Good for you. Good for him. But no thanks, Gerald. I'm fine."

"When you leave I'm going to tell everybody that I got you blow jobs every night with faggots."

"That's fine with me, Gerald," I told him. "But you and I will both know it's not true."

"Are you asexual?"

"That's it. I'm asexual. As far as you are concerned, Gerald, I am asexual."

The next morning he met me at breakfast and opened his wallet to show me a wad of five thousand dollars, all in crisp hundred-dollar bills.

"I told you to go with me to the dog races last night," he said.

"That's exactly why I didn't go with you, Gerald," I said, as he laughed.

This is the sleazy world of Alabama politics that Katherine captures with such relish as she contrasts it with the privileged enclave of Mountain Brook in all its quiet resplendence and refined serenity. Until I read her novels, Mountain Brook did not exist in my long overview of the places that define the bruised core of the Southern soul. Thanks to her, Mountain Brook has become a new territory in the many-faceted landscape of the Deep South. It is a misbegotten Camelot somehow parachuted into Alabama, where they don't talk about politics or the news of the day, but about their golf swings, their tennis strokes, new hybrids of gardenias, the status of the Crimson Tide football team, and whether the club is still serving lobster thermidor on Wednesday nights. Mountain Brook is a hideaway that has turned the absence of thought into an art form. In *All the Governor's Men,* Katherine Clark further establishes Mountain Brook as her literary domain for this ongoing series of novels. Her power as a novelist is on full display in her comic, shrewd and unflagging interrogation of the South on the cusp of reluctant but nonetheless metamorphic change.

PAT CONROY

Alabama
Summer 1982

From "George Wallace: Asking for One More Chance to Stand up for Alabama," by Powell Gaines, the New York Times, *June 7, 1982*

The George Wallace who appeared today on the campaign trail in Tuscumbia, Alabama bore little resemblance to the fiery demagogue seared into the national consciousness when he proclaimed "Segregation today, Segregation tomorrow, Segregation forever," as he stood in the schoolhouse door to block the entrance of two black students to the University of Alabama. That was in 1963, when Wallace was inaugurated for his first term as governor and sought to impede court-ordered integration of the public schools in Alabama. Much has changed in the two decades between then and now, as the 63 year-old George Wallace seeks the nomination for a fourth term as governor.

Although he still uses the slogan "Stand Up for Alabama," the Wallace of today literally cannot stand up himself, as a result of the assassination attempt during the presidential run in 1972 that left him paralyzed from the waist down and confined to a wheelchair. In his prime, Wallace used to burst onto stage as a band played "Dixie." Today he was pushed up a handicap ramp and wheeled on stage by a state trooper. Instead of whipping the crowd into a frenzy as he used to by railing about school busing, states' rights and federal intervention, he merely thanked his supporters for coming out in the heat and urged them to give him one more chance to serve the people of Alabama. His voice was soft and slurred, barely audible. The words were perfunctory and polite, with no trace of the incendiary rhetoric that made him a hero to some and a public enemy to many others around the country and the rest of the world.

After Wallace was wheeled off stage, a campaign aide made a brief appearance to tout Wallace's achievements in the many years he served as governor. He proudly noted that George Wallace has international name recognition. A governor with a worldwide reputation is best equipped to bring jobs and industry to a state devastated by the ongoing recession, he claimed. At 14.5%, Alabama's unemployment rate is second only to Michigan. As the afternoon heat grew more oppressive in this small Alabama town, known primarily as Helen Keller's birthplace, the crowd grew restless and began looking around for the candidate himself, the man they had really come to see.

Although Wallace has been an engaged candidate in the current campaign, today he appeared to be slumping in his wheelchair on the sidelines of the front row. At one point his arms seized up and clutched at his side in pain. Wallace is widely believed to require a daily regimen of a least half a dozen medications, some of them powerful, to control the crushing pain left by Arthur Bremer's bullets. The campaign has released no medical report, but insists that Wallace is fit to be governor.

For some of those who remember the heyday of the Wallace era, the Wallace of today may seem more myth than man. However, the voters who came out in stifling summer heat to shake the hand of their living legend were not troubled by the prospect of a crippled man running a heavily contested race for governor in a wheelchair.

"We all got problems," said Ruby Davis, 47, a beautician in Tuscumbia.

"The wheelchair don't bother me," said Jake Billings, 33, a local auto mechanic. "The important part of the man ain't in his legs."

Gladys Hines, 67, a retired court reporter wearing several vintage "Wallace for Governor" buttons, said she was proud of George Wallace. "Thanks to him and Bear Bryant, folks know who we are," she said. "Them two put Alabama on the map." Paul "Bear" Bryant is the beloved head coach of the Alabama Crimson Tide football team who has won six national championships and 13 SEC titles.

Although Bear Bryant will remain Alabama's football coach for at least one more season, Alabamians believed the man they have always referred to as "the Governor" had retired after his third term concluded in 1978. The city of Montgomery hosted a "George Wallace Appreciation Day" in January of 1979, when a political newcomer, Fob James, was sworn in as governor. Wallace's retirement seemed to be official; hundreds came out to pay their respects and bid farewell. It appeared to be the end of one era and the beginning of another.

But Fob James, who has been an ineffective and unpopular governor in the eyes of both Republicans and Democrats, is not seeking a second term. Meanwhile, those close to Wallace say that private life outside of politics holds no charms for him. Marshall Frady, author of the 1968 unauthorized biography *Wallace*, observed in his book that life without politics is blank and meaningless for George Wallace.

The crowd in Tuscumbia seemed for the most part happy to have their old warhorse re-enter the political arena. When asked about Wallace's controversial past, Lyle Kincaid, 53, a sales associate, said, "Segregation was wrong. Public education and public facilities ought to be open to the public. Even the blacks. That's what 'public' means. And that's the law, like it or not. But everybody makes mistakes, and people got a right to learn from their mistakes."

Wallace, a self-professed born-again Christian who faces formidable opposition in this campaign, has acknowledged making mistakes in the past. He now considers segregation a "mistake," and is actively courting votes from the black people of Alabama. . . .

~ 1 ~

Daniel Dobbs had had his doubts about the Chevette ever since that night in the Boston hotel room where he'd opened the blue box with the Cross logo containing car keys instead of the pen and pencil set he'd received at his high school graduation. He had no doubt this was the same box he'd opened four years ago. As children of Depression-era sharecroppers, his parents had learned to conserve whatever resources they managed to acquire; and while his mother did not save the wrappings from the white Wonder Bread loaves like his Mamaw still did, she would definitely keep a nice box like the one his Cross pen and pencil set had come in. According to his mother, his father had looked forward to the moment when his son would tear the wrapping paper off and struggle to control his disappointment at getting another pen and pencil set for his *college* graduation—from Harvard, no less—only to open the box and find a totally unexpected set of car keys. The surprise, the delight and the gratitude that would overtake his son's face was a sight he couldn't wait to see. "So be sure to act surprised," his mother warned him after each phone call in which they'd debated the relative merits of a used Honda Civic compared to a used Chevrolet Chevette.

Ironically, the surprise he'd experienced had been genuine, but unfortunately, it was not pleasant. When his mother had stopped raising the subject during their weekly phone calls and coyly declined to tell him which car they'd finally selected, he assumed they'd purchased the Honda. It was a newer car, with fewer miles and of course the excellent safety and reliability ratings of all Honda automobiles. It was only $250 more than the Chevette, and was a sweetheart deal offered by one of his mother's colleagues at the high school. She had taken good care of the car, kept it meticulously clean and drove it only in town: to her job at the school, to the store, on her errands. It had never even been on the highway. Since his mother appeared to be giving him a choice, he had chosen the Honda.

But folks where he came from often had only the illusion of choice, and the keys in the box were to the cream-colored Chevette. He hoped he'd concealed his dismay and betrayed no chagrin in the glance he'd exchanged with his girlfriend in the hotel room. It was hard to gauge his parents' reaction to his reaction. They were all too nervous about their ability to stage one of those Precious Moments celebrated in Disney movies and Hallmark greeting cards. And one thing they hadn't learned by growing up on farms in South Alabama was how to enjoy life or any of its moments. Too few of their own moments had been at all precious or enjoyable. So he'd tried his best to give them their hard-earned moment; Lord knows they deserved it.

"Your mother sabotaged it," his girlfriend had pointed out later. "If you'd known nothing about the gift beforehand, you would have been overjoyed to open the car keys. Strange," she had mused. "What was the point of spoiling the surprise in order to find out what car you wanted, only to turn around and get the car you didn't want?"

"I guess there are 250 points," he had said, "and they all have dollar signs in front of them." This was the kind of comeback that had worked so well for him all during college with other girls. But Caroline was a Harvard student herself, even if only a freshman. Harvard girls were way too smart for him; he was out of his league. Normally he'd stuck with the Wellesley girls, who were no less smart, but a lot more lonely for male companionship on their all-girls campus. Loneliness could blind a girl to a man's limitations.

"No," Caroline had continued doggedly, not at all amused or sidetracked by his attempt at a clever rejoinder. "If the $250 more puts the Civic out of the question, then just get the Chevette, say nothing about it, keep it a huge secret, and spring the big surprise on you the day you graduate." She shook her head. "I think your mother created a situation in which you were bound to be disappointed, so she would be spared her own disappointment in case you weren't as happy or excited or thrilled as she thought you ought to be. She'd rather prepare for disappointment—by creating it, if necessary—than hope for happiness and end up disappointed."

"I think you're overanalyzing this," he had said.

"No," she'd replied calmly. "I'm just analyzing it."

Analyze. Analyze. Analyze. It reminded him of the campus joke: How many men does it take to fuck a Harvard woman? Answer: three. One to persuade her to do the deed by discussing it beforehand to her satisfaction. Another to perform the actual deed to her satisfaction. And a third to *analyze* it afterwards to her satisfaction. Of the three men required to get the job done, he was most suited to be the first, because somehow he could always persuade people to do what he wanted them to do without even trying. His was the gift of gab. However, he really wanted to be the doer of the deed itself, and didn't see the point of discussing it afterwards. It was for these reasons he had always gravitated toward the Wellesley girls.

But unlike most other Harvard females, Caroline was also beautiful. And her relentless probing of the whole scene in the hotel room had indeed helped him understand it better, though he didn't want to admit it. He didn't think he had to either, since Caroline hadn't gotten it exactly right. Perhaps there was some truth to her explanation, but it was more likely that his poor parents wanted him to know how much they wished they could afford to get him a decent car, but they just didn't have the money. His mother had demonstrated this by involving him in the long, drawn-out debate with the predetermined outcome. His father had demonstrated this by launching immediately into a description of the Honda Civic they did not buy right after his son had opened the keys to the Chevrolet Chevette they did buy.

"But as you know, son," his father had concluded. "I always prefer to buy American, and the mechanic who checked out the car gave it a thumbs up."

His mother had chimed in: "The mechanic even thought the Chevette was the better car."

Yes it *was* the better car—for the mechanic who stood to make money repairing it. No doubt the $250 his parents had saved themselves would come out of their son's pocket within the month.

Note for the campaign trail: DO NOT CLOAK YOUR POVERTY IN VIRTUE. FLAUNT YOUR POVERTY AS A VIRTUE.

This is what he himself had done back in his dorm room with his girl-friend.

"I don't understand," she had said, "how anyone could say that a dorky-looking, piece-of-shit automobile is better simply because it's American."

"What you don't understand," he had responded fulsomely, "is that $250 is probably my mother's monthly grocery money."

This had both silenced and impressed her all at once. She had even reached out to take his hand, indicating that he might be able to get laid within the hour.

"Then why couldn't they just be proud to buy you any car at all?"

He sighed. "Why can't we just stop talking about it?" The subject of the car was already behind him. Cars were neither very interesting nor important to him; he really didn't care what vehicle he drove. At least he had one of his own now. As for his parents, they had done the best they could and it wasn't their fault that their best wasn't very good. He judged them according to how he wanted to be judged himself, by effort rather than results. Even if their results were pathetic, their effort was heroic, and that's what counted with him. One day he hoped he could redeem all their struggles by achieving the heroic deeds that were beyond their power but had been put in his reach by all their hard work.

Meanwhile, if his girlfriend wanted to talk about something, he wished it could be the Class Day speech he had delivered earlier in the day, right before Mother Teresa had given the Graduation Day address. He had worked hard for months to make this moment come out right. At the same time he was finishing his senior thesis and preparing for exams, he had labored for weeks on drafting a speech. As International Key Club president in high school, he'd never written any of his speeches, just stood up and talked. Knowing that wouldn't get him anywhere at Harvard, which abounded in people who could just stand up and talk, he had hunkered down to put his thoughts on paper and rehearsed his delivery countless times. Still, he'd never dreamed he'd be chosen. The only reason he'd tried out was to please his minister, who'd urged him to audition and then hounded him until he did so. Given his upbringing, he always found it hard to say no to a Man of God. Likewise, he found it impossible to believe that the committee would choose someone as unrepresentative of Harvard as he was to represent his Harvard class at graduation. His accent alone marked him as something less than a true citizen of the Ivy League nation that would assemble for the ceremonies. When the committee had selected two finalists, Daniel fully expected the nod to go to the other guy, who was not only several inches taller than Daniel, but every inch a Boston Brahmin. However, Harvard had been a continual source of amazement since it had first amazed him four years ago by sending him an acceptance letter.

And he thought he'd done all right with his speech, whose theme had been inspired by the senior thesis he'd written under the direction of the eminent Dr. Francis Miles. The idea for this thesis had come along and clobbered him one day as he was auditing a graduate seminar on "The Role of Religion in Southern Politics" at the Kennedy School of Government. To the students in this class, a "religious" Southern politician was little more than a charlatan, just another form of televangelist, using God and Jesus to get votes from a gullible, God-fearing public. Daniel knew in his Southern bones that it was much more complicated than that. For his research, he had chosen four members of the Alabama Legislature known for their Bible-thumping: two elder senators, one young up-and-comer, and a middle-aged woman who'd once been president of the Eagle Forum. Last summer, after his junior year, he had driven over to Montgomery to conduct interviews whenever he had free time from his job at Joab Tucker's law firm. The life stories and professions of faith he gathered from all four of these people left no doubt in his mind that religion was no cynical tool in a political arsenal, but a deeply ingrained and important part of their consciousness and character. The problem was not hypocrisy. The problem was hubris. These people sincerely believed they were God's chosen and anointed, executing God's orders, doing God's work. To dismiss this as a pose, as the students at the K-School were inclined to do, was to misunderstand the whole phenomenon and underestimate the extent of the problem. So this was his thesis.

This thesis had got him to thinking about the danger of hubris, which afflicted the souls of country folk in a downtrodden Southern state no less than it did the high and mighty. So when it came to writing his speech, he figured his classmates didn't need to be told one more time how great they all were. Instead, as these particular graduates went forth into the world to achieve great things and accomplish great deeds, they needed to be reminded to keep a humble heart. It was basically a sermon on humility. Anyway, Mother Teresa seemed to have liked it. At least, she had nodded at him as he departed the stage while she waited to be introduced. For a brief moment, he had shared the stage with a bona fide saint, who had publicly recognized him with a nod of what he wanted to believe was approval. But perhaps this was just an act of beneficence, like ministering to the starving poor. He desperately wanted his girlfriend's opinion. And he had to admit: he also wanted to hang on to this moment just a little bit longer; it didn't deserve to disappear into the ether quite so quickly. It deserved to be savored and re-lived. If he had been able to meet his roommates at the bar, that's exactly what they would all be doing right now.

"I'm just trying to understand your parents," Caroline was saying. "Why they can't be proud of what they had to give you."

Still stuck on his parents. God bless her! he thought, grinning to himself. She couldn't let go of a subject until she'd taken it completely apart and figured out every angle. His mind raced and leaped ahead, bounding from topic to topic, and like the proverbial hare, had trouble finding the finish line.

"It's hard for people who grew up in poverty to be proud of it," he explained to her. "It's only people who get rich who can afford to be proud of the poverty they came from."

He thought he might have scored a point, because she had nothing to say. He hoped he hadn't been too hard on her, and tried to lighten up.

"It's the folks who have 24 karat gold bathroom fixtures who can brag about the outhouse they had when they were kids," he told her.

Although she remained silent, it was the silence of a Harvard girl thinking long and hard and carefully formulating her reply, as if she were in tutorial with her senior tutor, or in orals defending her thesis. When that time arrived, Caroline would sail through easier than he had. He came from the gut, shot from the hip, and usually hadn't done the reading. In some mysterious way, this had proven to be a winning formula, so much so that a boy who had been born in Eight Mile, Alabama, to a Baptist preacher and a Mini-Mart cashier, was now in possession of a diploma from Harvard. It was as if the Good Lord himself had chosen Daniel Dobbs to be the one who got to cash in on the poor white struggle into which he was born. Otherwise, there was no accounting for it. "Brilliant, hard-working, and extremely personable," were the three adjectives his high school history teacher had used to describe him in the recommendation letter he had glimpsed by accident. Until then, he was under the impression that Miss Niemeyer hadn't even *liked* him. There was certainly no reason for her to do so, since he was definitely neither brilliant nor hard-working. And he wasn't even sure what "personable" meant. One of his friends joked that Miss Niemeyer must have fallen for his looks, but Daniel never thought he had any looks to speak of; as far as he could tell, he was way too short to be good looking. It could only be that the Good Lord had hoodwinked her like he had everyone else where Daniel was concerned, because there was no other way around Niemeyer. And while Daniel was grateful to the Good Lord, he wished he could feel as lucky or chosen as he evidently was. Most of the time, he just felt nervous, as if his luck could run out at any moment. For example, if not for the fact that he was delivering the Class Day speech—which he strategically let slip to one of his (female) section leaders—he might not have graduated with the rest of his class.

"I'm not saying your parents should be proud they grew up poor," Caroline was saying slowly, as if still formulating her thoughts. "That's just as bad as being proud of growing up rich."

Now she wanted to get into a philosophical discussion!

"Only that your parents should be proud they can get you any kind of car at all. They shouldn't be ashamed they couldn't get the more expensive car. And they shouldn't try to cover up the truth with flimsy subterfuges or excuses. That makes the truth seem shabby. When it could be so dignified."

"Honey," he said. "I hate to disillusion you. But there ain't nothin' dignified about where I come from." He was affecting his most pronounced South Alabama accent, and it succeeded in diverting her like it always did. Actually, his accent had always done even more than amuse her. It had seduced her. He well knew that she did not love him for himself alone. (And why would she?) It was his South Alabama origins and accent she had fallen in love with. Because she came from the other Alabama, the "Tiny Kingdom" of Mountain Brook, where folks had money and read books. Caroline, apparently, had read them all, especially the ones by Faulkner, Flannery O'Connor, and Eudora Welty. The upshot of reading all that Southern literature was: she fell in love with the first redneck she met. Of course, if they had originally met on Alabama soil, she would have discerned no romantic glamour in his background of sharecroppers and self-ordained Southern Baptist preachers. But they had met at Harvard, where by definition, no student was average or ordinary. So he was not your average, ordinary Alabama redneck. He was an Alabama redneck at Harvard. It was an irresistible combination. Fortunately for him, she had fallen hard and fast. He could only hope that whatever it was he had would not desert him and cause her to desert him in turn.

"Coverin' up the sorry truth is my mother's whole philosophy of life," he continued. "She even crocheted one of those cozy things to cover up the spare rolls of toilet paper in the bathroom. And when she takes a dump? She sprays half a can of Glade in the air. That stuff smells worse than the actual shit she flushes down the commode."

Doubled over with laughter, Caroline had said, "I think we're saying the same thing."

But he was on a roll now. "And she tells herself, my poor mama, that this air freshener is better than the box of matches on top of the toilet tank at my Mamaw and Papaw's house in the country. She thinks this room fragrance makes her civilized. But tell me this. What do *you* have in *your* bathroom at home?"

The look of bafflement on her face was pure Mountain Brook. It was also proof of what he was just fixing to tell her. However, she was suddenly so clueless, he figured he might need to lay a little more groundwork first.

"What I'm asking you, honey, is what do you have in your bathroom at home to cover up the smell?"

"What smell?" he could hear her wondering, and had to stop himself from laughing.

"I'll tell you what you have," he said. "You have nothing. Am I right?"
She acknowledged this with a grin.
"Not even a crystal bowl of potpourri?"
She shook her head.
"But I also know what you do have. I haven't even been in your house yet, but I know that it has high ceilings and a central air system that stays on all the time because no one turns up the thermostat to save—uh—energy. So there's

plenty of ventilation. But most importantly," his eyes twinkled with impending merriment. "The people in this house think their shit don't stink. It has not even occurred to the people who live in this house that their shit might stink. Am I right?"

Instead of answering, she pushed him down on the mattress and bombarded him with affection. "Try not to be too hard on my parents," he said. "At the schools my mama and daddy went to, they didn't do such a good job of nurturing the individual's self-esteem."

After he got laid and she fell asleep, he managed to sneak out to the Hong Kong, where his four roommates had a scorpion bowl and a round of high fives waiting for him.

* * *

But there was still the matter of the piece-of-shit Chevette, which had made ominous unidentifiable noises even in the flat terrain and limited confines of the small South Alabama town where he came from. Opelika, Alabama was the kind of town where the local hardware store could run an ad like the one he'd seen recently: "Does Dad need a strap-on tool for Father's Day?," and no one would notice the (entirely unintentional) double entendre. Opelika was also the kind of town where most people didn't even know what a double entendre was. The Chevette did okay in a place like that. But on the highway and now in Birmingham, which was located, after all, in the foothills of the Appalachian Mountains, the Chevette was acting like a country mule overwhelmed by the unfamiliar big city. It was as skittish as he was as it turned onto the steep, winding driveway leading up to the house where Caroline Elmore lived. "Goddamn," he thought, while the Chevette chugged slowly, as if gasping for breath. The Elmore's driveway was longer than Opelika's Main Street. He found himself falling more deeply in love than ever with the girl who lived on top of this mountain. Even in Massachusetts, the mystique of the Mountain Brook girl had been powerful enough to make him jettison his well-established personal life—namely, Eleanor—for a freshman student he barely knew. But now that he was actually *in* Mountain Brook, the soul-stirring, heart-stopping appeal of the Mountain Brook girl was even more overpowering. As he caught his first glimpse through the trees of the large white house with its elegant white columns, it was hard to keep in mind that he was coming here as a suitor deemed to have as much to offer as he stood to gain. He struggled to suppress feelings of inferiority and even outright fraudulence. How could he ever consider himself equal to, or worthy of, any girl from Mountain Brook, let alone one like Caroline Elmore? This girl was one in a million, whereas his kind were a dime a dozen. On the other hand, he had known all his life that despite his lack of brains, looks or any real talents, he was somehow destined for greatness anyway. For some mysterious reason, the Lord had chosen him for a special task, which was why Harvard had chosen him and then this girl had chosen him. It was all part of some inscrutable plan that had not yet been fully revealed. Otherwise, he would probably still be bagging groceries at the Winn-Dixie in Opelika.

His heart began to pound slightly at the thought of his appointed mission. As badly as he wanted to excel, he mainly hoped he wouldn't screw up. But the very grandeur of his surroundings was making him nervous. It wasn't so much a driveway or front lawn as it was a narrow winding path up a thickly wooded mountain. Halfway up, the only evidence of human habitation he could now see was the palatial residence looming before him with the serene assurance of being the only place for miles around, although it was in the middle of a neighborhood full of equally grand, equally imposing Southern-style mansions. On his front yard in Opelika, he could look to his left and then to his right and see every house on the block. Here there was no sense that anyone else even existed. It was hard to believe that he was supposed to exist, and impossible to believe that he was supposed to be here even if he had the temerity to exist. And yet he knew it was his destiny. This girl from Mountain Brook, her white-columned house, and her tree-studded front yard were both evidence of it and part of it.

The Chevette, however, was not. The black maids in Mountain Brook drove better cars. He knew this for a fact because before he'd found the Elmore's driveway, he had spotted several black women coming out of other driveways, presumably in their own cars since it was 4:15 on Saturday afternoon. As he reached the top of the driveway at last, a man stooped over in labor with a shovel straightened up, turned around, and doffed a blue denim engineer's cap in greeting. "Holy shit!" he thought. "They've even got a white yardman." He parked his car next to a nice Buick that he thought probably belonged to the maid, and tried not to start sweating like a field hand.

* * *

The guest room where he'd been invited to stay for the next two nights turned out to be a guest *house* adjoining the second garage at the edge of the spacious parking pad at the top of the driveway. The rear wall of his quarters, comprised mainly of windows, looked out on the sloping woods at the back of the Elmore's property. A side window looked out on a large formal rose garden with four separate plots, containing—he guessed—about a dozen bushes each. Forty-eight rose bushes! So this was what it meant to be on one of those "estate-sized" lots in Mountain Brook. Three acres, Caroline had supposed when he asked her. "You've got to be joking," he'd said. Shrugging, she'd admitted that she didn't really know and was only repeating the figure she thought she'd overheard her father mention one night. Now he could see for himself that three acres it probably was. And one of those acres was entirely taken up by roses. They were being tended at the moment by a second yard-man, this one black. Yes, indeed, Daniel said to himself: You are in Mountain Brook. There were many people from his past he wished could see him now. Especially because he had to wonder how long he would last here before he was discredited as an imposter whose Ivy League degree was just a consolation prize for being born of poor white parents. Daniel had no illusions about either his acceptance to Harvard or his graduation from it: He had been a mission of mercy for Harvard's bleeding heart.

After Caroline had greeted him in a way that left nothing, for the moment, to be desired, she led him out of the guest house and introduced him to the white yardman, who turned out to be her father. As if this weren't confounding enough, Perry Elmore wanted to show him the vegetable garden. Daniel had imagined being offered a drink upon his arrival, being shown into an impressive but comfortable room in their elegant home, and then given a chance to let his soul—or at least his silver tongue—expand in an attempt to prove himself worthy of this man's daughter. Instead he was led in the hot June sun to admire a patch of vegetables that wasn't even half the size of the garden at his grandparents' farm in the country, where everyone grew vegetables as a matter of course and no one would have dreamed they were a spectacle worth gazing at in punishing summer heat. Did Perry Elmore believe that because Daniel's parents had both grown up on farms, that their son—who was now an official graduate of Harvard—would be fascinated by tomatoes and cucumbers? Was Daniel being insulted or put in his place?

On the whole, he thought not. Mr. Elmore seemed like a mother obsessed with her children—positively infatuated with the okra and squash he had managed to produce. From the way he carried on, you'd think he had personally carried each and every vegetable to term and was now surveying his progeny with a parent's hard-earned pride. Daniel did what he could to show enthusiasm for the vine-ripe tomatoes, but he came from folks who raised crops for a living, not as a fun little weekend hobby. While Perry Elmore's agricultural aspirations were endearing and even commendable, Daniel did not want okra to be his point of connection with a man who was one of the most highly regarded attorneys in Birmingham.

Unlike his parents, Daniel was no son of the soil, and he wanted his chance to impress not the amateur agrarian in grimy blue jeans and a sweat-soaked tee shirt, but the man who would don an expensive suit and drive an expensive car downtown to a fancy law office on Monday morning. As it was, Daniel couldn't even look the other man properly in the eye, because his face was shaded by the brim of his cap. Mr. Elmore was friendly enough, seemed to like Daniel just fine as he stood dripping sweat and explaining the various rows in his garden. But Daniel wanted to be respected. He figured it was better to be respected than liked by Perry Elmore. Mr. Elmore struck him as a man who could only like those inferiors he didn't have to respect, could only respect those superiors he wasn't asked to like, and would never acknowledge there could be such a thing as an equal. This made Daniel an inferior until he could establish himself in his future father-in-law's eyes as a young man doing vitally important work. He was already savoring the moment it would dawn on Mr. Elmore that this twenty-one year-old young man was in fact doing more important work than he was as a high-priced defense attorney. Because this young man was working for the candidate who was finally going to beat George Wallace and turn the state of Alabama around.

But if he wanted to impress all this on the older man, he couldn't keep standing outside in the heat and perspiring like a field hand. He needed to be invited into the main house, ushered into a cool, comfortable room, offered a bourbon or at least a beer, and sit talking gentleman to gentleman. It would be uphill at first, because Perry Elmore was a Republican, which meant that he would despise the teachers' union representing Daniel's parents, and the farmers' subsidies which his grandfather depended on. But Daniel knew he could win this man over if given the opportunity. And he really wanted that bourbon, or at least the beer.

"Well, I know Caroline's mother is anxious to meet you," said Mr. Elmore, removing his cap and wiping his brow. Muttering a curse, he looked right through the two young people in front of him and darted toward a tomato vine that had toppled its frame and crashed to earth. It appeared his vegetables were everything; his guest—*his future son-in-law*—nothing.

Daniel was not going to get his chance. Perry Elmore was not even going to give him a chance to show them who he was. The lord and master was not even going to grant audience to the peon. Daniel stood rooted to his spot in consternation. Meanwhile, Caroline was tugging him toward the house. But instead of taking him around to the front door, she led him through a back door straight into the kitchen, where the effusiveness of the mother's greeting instantly eclipsed the inadequacy of the father's.

"What took y'all so long?" she cried out in the wail of a young girl unable to contain impatience.

To Daniel's delight, she embraced him, quite literally as well as warmly, and at such length he could see Caroline scowling out of the corner of his eye. It was an odd, topsy-turvy moment, in which the mother behaved like a teenage girlfriend while her daughter was the mature elder frowning in disapproval at the inappropriate conduct of youngsters. Of course the two of them didn't get along! Caroline had spent hours trying to explain what he grasped now in a flash. The daughter had been born older than any age the mother would ever reach. And while the mother was a quintessential Southern girl, the daughter had spent most of her life kicking and screaming at the world she came into.

"Was everything all right out there?" Mrs. Elmore was asking him. "We've had such trouble getting that rod to stay up in the closet! It falls down as soon as you get your clothes hung! And the chest of drawers needs to be replaced. Only one of those drawers works properly. I was about to come out and see if you needed any help."

Bless her heart! he chuckled to himself. It never occurred to her that instead of putting up his clothes, he had been busy taking off her daughter's clothes and giving their relationship a proper Southern consummation on the Mountain Brook soil she sprang from, mediated by the luxurious big bed in the guest house. The mother was obviously one of those Southern women who had somehow remained a virgin despite years of marriage and numerous children. Sex had utterly failed to penetrate her personality. Her mind was still innocent and her imagination was chaste, like that of the young girl she sounded like when she spoke and acted like when she hugged him. She had all the enthusiasm and energy of a young girl, too, even if she no longer resembled one because her figure had plumped and her hair was teased at the beauty parlor. He had met many Southern ladies like that, who were really little more than overgrown girls, with the naïveté and sweet charm of youth perfectly intact. However, he had thought this was a small-town breed, and feared that Mrs. Elmore would be a much more sophisticated and complicated creature, full of Mountain Brook hauteur, reserve, and disdain for anything not of Mountain Brook, especially a runt like himself. But she was a hugger, someone who reached out quickly with open arms and a ready smile. He was a hugger too. And the only consummation she dreamed of for her daughter—marriage and a big Mountain Brook wedding—was the same one he wanted. They formed an instant bond.

There was a ten year-old sister, too, who crept silently into the kitchen and stood just as quietly in a corner of the room, staring at him with wide-eyed admiration as he dug into the bowl of peach cobbler her mother had placed in front of him. He was The Boyfriend. Apparently Caroline had never had one of these in high school. No one needed to tell him why, either. When he'd first met her, at the beginning of her freshman year at one of the Alabama brunches, she had been just the usual Harvard square: overweight, with eyeglasses that were too big and hair that was too short. He'd exchanged few words with her beyond the polite introductions and pleasantries he presided over at the beginning of the meal. Since she had not come to many more of the Alabama brunches he hosted once a month on Sundays in the Eliot House private dining room, she had slipped from his mind. By the middle of spring semester, he had so completely forgotten about her and she was so transformed that he failed utterly to recognize her. She was the one who greeted him as they stood in line together at the Coop in late March.

"You don't remember me, do you?" she had smiled on his confusion.

He did not. Not at all. How could this happen? He never forgot a face. It was perhaps his one and only talent. He prided himself on this ability, and he depended upon it too. His failure to recall her troubled him more even than the grade he'd just received on his soc/sci midterm. To forget someone was to deny the significance of their existence. It was the ultimate offense. The only thing worse than doing this to someone else was having it done to you. Especially because it was so easy to avoid. If you talked to anyone long enough, you could always find something interesting about them. Luckily he always enjoyed talking to people long enough. And this girl was beautiful. She had a face and figure that no man would ever forget. Yet apparently, he had.

"I came to one of your Alabama brunches," she was saying. "I'm Caroline Elmore. A freshman. From Birmingham."

He was not sure he'd been able to conceal his astonishment. This could not be the same girl he had met in the fall, a mere six months ago. There was no way this was the same girl. That girl had been an awkward, heavyset wallflower, with a dyke's haircut and a librarian's glasses. This girl was a beauty. A slim-waisted, full-breasted, blonde-haired, blue-eyed beauty. A Southern belle. It had to be the only time in the history of Harvard that a girl had gone in ugly and come out beautiful. Usually it was the other way around. The pretty ones got ugly and the ugly ones just got uglier. And the Southern ones became a lot less Southern. But somehow, Harvard had taken a little bookworm from Birmingham and turned her into a Southern belle. He couldn't believe it.

It was miraculous, it was mind-blowing, and above all, he knew: it was for him. Somehow the universe always presented him with what he needed at the exact moment he needed it. He was born knowing he had won some kind of cosmic lottery and was marked out for a special fate, and these gifts of the universe were both a sign of his favor as well as the means through which he was to achieve his destiny.

As his senior year was winding down, he had found himself in an unaccustomed fog. Every law school to which he'd applied had turned him down, except the University of Alabama. But Eleanor, his girlfriend at the time, didn't want him to go back to Alabama, and she certainly didn't want to go there herself. Although he had always assumed he would return to his home state, he did not want to go to law school. He just didn't know what else to do with himself. To Eleanor, his rejections from law school were a sign that he should do what she and her parents had long wanted and expected him to do. Marry Eleanor, move to Greenwich, and join her father's venture capital firm, which years ago had put up some of the original venture capital for UPS. Although Daniel knew nothing of what her father actually did on a day-to-day basis and wasn't entirely sure what venture capital was, he had been assured that he would be a welcomed addition to the family firm. Apparently his marriage to the founding partner's daughter would be all the qualification he needed, and the Harvard degree would pass as a credential.

It was in some ways a tempting vision of his future. But he wasn't sure it was the right one. Money had never meant that much to him, and making money had never appealed to him as a worthy way to spend his limited time on earth. More importantly, he had always assumed that his fate was bound up with his native state. Not for nothing did they call him "The Governor." And not for nothing had the Good Lord enabled Daniel Dobbs to rise in the world. Daniel knew there was no way he had gone as far as he had in life on his own meager merits—assuming he had any at all—and there was even less chance that the higher power which had made his advancement possible had done so simply in order to give one insignificant individual a comfortable life of leisure. No, Daniel knew he had been catapulted so far beyond the realm of the society he came from so that he could then be in the best position to serve this society and help others rise in the world the way he had been able to. Daniel was merely an instrument of the Good Lord's plan for progress. This conviction was the very lifeblood that flowed through his veins. Others called it "ambition"; he was always described as "an ambitious young man." Somehow it was just written all over him. So be it. He wasn't ashamed of it and saw no reason to make a secret of it either, though he never really talked about it. But to accomplish this ambition, he needed to go back to Alabama. Marry an Alabama girl, not a Yankee woman with eyes shaped like two big tears dropping down the sides of her heavily freckled face. Somehow, the downward slant at the corners of Eleanor's eyes brought her whole face down with it, so that not just her eyes, but the corners of her mouth and the balls of her cheeks seemed to sag down as well. It was a most unfortunate countenance, which conveyed an impression of either deep unhappiness or profound displeasure. And after twenty years of wearing this face, that had become Eleanor's default disposition. But the current momentum of his life was pulling him in the direction of a life with Eleanor in Greenwich. And anyway, he had never met an Alabama girl he actually wanted to marry. Above all, his political aspirations were only intangible dreams, whereas Eleanor and her family's money were quite real and substantial. Two of his college roommates were from wealthy, prominent New England families. One was even a DuPont, and the other was a Thayer. He still didn't know exactly what a Thayer was, but there was a freshman dorm with that name at Harvard. At any rate, it wasn't hard to imagine a life of ease and pleasure as a respected rich person who was part of the highest social circles in New England.

And then, that day in the Coop, he had run into an Alabama girl he could have married then and there. He knew instantly that this girl was intended for him. Why else had the universe disguised her as an ugly duckling up until this very moment? Why else had the world camouflaged her beauty and kept it hidden from view so no other man could seize it before he was ready to receive the delivery of the beautiful swan into his own hands? His future now lay revealed before him, and he knew what he needed to do.

At the moment, this meant consuming peach cobbler in the Elmore's kitchen. Mrs. Elmore hovered nearby, ready to dispense more of the cobbler that had been made, she said, especially for him. Caroline stood with her back leaning against the stove, absently popping one just-fried piece of home-grown okra after another into her mouth from the grease-stained paper towels on the counter where the maid Pearl had just placed them. The little sister Laura remained silently staring at him from her corner of the kitchen. In fact, all eyes seemed to be on him while he ate.

These Mountain Brook women were no different from his female relatives in the country. It must be a Southern thing, he thought, universal to all Southern women regardless of their social class. Even rich and well educated Southern women liked to watch a man eat, make sure he enjoyed his food and got his fill. As a result, he ate a lot more than he really wanted to, and asked for a second helping although he could barely finish the first. It was the least he could do; after the upsetting encounter with the father, he had not expected it to be this easy with the mother. He had hoped that at least she would give him a chance to prove that a penniless nobody from a small town was worthy of her daughter. But he'd been instantly accepted and plied with home-made peach cobbler and iced tea. He knew better than to think it had anything to do with him personally. A lot of it was Harvard, which went a long way toward cancelling out Opelika. Another part of it was simply being a male coming to call on a girl whose mother had written her off as an old maid the day she decided to go "up North." He had thought Caroline must have been either exaggerating or joking when she told him that. But obviously not, he realized now. He had forgotten how hard life could be on a Southern girl who wasn't either pretty or "sweet," as in "She's so sweet," meaning she had the face of a road-killed raccoon, but made up for it by doing whatever she was asked or told to do. Although she was beautiful now, Caroline had not been pretty for most of her life, and there was nothing "sweet" about going to Harvard. Harvard students had many fine and wonderful qualities, but being sweet was usually not one of them.

But this wasn't just a Southern thing, either, he mused. It hadn't been too different with Eleanor, whose parents had worried about her because she had a bad case of the uglies that wasn't going away. Super-rich and sophisticated as they were, they had welcomed him with open arms into their Greenwich mansion and their Cape Cod summer house without one raised eyebrow at his Alabama origins or accent. Again it was that winning combination of the Harvard status coupled with the male gender. He was a Harvard man. He had entrée wherever he wanted to go. He could only thank the Good Lord that life wasn't fair; otherwise, he'd never have wound up on top, especially considering where he came from.

Gazing out the kitchen window at the four plots of rose bushes, he realized he had gained entrée to the very place he'd always wanted to be. It wasn't Greenwich, Connecticut or any place in New England, either. It was this house that looked like Tara, with a maid and a yardman and forty-eight rose bushes out back making roses in the hot summer sun.

Caroline's brothers were another matter. They had greeted him politely but perfunctorily as they diverted their gaze for the necessary moment from the Braves game they were watching in the room called the library, because it held rows and rows of books along with a huge television set. Although this room adjoined the kitchen where he sat eating his cobbler, the brothers showed no curiosity or even awareness of his continued presence in their home. Rather, they remained sprawled on the sofas in comfortable indolence, laughing and shouting in amused outrage as the Braves headed for another monumental defeat with one signature blunder after another. He himself had never known such careless, carefree laziness. When he was in high school like they were now, he was always on the go, even in summer, without one truly free moment. If it wasn't his duties as International Key Club President, it was his part-time job, his studies, his track meets, or his girlfriend. He'd never been without something he urgently needed to do every waking moment. Either it had changed his metabolism for life, or had been his metabolism since birth. Now he had to be on the go every minute. At this very moment he was working on the chore of consuming a second helping of peach cobbler. It would be constitutionally impossible for him to spend an entire Saturday afternoon on the couch watching the Braves lose yet another game. These boys were definitely products of a leisure class he didn't belong to or fully understand. It wasn't that he really wanted to join it either, because he distrusted and even disliked leisure. But he enjoyed proximity and acceptance to the leisure class, and these boys' indifference to him was troubling. He had work to do there.

Not to mention with the father, who rapped on the kitchen door and asked for a glass of iced tea to be brought out to the hammock. He didn't so much as stick his head in the house to see how Daniel was getting along, as if he'd completely forgotten his existence; or else Daniel was of so little consequence he could be treated as nonexistent. The little sister abandoned her corner at last, and bustled importantly about to comply with her dad's request.

"Don't forget the mint," said her mother, as Laura headed out the door.

He could see her through the window as she bent down to pick a sprig of mint from a large pot by the steps. For the life of him, he couldn't fathom Mr. Elmore's behavior. When his parents had guests or visitors, it was treated as an important occasion and planned for carefully in advance. Guests rang the doorbell and were greeted at the front door. They were entertained in the living room, where all members of the household were expected to be present, sitting respectfully as in church, with straight-backed posture, paying close attention to the conversation. At a given moment, his mother and sister might excuse themselves in order to bring in some home-made treat served on the best china. Here in this Mountain Brook household, he had expected even more formality, not less, than he was used to at home. It wasn't that he really liked formality, because he didn't, and certainly wasn't a formal person himself, but he wasn't sure what it meant that he was being received in the kitchen by the women of the family while all the males of the house ignored him. Truly, he'd expected better manners from those at the pinnacle of society. At the same time, he knew that those at the top had no need to be polite to the likes of him. Wiping his mouth, he told Mrs. Elmore that was the best peach cobbler he'd ever had in his life, only please not to tell his mother or his grandmother he said so, if she ever met them.

"I wish y'all were staying for dinner!" she exclaimed by way of reply. "Do you have to go out? Pearl fixed something special, in case you changed your mind."

She placed his empty dish in the sink, and turned back around to plead with her eyes for him to stay, as if he were *her* suitor, and she was the girl he needed to please. Her look of longing was as unabashed as it was abject. It flattered him silly, and he found himself wondering how old she would be. Calculating quickly, he put Mrs. Elmore at about thirty-six or seven; thirty-eight at the most. Not to put too fine a point on it, but he'd slept with women older than that. In other words, he was not too young, and she was not too old, for sex to be a possibility. And the mere possibility of sex was always an exciting thing; perhaps the most exciting thing in the world, more than even the sex itself. This was the problem with relationships: the possibility of sex with someone new was always more thrilling than the inevitability of sex with someone you'd known for awhile. It wasn't that he would ever want to sleep with Mrs. Elmore, and of course this idea would never occur to her virginal Southern imagination *as an idea.* But he could feel the pull that drew one body toward another. He could always feel the pull, and he could never fail to respond. It didn't need to be sex all the time, either, although this was perhaps the most rewarding response. Often it was just a smile, a touch, simple human warmth or a kind word that people needed. It was all so easy to give, because he loved doing it and got back the same in return, with interest. But what Mrs. Elmore needed was company for dinner, poor lady. Maybe the Mr. didn't treat her any better than he'd treated Daniel.

He exchanged glances with Caroline, who had remained standing by the stove and continued to eat the fried okra. Half of what had initially been cooked was now gone. In reply to his inquiring glance, she gave him a shrug which said, "I tried to tell you."

So she had. "The first night you're here?" she had said.

At the time of that phone conversation, he had naïvely assumed that the best way to make the biggest impression on her family was to pop in just long enough to scoop her up and whisk her away to meet the future governor of the state of Alabama. Not only did Daniel Dobbs have places to go and people to meet, these people—or this person—happened to be the future governor of Alabama. And this future governor of Alabama happened to be Daniel's employer. What better way to impress all this—as well as himself—upon his future in-laws than by dashing off for the appointment with his destiny, their daughter in tow? It would be like a metaphor: she had hitched her wagon to a rising star who was already going somewhere the minute they first met him. How lucky she was, they would think, to be with a man like him.

Fool! he castigated himself. You don't just breeze into a prominent Mountain Brook household in your rattletrap Chevette and treat it like your motel, dashing off to a more important appointment with more important people. That did not impress people. Or even worse, that only impressed people with your rudeness. You had to pay your respects first and foremost to your hosts. It was an egregious error, one he would not make again. Now he understood that it was dinner, probably preceded by a cocktail hour, which would have been his official and formal family welcome, staged, no doubt, in that large, stately dining room with its salmon pink walls. It was the kind of color only an expensive Mountain Brook decorator would choose for a big Mountain Brook house. No real person would ever even think of that color for dining room walls. He'd like to see his mother's face if she ever caught a glimpse of that room. And he really would have liked to eat dinner in that room with pink walls. It was his own fault: he had done his own self out of his chance at that experience. It wasn't Mr. Elmore but Daniel who had shown no manners by barging in just long enough to take himself and the daughter immediately off somewhere else. Had he been slighted in return? Was he being written off as a hopeless country boy who wasn't worth bothering about? Was that why the father was in the hammock, the boys were in the den (or library), and he was in the kitchen?

Sensing his hesitation, Mrs. Elmore pressed further. "It's Pearl's fried chicken," she said. "Doesn't get any better than that. Not even from Brodie's."

He didn't know who or what Brodie's was, but he did know he was being given a second chance to undo his faux pas and eat dinner in a room with pink walls. Again he looked for help from Caroline, who was still eating pieces of fried okra one at a time. This was *her* chance to help him out and at the same time help him impress her family with who he was and what he was doing.

"Aaron Osgood!" he pleaded in his mind, hoping this plea would reach her by some telepathic process. "The Alabama attorney general! The man running against Wallace! My employer! The future governor!"

But his appeal didn't make it through. Fried okra was all she was taking in at the moment. He couldn't help frowning. If she didn't watch out, she'd put back on those thirty pounds she'd lost from the stress of her freshman year. While she looked like a beauty, with her Southern suntan in a pale blue sundress, and her blonde hair still growing out in the most delicate wisps and tendrils down her long, elegant neck, she was eating like a fat woman.

"There won't be any of that left come dinner time," he told her, irritation creeping along the edges of his voice.

"We're not going to be here for dinner," she said. "So I'm getting my fair share now. It's best just out of the skillet anyway."

So that was the verdict: they weren't going to be there for dinner. Out of the corner of his eye, he could see the crestfallen look that had descended on Mrs. Elmore's face. Caroline had a way of flatly stating what was what that put an end to all debate and discussion and killed the illusion of multiple possibilities that many people, himself included, like to juggle in their minds until the very last possible moment. He would have been happy—and he could have kept Mrs. Elmore happier for longer—if they could have entertained the idea that they might indeed stay for dinner, up until the minute they needed to leave the house. Until Caroline spoke, he had been on the verge of saying he was going to make a phone call, to see if he could re-schedule the dinner engagement he had made for tonight. If he had actually placed the call, this would have given him a number of options, according to what came back at him from the other end of the line. He could simply have felt out the situation, asked point blank for a different time to meet, stated his wishes or sheepishly told the truth, depending on which tactic he thought was most likely to get him what he wanted without alienating anyone. The trouble was, he wanted it all, everything at once, and he didn't want to alienate anyone ever.

Caroline was different. Although she had initially objected to his plan for the evening, once she had agreed to it, she would stick with her decision and not re-visit it or second-guess it. That's the way she was. She was decisive and unwavering, and there was a lot to be said for that. However, she didn't know what it was like to try to make everybody happy all at once. One year he'd eaten three different turkey dinners in a six-hour time span on Christmas day. What's more, he had enjoyed each and every one of those three turkey dinners. It wasn't the food, although he had the metabolism of a hummingbird and could always consume whatever was placed in front of him. What had made that Christmas so special was the chance to spend it with three different sets of people, instead of being stuck with the same group all day. Life was a lot more rewarding, if somewhat more complicated, when you couldn't say no.

Fortunately, he hadn't been the one to say no to Mrs. Elmore. Her daughter had. He gave the mother a look of commiseration, as if it were all Caroline's doing, none of his own.

"We'll be here tomorrow for sure," he assured Mrs. Elmore.

But instead of brightening, her countenance appeared stricken, and she looked over at her daughter in alarm and confusion. What had he said now? How had he put his foot in it this time?

"Tomorrow's Sunday," Caroline reminded him, her mouth full of fried okra.

The problem with Sunday wasn't immediately clear to him. After all, that was the day his parents had their biggest dinner of the week.

"Pearl won't be here," Caroline explained.

The relevance of this wasn't immediately clear to him either. What did the maid have to do with anything? When he glanced back at Mrs. Elmore, her face offered no clue. Indeed, she looked like she'd just been slapped, as if what her daughter said had been a deliberate attempt to expose and humiliate her in some way.

"We'll be going to the club," Caroline added.

Only then it dawned on him that of course Mrs. Elmore—unlike his mother and the mothers of everyone he knew—was useless in the kitchen and did not cook. Obviously she did not want this astonishing fact of her Mountain Brook life to be thrust so unequivocally upon him, especially after they had both collaborated in the illusion that it was she who had made the peach cobbler she had just served him. But all was not lost, he reflected, if they were planning to take him to the Birmingham Country Club.

~ 2 ~

Half an hour later, when he and Caroline were headed downtown, he was still unsure of both the Chevette and the way he had mishandled his own introduction into her family. He made the additional mistake of trying to defend himself out loud, to her, rather than silently, to himself. Caroline only looked like a Southern girl. But she was more Harvard than Southern, more inclined to be analytical and critical instead of soothing and comforting. Normally her unique combination of Southern beauty and Ivy League brains made him think he was the luckiest man alive. And most of the time, he appreciated her brains even more than her beauty. But sometimes, he just needed a woman to tell him that everything was okay.

"The whole reason I'm here is to see Aaron Osgood," he reminded her.

"Thanks."

"You know what I mean," he said irritably, unable to suppress his agitation. "I'm on the payroll starting Monday. And this man is not just my employer; this isn't just any job. This man is trying to beat George Wallace, and he's hired me to help him do it. If he wants to meet with me on Saturday in Birmingham before I start work in Montgomery, then I have to meet with him on Saturday."

Caroline said nothing as she gazed out the window.

"Well?" he demanded.

"Well what?" she said, looking over at him.

She knew what he wanted, but she was going to make him beg for it.

"Do you think your mother understands that?"

"My mother has never understood that some people have to work for a living," she said. "Including her own husband."

Spoken like a true daughter of Mountain Brook. He sighed.

"You could have come on Friday," she added.

"Friday?"

"Yes. If you had to meet someone on Saturday, you should have come on Friday to meet my parents first."

"Someone," she had said, with absolutely no acknowledgement that this "someone" he had to meet could—probably would—and certainly should—be the next governor of Alabama. The governor that Alabama had been waiting for, the savior who would rescue the state from the highway to hell and put it on the road to redemption. Still, she had a point. But he was so irritated at her for making it and so mad at himself for his stupid mistakes that he continued to argue.

"I had things to do to get ready for my job." This was mostly true; however, he could have come on Friday if he'd only known. And he should have known.

"Look," he said, appealing to her mercy. "I'm just a stupid redneck who doesn't know any better. People where I come from don't think of scheduling leisure time on a week day. Leisure is whatever's left over after we work our asses off all week."

"If you plan on being a politician," she said, "you better learn how to schedule time so you can be polite to people. Being polite is a form of work too, you know. Hard work. You'll find that out soon enough."

She was right, of course; she always was. It never paid to forget that she was always right and that he really was a stupid redneck. Caroline was just trying to teach him what he needed to know, as she had during the phone call when they'd discussed his visit. He should have listened and followed her suggestions. Instead, he had been deluded by visions of the grandeur he could achieve by sweeping her off to meet the future governor of the state while her family waved good-bye with looks of awe and admiration on their faces.

The reality had been quite different from his fantasy, as reality usually was in his humble experience. The very house itself with its long tall columns at the top of the hill had shown a supreme indifference to the existence of both himself and his little Chevette too. And the gubernatorial race which he had assumed would be the one and only topic on everyone's mind might as well not be taking place. The name of Aaron Osgood had never even been mentioned. No one had shown the slightest awareness, and certainly no interest, that a historic campaign was taking place that could alter the fate of their state forever. But for him there could be no bigger drama, especially since he was going to play a role in it. On the one hand, there was the heavily-medicated, wheelchair-bound Wallace who had once proclaimed that he would never be out-niggered again. On the other, there was a progressive, forward-looking young man who had recently been named one of the top five attorneys general

29

in the nation. This was history in the making. This was their future at stake. This was a chance for Alabama to break with its past, turn away from evil, renounce its sins, and be born again.

At the very least, this was exciting. When he was still up in Cambridge, before his graduation, he and his thesis advisor, Dr. Francis Miles, had spent many hours, some of them in a bar, discussing the work he would be doing in the campaign against Wallace. Fists had pounded the table, beer had sloshed out of pitchers and frosty mugs had been raised to the prospect that Daniel would be a part of helping to save the world, or at least, a small portion of it named Alabama. But in Alabama itself, the subject didn't even seem to enter into anybody's mind. It was possible, he supposed, that people in Mountain Brook could literally afford not to care who their next governor would be: It was all the same to them, because whoever it was would not be able to change their lives in any significant way. They had enough money to buffer themselves from most vicissitudes of life and live their lives exactly as they wanted regardless of whatever buffoon took charge of Goat Hill, as the Capitol was called. In fact, it suddenly occurred to him, these rich folks probably preferred to have a dunce in the governor's office. That way, nothing would ever get done, nothing would ever happen, and nothing would ever change. The good life they already had would remain theirs.

But he had to admit, after spending a week in Opelika: People there weren't interested in the election either, with the single exception of his neighbor across the street, who was a Harvard Law School graduate as well as an Opelika native and small-town lawyer with the soul of an Atticus Finch. He was the one person in town who'd shown a keen interest in the campaign. He also knew what a double entendre was. Except for Joab Tucker, though, no one had shown the slightest curiosity about the race beyond the polite formality of inquiring when he was to start his work for the campaign.

It was easy to come up with reasons why. It was summer. It was hot. People were on vacation. And unfortunately, the primary had been scheduled for the Tuesday after Labor Day. Labor Day meant football season; that's what people were concerned about. Would Bear Bryant announce his retirement? How would his final season turn out? Who would be Alabama's new head football coach? These were the most pressing issues of the day. The topic of Alabama's next governor was of little interest. A thousand miles away, in Massachusetts, you could find people who were curious and concerned about George Wallace's fifth bid to become governor of Alabama. But Daniel had not found many of these people in the state of Alabama itself. It was this kind of apathy, if he remembered correctly from a European history class, that had allowed

Adolf Hitler to gain power in Germany. Between their troubles on the one hand and whatever distractions they could find on the other hand, the general population was too self-absorbed to notice or care that a monster had seized control. Here was the same apathy, and the same monster; Wallace might be a "little Hitler," but that was bad enough, and no one in Alabama seemed to mind.

In the four years he'd been away from home, he'd forgotten a fundamental truth about it: It was much easier to be a Southerner in the Northeast than it was to be a Southerner in the South. And the South itself was much more compelling when you were outside of it rather than in it. On the outside, you could always find an eager audience for whom Southern culture was a spectator sport which provided a satisfying outlet for a full range of emotions: anger, outrage, disbelief, horror, fear, disgust, and righteous indignation. Even sympathetic outsiders were always happy to peer closely at the South and examine it under the microscope as a fascinating bacterium which flourished in the warmer climate below the Mason-Dixon line and far below any place they would ever consider making their own home. They welcomed him as someone who had survived infection from the plague zone and was surprisingly free of contamination himself. He was something of hero to them, and he had enjoyed their admiration and the fascination with which they regarded the primitive territory he had miraculously escaped. George Wallace's latest bid to reclaim the governor's mansion of Alabama was a striking new mutation of an already bizarre bacterium that had them gathering around the specimen slide and gawking openmouthed in astonishment. Because of his impending involvement, it was almost as if he had discovered the latest development and presented it to them. And then he was twice a hero: once for making his initial escape, and then for volunteering to go back to contain and perhaps stop the spread of new damage.

But back home, he was no kind of hero. He was just one of them. And very few of them were given to the intense self-scrutiny with which they were scrutinized by others. The Wallace campaign did not alarm or interest them in the least. It was all just so much white noise in the newspapers and on the airwaves. This was proving harder than he supposed, and the Lord hadn't shown him the way yet.

He gnawed his cheek, bit his lip and wished for a piece of the gum he wasn't supposed to chew anymore because he chomped so hard it often threw his jaw out. But he needed something besides his teeth to gnash when his anxieties got the better of him or the specter of his mother and father crowded in on him. In the apathy of Alabama, how would he ever explain to his parents that instead of starting law school, he wanted to stay with the campaign? To them, his work for the campaign was just a summer job. For him, it was a calling he did not intend to abandon when law school began on August 30th. With the primary scheduled for September 7th, there was no way he could both embark on a law school education and continue to be an instrumental part of an important political campaign as it entered its most crucial and decisive phase.

He knew what his parents would say to that. First, they would tell him that working for a political campaign was all well and good for a summer paycheck; but two, putting off law school, along with the day he could start making real money, would be nothing short of insane. If he persisted, they would advise him to hedge his bets. Start law school on schedule, do what he could for the campaign on weekends. After all, no one had defeated George Wallace in Alabama since 1958. If his candidate did do the impossible, defeated Wallace and offered Daniel Dobbs a job in the new administration in Montgomery, he could make a decision then—and only then—about deferring law school. But if his candidate did not make it, then Daniel would still be on track with his first year of law school, and his future ahead of him assured—no time lost, no bridges burned, no opportunities wasted.

He didn't even want to imagine what they'd say if he told them he didn't want to go to law school no matter what the outcome of the campaign.

To them a law degree was the blank check that would vouchsafe his future. But he didn't want to do the work required to get the degree any more than he wanted to do the work he'd be qualified for with the degree. What he wanted was—. Well, it wasn't that simple. It couldn't be summed up by a professional degree or a job title. He could explain it only by example. The best example that came to mind was the Civil Rights Movement. In particular, the hordes of young people who had put their education and careers aside in order to fight for their values and ideals. They had fought to make their country—and the world—a better place. What he wanted was to be a part of that kind of noble, heroic struggle. He wanted to be a soldier fighting the good fight. Well, okay, if he was going to be really honest, he wanted to be a hero who helped conquer evil. The campaign to defeat George Wallace represented the best opportunity he knew of to be involved in that kind of epic battle between good and evil, and he considered himself fortunate to be a part of it.

He didn't believe in doing it half-ass, either; hedging his bets, as his parents would say. That was not the way to fight the good fight, certainly not the way to win it. Nothing less than whole-hearted dedication and commitment were required. If he didn't make sacrifices to further the cause, then he wouldn't be truly giving himself to it; he would simply be exploiting it for his own benefit, then discarding it if there was no benefit. Although some of those young civil rights marchers had been carpet-bagging opportunists like this, others had put their lives on the line, and actually lost them. These were the young people he admired, especially because their sacrifices had succeeded in making a difference. They had succeeded in changing the world. Their efforts had made the world a better place. As far as he was concerned, that should be the task every young person confronted: Figure out the best way or the best thing you can do to change the world and make it a better place. And then do it. Let nothing stop you or get in your way. Don't quit until you're dead.

If he had ever attempted to communicate any of this, his literal-minded mother would have dissolved in hysterics.

"You want to be a *civil rights worker* instead of going to law school?!"

"No, no, no. . . ."

"What do you mean, you want to be a *soldier*? Are you saying you want to join *the military*?"

His mother would need a Valium, along with repeated assurances that her son had not enlisted. Where she came from, the military was one of the best ways out: her own brother had fought in Nam. Everything she had done, she would tearfully remind him, had been designed to spare her son that mortal danger. But once her fears had been put to rest, the discussion would boil down to this essential question: "Why did you go to Harvard if you don't want to go to law school?"

Law school was the last thing he wanted to do with his life; he'd rather have stayed in the Northeast and joined Mr. May's venture capital firm. If his parents had known what venture capital was, they probably would have wanted him to stay in the Northeast and join the firm too. Somehow this summer, he had to defeat both George Wallace and his parents. Of the two opponents, his parents were the more difficult by far. He could defeat them only by defeating George Wallace. Wallace had to go down. The state of Alabama needed it, and one Daniel Dobbs needed it too.

* * *

When they reached the downtown building where the law office of Osgood, Oliver was located, the fond figments of his overactive imagination suffered another bracing encounter with reality. Although he had committed his mind, body and soul to the man who was trying to beat Wallace, he suddenly remembered that he didn't know this man at all. In fact, he'd only met him once. And that had been several months ago, back in December when he'd interviewed for a job with the campaign. But it hadn't been the typical job

interview. Before Daniel could even begin to sell himself, Osgood had proceeded to sell *himself*, as if Daniel were the prize and Osgood the supplicant
for his favor. Leaving the Capitol building, Daniel felt like he'd just been
knighted and asked to join a holy crusade. This image of himself as one of the
heroes riding to rescue his fallen state from the evil snares of George Wallace
had taken deep root in his imagination. He had not been able to resist the
urge to talk of almost nothing else when he arrived back on campus for his
final semester. True to form, his Harvard classmates had been so impressed
with the role he was going to play in the attempt to take down Wallace that
Daniel had spoken of Aaron Osgood as if the two went as far back in the past
together as they planned to go in the present and future. But the reality was,
Daniel had spent a mere few hours in the man's company. And he had never
been in this imposing high-rise office building before, never seen anything
like it in Opelika or Montgomery.

Once inside, he felt even more puny, and everything he'd been so certain
of a moment before was thrown into doubt and confusion. Could it really be
that Daniel Dobbs was about to start working for the candidate who might
become the first New South governor of Alabama? And if so, how could this
candidate be the man Daniel supposed him to be if he was hiring a twenty-
one year-old with no prior experience on a professional campaign to play
an instrumental role? While Daniel wanted to believe that Aaron Osgood
had instantly recognized his natural gifts, Daniel himself didn't even know
what these were. Indeed, he couldn't even say for sure that he'd got the right
time and place for the appointment that evening. Except for a lone security
guard, the spacious lobby which could easily hold a couple hundred people
was completely deserted and so silent they could hear the soft hiss of the air-
conditioning. It all began to seem so unlikely and unreal. It did not even seem
likely that they were supposed to be there; no one else was. The sound of their
footsteps on the marble floor made an accusing echo, as if reproaching them
for going where they shouldn't have presumed to go. Daniel began to feel like
it had all been nothing more than an indulgent daydream: that he would be
working for the next governor of Alabama. That he would one day become
such a governor himself. Who did he think he was? Who had he been kid-
ding, besides himself?

"Does he still practice law?" Caroline whispered.

"Not since becoming attorney general. But he uses the office for campaign
business when he's back in Birmingham."

Faking a confidence he didn't feel, Daniel pressed the elevator button
and wondered what really awaited him several floors above. Stepping off on

the tenth floor, he was relieved to see the double doors straight ahead with OSGOOD, OLIVER superimposed in grand gilt lettering, just as Aaron had described, unlocked as promised. He and Caroline entered a gracious reception area with a thick, noiseless carpet and a three-quarter round polished wooden desk. Supposedly there was a button he could press to summon Aaron from his own private quarters.

But no sooner had he approached the desk than Aaron himself burst unexpectedly out of the shadows. Well over six feet tall, he was a huge man whose presence overwhelmed all at once, like a star tackle materializing suddenly out of the backfield. He pounced on Daniel with his arm outstretched and a hearty welcome that instantly pulverized the doubts and fears Daniel had felt moments earlier. Pride and adrenaline pumped through his veins. Daniel felt himself melting into a puddle of gratitude at the feet of this man whose forceful presence alone revived all his hopes and dreams, and whose vigorous handshake, prolonged smile and voluble greeting were making Daniel look good in front of his girlfriend. At least, it made Daniel feel as if he was looking good, as if he had been every bit as important in Aaron Osgood's mind as the other man had become for him.

It was also exhilarating to enter the sphere of a man who could shape the future, both for an entire state as well as for a certain Daniel Dobbs. One look at this man and it was obvious he had what it took to be a governor in the South. In other words, he looked like a football player. Wallace in his wheelchair could not possibly compete with this. His day was over and done. The current governor of Alabama, Fob James, had been a starting quarterback at Auburn. Anyone who aspired to be the next governor would do well to look like he could have played football, even if he never had. Aaron Osgood not only looked like a football player, he looked like one who could *win*. One glimpse conveyed the powerful image of a man who could carry the ball, not just to win an election, but to resurrect an entire downtrodden people. Whenever the newspapers spoke of "the formidable opposition" Wallace faced in the current election, this is what they meant: Aaron Osgood.

Osgood's eyebrows shot up when he looked at Caroline, and he turned back to Daniel.

"What have we here?" he cried. "You've brought a much better looking companion than Will Hill, I see," he said, smiling broadly.

Will Hill? "This is Caroline Elmore," said Daniel.

"I know! I know!" said Aaron, turning toward her and pumping her hand enthusiastically. "When Daniel said he'd met you, I told him it was undoubtedly the smartest thing he'd ever done in his life. And did he tell you? I know your daddy. When I was fresh out of law school, I interned at his firm. Wonderful firm. Best in the city. For that matter, best in the state of Alabama. I would say: tell him I said so, but he doesn't need anybody to tell him so. He knows it. Everybody knows it. At least tell him I said 'hello.' Now why don't y'all come sit down in my office for a minute?"

For a minute? Something's wrong, Daniel's radar told him instantly. But he didn't have time to identify it as Osgood herded them quickly across the hall and into a large, richly-appointed room where opera music was blaring from speakers mounted on the walls.

For the first time Daniel noted that Aaron was padding about in sock feet. Otherwise, he was dressed in a suit that looked at least half a size too small for his six foot four inch frame. Osgood looked like he could bust out at the seams any minute. Somehow this was endearing. The contradiction between the elegant and beautifully tailored suit and the stocking feet was equally endearing, probably because it was the very same contradiction of Aaron Osgood himself. While the newspapers invariably called him "an urbane Mountain Brook attorney," since this is the part he was—mostly—dressed to play, as soon as he opened his mouth to unleash his affable volley of speech, you knew you were dealing with nothing more than a country boy made good. He might have a torrent of high-falutin words he'd learned in college and law school, but they were uttered in an accent so raw, flat and nasal that he sounded like a complete redneck. It was a perfect combination. He was the absolute incarnation of the Southern cliché that you could take the boy out of the country, but not the country out of the boy. Clichés worked in politics if not in literature, and this was the perfect cliché for Alabama voters.

In some way the very size of the man was a reflection of his background in the country, like he'd been left on the vine too long and grew too big as a result. And so now, what was he to do with himself? A high school basketball coach had once wanted to make a player out of him, but Osgood hadn't been inclined in that way. Even if politics was the best way to channel himself, nothing seemed capable of containing him properly, down to the suit he wore or the chair he sat in. And no frame could capture the whole man, Daniel had noticed. Whether it was a photograph in the newspaper or television footage from the campaign trail, no camera angle seemed to get the big guy in all his physical glory. He seemed larger and therefore more capable than any others in the picture. There was also a restless energy, as if he needed to be doing something more, something else besides what he was actually doing at the given moment. Instead of offending, this restlessness made him only more impressive. It was a constant reminder of how many pressing and important matters this man had to attend to, both as attorney general and gubernatorial candidate. It was hard to believe that even the state of Alabama could hold him. Indeed, there were some who were already whispering "President" even before he'd been elected governor.

The only truly unfortunate aspect of his demeanor was his prematurely and nearly bald head, shaped so much like an egg you couldn't help but think "egghead." So far as Daniel knew, George Wallace had not yet recycled the infamous epithet he had used in the sixties to deride Ivy Leaguers coming down from the Northeast to join the Civil Rights Movement. "Pointy-headed intellectuals," he had called them. Later it was a populist rallying cry during Wallace's presidential campaigns. It wouldn't be long before the current Wallace campaign began using the familiar catchphrase against this latest opponent, who literally and physically fit the description of a "pointy head."

Fortunately, there was no indication that Osgood was "intellectual," except perhaps for the opera music he loved. Daniel had never understood people who always had to have music playing, and opera was the very worst. Whenever subjected to it, Daniel found himself annoyed and confused. Instead of relaxing him or giving him pleasure, it only made him tense and unable to think or concentrate. Plus he did not know how in the world he was going to make his voice heard above the din. He even found himself fumbling a bit as he sat down in one of the chairs Aaron indicated across from his desk.

Meanwhile, Aaron had crossed his long legs on top of his desk and was leaning back so far in his own chair that they had a better view of his sock feet than his face. His long slender hands were clasped behind him and his elbows jutted out at odd angles. "So where is our friend Mr. Hill?" he was asking. "Have you met Will Hill?" he looked at Caroline.

She shook her head. "Not yet," she said, staring blankly ahead as if dazed by the spectacle in front of her.

Daniel remembered a similar sensation from his first meeting with Aaron Osgood, when he knew at a glance that here was a man who could truly be king of Goat Hill. And where others with Aaron's physical gifts might make mere mortals feel diminished, Aaron somehow managed to enlarge those in his presence, as if sharing his surplus height and bulk instead of hoarding them for his own advantage. Suddenly, Daniel hadn't felt so short anymore, and this was truly a wonderful feeling. And now, watching Caroline respond to this man, he felt as proud of himself as he did of Aaron Osgood, as if Aaron were an accomplishment he was laying at Caroline's feet, just as Caroline was an accomplishment he was laying at Aaron Osgood's feet. With so few assets to offer others, Daniel felt the most he could do was offer them someone else as proof of his worthiness.

"You're in for a rare treat. A rare treat," Osgood was telling her. "Will Hill is a very special young person. I was a changed man after Will Hill came to intern in the Attorney General's office last summer. But the most important thing Will Hill has ever done for me so far is to introduce me to his good friend Daniel Dobbs. Just like one of the smartest things Daniel Dobbs has ever done in his life is to meet Caroline Elmore, and bring her here to meet me. Let me tell you all something: Young people like you are the future of this state! The future of this state! It used to be said, that anybody with brains in the state of Alabama would get themselves out of Alabama as soon as they could and stay out of Alabama for as long as they could. They used to say, if you lived in Alabama, that was certain proof you had no brains, and that if you *chose* to live in Alabama, you had shit for brains. But that's changing! That's changing! With young people like you, it's changing! Young people like you are exactly what we need in this state! Native sons and daughters who go away and *choose* to come back. Because you don't come back the same. Do you?" He paused briefly to give them a chance to shake their heads. "No, you're not the same," he affirmed. "But." He held up a long index finger. "Here's the key," he said, lowering his voice. "You're still one of us. You're still one of us, so folks aren't going to notice at first that you're *mavericks*. You're mavericks! Because you've been away, you've seen a different world, a better world, and you've come back to make your state of Alabama a better world. And that's what I need. Young people like you. Mavericks!"

Suddenly Aaron's feet hit the floor and he sat upright, as if electrified by an important new thought. "You know," he said musingly, pulling himself up to the desk and addressing Caroline intently. "Someone was telling me something about your family the other day. Something I didn't know. Now what was it?" He put that index finger on his lips and pondered briefly before crying: "Oh! I know!" and looking back at her. "I heard that your family is related to the Petsingers. Is that true?"

The name was familiar somehow, but Daniel couldn't quite put his own finger on it. At the moment, he was trying to put his finger on something else. In spite of all that seemed so right about Aaron Osgood, something seemed wrong somehow, at least with the way this meeting was progressing. Perhaps because it wasn't very much like a meeting. Osgood was treating it like a social call. Although he was grateful to the man for making such an all-out effort to cater to Caroline, there was something odd about it too. And back there in the hallway outside his office, he had invited them in for *a minute*. What had happened to *dinner*?

"Julian Petsinger—little Julian—is married to my cousin Lena," Caroline was telling him.

"Is that right?" Aaron responded as if this were truly one of the most fascinating facts he'd ever learned.

"Now, is this on your mother's side, or . . ."

"My father's. Lena is the daughter of my father's sister. My aunt Libba Albritton."

"You know, I grew up eating Dixie pecan pies?" Aaron said fondly. "I'll bet you did too, Daniel?"

"What? What's that?" He was still having trouble hearing over the noise of the opera music, and still trying to figure out how a man who had wasted no time as attorney general prosecuting the battalions of corrupt Wallace cronies could be sitting here so lazily doing nothing and talking about nothing—as if there were all the time in the world instead of a few short months to beat Wallace for once and for all.

"Dixie pecan pies," said Aaron. He made a small circle with the fingers of both hands to indicate the size of a small pie. "Dixie pecan pies were in all the fillin' stations when I was growing up in Andalusia."

"Oh, those," said Daniel, inching nervously toward the edge of his seat. Neither he nor Caroline had come to a deserted downtown Birmingham on a Saturday night to talk about pecan pie. What he wanted to talk about were the latest poll numbers, which had Aaron Osgood within four percentage points of George Wallace. Considering the crowded field of contenders in the Democratic primary, including the speaker of the house and the lieutenant governor, Aaron's success in narrowing the field and pulling so close to Wallace was a clear sign that victory was possible. But it was by no means certain and there wasn't a moment to lose. In Alabama, the primary *was* the election. If Aaron Osgood could pull off a victory against Wallace in September, he could consider himself the governor. What happened later in November would only ratify it. But this meant they had less than *three months* to make it happen.

"Yes, those," said Aaron, staring nostalgically into the middle distance. "Growing up, every afternoon after school, my mother took me to the fillin' station for a cherry Coke slush and a Dixie pecan pie." Aaron formed a circle again with his fingers. "I could eat one in four bites. Beg for another with my mouth full. Bet the same thing happened in Opelika."

Well, yes, of course Daniel had grown up eating Dixie pecan pies like everybody else. As Aaron had said, it was what you got from the fillin' station, because there weren't the rows and rows of candy bars and potato chips like there was today. So what? Food had never been that interesting to him.

"You know that's her family's business?" Aaron nodded toward Caroline. "Dixie Pies & Pastries."

Daniel hoped his face did not betray the jolt he felt. Dixie Pies & Pastries? Her family's business? She had never told him that.

"Well, not exactly my family's business," Caroline was saying. "My aunt married the son of the man who founded the company. And it was sold a few years ago to Nabisco."

"You can still get a Dixie pecan pie in a fillin' station in Andalusia," Aaron said, becoming lost again in nostalgia. "You know, everybody has their mad-a-lynn," he continued affectionately. "Mine is a Dixie pecan pie. If you put one in front of me right now, I would eat it in four bites and it would take me right back to grade school in Andalusia, Alabama and my mother's second cousin's fillin' station at the corner of 2nd and Main."

The allusion to a "mad-a-lynn" appeared to mean something to Caroline, who smiled. Daniel didn't know what the hell was going on and was becoming more and more bewildered by Aaron's behavior. Did this man feel any sense of urgency about his campaign? Something was fucked up, and Daniel hoped it wasn't his fault. It was hard to rack his brains and figure it all out while the music was already racking his brains.

Aaron leaned forward and slapped the desk with the palm of one hand. "Now tell the truth young lady," he said, addressing Caroline with a gleam of amusement belying the intensity of his gaze. "Have you ever in your entire life eaten a Dixie pecan pie?"

She shook her head as a sly grin crept across her face.

Aaron slapped again at the desk. "I knew it!" he cried. "I knew it!" He looked over at Daniel. "What are we to make of this?"

Aaron's amusement was becoming infectious, and Daniel decided it wouldn't hurt to join in a little. "Folks in Mountain Brook can start a company that makes a fortune selling miniature pecan pies to everybody else in the state, and never even touch one themselves."

"Bingo!" said Aaron, pointing his finger at Daniel. "This is exactly the disconnect between the Tiny Kingdom of Mountain Brook and the state of Alabama I'd like to resolve!"

Suddenly Aaron seemed serious, like the serious contender he had become.

Daniel felt his spine stiffening with pride, and noticed a sparkle coming out of Caroline eyes. But just as suddenly, Aaron changed the subject.

"Now tell me about your cousin Julian," he said to Caroline. "Julian Petsinger. He's got two sisters, I believe . . ."

Daniel knew he should keep paying attention, but the fear that he had screwed up began to overtake him again. As his uneasy mind wandered, his eyes scanned the room anxiously, as if it could provide clues to help him interpret what was amiss. For the first time he noticed a tumbler with a half-finished drink on the desk in front of Aaron. Not one sip had Aaron taken since he'd been in the room with them. Nor had he offered them a drink; Daniel realized he could definitely use one. Why hadn't Aaron Osgood offered them anything? Searching the room further, he spied a row of crystal decanters and tumblers on an elegant side table which also contained the family portrait of Aaron's wife and two children.

Daniel had met Aaron's wife once, very briefly, and she had treated him as if she'd barely noticed his existence. It was quite possible this was literally the case, since she was six foot two and closer than not to being almost a foot taller than he. Will Hill called her "the Ice Maiden." Not only tall, she was also strikingly beautiful, with hair a color he couldn't even name. It wasn't blonde, it wasn't red, it wasn't auburn or brunette or anything he'd ever heard of or seen before. And it looked real. "Strawberry blonde" was the phrase used in the newspapers to describe her. But it didn't do justice to her unique, show-stopping looks. However, Mary Winston Osgood carried herself like a woman who didn't need justice. She had beauty and she had money—her own money. She also had brains. She didn't need justice. She didn't need anything from anybody. Indeed, she didn't need anybody at all, certainly not a no-account little thing like him she could barely see way down there on the ground where he lived like a worm. Harvard? What was Harvard? She might have heard of it, once or twice, from somebody somewhere. She had been everything he'd feared Mrs. Elmore would be: the rich bitch, the society lady, the Mountain Brook matron. Ice Maiden exactly.

It was common knowledge that she had married a South Alabama boy with no money or name to speak of for one reason and one reason only: he was a few inches taller than she was. For her generation, it was still true that a woman who was too tall was as damned as a woman who was too smart. Men would not go near a woman who was taller or smarter than they. So Mary Winston Cargill had been doubly damned. Luckily she was also rich: Cargill Clothiers had been a lucrative family business in Birmingham before selling out to a national apparel company. Mary Winston and her brother were the sole heirs to the fortune paid to buy out their business along with the prime commercial real estate owned by the Cargills in downtown Birmingham and Mountain Brook Village. Mary Winston's brother had devoted his life to investing and managing his and his sister's inheritance. Of course, with all that money, it was only a matter of time before some (very tall) man plucked up the courage to approach Mary Winston. But she had made it all the way to her final year in the MBA program at the University of Alabama before meeting Aaron Osgood, a law student.

Now she was the director of the United Way in Birmingham, which couldn't have been a more perfect job for the wife of a politician. It was nonpartisan and philanthropic, and for some reason, people assumed it was run by volunteers. So Mary Winston escaped the censure for having a full-time job with a handsome salary while she had two young children, at the same time she defied the image of the idle rich wife who did nothing but shop and play tennis. Aaron still seemed smitten with what he called his "bride," whom he always referred to as "the lovely Mary Winston," as if he were still trying to win her favor.

He must have noticed Daniel's gaze trained on the sidebar, because he suddenly popped up from his chair like a jack-in-the-box. It was a typically endearing burst of energy: however elegant his clothes or his office furnishings, this was like window-dressing applied by his rich city wife to which he amiably acquiesced. But always his raw power and enthusiasm popped through the veneer. "This is more like it," Daniel thought to himself. "Now we're going to get a drink and get down to business." But to his astonishment, Aaron Osgood did not offer a drink. Instead, he extended his long arm across the desk to each of them in turn, and beamed his wide smile, while thanking them effusively for sharing a small part of their Saturday night with him.

"We're going to turn this around," Osgood said as he joined them on the other side of the desk. "We're going to turn it around. With young people like you, we can turn this state around." As if to emphasize his point, Osgood interposed himself between the two young people and turned them both around toward the door of his office. "This campaign is not about me," he said as he moved them all closer to the door, his arms still around the young people. "This campaign is about taking a poor, backward state and turning it around. It's about taking a state that ranks 49 or 50 when it comes to the positives, and number one or two when it comes to the negatives. I don't have to list them for you. I don't have to spell them all out. You know them as well as I do. Infant mortality: we're number one in the nation. Ratio of education

42

dollars per school child, we're number 49. Number 49. That's abysmal. The only good thing we're ever number one in is football, and that is not enough. Football can take our minds off our troubles, make us feel better about ourselves, make us feel like winners. But we're not winners. We're the 'Thank God for Mississippi' state. And you know what? Soon enough, we won't even be able to say 'Thank God for Mississippi,' because I do believe they are progressing in ways we aren't over here. It's abysmal. And it doesn't have to be this way. Alabama is a wonderful state. A beautiful state. We got so much to offer here in this state it just takes my breath away. Sure, we got our problems and faults like everybody else. But the main problem is: we've never had any real leadership. Let me tell you what: The state of Alabama is like a young kid, full of potential and promise, with its future before it. But like a kid, it needs to be guided. It needs good discipline, somebody to steer it the right way and teach it good values, show what's right from wrong. The state of Alabama's like a kid that ain't got a mama or daddy. Or it's got a no-good mama'n daddy, and had nothin' but lazy, incompetent teachers. Most of the leaders we've had—especially my current opponent—have brought out only the worst in Alabama. Nobody has shown the folks of this good state how to bring out the best we've got. But it *can* be done. We can turn this around. And we will. We will. With young people like you coming back to serve their state, we will turn this around. And that's what this campaign is going to do."

By now they had reached the reception area. When Aaron stopped and dropped his arms from around them, they turned to face him.

"I think it's great you have your Harvard education," he told them. "But it's even better that you're bringing that Harvard education back to Alabama. I don't have to tell you, Caroline, that with their Harvard degrees, Daniel and his friend Will Hill could be at Harvard Law School right now. Or Yale or Stanford. They could be anywhere they wanted to be. And they could take those fancy degrees and go to New York or D.C., Chicago or L.A. And they could walk the corridors of high finance or national government. And there's nothing wrong with that! Nothing wrong with that a-tall! But I think they've done the greatest thing they could possibly do by coming back to Alabama."

Will Hill could have been at Harvard Law School right now, but the truth was, Daniel Dobbs had shit for brains. For one thing, he'd had no choice but to return to Alabama for law school, and for another, he still didn't have the slightest clue what he'd done so wrong he didn't even rate a drink, let alone dinner.

"We all know what happens to outsiders with Ivy League degrees who come to the Deep South trying to change it," Osgood continued as he moved them toward the elevators. "Fifteen years ago, the Civil Rights Movement showed us what happens to those people. Some of them don't even make it out of here *alive!* It's young people like you that we need, to get this state moving in the right direction. *You* are our greatest asset! *You* are our future! And that future is not about winning a campaign but lifting up an entire body of people from the depths of despair, poverty, disease, ignorance, prejudice and racism. Together, we can do it!"

Osgood thrust out his hand again, first to Caroline, then to Daniel.

"I look forward to seeing you and Mr. Hill in Montgomery on Monday," he said to Daniel just as the doors to the elevator opened in front of them. He stood there beaming until the doors closed between them.

"I thought he was taking us to dinner," observed Caroline.

Daniel sighed as he pushed the elevator button. It had been too much to hope for that she would overlook that detail. "I did too," he admitted. "Is it too late to have dinner with your family, do you think?"

In reply she only rolled her eyes. "I don't get it," she said. "It was necessary for you to come all the way to Birmingham for *that*?"

Daniel could only sidestep this question. "So what did you think of him?"

To his annoyance, she only shrugged. "I don't feel like I met the real person," she said. "Just heard part of his stump speech. If you want to know the truth, he reminded me of an Amway salesman."

He fought hard to check the outburst of indignation rising up his windpipe. How could she not see it? She had just met the man who could finally beat Wallace, the man who could win. So what if he reminded her of an Amway salesman? That was probably a good image to project in the state of Alabama. The main thing was this man had what it took to get elected governor. As much as Caroline claimed to disdain the elitism of Mountain Brook, she herself was still Mountain Brook through and through. Of course, this was why he loved her, he reminded himself sternly. Still, it was galling that all she had was a shrug for the man capable of hauling her own native state out of the mud.

"He seemed much more like a salesman than anything else," she added.

Well, in a way he was a salesman, Daniel defended the man silently. He had to be. The ultimate salesman. The one who was selling himself. Yet he knew what she meant. Aaron Osgood had not come across like a fierce competitor in the grip of a vital campaign that would determine the fate of himself and an entire state that desperately needed his victory. The man had not even been wearing *shoes*. The only topic he'd discussed with any passion had been *pecan pie,* for Christ's sake.

44

"Anyway, the real reason I came to Birmingham was to see you," he told her as they plunged through ten floors.

As soon as he said this, he suddenly remembered he'd said something directly contradictory in the recent past. Something about coming to Birmingham to see Aaron Osgood. Usually Caroline pounced immediately on his minor inconsistencies as if they were evidence of a major character flaw. For the moment she made no use of this latest discrepancy, although it was too much to hope she would overlook it altogether. Through painful experience, he had learned she could store these up and use them to maximum effect at a later, more strategic, date.

Hoping to forestall this moment and perhaps mute its effect, he said, "I thought you of all people would like to meet Aaron Osgood," with an air of reproach. "Still, it *was* strange," he ventured also, hoping she could help him figure out why. He chewed the inside of his cheek.

"Why did he think Will Hill was going to be with you?" she wondered. "He seemed so surprised to see me. Downright disappointed, even."

And then it hit Daniel as he stepped off the elevator on the ground floor. "You two," Aaron had said during their phone conversation last week. He had called from his campaign office in Huntsville to set up a time and place to discuss the logistics of Daniel and Will beginning their work for his campaign. Multiple phones had been ringing in the background every few seconds. There were constant interruptions as Aaron was pulled away from the phone to answer a question or speak to someone on another line. Either he did not hear or failed to register what Daniel had said about the funeral of Will Hill's aunt preventing him from coming to Birmingham over the weekend. And when Aaron had said "I'd like to take *you two* out to dinner," he had been referring to Daniel and *Will Hill.* Not Caroline, as Daniel had assumed after telling Aaron about her in the course of the call.

Now it was all clear: Aaron Osgood had wanted a meeting—a *business* meeting—with his two new campaign workers before they officially got started on their duties in Montgomery. After all, he still needed to outline exactly what their duties were to be, what role he needed them to fulfill for the summer and possibly beyond. No doubt Aaron had wanted to lay this out before them in person, when it could all be more easily explained, discussed and agreed upon.

As soon as they left the ice-cold air conditioning of the office building, Daniel found himself sweating from every pore, not so much from the hot, humid night air of summer as from the humiliating blunder he had stumbled into. It didn't matter that it wasn't his fault. Politics, at the end of the day, was about winning or losing. Whether you were right or wrong was of no importance as soon as you'd lost. And he had been the loser, like some clueless high school kid showing up with his prom date. Clearly what Aaron had in mind was a bull session over bourbon, followed by a late steak dinner somewhere downtown. It didn't matter where. It wasn't about the food, the restaurant, your girlfriend or your wife. It was about winning this governor's race. He *knew* something had gone wrong with that meeting. He'd been right about that; the only problem was that it was all his fault. Dammit! He could feel his teeth clenching.

At least Will Hill had been at a funeral. At least he could demonstrate that he had been *working*. Not jerking off like some stupid kid.

"Well, the night is unexpectedly ours," said Caroline with a smile, when they reached his car. "What should we do?"

"Are you sure it's too late to have dinner with your family?" He looked at his watch. "It's only seven-fifteen. Don't you think they'll still be eating if we head straight back?"

Laughing, she shook her head and got in the car. What kind of answer was that?

"Well?" he demanded as he got in the driver's seat beside her.

"Daniel," she said. "You can't be serious. This isn't the way to do things. Plan A doesn't pan out, so you fall back on Plan B."

"What's wrong with that?" he said, staring through the windshield, keys still in hand. "What else are you supposed to do?" He honestly did not know. If he couldn't make headway with his employer, at least he could use the time to make headway with her parents. Call him a dumbass—it's what he was—but what else could you do besides go to Plan B when Plan A had failed?

"You do not treat people—least of all my family—as your Plan B," Caroline explained with annoyance. "It's rude. That's what's wrong with it. And coming in at the middle of the meal—or even at the beginning—when my mother doesn't expect us?" She gave him a look suggesting this was the worst mistake he could ever make. She was the wise and experienced teacher and he was the ten year-old boy. She was the Southern lady and he was the bubba. "Trust me," she concluded on a softer note. "My mother would be more upset than glad to see us."

"But why?" He thought of the way Mrs. Elmore had pleaded for him to stay with her eyes and every ounce of her body language. He couldn't believe that she wouldn't be glad to see him at the dinner table. And he thought of the way his own mother was always glad to have him for a meal at home—at eight, ten or even midnight—whenever she could get him. She had not wanted him to "go to Birmingham on his only weekend home before starting his job." If he were to show up suddenly and unexpectedly in Opelika two hours from now, his mother would gladly welcome him for a meal, even if she had to get out of bed, put on her bathrobe and go pull out leftovers from the refrigerator as she rubbed the sleep out of her eyes. There was a part of him that actually wanted to get on the interstate—alone—and drive like a bat out of hell back home to Opelika and put the whole mess of the evening behind him.

"Well, let's see," said Caroline, getting even more annoyed. "My mother would be embarrassed first that they were eating at the breakfast table instead of the dining room. Then, the napkins would be the cotton ones, not the linen. Same for the wineglasses, because she doesn't use the crystal unless she's *expecting* company."

So: no formal dining room with salmon pink walls. Suddenly he realized that the downtown was even more deserted, if possible, than when they had first arrived. "Where should we go, then?" he asked, looking over at her.

"Where do you want to go?"

Somewhere cheap, he thought. "Anywhere I can finally get a drink," he said.

"Just get back on the expressway, and I'll think of something," she said.

It was several moments after he'd started the car before he noticed she was laughing not so softly to herself.

"What's funny?" he said, irritated.

"You," she said. "In college you were a party boy," she said, "but now that summer's here, you can't relax and have fun." She pointed. "That's your entrance ramp there. Up ahead to the right."

"That was just senior year," he said. "It's supposed to be a party year. But now it's like real life has started. I've got to work, and not just at a summer job. I've got to help get a man elected governor of this state. I've got to—" He bit his lip. He was about to tell her that he had to make sure he never needed to go to law school, but now was not the time. Unsure of her reaction, he did not want to risk opening a second battlefront on the issue, and find himself fighting her as well as his parents.

"What are you thinking?" She reached for his hand.

"You're the one who told me back in Cambridge I wouldn't succeed unless I could learn to buckle down," he said.

"Well, I didn't mean you couldn't relax and have fun on a Saturday night." She squeezed and let go of his hand as he changed lanes to pass a straggling pickup truck trailing something that looked like collard greens or lettuce leaves.

Having fun on a Saturday night was no longer his ultimate ambition, as it had once been only a few short weeks ago. Having fun on Saturday nights had been a temporary, four-year aberration while he was in college in Massachusetts. Now he was back in Alabama, where he needed to be accomplishing something toward his life's goals every waking minute. It was the way he'd been raised. And it was the way to get what you wanted. Aaron Osgood, he noted, was neither at home with his family nor prepared to sacrifice his Saturday night for a purely social occasion. For example, he could have followed through with his invitation to dinner regardless of Will's absence and Caroline's presence, but had chosen not to. Daniel understood this. He respected it. And now he understood the whole scene in Osgood's office. Aaron Osgood had forced himself to be polite and sociable to Caroline for the minimal amount of time before showing her back out the door so he could get back down to business. Which is why Daniel—*not Daniel and Caroline*—had been summoned in the first place. He had royally fucked up. And the irony was: he *should* have called Osgood from the Elmore's house to find out what would come back at him from the other end of the line. Then the misunderstanding would have been discovered, the pointless "meeting" could have been averted, and he could either have met alone with the man who was going to be written into the history books, or eaten dinner with the Elmore family in the formal dining room with the salmon pink walls. Dammit! He thumped the steering wheel.

"What's wrong?" she said.

He couldn't tell her; it wasn't her fault that her presence had derailed his meeting with Aaron Osgood. "It's being back in Alabama," he sighed.

"What do you mean?"

"Being back here makes me feel like I need to be working toward something every second."

"That's ironic," she laughed. "Harvard is where you went to party, and Alabama is where you plan to buckle down and work." She laughed again.

"It's also being back around my folks," he admitted.

"What do they have to do with it?"

"It's the way they are," he said. "They both grew up on farms. There was always something to do until it was time to go to bed. Then it was time to wake up."

"Life is hard and then you die," she murmured, alluding to the tee shirt she'd pointed out to him in the gift shop of the Boston hotel where his parents had stayed for graduation. This could have been his parents' family motto, she told him: Life is hard and then you die.

"It's not their fault they could never get away from it," he said.

"No," she agreed simply.

And it was to their credit, he argued silently with her. Even if much of it was bullshit: the elocution and comportment classes his mother had taken on weekends, hoping to rise from being a secretary into something more at the office where she worked. And when this promotion hadn't come, the education degree that took her four years of nights so she could teach "business administration"—meaning typing and shorthand—in the public school system. The E.D.D. that had taken his father ten years so he could quit preaching and become a high school principal. Now he was an assistant superintendent, and one day, when God finally realized that Cloyd Mullins was already dead, Bobby Dobbs would finally become in title and salary what he'd already been for a dozen years in practice: the Superintendent of the Opelika Public School system.

He was proud of his parents: their drive, their sacrifices, their ceaseless, tireless, relentless labor in service to their goals. And he was proud they had instilled all this in him. He could feel his hands tightening around the steering wheel and his whole body clenching with the fierce pride he felt in defense of his parents and their middle-class dreams. If they'd had no vision or drive and had not pulled themselves up from where they were born, he wouldn't be where he was today. He certainly wouldn't have had a shot at a Harvard degree or a Mountain Brook girl.

"Well, I know what I have to do when you get like this," she teased, unbuckling her seat belt and sliding over next to him.

"Oh, God," he grinned, his grip loosening on the wheel. Already he was a changed man, as lust suddenly flooded his bloodstream like a powerful drug, half opiate, making his eyes want to roll back in his head, and half stimulant, making him almost bust out of his very skin, not just his pants. "Honey," he said weakly, almost incapable of coherent speech. "Before you go down. Could you just tell me. What's my exit? Where do I get off?"

"Mountain Brook," she said, tugging at his zipper. "That's where you get off."

Mountain Brook, he thought peacefully a few seconds later. It was a great place to get off.

From "Aaron Osgood: Man of Town and Country" in the Montgomery Advertiser, *June 14, 1982 This is the second in a series of profiles of the gubernatorial
candidates competing in the Democratic primary on September 7th. Last week,
the* Advertiser *profiled Percy Atchison of Mobile; next week: former governor
James "Big Jim" Folsom.*

ALABAMA ATTORNEY GENERAL AARON OSGOOD'S MOTHER PEGGY was a country
girl, raised on a farm with five siblings in the unincorporated South Alabama
community of Libertyville, ten miles outside Andalusia in Covington County.
His father, Aaron Sr., grew up in town, son of a respected Andalusia physician
whose own father was also a beloved country doctor.

Family and friends closest to Aaron Osgood Jr. say this simple bit of
background information best explains the man now running for governor of
Alabama, who, at 39, is the youngest candidate in the race. Although Aaron
Jr. lived in town during the school year, he spent his summers "running wild"
on the farm where his mother grew up, recalls Peggy Osgood.

"As soon as school let out for the summer, we would take Aaron, his
brother and sister out to the country," she said recently. "Open the car door,
and it was like letting caged animals loose. Three months later, we'd go pick
'em back up, and it was like trying to corral wild beasts. They loved it out
there. The barn, the fields, the creek. The freedom."

But in Andalusia, Aaron Osgood Jr. was known as a scholar and dedicated
musician. The only instructor in the Andalusia Public School System he ever
disappointed was the chemistry teacher, Phil Douglas, also the basketball
coach, who had hoped the six foot tall and still growing young man would
prove the star center on the high school team. Instead, Aaron Jr. joined the
marching band. Because of his height, he agreed to learn the tuba, but the
flute was his favorite instrument, according to his sister.

"Books and music. Those were his passions," said his sister, Andrea Osgood Willis, 35, of Montgomery. "At home, he was either reading a book or
playing the flute."

But during the summer, he helped his grandfather with farm chores, and thought of it as fun. "It was a game to them kids," said Owen Woodrow, 75, who still lives out on the old place, though he has leased his farm land to an agribusiness.

"We still kept a few pigs then," said Mr. Woodrow. "Some chickens in the yard. Maybe half a dozen milk cows. Two or three goats. Aaron and 'em thought they was pets. Playthings. They loved helping with the animals. Got to the point, I had to keep enough goats so they could each have one or two to call their own come summertime."

The man who wants to be "king of Goat Hill," as the governor of Alabama is known colloquially, grew up taking care of a pet goat in the summer. But he was also a straight-A student who made every Honor Roll.

Aaron is both a farm boy and a city boy," said his brother Owen Osgood, 37, an insurance executive in Andalusia. "Same as me and my sister. We grew up thinking of both places as home. We were equally at home in either place. This is one of the keys to Aaron's success. He feels at home everywhere he goes, and can get along with anybody."

Aaron Osgood says he was shocked when he first began attending the University of Alabama in Tuscaloosa as an undergraduate and discovered the many different divisions between those from different parts of the state. "I never realized the way city folks would look down on country folks, who in turn were intimidated by city people. And coming from Andalusia, which is really a small town, I was devastated to learn that I was a redneck to the Brookies," he laughed, referring to the residents of Mountain Brook, where he now makes his home. Osgood calls it a rude awakening. "I had not grown up with any divisions like this in my own mind or in my upbringing," he explained. "And I didn't like it, that people from some parts of the state looked down on people from other parts, distrusted them, or even hated them. I feel the same way about racial fault lines as I do about the social lines people draw."

In a lengthy interview conducted last month, Aaron Osgood detailed the way his initial introduction to a more diverse Alabama community on the Tuscaloosa campus helped shape his political vision. "In the past, some politicians have used racial prejudice as a way to bring all of white Alabama together in a united front," he said. "But this created a false sense of community that accomplished no good and did an awful lot of harm. I'd like to unite all of Alabama—black, white, rich, poor, town, country, city—in a common cause to address our issues. Stagflation, unemployment, the recession are hurting us all in Alabama. We need to move beyond the past and our differences to confront the problems that are affecting all of us."

IN ANDALUSIA, THE OSGOOD NAME is synonymous with the power of healing. Both Aaron Osgood's grandfather and great-grandfather were revered as physicians known to make house calls, in all weather and all times of day or night, even deep in rural Covington County, where the wives of black sharecroppers were giving birth in two-room shacks.

"There was a story my great-grandfather used to tell, when he was still alive," said Andrea Willis. "About the time he was woken up at 2 A.M. one cold winter night by a 16 year-old black boy who had walked 20 miles to fetch him. Seems the midwife was having trouble delivering his mama's twelfth baby, and they feared for her life.

"It's sad to say, but this was a time when some white people would have said 'Why bother?' about a black woman 20 miles deep in the country laboring to bring her twelfth black baby into the world. But Daddy Jim didn't hesitate. Hitched his wagon, drove it across fields and even on a path through the woods to get to this sharecropper's shack where they had this poor black woman on a pallet filled with corn husks in front of an open fireplace. The baby was stuck coming face first, and the midwife had given up. Daddy Jim turned that baby, and both the mother and the baby survived. Next day, someone left a basket on his front porch filled with winter squash. That was his payment. But he always said, his real payment came 20 years later, when that face-first baby moved to town and got a job [as handyman] with Mr. Buchanan."

The doctrine of service to others could be called the creed of the Osgood family, who helped found the First Baptist Church of Andalusia. Senior male members of the family have always served as deacons. Currently, Aaron Sr. and Owen Osgood are both deacons.

"We were taught from a very young age, that our gifts were given to us by God so that we could help others, especially those less fortunate," said Owen. "Nobody embodies that spirit more than my brother Aaron. He is in politics for one reason only, and that is public service."

Aaron Jr. is not the first to put the family philosophy to a somewhat different use. Aaron Sr. was expected to become a doctor himself, help out with his father's practice and eventually take over. Instead, he went to veterinary school at Auburn University, and came back to Andalusia to treat sick animals rather than people.

"Those were the days when being a vet did not mean taking care of the pet poodle," he chuckled. "Back then, it meant going out in the country to the farms and seeing about Buddy Sloane's sick milk cow."

Aaron Sr. met his future wife on just such a call to her father's farm, to tend a mare bleeding to death after a difficult delivery.

It was political healing that appealed to Aaron Jr. from an early age, according to Kendall Oliver, his college classmate and now his law partner. "We were juniors when George Wallace stood in the schoolhouse door," he recalled. "The next year, Aaron told me he wanted to run for student body president, because he wanted to ease the process of integration for white and black students alike. He saw politics as a way to heal the scars from Alabama's painful past." . . .

~ 3 ~

When Daniel Dobbs awoke the next morning in the Elmore's guest house, he sensed none of the getting-ready-for-church bustle that would be going on his in own household in Opelika. What did these folks in Mountain Brook do with their Sundays if they didn't go to church? Lifting a slat in the blinds, he saw Caroline's father just as he emerged from the back door, dressed like the yardman. Apparently he was preparing for another day in his vegetable garden. This is what Perry Elmore did with his Sundays. "So be it," Daniel chuckled to himself. He should have known he was going to have to spend some time in that damn garden.

Five minutes later, he was dressed in jeans and offering Perry Elmore a hand with those twenty pound bags of fertilizer he was lugging from the garage. Although it was only seven o'clock, Mr. Elmore was already sweating profusely, and took off his engineer's cap to wipe his brow on the sleeve of his tee shirt.

"Sure," he said, in reply to Daniel's offer. "First thing: move your car so we can use that wheelbarrow to cart these bags." He gave Daniel a friendly wink and replaced his cap.

With a feeling of chagrin quite similar to the one he'd experienced last night, Daniel realized that the car Caroline had urged him to park in the second garage had pinned in the wheelbarrow her father now needed to use.

"If you'll just load up the rest of those bags," said Mr. Elmore. "It may take two trips."

So this was what it felt like to be a junior associate in Perry Elmore's law firm, Daniel grinned to himself. His assistance taken for granted and immediately put to use, with no time wasted on formalities or pleasantries. Well, Daniel thought, he'd have to be the best damn junior gardening associate he could be. At the moment that meant loading a wheelbarrow with twenty pound bags of fertilizer.

"Right over there," Mr. Elmore pointed in reply to the question Daniel had not had time to ask when he arrived at the garden with the wheelbarrow. As he maneuvered the rather unwieldy wheelbarrow between haphazard tools and various supplies, Mr. Elmore went right back to spreading fertilizer from the half-empty sack he held in his hands. "Take a bag and just lay it on," he said cheerfully. "It's pretty self-explanatory. It ain't brain surgery. I'd like to get the whole garden done before ten o'clock." He looked up at the sky. "It's supposed to rain like the dickens then."

No wonder it was so muggy: it was going to rain, and rain heavily. Daniel could feel it now, the moisture in the air drenching his clothes and calling forth the moisture in his body. Soon he was as wringing wet as Mr. Elmore, and felt like he'd been out in the garden for hours. Unfortunately, it had only been a matter of minutes. Ten o'clock? Would it take that long? Surely not, Daniel thought, trying to summon his natural optimism. Because he wouldn't last that long. He'd be dead first.

For some time they worked in silence punctuated only by the occasional grunts Mr. Elmore made as he tugged to rip open a new bag or lug one over from the pile. All Daniel's efforts at conversation were met only with monosyllables that discouraged such idle chatter. Perry Elmore had a mind only for his "cukes" and his "maters," as he called them when directing Daniel to the row he should attend to next. To make matters even more miserable, the fertilizer was not of the synthetic chemical variety. It was the real thing. Nothing but the best for his "cukes" and his "maters." Unfortunately, Daniel had not even eaten breakfast. And he never in a million years imagined spending any part of his time in Mountain Brook shoveling manure. Instead of the highbrow intellectual conversation he'd imagined conducting with Caroline's father over a polite bourbon or two at twilight, he got only the groans, grunts and the "ain'ts" Mr. Elmore enjoyed sprinkling into every other sentence. Daniel had it better when he visited his grandparents on their farm in the country. They took pride in treating him like a college boy with professional prospects. And his mother would have bristled if he'd ever been asked to perform any manual farm labor. She frowned whenever anyone used the word "ain't," and it went without saying that he had never once in his whole life heard her commit such a damning grammatical error.

"So," Mr. Elmore said unexpectedly, straightening up and massaging his back. "Aaron Osgood, eh?" He took out a handkerchief from his back pocket and wiped his face.

"Yes," said Daniel, trying quickly to rise to the occasion he had almost despaired of. "I think he's going to do it."

"I like Aaron," said Mr. Elmore, blowing his nose on the same handkerchief. "He interned at our firm." Perry replaced the handkerchief in his back pocket. "Nice guy. Really nice guy. We didn't offer him a job, but he's a really nice guy." Massaging his back with a wince, he made for the diminishing pile of fertilizer bags.

Daniel suppressed a grin. So this was how Perry Elmore thought of Aaron Osgood: not as the Attorney General of Alabama—which he was—nor as the governor of Alabama—which he might well become. To Perry Elmore, Aaron Osgood was the really nice guy who wasn't good enough to be offered a job in a top Birmingham law firm. To his daughter, Aaron Osgood was more like a door-to-door vacuum cleaner salesman. Although this might endear him to most of Alabama, she hadn't intended it as a compliment. How could he make it through to them? They weren't talking about an ordinary human being; they were talking about the man who would be governor; the man who would be king of Goat Hill.

Daniel gave it his best shot. "Aaron Osgood may not be in your law firm," he said with good humor. "But I think he's going to be your next governor."

Perry Elmore stopped in his tracks and looked over at Daniel with serious surprise. "Aaron?" he said quizzically. "Pshaw." He took out his handkerchief and wiped his face again. "Aaron's just lucky his wife's got the money to underwrite this foolishness." Perry stuck the hankie back in his pocket and bent down to get the next bag.

This foolishness? Daniel thought. Defeating George Wallace? Starting a new chapter in Alabama politics? A new day in Alabama? Electing an educated, forward-looking, well-intentioned politician like other Southern states had already done? Proving to the world and the rest of the country that Alabama could turn its back on a shameful past and work toward a better future? If that was foolishness, then what wasn't foolishness? Given these impossible standards, Daniel Dobbs felt like a piece of foolishness himself.

Not ready to give up, he waited until Mr. Elmore was positioned at his next row with the new bag of fertilizer. "Did you see where the latest polls have Aaron Osgood almost even with Wallace?" he said.

"Really?" Perry poured from the bag. "Is that so? Well good for Aaron."

Daniel waited, but Perry had nothing further to add. "So who will you vote for?" he asked, amused.

"Me?" Mr. Elmore straightened up as if in astonishment, as if the idea of voting had never occurred to him. Possibly it had not; perhaps he didn't plan to vote. Maybe he wasn't a voting man. Massaging his back again, Perry simply shook his head, as if voting for governor was an act of foolishness no less extreme than running for governor.

"You can't vote for Belton Collier," said Daniel, referring to the unchallenged Republican candidate who would face the winner of the Democratic primary. Belton Collier was a millionaire businessman who was currently mayor of Montgomery and widely regarded as just a few episodes shy of a trip to the loony bin. Despite his self-made millions—maybe in defense of them?—he packed several pistols for his daily duties as mayor and conducted himself more like a vigilante sheriff in a Wild West outpost than a mayor of a small Southern town.

"No, I can't vote for Belton Collier," conceded Mr. Elmore, pointing to something just beyond Daniel and outside his range of vision.

Turning around, Daniel saw a pitcher of water as beaded with sweat as he was. It lay on a large stone barbecue pit so studded with moss or fungus that it was obviously no longer used as a grill. In fact, Daniel had assumed at first it was some decorative piece of stonework he didn't understand jutting out from the wrought iron fence separating the patio from the sloping woods below. Far in the distance was the city of Birmingham, which last night when he returned home had lived up to its nickname of "the magic city," as it appeared a million pinpricks of light to those staring down at the valley from atop the mountain. During the day, however, the distant downtown and the even more distant steel mills were impossible to see, as if they didn't even exist. Indeed, this was the whole point of Mountain Brook. From his vantage point now, there was nothing to be seen except for the thick green wisteria vine running along the fence. It was hard to believe that an industrial city was just a few miles away; he felt like he was on a country estate. Dropping his sack of fertilizer, he joined his host as he drank off a whole glass of water in three large swallows. There was only the one glass, which Mr. Elmore re-filled for his guest and handed over. Stale, tepid tap water had never tasted so good.

"You can't vote for George Wallace," said Daniel, handing the glass back.

"Nope," Perry agreed, pouring out the last of the water.

"So why not Aaron Osgood?"

Instead of answering, Mr. Elmore drank half the glass in one gulp. "Daniel," he said, extending the glass and thrilling his guest with the first use of his Christian name. "I have never voted for a Democrat in my entire life."

In his dirt-stained, sweat-soaked clothes that reeked of manure, Perry Elmore resembled nothing so much as a yellow-dog Democrat, tilling the soil like a humble Alabama farmer. But this was just a pleasurable pastime for a

Republican, who could afford to love tending crops because he didn't need to sell them. Daniel's grandfather, still a cotton and soybean farmer in South Alabama, had never truly enjoyed one day of farming in his whole life.

"But in a situation like this," Daniel persisted, "with Belton Collier as the Republican candidate . . ." He put the empty glass back on the stone fire pit.

"Daniel," said Mr. Elmore, thrilling him again with the use of his Christian name. "I have never yet met a Democrat who didn't want to raise my taxes."

Daniel grinned. "If that's your only gripe with the Democrats, you should give them another look. Because the Republicans are going to raise your taxes too; they're just going to deny it. Even after they've done it."

Daniel was rather proud of his comeback, but Perry Elmore only shook his head ruefully.

"I have never known a Democrat who didn't hold hands with the God-damn teachers' union," he said. "And thanks to the Democrats, we're paying farmers in Alabama to raise cotton that rots in warehouses. I like Aaron Osgood just fine. He's a nice guy. I'll shake hands with him anytime. But I just won't vote for him." Mr. Elmore removed his cap and wiped his brow with his handkerchief. He pointed to the garden. "If we make one final push, I believe we can finish this job before the rain comes. What do you say?"

Daniel nodded and didn't even try to suppress his grin this time. He had pegged Perry Elmore from the start. He knew the man better than the man knew himself, and that was always an advantage. Perry must have seen Daniel's look of amusement.

"Next thing you're going to tell me: your parents are teachers and they grew up on farms." Mr. Elmore picked up a hoe and began smoothing out the clumps in the fertilizer.

Daniel grinned again. "That's just about right," he said.

"Yeah, I think Caroline said something to me about all that," said Perry, continuing with his work. "And I should have remembered. But I—" he looked up at Daniel—"I am no politician." He bent over again and looked back down. "And I still hate the way incompetent teachers get tenured and farmers get paid to plant too many crops. Now. How about we finish this job and go get some breakfast?"

~ 4 ~

In the polite pandemonium of the Sunday buffet in the grand, cavernous rooms of the Birmingham Country Club, no one noticed that Caroline Elmore and her mother had brought a guest, and Daniel was introduced to none of the other patrons, who were intent only on getting in line or chasing down well-dressed children running wild. Amidst this genteel uproar, people only nodded in passing with plates piled high or waved from across the room as they lifted a fork. Even from inside one of the inner sanctums of Mountain Brook, Daniel was finding it difficult to penetrate the society. It wasn't a simple matter of being there, he realized; you had to *belong* before they really let you in. But how could you ever belong if they never let you in? he wondered. It seemed a hopeless conundrum. And you couldn't just stake your claim through marriage. Foreigners who married Americans might automatically become U.S. citizens, but small-town country boys who married Mountain Brook girls did not automatically become Brookies. To become a Brookie, you had to be a Brookie. It wasn't impossible, but it was going to be a hell of a lot harder and take a lot longer than he'd anticipated.

As soon as they returned, the younger brother came out of the house to report that Daniel's mother was on the phone. Even as Daniel rejoiced in this first tangible evidence of the brother's awareness of both his name and his existence, he was flooded with dread as he went to the "Hideaway" to answer the call. His mother never dialed long distance if she could help it, and strictly rationed her telephone time with her parents and her son in college to five minutes apiece on alternating Sundays. Unless there was an emergency, these were the only long distance calls she ever made. The only ones she received were likewise from her parents and her son every other Sunday, when it was their turn to call her. So he was afraid there must be some catastrophic piece of news. The stress his father had been under lately, combined with the number of cigarettes he smoked every day, had led the doctor to take Shaye Dobbs aside last month for a serious conversation about her husband's health.

"Daniel?"

"Yes, Mother. What's wrong? What's happened?"

"Nothing's happened. Am I no longer allowed to call unless there's a calamity?"

"Mother." On this one word he dumped his entire load of relief, anger and outrage.

"Yes?" she said sweetly, with perfect innocence.

Refusing to take the bait, he kept quiet.

"It's my Sunday to call you, Son."

Daniel sighed heavily. "I wasn't expecting you to call here."

"Well why not?" she said, treating him to her own special recipe of righteous indignation. "Is there something wrong with calling you there?"

"Of course not. Like I said: I just wasn't expecting it."

"Well I don't know why not. We talk on the phone every Sunday when you're away from home. Why wouldn't you expect me to call?"

Well, let's see, he thought to himself, his initial relief evaporating while his anger and outrage mounted. First of all: he had just spent the entire previous week at home. Secondly, it was barely twenty-four hours since he had last seen her, as he'd had lunch with her right before leaving for Birmingham. On top of that, he would be seeing her again next weekend, when he brought Caroline to Opelika. Otherwise, there was no real reason he wasn't expecting her to call, except that she pinched every possible penny and always complained of long distance calls as "budget breakers."

"Daniel?" she said. "Are you all right?"

"So how was church?" he asked her.

"Very nice, thank you. Of course, everyone asked about you, expected you to be there. Old Mr. Bates said the only reason he got out of bed, came to church today, was to see you."

"I'll be there next Sunday, with Caroline."

"Joab and Janet were particularly upset."

"I spent Wednesday afternoon with Joab, at his office."

"It was Janet I spoke to. Said she would have paid a special visit to the house before you left if she'd known you weren't going to be there in church today."

"It's not my fault that Aaron Osgood needed to see me in Birmingham. The man *is* running for governor. And it's my job to help get him elected. I'll see Janet plenty next weekend, at the party."

"How was *your* Sunday, Son? Did you have a chance to worship?"

"Mr. Elmore needed my help on something. I spent the morning with him."

"You didn't go to church?"

"No, Mother. I didn't."

"Did the rest of the family go to church?"

"I'm not sure that's any of your business."

"If you're as serious about this girl as you say you are, then it *is* my business."

"I don't follow you."

"If you marry her one day, then her family will be part of our family. That makes the faith of her family my business."

Daniel said nothing as he gazed out the window at what had turned into a gorgeous, mild summer afternoon thanks to the morning's earlier storm, which had cooled things off for once. At the top of the driveway, Caroline's two brothers were strapping water bottles and other gear onto the backs of their bicycles. The two sisters and their mother were cutting roses from the garden. The father was plucking ripe vegetables and placing them in a big straw basket dangling from his arm. Only Daniel was indoors, having a conversation about church. He'd had this kind of conversation with his mother before. If his father actually *had* suffered a heart attack or stroke, that conversation wouldn't have been much worse than this one.

"There are many different ways to worship, Mother."

"What are you trying to tell me, Son? How does Caroline's family worship?"

Any response involving flowers, vegetables or bike rides would only confuse or horrify his mother, who came from a place that sprouted crudely lettered homemade signs like the one he'd seen yesterday on the way to Birmingham: "Go to Church or the Devil will GET You."

"Is this really what you called me to talk about right now?"

"Are you suggesting there's anything more important? You know what we went through with you on this subject just a few months ago. Your father is still upset at the way you handled it, how you shut us out, didn't consult with us or tell us the first thing about it until it was all over. If you're going to choose another faith now, so you can worship with Caroline, your father and I would like to be told right away. Do I need to remind you that he can't handle the stress of any more shocks to his system?"

If he hadn't felt so sorry for himself right now, perhaps he could have felt sorry for his poor mother. Half of her lifelong struggle had been spent in the enormous effort to get off her father's farm and out of the "country." The rest had been directed toward maintaining a financially precarious place in her small town society, and convincing everyone that she belonged. But her son, she had always told him, could go all the way to "the top." She had never defined what she meant by this, nor had she reckoned on its consequences, especially after he was actually accepted at Harvard. She must have imagined that his rise in the world would both complete and call greater attention to her own. Unfortunately, what she also seemed to want was a simpleminded mama's boy who never really grew up or left home, certainly not his hometown. Already he had traveled so far away from her—geographically and otherwise—she could no longer reach him. These phone calls which were her pathetic, desperate attempts to get him back only drove him further away.

During one of these conversations this past semester, he'd informed his mother that he had been officially confirmed in the Episcopal faith. He had assumed this would please his parents, who had never understood why he wasn't attending church, or why a Sunday morning in Massachusetts should be different from a Sunday morning in Alabama. Of course he believed in God, he assured his parents. He had to. If there were no such thing as God, Daniel Dobbs would still be bagging groceries like he'd done every summer since he could remember. But while he was away in college, he usually didn't get back from his Saturday night until Sunday morning. Dawn meant getting to sleep, not rising for church. He was working so hard, he just didn't have time for it, he told his parents, and thought no more about it until this past fall, when Eleanor pointed out that there was really no such thing as a Southern Baptist in New England. All of his family on both sides—grandparents, aunts, uncles, cousins—every single relative he'd ever known or met—was Southern Baptist. His father had once been a Southern Baptist preacher. But if he planned to make this part of the country his home, Eleanor observed, then he would need to choose a different "spiritual home" as well. He certainly saw the wisdom of her point, especially after he attended Sunday services with her in Greenwich at St. Paul's Episcopal Church, to which her family belonged. Without hesitation or hyperbole, he could safely say it was the largest group of well-dressed, well-heeled and well-to-do people he'd ever been around in his life.

Eleanor advised him to begin confirmation classes. As far as he was concerned, he had more than enough classes with his college course work. But she investigated. The Episcopal chaplaincy at Harvard offered a five P.M. Sunday service, she told him. As for the confirmation classes, which would begin again in January following the holiday break, these were conducted after the five o'clock services, at the rectory, over sherry. Then came a light cold supper of catered sandwiches, which—though modest—was still far better than the dining hall fare he would have gotten at Eliot House. At five P.M. on Sunday afternoon, what else was there to do except find some way to avoid studying and eating in the Eliot House Dining Hall? Best of all, the thirty-five year old chaplain, Lewis Holditch, was the father figure he had never found in any one of his college professors, including his beloved senior tutor and thesis advisor, Dr. Francis Miles.

Lewis was probably the first person Daniel had met on the Harvard campus who wanted to listen more than he wanted to talk. Daniel had a lot to talk about; there was much on his mind. For one thing: How could a Southern Baptist from Alabama ever really become an Episcopalian like the ones he'd met in Greenwich, Connecticut? But there was an even bigger question. After meeting with the Alabama attorney general and gubernatorial candidate Aaron Osgood over Christmas break, did he really want to move to Greenwich, Connecticut anyway? And then, in March, after running into Caroline Elmore again, did he really love Eleanor? Lewis helped him find answers to all these questions. After the others had departed from the sandwich supper, Daniel often stayed for hours on Sunday evenings talking to Lewis. It was Lewis who helped him understand that he had already abandoned his Southern Baptist faith; his belief in a God who did not demand regular churchgoing made him an Episcopalian at heart. It was Lewis who pointed out that he'd already decided to move back to Alabama by accepting a job there. It was Lewis who told him that if he was in love with Caroline Elmore, he couldn't really be in love with Eleanor May, despite the fact that if not for her, he would never have met Lewis in the first place. And it was Lewis who suggested that he audition for the role of Class Day speaker. The chaplaincy was even the site of his first date with Caroline, whom he'd asked to accompany him to Easter Sunday services. Figuring that an Alabama girl, even one from Mountain Brook, could not turn down a date for church on Easter Sunday.

It was the Easter Sunday phone call that had gone so badly awry with his parents. Instead of being pleased by the news of his confirmation, his parents reacted as if he'd just made a pact with the devil and was headed directly to Hell. He'd forgotten that for folks where they came from, there was only one true faith that confirmed your place both in Heaven and in small-town Southern society. What did his confirmation in the Episcopal faith do to his baptism by total immersion when he was eleven years old? his mother demanded to know.

He attempted to change the subject by telling them of his date with Caroline Elmore of Mountain Brook. The results were equally disastrous. What about Eleanor? they wanted to know. Why was he taking one girl to the afternoon services when he'd already attended the morning services with another?

Was he going out with two girls at the same time? On the same day? On *Easter Sunday*, of all days? And if he was no longer planning to spend the rest of his life with Eleanor, then why did he need to be an Episcopalian?

Despite the eagle eye his mother kept on her budget, this phone call had lasted almost two hours. His mother thought he was damned, juggling two different religions and two different women, all on *Easter Sunday*. Later, it was Lewis's soft, gentle voice that explained their son's entire spiritual journey to such an extent and in such compelling detail that any objection would have seemed un-Christian. His parents had no choice but to accept the news, and no real reason not to after Lewis pointed out that Daniel had no obligation to proclaim this new faith or avoid the First Baptist Church when he was in Opelika. For the sake of "family togetherness," he could always worship with them at their church. Bitter reproaches turned into perfunctory congratulations. Lewis had pulled off a miracle akin to changing water into wine.

But Lewis wasn't so readily available at the moment.

"Mother, I'm being rude to my hosts, and I shouldn't tie up their line much longer. If there's nothing else, we should probably get off the phone now."

"Actually there is something else, Son."

He sighed. "What is it?"

"Ricky Jill called here last night. Wanted to know how she could reach you."

"Ricky Jill!" he exclaimed, amazed.

"She wanted to know if you were living in Montgomery yet, and how she could get in touch with you there," said his mother, her voice full of unstated accusation, no doubt primed by the sermon she had heard that morning, which would not have consisted of polite abstractions. Sin, sin, sin was ever the theme, and it was always illustrated in vivid and graphic detail. For many Southern Baptists, going to church was the closest encounter with Sin they were likely to get.

"I wasn't aware that you were still in touch with Ricky Jill," said his mother primly.

"I'm not," he protested. "I ran into her last December in Montgomery. When I had the job interview with Aaron Osgood. That's all."

"What was she doing in Montgomery?" said his mother suspiciously.

"She goes there once a month apparently," he said nervously, wishing he had more time to craft his answers. "With her family," he added. "When I told her I'd be working there this summer, she said we'd all have to get together. She might have been there this weekend. With her family. Or they could be coming next weekend. That's all I can think."

"It's just strange," said his mother. "In the whole two years you dated her, I don't think she called this house once."

"She was just a high school kid then," he explained reasonably. "Now she's a married woman with a three year-old daughter. No reason for her to be shy about calling the house to arrange a get-together. I've always wanted to meet her husband and see her baby girl," he added as a final flourish.

"I still think it's strange," said his mother.

Yet her suspicions sounded allayed by his strategic and repeated references to Ricky Jill's family, marriage and child. In his mother's mindset, allusions to "family" laid all concerns instantly to rest. It was truly a magic word. In the Southern Baptist lexicon, the word "family" was the antonym of "sin," the opposite of "sex."

But his mother was right: It was strange.

Ricky Jill Johnson had been his high school sweetheart, his girlfriend for two years, although she lived a few hours away in Brewton, where she attended Brewton High School and was a member of the cheerleading squad. They had met when he came to Brewton for a statewide Key Club convention being held at the school. A junior then, he was president of the Alabama chapter. She had been part of the hospitality committee greeting all the arrivals, handing out nametags, setting up the banquet and directing out-of-towners around the campus. She was a year younger than he, a mere sophomore then. That hadn't mattered.

It wasn't that Ricky Jill was what was called "pretty in the face." She wasn't. Her long, dirty-blonde hair was parted in the middle and feather cut in the style made famous by Farrah Fawcett and enthusiastically followed by a generation of cheerleaders, baton twirlers and majorettes, especially in the small Southern towns like the one Ricky Jill, and Farrah Fawcett herself, came from. Her breasts were not particularly remarkable either. It wasn't that they were small, but they weren't large and were somehow lacking in any quality that could make them stand out as erotic body parts. They were just absolutely average, ordinary breasts that formed a bit of a shelf on her chest. That was all. So most other females failed utterly to understand why men had been wild for Ricky Jill since she was about fourteen and her hips spread out. But boys noticed instantly: Ricky Jill was all crotch. In the same tight jeans and short shorts that all the girls wore, her crotch appeared like a continent unto itself, bound on either side by her widespread yet slim hips and supported by her strong yet slender legs. Years of gymnastics and cheerleading had taught her body how to maximize the impact of even its slightest motion or action. When she walked down the street it was more provocative than a Playboy centerfold doing a striptease. Men caught one glimpse and they just *knew*. At any rate, that's what had happened to him when he first laid eyes on her. And those eyes had never even traveled upwards to her breasts or her face. They didn't need to. That part of her was irrelevant.

Ricky Jill had not been a virgin when he met her at sixteen. That didn't matter. Ricky Jill had never been a virgin, not even when she was born. There were the Southern girls who stayed virgins no matter how long they'd been married, and the Southern girls who never had any virginity to begin with. Ricky Jill had not been able to lose what she never had, so it didn't bother him a bit that he wasn't her first, though she was his first and they were both young teenagers in high school. Being Ricky Jill's first wasn't the point. With a girl like Ricky Jill, you didn't ask to be the first or the only. That would be asking too much. This girl was built to fuck, and instinctively, all males regarded her as a natural resource open to the public, not meant to be hoarded as a private possession or a piece of private property.

To Ricky Jill, sex was just a spontaneous show of affection which came as naturally and easily as hugging a good friend, of which she had many. Fucking was just a different kind of hug, with the legs instead of the arms. It was not fraught with moral implications, future obligations or religious strictures like it was for most other girls. She taught him how without actually teaching him—just by doing him. Even when he was on top, it was somehow she who did all the work in her practiced, easy way. Cheerleader that she was, she swiveled her hips, tightened her muscles, thrust her pelvis into his and before long he would collapse on her chest in a grateful heap. When this happened too soon, like it did at first, she would playfully shove him off, prop herself on an elbow and watch him fall almost asleep until she judged he was rested enough. Then she would take his hand and touch herself with his fingers until the next thing he knew, he was on top of her again and she was coming like a freight train. The first time she did this, he was frightened out of his wits. As she hollered and writhed from side to side, her head thrashing wildly to and fro, he thought she must be having an epileptic seizure, and didn't know how he would explain this to her parents, especially if she ended up dead. When she was done, still very much alive and well, she laughed at the alarm and confusion written all over his face.

"Guess you didn't know you could get a girl to do that, did ya?" she grinned at him.

No, he did not. And more importantly, he had not known that girls could do that. Nothing and no one in all sixteen years of his Alabama life had ever so much as hinted that girls could do that. He figured it must be something that only Ricky Jill could do, and she had let him in on her little secret. It was impossible to imagine that almost any other woman or girl he'd ever met could be possessed by sexual feelings in that way. Ricky Jill had looked exactly as if possessed by the very devil folks in Alabama were always trying to steer clear of. Impossible to believe that his own mother, for example, who had worked so hard to learn to carry all five feet of herself like a department store mannequin, would flail about in an unmade bed like a mad dog with rabies. But now he knew it was possible, at least for some girls. At least when they were with a man who knew what he was doing. Afterwards, he'd swell with pride at what he'd been able to do just as earlier he'd swelled with lust.

He made it over to Brewton about once or twice a month, right after early church on Sunday mornings, when he could borrow his father's car. The round trip from Opelika to Brewton and back was not an easy one to make in one day. But Ricky Jill made it worth his while. Everyone thought it was sweet, innocent young love. He came by her house and took her to the Youth Fellowship gatherings at the First Baptist Church of Brewton. But Ricky Jill's mother worked as a hostess at the Ramada Inn restaurant, and the Sunday lunch shift was her busiest time of the week. She didn't get home till four or four-thirty, when she'd find them sitting on the couch in the rec room holding hands and watching TV, as if that's all they ever did after the Fellowship meetings. Ricky Jill's father spent his Sunday afternoons going fishing in the spring and summer, or hunting during the fall and winter. If it rained, the men played poker in the fishing camp or the hunting lodge. Her father was never back till after dark. Ricky Jill's two older brothers had moved out on their own years ago. So there was no one at the house to know that he and Ricky Jill didn't stay at Youth Fellowship too long.

Whenever he visited, Ricky Jill was always ready for him, and she never seemed to have vaginal infections, menstrual periods or headaches. After they'd been seeing each other more than a year, she really did stop having periods and it appeared she had turned up pregnant. By then, he had been accepted into Harvard and was about to graduate from high school. Of course he offered to marry her, but she knew his parents were set on him going to college, and she herself was set on graduating from high school. She had another year to go, and it would be the best year of her life. She would be head cheerleader and might even get to be the homecoming queen. There was also the Senior Prom. No way was she going to miss out on any of that. After she'd enjoyed the peak experiences of a girl's life, that would be the time to settle down with someone and get married.

So he gave her the money, and her cheerleading coach drove her to a Planned Parenthood in Montgomery one Saturday, when her parents thought they were attending an all-day training camp like they'd done before. When he came over the next Sunday, he was surprised to find that she was neither sad, subdued, nor scared by what had happened, and didn't seem to see why they shouldn't behave as usual. He had not anticipated this. He had assumed that she would at least be sore, perhaps in more ways than one, and he'd spend his whole time stroking her hand while they watched TV on the couch in the rec room until her mother came back from the Ramada Inn. But Ricky Jill shucked her clothes like she always did and expressed amazement when he hesitated to do the same.

"There's nothing wrong with me, boy," she had teased. "What's wrong with you?"

What was wrong was the harrowing two weeks he had spent between Ricky Jill's announcement of her pregnancy and the abortion which terminated it. During that time, every waking moment was spent in dread that Ricky Jill would change her mind and accept his proposal, or that her parents would learn of her condition and force her to do so. Although less likely, it was also possible that his parents would find out, and then there would be hell to pay. While his father was no longer a Southern Baptist preacher, both his parents were still devout Southern Baptist churchgoers, and the concept of a separation between church and anything else had never made it that far south. His parents lived in fear that all they had ever gained—their jobs off the farm, their homes off the farm, their meager possessions and even more meager savings—would be instantly stripped from them by either the force of a wrathful God or by the earthly powers that acted for God if they so much as strayed one whit from the Christian life. The further they moved away from their own origins and upbringing, the more they stood to lose and the more they had to fear. If they knew their son had committed the worst sin of all and gotten a girl pregnant, it would have killed them. Every time the phone rang, it would be the bank calling in their mortgage. Every time the mail came, it would be the letters informing them that their job performance was unsatisfactory.

His own future would be equally blighted, he now realized, if he ended up having to marry Ricky Jill. Although he'd just as soon marry Ricky Jill as any other girl he'd ever met, he wasn't ready to get married and had the sense to know it. Marriage wouldn't be all pussy, like his relationship with Ricky Jill was now. Marriage now would mean either Opelika or Brewton for the rest of his life, and the kind of job like the ones he had now, but not just after school or over the holidays and during the summer until he went away to college. There would be no college. There would be a baby instead. And soon enough, there might not be so much pussy, either. Was this what the youth counselors had been trying to get at when they preached abstinence and said there was more to life than sex? If so, he now understood there was more to life than Ricky Jill's pussy. No one could have told him that a year ago. It had been his whole life. Well, that and Key Club. And he hadn't asked for anything more. But if he kept going with that, it would bring a whole lot more, none of which he wanted. So for the first time, he didn't want Ricky Jill.

But she was a girl who thought that sex was just something people did when they felt like doing it, and she always felt like doing it. Afterwards she thought no more about it than she did of the cereal she ate for breakfast when she woke up hungry. She had a boy's attitude about sex in a woman's body. It was an irresistible and overwhelming combination. There was no way not to fuck when he was with Ricky Jill.

So that Sunday after the abortion was the last time he'd been to see her. In the middle of the following week, he called to tell her that he'd managed to get his hours extended and would now be working on Sundays as well as Saturdays in order to save as much as possible for college. Come summer, he'd be working full-time, of course, including on the weekends, but he'd try to make it over to Brewton when he could.

Ricky Jill accepted this news matter of factly, without question, without protestations, without tears and without demands. A man who buckled down and worked hard—that was what a good man did, and she expected no less of a man who had been International President of the Key Club. In a few short months, he would be heading a thousand miles away, to college in Massachusetts, and she would be heading into her senior year at Brewton High School. He didn't need to break up with her; circumstances did it for him. The few times he called over the summer, she was cheerful as ever, without reproach or recriminations. Soon enough, he suspected, there would be another man in her life. Probably there already was. Only later did it occur to him that there might have been another man besides himself in her life when he was still in it.

At any rate, she hadn't pressed him and they hadn't seen each other again. The year after she graduated from high school, he heard from his mother that Ricky Jill had dropped out of the junior college to get married to Kirk McNeese, whose father owned the Shell station and carwash on the county highway. A few years older than Ricky Jill, he was a good-looking, hard-working young man who would be what was called "a steady husband." Not quite nine months after they were married, when Ricky Jill was eighteen years old, she had a baby girl.

He had never expected to see her again and so didn't recognize her at first when he ran into her in Montgomery before last Christmas. That was when he'd come to meet with Aaron Osgood, and she'd come to do her Christmas shopping at the mall in Montgomery. Her mother was keeping the baby, now three years old, until Ricky Jill's husband got home from work.

She looked exactly the same except her hair now had blonde streaks that didn't seem intended even to resemble natural hair color. He couldn't help but notice that neither pregnancy nor childbirth had affected her figure. Perhaps her hips were just a little bit more wide spread. The better to fuck a man's brains out, he couldn't help but think to himself. He got a hard-on then and there so bad it hurt and he couldn't think of a thing to say. Meanwhile, she just greeted and hugged him like she used to do on those Sunday afternoons when he'd picked her up at her house in Brewton to take her to the Fellowship meetings. Like there had been no four years absence and silence, no marriage and baby with another man, no abortion of their own baby.

"Where you stayin'?" she had asked him.

He wasn't staying anywhere, but was supposed to be driving back to Opelika—in his father's car—after he picked up the stuffed animal from the Hallmark Shoppe his mother wanted him to get for his sister's Christmas present.

"I don't know where I'm staying yet," he had said. And this was no lie.

"I'm at the Crowne Plaza downtown," she said. "They got this beautiful new bar and restaurant made outa this old railroad depot they converted. Why don't you meet me there for a drink after we're both done shopping? Say about six o'clock?"

He had called his mother from a payphone in the mall to explain that his meeting with Aaron Osgood had gone extremely well, and he'd been offered a full time job on the campaign, to begin in the summer right after he graduated. This was no lie either. But Aaron had suggested he stay in town for dinner tonight to meet some of the other people who were already working on the campaign. Although this *was* a lie, it was a plausible one, and his mother was primarily concerned about his night's lodging. Yes, his father could do without the car just this once—she would drive him to work—but they could not afford for the price of a hotel room in Montgomery to go on their credit card, especially this time of year.

"Oh, that's all taken care of," he had assured her.

The drink at the depot restaurant and bar of the Crowne Plaza in downtown Montgomery turned into dinner. The food was good and the atmosphere was nice. He fumbled a bit with the tab, because he didn't have the cash to cover it and the only credit card he now possessed was in his parents' names. Since he'd been with Eleanor, he hadn't needed his own card anymore, and he only got in trouble if he had one. So after he'd paid off the last one, he'd cancelled it. He'd have a lot of explaining to do with his parents when the meal he was supposed to be taken out for showed up on their statement. But Ricky Jill said the bill would be charged to her room number.

"We have an account," she explained. "I come here at least once a month for shopping, doctor's appointments, things like that."

"It's a nice place," he said, looking around the restaurant. "Are the rooms this nice?"

"Why don't you come see for yourself?" she said.

There were no hollow pretenses, no soul-searching discussions, no convoluted rationalizations or justifications, no apologies, no explanations, no shame, no guilt, no whiff of sin and no sense that what they were doing was at all wrong or unnatural. There was just good hard fucking such as he had not experienced since he'd last been with Ricky Jill. He had forgotten just how good that could be. She wrung him out of his very last drop, and then some. Whereas with Eleanor, sex was just a maintenance chore, something he had to do, like saying "I love you," to keep the relationship running smoothly. But lately with Eleanor, he hadn't even been able to get it up. And he had never yet been with a girl who could come like Ricky Jill. Most girls did not know how to come, or for that matter, how to fuck, and they probably didn't even like to. As far as he was concerned, when a man was lucky enough to find himself with a girl who really liked it and really knew how to do it, then all bets were off. No man should be expected to deny himself that pleasure, and the fact that she was married now meant he wouldn't need to worry if she got pregnant. He fell asleep thinking how convenient it was that she came to Montgomery at least "once a month," she'd said, and he would be spending most of his summer, if not the foreseeable future, in that same city.

The next morning he woke up with a hard-on poking right into the firm flesh of her perfect ass. Obviously it woke her up too, and she knew exactly what to do about it, rising up on her knees and letting him take her from behind right where he wanted her at that very moment. Any other girl would have wanted to go to the bathroom first and then talk for hours about contraceptives. Ricky Jill knew how to seize the moment like she could seize a man's dick and make the absolute most of it.

He could not deny that even after he had met Caroline Elmore in March, he had not forgotten that Ricky Jill came every month to Montgomery, where he would be living this summer and possibly for the near future if Aaron Osgood was elected governor. This wasn't to say that he planned to be unfaithful or even to contact Ricky Jill. He considered himself committed to Caroline, and Caroline, with her beauty, her brains, and her Mountain Brook background, was obviously the woman who should be his wife. Of course, he never intended to be anything but faithful to his wife or the woman who would be his wife. He believed wholeheartedly in the concept of monogamy.

Unfortunately, the vestigial Neanderthal part of himself had difficulty with the actual practice of monogamy, and did not at all comprehend the necessity of limiting himself *for the rest of his life* to just one woman when the world was full of available, eager and attractive women who were all potential sex partners. Why did all these beautiful women inhabit the world if he was not supposed to have sexual intercourse with them? His inner Neanderthal simply could not suppress the urge to fulfill his male destiny, especially if the female was equally intent on fulfilling her destiny. In short, it would be impossible to prevent the spontaneous combustion of two explosive elements like himself and Ricky Jill. If he ever ran into her again, he could not guarantee that his commitment to Caroline would be enough to prevent the inevitable. Sex with Caroline was just fine—there was nothing wrong with it, like there had been with Eleanor. It just wasn't the earth-shattering experience it was with Ricky Jill. And why should he deny himself? His commitment to Caroline was genuine and his intentions were good and pure. So if he failed to live up to them every once in a while, he didn't see how anyone was harmed. The sin would be in the planning of it, and this he most certainly would not do.

It wasn't like Ricky Jill either. She had not even telephoned his house in high school when she first learned of her pregnancy all those years ago, but had simply waited till he got there on Sunday to tell him. As his mother had pointed out, he had never known Ricky Jill to call his house at all.

"She left a phone number for you, Son. Do you want me to give it to you?"

"No, that's okay. I can't imagine it's anything important. We haven't been in contact for four years." (Not counting the time a few months ago he'd slept with her in Montgomery.)

He prayed that she wouldn't be in Montgomery next weekend, when Caroline would be with him.

~ 5 ~

Daniel's imagination had conjured Caroline's aunt Libba in the image of Aaron Osgood's wife: tall, beautiful and utterly imperious in the security of her wealth, looks, and social position. This preconception stemmed not just from his own fears, but from those of Caroline's mother, whose flustered and anxious preparations made Daniel feel as if they were headed to Buckingham Palace to wait upon the Queen. What he encountered when he arrived at Libba Albritton's house for the dinner party on Sunday night was completely different from his expectations, yet all the more fascinating as a result. A grey-haired woman dressed in loose black silk, she sat perched on a floor cushion with feline grace and elegance, smoking a cigarette, sipping from a glass of wine, and paging through a *New Yorker* magazine placed on the living room rug. Twin black standard poodles named Nip and Tuck sat like sentinels guarding her on both sides. She didn't rise to greet him, but waved cheerfully as he entered the house. "Hello, Daniel," she called out, as if he were an old friend she'd known forever. He was beginning to understand that people in Mountain Brook had no need to be formal, because folks at the top could behave exactly as they pleased. With nothing to prove to anyone, they could afford to be relaxed. In a way, this was a much more thrilling welcome than the usual introductory fuss, as if he were being immediately initiated into an intimate family circle.

Although sitting cross-legged on the floor, this woman still managed to command the room. Indeed, she did possess the presence of a queen, despite a complete absence of make-up, nondescript clothes, and no jewelry except for a gold safety pin encrusted with tiny diamonds on the collar of her silk blouse. Instead of the large diamond wedding ring he had expected on a woman who enjoyed the benefit of millions, she wore only a gold band. Unsophisticated as he was, he somehow understood that she was the essence of sophistication. Her glamour came from herself alone—the force of a strong personality permeating the room. He had never seen a woman like this anywhere in the state of Alabama. She looked like someone who belonged in a Manhattan apartment or a Paris salon.

It was her husband Milton who came to greet him formally and shake his hand.

"What can I get you to drink, sir?" he asked.

Afraid he was being mocked, Daniel looked around in mild panic. But no one was sniggering or at all surprised by Milton Albritton's manner. Unlike his wife, Milton was the one who looked straight out of central casting: the quintessential Southern gentleman—tall, courtly, and handsome as an old-fashioned movie star, a Cary Grant or Gregory Peck. Yet he was polite and deferential as a black waiter at a country club, coming right over to take a drink order. Suddenly it occurred to Daniel that this was none other than that famous Southern hospitality, which he had completely failed to recognize.

He was further disconcerted when one of the guests he had not yet even met proudly proclaimed his intent to depart almost as soon as Daniel walked through the door. Did this man's departure have anything to do with Daniel's arrival? He was a large, heavy-set, red-faced man who moved slowly but forcefully toward the door, as he pulled on the arm of his wife, who was still engrossed in conversation. The other arm he stuck out at Daniel when he reached the door.

"Julian Petsinger," he said gruffly. Without waiting to hear who Daniel was, he turned around. "Come on, Lula!" he called out with affectionate firmness. "Let's get out of here and go get some good American food at the country club!" He tugged on her arm and turned back around to the front door. "I gotta get outa here before that woman brings out that fancy French food she always serves even when she's invited me over to dinner. I don't like it, I don't eat it and I don't even want to smell it or be around it. Just the sight of it upsets my stomach. I don't know why that woman even keeps inviting me over!" He jerked his thumb to indicate Libba Albritton, his imperturbable hostess, who remained seated on her cushion, calmly smoking her cigarette and taking no notice of him whatsoever.

"I think she invites you because her daughter is married to your son— namely, *Me,*" yelled a tall, ruddy-cheeked young man with blond hair parted straight down the center. The red face that looked like a heart attack waiting to happen in the father looked like wholesome good health in the son.

"Then she ought to fix me something I can eat, dammit!" yelled the father. "She knows I cain't eat that French glop!"

"Mother has lasagna for tonight!" called a young woman who was obviously his daughter-in-law. "Eggplant lasagna. Just for you!"

"Eggplant!" he bellowed, reaching for the doorknob. "I've never eaten an eggplant before in my life! What kind of food is that? Come on, Lula!" His tone was losing its hint of playfulness and becoming more belligerent. While his son and daughter-in-law exchanged glances behind his back, his wife broke free of his grasp and scampered over to give her hostess a brief embrace. There was a tremor at the corners of her mouth as she bent down, and bald spots at the back of her head where her beauty parlor hair had been slept on and insufficiently restored afterwards. Daniel could even see flakes of dandruff clinging to stray strands of hair like flakes of snow in the bare branches of a tree in winter. She seemed a wreck. No doubt she would look somewhat better tomorrow, after her Monday morning appointment at the beauty salon. But she would still be a nervous wreck.

"Come, on, Lula!" her husband commanded, with even more menace creeping into his voice.

Lula hastened over to join him, anxiously waving to everyone without looking at anyone. As soon as she reached her husband, he flung open the front door and charged through it like a bull, dragging his wife after him.

When the door slammed behind him, there was some scattered laughter followed by the general hum of conversations resumed. Obviously the man's rude and untimely departure was a commonplace occurrence. But Daniel had never seen anything like it and was flabbergasted. He couldn't help but steal a glance at his hostess to see how she would respond now that this boorish blockhead was gone. Throughout the scene, she had simply observed it unfold as if it were no more than a movie she was watching that had nothing at all to do with her personally. It was somewhat amusing, but in no way deeply affecting and certainly not troubling.

Now she stubbed out her cigarette and rose gracefully to her feet without the slightest sign of effort. To his surprise, she came straight over to him.

"I'm sorry I didn't get up earlier," she said, grasping his outstretched hand with both of hers in a gesture of warmth he no longer expected. "I only give myself two cigarettes a day, now, and I'm determined that nothing will interfere with my enjoyment of *every single puff.*"

It was then the charm of Libba Albritton hit him full force. The grey hair was smooth as the silk of her blouse, parted on one side and held back on the other with a bobby pin covered in tiny pearls. The locks at the jaw line on either side of her face jutted forward like the buoyant, bouncing hair of a schoolgirl. Her supple figure was equally youthful. He'd been told she was almost sixty, but this didn't look like the sixty he'd seen on any other woman.

However, there was nothing childlike about the implacable force of silence and indifference with which she had countered her guest's rude bluster.

"I'm glad that man I just met didn't interfere with your cigarette," he said.

"Oh, him." She gave a curt, dismissive wave of her hand and a short bark of contemptuous laughter. "So much for being one of the richest men in Birmingham," she said. "Look what it's done for him."

One of the richest men in Birmingham?

Seeing his frown, she repeated the man's name. "Julian Petsinger," she said.

His mind staggered as an incredible thought crashed in. "Is that the Petsinger. . . ?" He looked over at Caroline, unable to believe that she would have failed to inform him of her connection to one of the original Big Mule families of Birmingham. While Caroline accepted a glass of wine from her uncle, her aunt was nodding with a smirk in reply to his question.

"The Petsinger of U.S. Steel?" she said. "Yes. The very same. You've just seen one of the richest men and one of the biggest rednecks in the entire state. Welcome back to Alabama, Daniel. Ta-ta, darling," she said to her husband, who handed her a fresh glass of wine. She nodded at Daniel and lifted her glass slightly toward him before taking a sip. Daniel noticed that he now had a glass in his own hands, though he didn't remember accepting it.

"But, but . . ." he found himself almost sputtering, and the aunt trying to stop her smirk from spreading across her face. He had just met a member of a family that was already in the books of Alabama history? Even the beginning fourth grade textbooks on Alabama history now contained the name Petsinger, one of the founding captains of the iron and steel industry in the city of Birmingham. And Libba Albritton had just sat there on a *floor cushion,* smoking a cigarette, cool and unconcerned, while one of the Big Mules of Birmingham berated her and her hospitality? He had to hand it to her. Mrs. Elmore would have been fluttering and hovering about, wringing her hands and emptying her kitchen to try to please a man who could not be pleased. And any other Southern hostess he knew would be firmly ensconced in an apron at the stove where she'd spent the majority of the day in hopes of pleasing a rich and important man who couldn't be pleased. It was all hard to believe, and he could not believe he had just been in the room with an actual Petsinger. Just then he remembered he was still in the room with one, and turned around to look for the man who'd married Caroline's cousin. The aunt followed his gaze.

"There are two sisters also," she said, reading his thoughts and sipping her wine. "One is quite attractive and won't have any trouble finding a husband. And the other is . . . well . . . not as attractive." She paused to take another sip of wine. "But Big Pet is a b-i-i-i-i-i-i-i-i-i-g donor to the Republican Party, and the older girl has been given a thank-you job with George Bush. She wanted Reagan, of course, but she'll have to make do with Bush. Maybe she'll be able to find a husband in Washington. I'm told the men aren't as picky up there."

"They can't afford to be," he said, thinking, Reagan? Bush? He had known these folks would be Republican, but he hadn't figured they'd be quite such Big Republicans.

Right then there was a large disturbance as if a herd of elephants had just stampeded into the room. He wasn't sure what, or who, it was. When he looked back at his hostess, he saw he'd lost her attention. She now had a hand clamped down on her niece's arm and was leaning over toward her ear. He heard her mutter something to the effect of "Drop dead good-looking," but wasn't sure he'd heard right or who this referred to. It certainly couldn't refer to the new arrival, who turned out to be the high school English teacher he'd heard so much about. Caroline had spent hours and hours telling him everything about this all-important man named Norman Laney. She'd left out only one tiny detail: he looked like he weighed over 500 pounds. He looked, in fact, almost exactly like that picture in *The Guinness Book of World Records* of the fattest man in the world.

For such a fat man, Norman Laney moved with surprising swiftness and came straight over to Daniel to seize his hand and wring it to a pulp. "I've been waiting to meet you for years!" he cried. "Years!"

"Years?" Daniel echoed. He'd only known Caroline a matter of months.

"You know Susan Ritchie?" Norman Laney said. Everything about him was large, including his voice, which boomed out over the room and tended to stop any other conversations and draw all eyes over to what was now the most commanding presence in the room.

"Susan Ritchie?" He thought for a minute. "Is that the woman who interviewed me for Harvard?"

"Exactly!" shouted Mr. Laney, as if Daniel had just aced an impossible exam question. "She's the *head* of the committee, in fact, that interviews all the applicants to Harvard from Alabama. And she told me years ago that a boy named Daniel Dobbs from Opelika, Alabama was *the* most exceptional, stellar candidate who had ever come before that committee in all the years that she had been on it. 'Norman,' she told me, 'We felt like we had just met a future president of the United States. He is *that* impressive,' she said. So, naturally, you can imagine, I've been desperately wanting to meet you before you're off to the White House. I understand you're on the side of the angels, working for Aaron Osgood?"

Had Daniel's moment in Mountain Brook arrived at last? Mr. Laney was the first person Daniel had met in Mountain Brook who had raised the subject of the election, and seemed to grasp the importance of this moment in Alabama history, when the people of the state could choose either to go forward or sink back into the dreadful mire of the past.

"Now, Norman," said Mrs. Elmore, as if admonishing a small child instead of a ten-ton grown man. "I'm sure Susan meant what she said about Daniel at the time," she wagged her finger at him playfully. "But that was three years before Caroline's application." Her tone was that of a young mother trying to salvage or encourage the self-esteem of a five year-old child. Caroline rolled her eyes.

Ignoring both daughter and mother, Mr. Laney addressed Daniel. "You've come not a moment too soon. The Reagan/Bush crowd around here could use an infusion of **democracy**."

"Watch it, Norman," called out the six foot two (little) Julian Petsinger.

"Oh, I know, I know," said Norman, with great good humor and a smile that pushed up big balls of fat on either side of his face. "I know I'm just the token Democrat! But I'm determined not to be a mere decoration, you know, no matter how ornamental my appearance may be! I've got to speak my mind. I won't let you have me just for my good looks alone!" He turned around abruptly to Caroline, the supposedly beloved pupil whom he had not yet even greeted. "Come with me, darling, out to my car. Will you? I could use your help."

If that had been Daniel's moment, then it was snatched away no sooner than it was given. Perhaps he was still suffering from some cultural jet-lag after his return from Harvard, but Daniel really had assumed that once the topics of Aaron Osgood, the Wallace campaign and the future of Alabama had been introduced into conversation, these issues would at least spark some *recognition,* if not outright discussion. After all, what could be more important? And if people in Mountain Brook—with the education and enlightenment that their money could buy—did not care about these topics, then who in Alabama would?

But to his dismay, the name of Aaron Osgood was not taken up, and the name of George Wallace never came up. Instead, a man he'd never heard of named Warren Ritchie became the subject as Perry Elmore embarked on a hilarious description of Susan Ritchie's husband, who had been seen on the streets of downtown Birmingham wearing a gas mask to protect himself from the pollution in the city. This was followed by a series of anecdotes testifying to the obnoxious behavior of this Warren Ritchie, who appeared to be the man everyone loved to hate. Everybody had their own Warren story of recent vintage. After his years in the Harvard dining halls, Daniel had really forgotten that people in the South didn't like to talk about ideas or current events. They liked to tell stories about people they knew. Eventually he began to wonder where Mr. Laney and Caroline had actually gone; they were taking an awful long time bringing something in from the car.

Ostensibly in search of the bathroom, he wandered out of the main room where the guests had gathered and entered the narrow hallway pointed out to him. Just as he spotted the unoccupied powder room, he heard the voices of Caroline and Mr. Laney coming from behind the closed door next to it. Had they taken whatever it was from the car in there, or never gone to the car at all? Their voices were both urgent and intense. What were they talking about? He paused to listen, as the voices flowed on unmindful of his presence, thanks to the thick Oriental runner and the equally thick carpet pad underneath it.

"You know I love you," Mr. Laney was saying. "I love you as much or more as any student I've ever had. I love you as much as if you were my own daughter. Even more than that, because my own daughter probably wouldn't have turned out so well. But I cannot approve of the way I saw you looking at your mother, especially after our last discussion. You agreed you were going to put the past behind you. But there was not one ounce of respect for your mother anywhere on your face."

"I'm sorry. I just don't have any respect for her." Caroline's voice was soft and sullen.

"Then fake it!" Mr. Laney ordered sharply. "Do you hear me? Fake it! I won't have this! Assume a virtue if you have it not and fake it!"

Daniel wasn't sure whether or not Caroline replied to this command. All he heard was a sound like a sigh.

"Perhaps if your mother had not dropped out of the University of Alabama in order to *give birth to you at age nineteen,* she might have more than a few scattered wits in her head," continued Mr. Laney. "And I do admit that there are plenty of times when I seriously wonder if she has even two brain cells to rub together to spark a single intelligent thought. But she obviously did something right, because that daughter of hers is now a *Harvard student.* While the vast majority of other people's daughters all over the country *are not* Harvard students. **DO YOU READ ME?**"

Caroline must have simply nodded, because he heard nothing from her.

"This is a woman who sent you a box with homemade banana nut bread and biscuits every single week of your freshman year."

"But Mr. Laney, that's just it. I don't even *like* banana nut bread," said Caroline.

"What the hell does that matter?" he erupted.

"She doesn't even know who I *am*. Despite the fact that I have never ever eaten banana nut bread **and** told her repeatedly that I don't like it, she still doesn't seem to realize that *I don't like banana nut bread*. If she ever really cared or stopped to think for one minute about who I am, maybe she'd know what I like and what I don't. Maybe she'd know me just a little bit. It isn't just the banana nut bread; it's a metaphor."

"It is not a metaphor; it's banana nut bread," he said emphatically. "And I don't care if you like it or not. I'm not asking you to like it. I'm not asking you to eat it. For all I care, you can take it down and throw it in the Charles River, week after week. What I demand is that you show some respect for the woman who sent you a bubble-wrapped package from home every single week you were gone. Are we clear on this?"

He could hear the murmur of Caroline's voice, but couldn't make out any of the words. She spoke a lot more softly than Mr. Laney, and the closed door was obviously made of solid wood. No hollow-core doors in this part of Alabama.

"Good," said Mr. Laney finally. "Now what about this boy?"

Suddenly Caroline spoke up with eagerness; he could hear her voice now. "Tell me what *you* think about him," she said.

"I think he has more good looks than any one person is entitled to. Are you sleeping with him?"

She must have nodded; Daniel felt his pulse quicken. He had not anticipated this degree of intimacy between his girlfriend and her former teacher.

"You aren't the first to be sleeping with him; I can promise you that," Mr. Laney said. "And you may not be the last. I hope you realize it."

Her voice devolved again into an unintelligible murmur.

"What are you using for birth control? I trust it's more than just your good luck!"

The muffled sounds of her words thrummed for some time behind the door.

"What do you mean you haven't had a chance yet?" exploded Mr. Laney. "Why in the name of the Father, the Son, the Holy Ghost and Mother Nature did you not go to the student health services when you were still at Harvard?? If there's one thing they don't blink at up there, it's birth control, and it would have been *free-ee-ee-ee*. Oh, Mary, Mother of God. The two things that Harvard Student Health Services handle better than anybody else are **Human Sexuality** and **Mental Illness**. And if you don't deal with your Human Sexuality, you'll be dealing with Mental Illness next. So why did you wait till you came back to the Bible Belt to procure your contraceptives? With no money, no car, no relative you can ask! Why is it that the smartest people do the dumbest things? Especially when it comes to sex! If you'd taken yourself to the health services and gotten yourself on birth control *up there,* you wouldn't *have* to worry about a doctor here gossiping or rumors getting back to your parents. And why hasn't *he* taken the lead on this? I sure hope he's at least taking what *inadequate* and *unreliable* precautions he can in the meantime, because if I find out he's not, there will be one less Romeo in the state of Alabama! Now listen to me and listen good!"

He must have given Caroline a moment to indicate that she was listening good.

"Tomorrow morning," he said. "Bright and early. Right after he leaves, and it can't be soon enough. I want you down at Planned Parenthood getting yourself on birth control if you have to sit and wait all day. You get that prescription, you get it filled, and you take a whole pack of pills if necessary!"

The whispery sound of Caroline's muted voice must have reminded him that she no longer had a car of her own since she'd left for college.

"All right then," he said. "Lunch tomorrow. I'm coming to pick you up. Just you. I will take you down there myself and will personally see to it that you get yourself squared away. Can I at least count on you to come up with some *polite* and *plausible* reason why I am not including your mother in this invitation *to lunch?*"

There was barely a murmur before Mr. Laney said "Good! Because if you're not careful, you will find *yourself* dropping out of college at an earlier age than nineteen to give birth. And twenty years later, *you* may not have *your* wits about you either. And most likely, you would not be married and *your* child would not be a student at Harvard. And then we would be talking about your lack of *self-respect!* And with good reason!"

Suddenly the door flung open and Mr. Laney barreled out with unexpected violence. Daniel barely had time to escape unnoticed into the bathroom, where he waited a few moments to gather his wits. This fat man was no ally, he realized, but a potential adversary. The only person he'd encountered so far who had shown the slightest interest in his work for a historic governor's race had only done so in order to ingratiate himself. It had been mere cocktail party chatter just like all the rest, only of a slightly higher order and with an ulterior motive that Daniel was only beginning to comprehend. He knew to be on guard when they were all seated for dinner and Mr. Laney made a flattering reference to Daniel's participation in Key Club.

"Tell me," said Milton Albritton to the table at large. "What is the *Key Club?*" He laid emphasis on those words, as if simply underscoring what he didn't understand. His expression was that of genuine bewilderment, and he seemed to be waiting patiently for the answer which would clear it all up. His whole demeanor was like that of an old school British gentleman: careful, polite, somewhat out of it and asking only to be made current. But something about his manner and means of expressing himself—however genuine—had the effect of making a slight mockery out of the *Key Club,* and by association, Daniel himself. He had no doubt that Mr. Laney had set him up, and that laughter was brewing just below the surface of the conversation. If it erupted, he feared it would be at his expense.

"It's a *service program* for young people," said Mr. Laney, making what to Daniel seemed like a deliberate mockery by speaking with his mouth full of French bread, which he tore off in big hunks with paw-like hands. (If Daniel's parents could have seen this man, they would have been aghast at his willfully bad table manners and his open disrespect for the Key Club.)

"Think 'Kiwanis Club,' Milton," said Perry Elmore. "Key Club is like Kiwanis at the high school level."

"Isn't Key Club part of Kiwanis?" asked (little) Julian Petsinger. "I mean, didn't Kiwanis start these high school programs? Don't they sponsor the Key Clubs?"

"Exactly right," said Mr. Laney, chewing noisily.

"Thank you," said Milton, inclining his head toward the table in a nod of thanks. "Kiwanis Club. I know about Kiwanis. Community service. Citizenship. Volunteering." He peered around the table. "Is that right? Or do I have it mixed up with Rotary?"

Again the question was perfectly straightforward and legitimate, but something about its very transparency and simplicity was making others at the table exchange glances of amusement. Daniel was even beginning to feel amused himself. His own father would practically have killed to get into the Rotary Club of Opelika, but had to settle for Kiwanis. Meanwhile, here was a man who obviously did not see much point in either, though he was not actively making fun of them. Daniel could not deny there was something refreshing and liberating about this attitude. It was cavalier in an older sense of the word. This man was naturally above it all by sheer birthright, and had no need for arrogant contempt to distance himself from the petty doings of middle-class strivers.

"You've got it right," said Mr. Laney. "The core values of Key Club are: Number One: leadership." In punctuation, he savagely tore off another hunk of bread. "Number Two: Character-building." He crammed the bread into his mouth and chewed with equal savagery. "And Number Three: Caring. Then we have the Key Club colors. Gold, for service. Blue, for *unwavering* character. And white, for purity." He trained a savage stare across the table at Daniel. "Did I remember them all, Daniel?" His politeness was sarcasm in thin disguise.

"Well," Daniel began sheepishly, fully aware that the laughter he'd feared was already beginning. "You left out the one that really drew me in. The one about college scholarships."

Now the table *did* erupt with laughter, and it was not at Daniel's expense, either.

Mr. Laney narrowed his eyes, as if he knew he'd lost a round he'd expected to win. "And the motto of Key Club is: 'Caring—our way of life.'" He bored his eyes like two bullet trajectories aimed straight through Daniel's skull.

"Daniel," said Perry Elmore, a bit drunkenly. "Did you *care deeply?*"

"About the college scholarship?"

Again there was laughter all around, except from Norman Laney, who was still tearing the entire baguette of bread apart hunk by hunk as if he wished it were a certain young man he was dismembering instead.

"It's so important to *care,*" continued Mr. Elmore. "And I for one am so glad to know that we have in our high schools in America actual organizations that teach people to *care.*"

Mr. Laney ignored the laughter and prepared to aim his next bullet. "Every two years the Key Club has a different *service initiative,*" he said. He was down to his last chunk of bread, which he now tore off in small bits. He formed these into pills with his fingers and then flicked them with disgust onto his plate. "What was the initiative when you were president, Daniel?" He asked in a super-polite voice Daniel immediately distrusted. "Was it 'Reducing Teenage Pregnancy,' or something like that?"

Little Julian saved him. "How do you know so much about it, Norman?"

Norman gave Julian a withering look before explaining that he'd once been the supervisor of his school's Key Club chapter until he'd fobbed off the job on the soccer coach.

"Okay," said Milton. "Now tell me this." He paused to look around the table.

"*International* president," he said.

This time laughter couldn't help but break out at his mere emphasis, although once again, he wasn't trying to be funny.

"President, I understand," Milton continued. "Organizations usually work this way, I believe. You have a treasurer, to take care of the dues. And a secretary, to take notes of the meetings. A vice-president, in case anything happens to the president. And a president, because . . ." His voice trailed off, as he couldn't come up with the reason for the president.

"You have a president because the rules say you must have a president," said Perry Elmore.

"Thank you," said Milton. "The rules require an organization, if it is to *be* an organization, and *to function* as an organization, to have a president. So I understand the president. But *international* president? Now what does *that* mean?"

At this point Daniel had the feeling that the others were attempting to withhold laughter they feared might hurt his feelings. Meaning: he was doing okay here.

"It means there's a Key Club chapter in Puerto Rico," snapped Mr. Laney.

"Ah," said Milton. "So this young man here," he inclined his head toward Daniel. "Was president over all the Key Club chapters in the U.S., *and* in Puerto Rico? I see. I see."

"Tell us what it was like, Daniel, being the president of Puerto Rico," said Perry Elmore.

"Well," he reflected. "I did get to fly there for free once."

He was surprised at what a good time he had laughing at and making light of matters he had held very dear and took very seriously just a few years ago. It was like taking off clothes he didn't even realize were too hot and uncomfortable until he was no longer wearing them. He had not done too badly, here, either, and this was what he loved: the thrill of engagement. The friendly encounters of thrust and parry when he could conquer hearts and minds that were new to him.

"He fits right in, doesn't he?" He overheard Libba Albritton whisper to her niece on the way out.

The idea that he fit right into Mountain Brook sent his heart soaring until Mr. Laney caught his eye and stopped that heart cold in mid-flight.

From Aaron Osgood's campaign brochure

AARON OSGOOD BELIEVES IN THE FUTURE OF ALABAMA
AARON OSGOOD BELIEVES IN REDEMPTION, IN CHANGE, IN PROGRESS

Aaron Osgood Believes

- In **TAX REFORM,** so that the poorest of our citizens do not continue to pay more through sales taxes than our biggest corporate landowners pay in property taxes.
- In **ETHICS REFORM,** so that state contracts are subject to competitive bidding in an open, transparent process.
- In **PRISON REFORM,** so that our state correctional system complies with federal regulations.
- In **EDUCATION REFORM,** so that underfunded schools, overcrowded classrooms, poorly trained teachers, run-down, antiquated buildings and textbook shortages do not continue to shortchange our schoolchildren.
- In **PUBLIC HEALTH REFORM,** so that our citizens do not succumb to the maternal and infant mortality statistics that put our state on par with undeveloped nations.
- In **CONSTITUTIONAL REFORM,** so that our outdated state constitution from 1901 can better serve the needs of **ALL** Alabama's citizens in today's world.
- In **IMAGE REFORM,** so that our state can attract the tourists, the retirees, the industries and opportunities it needs and deserves.

~ 6 ~

The following weekend, when Daniel and his girlfriend arrived at his parents' house in Opelika, they were forty-five minutes late, and his parents were both sitting stiffly on the loveseat in the living room, staring straight into the carpet without speaking to one another. It was like walking into a death watch. Instead of preparing to greet guests, his parents looked like they were in the middle of a grim vigil in the waiting room at a cancer hospital. There was no change in their demeanor when their son and his girlfriend entered the room at last. Rather than a warm welcome, they were met with looks of stern rebuke and words of reproach.

"Son," said his father in his deep, gravelly voice. "Your mother and I have been waiting this past hour."

Daniel had imagined this moment as the triumphant finale to an exhilarating first week of work for the Osgood campaign. But unfortunately, it had not been that kind of week, and the look on his parents' faces was only the crowning blow. Daniel launched at length into a protracted apology involving Caroline's tardy arrival in Montgomery; her belated tour of the attorney general's office, the campaign office and the apartment where he and Will Hill were living. Then there was all the traffic jamming the interstate at rush hour. But it was all to no avail; his explanation received only a stony silence.

"Son," said his mother finally. "We had no idea where the two of you were. If Caroline's parents had called this house, we would not have been able to tell them where their daughter was. While she is our guest, she is also our responsibility. If anything were to happen to her, we would be liable."

Liable? he flinched, as he looked from the tense countenance of one parent to the equally tense countenance of the other. Liable for what? If he and Caroline had been in a car crash, for example, did his parents think her father would sue *them*? Searching their faces again, he quickly deduced that this was precisely their concern. After all, Caroline's father was a successful "big city" lawyer, and to them that meant unscrupulous ambulance chaser or personal injury opportunist; they had no knowledge of the rarefied practice of a corporate defense attorney. So the fact that their son was dating the daughter of a prominent Mountain Brook attorney meant that one day they could be sued by him and stripped of everything they possessed. He had been utterly mistaken in his assumption of what she would mean to them. They derived no joy, satisfaction, or even vicarious fulfillment in his girlfriend, and they didn't even ask themselves if they liked her. By virtue of where she came from and who her family was, she aroused in them nothing but their numerous fears and insecurities. Although they had passed these down to him in full measure, he was never incapacitated to the point of quaking on the couch for an hour on a Friday evening. Get a life! he wanted to shout at them. Have a drink! Watch some television! Read a book! His mother, in particular, was always complaining that she never had time to read. So go read a book for an hour in your favorite chair instead of sitting on that miserable loveseat and staring at the wall-to-wall carpet! Glaring at their frazzled faces, he realized that they were constitutionally incapable of relaxing. And keyed up as he always was, he was just like them. It was a terrible way to be.

Somehow he managed to restrain himself from even looking at Caroline, who was standing beside him like a statue, no doubt frozen in disbelief. Her presence had been neither greeted nor acknowledged, certainly not welcomed. Neither of his parents had made eye contact or even looked at her. She might as well not have been in the room, and was probably wishing she wasn't. He himself was wishing he were anywhere else but where he was. The happiness he had anticipated in bringing his girlfriend home had changed into dread of going through the motions of their carefully scripted visit. Now all he could think about was leaving at the earliest possible opportunity on Sunday. Indeed, he was already looking so forward to leaving that he almost began feeling sorry for his parents. At least he *could* leave; they couldn't. They were stuck with their miserable selves and their miserable lives. The only real diversion they had was their children. They put forth so much effort securing and planning for his visits home, but as soon as he got there, they couldn't help but make him yearn for departure.

He always forgot, until he crossed the threshold of his house, that his love and admiration for his parents existed only in the abstract and in their absence; whenever he was actually with them, he couldn't stand it. The spectacle of their desperate behavior was bad enough, but was always made a thousandfold worse by the pity and horror the spectacle aroused in him, especially now that he had lived away from home for four years, and been exposed to the behavior of those who had not grown up on farms in a South Alabama still suffering from the Depression. The worst thing about his parents' rudeness was they weren't even aware of it. Although his mother thought she had made a careful study and mastered all the rules of proper decorum, deportment and etiquette, she was as incapable of true good manners or courtesy as she was ignorant of her shortcomings. Chronic stress, anxiety and worry had so twisted the insides of both his parents that social grace was impossible for them and simple politeness got lost in the constant churning and grinding of their inner gears.

As if reading his son's mind, Dr. Dobbs—as he preferred to be called—stepped forward to give his son a belated embrace. Briefly he cupped Caroline's chin in his hands and treated her to one of his serious, searching, silent gazes. This was his signature method for saluting close female relatives and friends, and had earned him a reputation for "having a way with the ladies." Where another man might have winked at this moment, he raised his eyebrows to comical heights. "Now I can finally have a drink," he said.

So that was it! Daniel thought. Or part of it: his mother had refused to let his father start in on the bourbon until they arrived. Probably she didn't want it being said there was liquor on his breath when Caroline arrived. With her Southern Baptist background, she failed to understand that where Caroline came from, there was nothing shameful or sinful about bourbon, gin or Scotch on a man's breath, especially after five o'clock. There, the shame was more in not drinking, even if you were notoriously unable to hold the liquor you drank. As a patchwork graduate of small community colleges, his mother was also unfamiliar with the fraternity system at Bama, which specialized in producing graduates who at least knew how to imbibe large quantities of alcohol, even if they did not know what to do with it afterwards. She mistakenly believed the most socially acceptable behavior to the upper class of society was to be stone cold sober, so as to ensure that all your actions were controlled, polite, responsible and mature.

So it was no wonder his father had been in a foul mood when they arrived. He needed his bourbon, and already seemed more relaxed and convivial at the mere prospect of an imminent drink. His mother likewise soon relented. Her face softened and her sharp shoulder blades lost some of their edge and curved into a more comfortable posture.

"I think *everybody* needs a drink," she said. "I'll bring those in, Daniel, if you'll go get the bags from your car and put them in the rooms. Bobby, if you'll keep Caroline company, I'll excuse myself for just a minute."

And so his mother switched from harried over-anxiousness to machine-like efficiency, her two most common modes of being. They could hear her whizzing from one point to another in the kitchen, like a pinball hitting its targets in an arcade game. Whenever anyone marveled at her energy level, she would gladly inform them that she had a borderline case of hyperthyroidism, which kept her as tightly wound as the Energizer Bunny. Even after years of being on medication, she still sometimes got up at three in the morning to clean her house from top to bottom. Before her diagnosis, she always got up at three in the morning and thought nothing of it, because this was necessary for her to get ahead in life. Now she bustled around her kitchen with the pride of someone who had indeed gotten ahead in life. But to her son, it was so unbearably sad he wanted to bolt out of the house then and there. Her definition of success was akin to racking up points in a pinball game: so many for getting off the farm, so many for having a house in town. The prize for winning that kind of game was nothing but a cheap plastic toy, as useless as it was worthless; and all too soon, the points she had scored would be erased and the pinball itself would fall from view.

He had no doubt this moment would occur before she had ever known genuine joy or happiness. If he could have given this to her, he would have done so on the spot. Knowing this about him, she never failed to tell him what it was that would give her such joy. "Law school," was what she said these days, and he would have agreed to this but for his absolute certainty that it would never bring either of them what she thought it would.

There was no need for his mother to ask what anyone wanted to drink, because she had quizzed him on Caroline's preferences well before the visit and had long planned exactly what to serve when that time came. She had also choreographed Daniel's bringing in the bags while his father entertained Caroline in the living room. So after the trauma of the late arrival had been overcome, this plan was put into action. No doubt, Daniel realized as he executed his role, one reason his parents were so put out by the delay was because their action plan for the evening was not following the pre-arranged timetable. Plus his mother was never comfortable sitting still, no matter how faithfully she took her medication. Sitting down was sloth, a deadly sin.

But once everyone was seated in the living room with drinks in hand, his parents did appear to unwind a bit. The only problem was: his parents had no conversation. For example: What was the office of the attorney general like? What had Daniel been doing in his first week of work? What had Caroline been doing with her summer so far? How was Will Hill? What was the news from the campaign trail? All of these were automatic topics of conversation.

None of them occurred to his parents. And there was a simple reason why: they were not the least bit interested in the answers. And they had never learned to simulate an interest in obvious topics for the sake of a guest, if not for their own sake.

Instead, it was straight to business and Serious Discussion, as if a guest were not in the room and private family matters could appropriately be aired. His parents so seldom got to see their son, and when they did, they always behaved as if there were no time to waste. In general, they always behaved as if there were no time to waste. They would have told you this was how they'd gotten where they were.

"Daniel," said his father heavily, setting down his glass. "Remind me to ask you. There are some charges on my MasterCard statement that I don't understand. Have you been using the card, Son?"

Last week, in Birmingham, when Aaron Osgood had not taken them out to dinner and he'd had to pay for their meal instead. "I ran into a few emergencies," he said nervously, hoping Caroline would not connect the dots. "These are nice glasses, Mother," he added, holding up the pilsner glass that contained his beer. Too late he realized that his gambit wouldn't please his mother, who did not want it known that, prior to this weekend, she had no beer glasses or had specially purchased some before Caroline's visit, although Caroline was drinking white wine, his father was drinking bourbon, his mother was sipping her wine cooler and he was the only one using a single pilsner glass from the set of six his mother had found two days ago, on sale, at Gayfer's Department Store.

"A letter came to the house for you this week," she said in reply. "Did you see where I put it in your room, Daniel?"

Right there on the middle of his pillow? The letter from Eleanor? Yes, he had somehow not failed to notice it when he took his bag downstairs. Meanwhile, he could only hope that Caroline would fail to ask him about it later.

"Did you hear me, Son? Did you see the letter? Daniel?"

"Yes, Mother. Thanks," he said irritably. He really hated the way she pronounced his first full name as if to prove a point because the name on his father's birth certificate was only "Bobby," not "Robert." (Poor Granny had thought "Bobby Dobbs" was pure poetry, and where she came from, "Bobby" was a fuller first name than most people got.) But people were always wanting to call Daniel "Danny" or "Dan," and his mother wielded his full name like a two-by-four to clear the room of anyone who tried to use a common nickname. And she also enunciated all the vowels so carefully that the masculine name of "Daniel" turned almost into the feminine name of "Danielle." This was the result of those elocution classes she had taken to rid herself of her country accent and make herself sound more educated and cultivated. Now she never dropped a "g" even when a Yankee would have dropped the "g." And she included some vowel and consonant sounds that even an upper-class Englishman would have glossed over. The result was a stilted, unnatural form of speech that seemed to come from the computerized voice of a robot. But to his mother, the fact that she never dropped a "g" meant she was "educated."

"After dinner," said his father, sipping deeply from his drink. "I need to get with you on the MasterCard statement. Remind me."

His father had the perfect preacher's voice: a baritone so deep it sounded like the voice of God himself. It was as full of authority as it was devoid of humor: ideally suited to proclaiming the Ten Commandments from the pulpit. Whenever he spoke, the subject matter seemed all-important and utterly serious, especially because his somber, earnest manner struck the same deep, low note as the pitch of his voice. So it was difficult to go up against that and point out that the charge for $32.78 at the pizza place was a trifling expense that could easily be resolved with two of the twenties he now had in his pocket, courtesy of his first paycheck.

"We can't afford to pay Daniel's bills or have him using our credit card," his mother informed Caroline, in what may have been the first sentence directly addressed to her since their arrival. And it was no idle conversation, either. Caroline had now been put on notice that she could not condone the use of the parental credit card if Daniel tried to use it for her benefit or even just in her presence. If this were to happen from here on out, Caroline would also be held responsible as an accessory to a grievous offense.

His mother tensed her body righteously as she sat in her studied fashion: knees and legs pressed together, ankles crossed, back straight as a ruler, hands folded on her lap. She looked exactly as she did in the photograph taken at the Olan Mills Studio. His father had no choice but to like it and keep a framed copy of this portrait on his desk at work. But as far as Daniel was concerned, the Olan Mills posture did not do his mother any favors. Instead of appearing elegant or sophisticated, she just looked uncomfortable, which then made others uncomfortable when they looked at her.

Daniel stole a look at his girlfriend shifting awkwardly in a straight-backed chair without arms. He was in the identical twin chair, while his parents were in the matching loveseat, all upholstered in the same fabric. Along with the chairs and the loveseat, the two side tables next to the chairs and the coffee table in front of the loveseat—all sharing the same wood veneer—had comprised the living room "suit"—as it was mispronounced in the country—proudly purchased by his parents when they moved up in the world to Opelika. They had been thrilled to find such a nice-looking living room "suit" on sale, and never admitted that it had been heavily discounted because it was so uncomfortable. As soon as you sat down on either the thinly cushioned chairs or the loveseat, your first impulse was to get right back up and go sit somewhere else. Only there wasn't anywhere else. The size of the room allowed for no other furniture, only what his mother called "accessories," such as the artificial peace lily and the equally artificial brass magazine holder. And as for the tables, their lightweight legs were no match for the wall-to-wall carpet, and failed to penetrate it deeply enough to support properly even the glass of wine Caroline tentatively placed on the table beside her. Usually the Dobbs did not subject themselves to the discomforts of this room, but used it solely to entertain their guests.

Daniel couldn't stand it anymore. He snatched up the brand-new pilsner glass. "I'd like to show Caroline around. If that's okay," he said to his mother, although this had not been part of the game plan his mother had evolved for the evening.

"That's a very good idea," she agreed nevertheless. "That will give me a chance to put dinner on the table. I've been cooking all week," she explained to Caroline. "And everything has been on 'warm' for over an hour now. So all I need to do is take it out of the oven. Don't worry about helping in the kitchen, but don't be surprised if the casserole is burned on the bottom. We expected you an hour ago, you know."

Dinner was served in the tiny dining room that was also hardly ever used and did not have salmon pink walls, although there was a wallpaper border trim his mother was very proud of. Caroline had the presence of mind to compliment the floral centerpiece his mother had bought at the supermarket. "I just love fresh flowers," his mother proclaimed proudly in return, as if there were people on the planet who did not. Actually, the people on the planet his poor parents came from had plastic flowers if they had any at all; it would have been an unthinkable extravagance to spend money on anything that had to be thrown away after three days.

Once they were seated, he soon found himself wishing that his sister Tanya had not been banished to her best friend's house to spend the night. Only eleven years old, she would not have sat still at the table for the duration of the meal, but would have been bouncing all over the place, complaining about the food, demanding a different menu, interrupting conversation and generally ruining all possibility of an adult evening. As it turned out, this would have been preferable to what developed instead.

At first there was an awkward silence after his mother instructed everyone to avoid the last layer of the casserole, which did appear to be somewhat burned. This was doubly unfortunate since the last layer contained whatever meat substance had been placed in the casserole dish. The awkwardness grew when his father's request for more bourbon was refused by his mother, who darted her eyes toward Caroline by way of explanation. Without excusing himself, Dr. Dobbs stormed from the room and returned moments later with a replenished glass of bourbon filled defiantly to the brim. His wife's mouth hardened into a firm, thin line. It was clear there would be a reckoning between them later in the evening.

Daniel thought back to the family dinner party in Mountain Brook he had attended less than a week ago, which seemed to have taken place in a different universe. The dining room in Libba Albritton's house had mysteriously sprouted a profusion of food, none of it requiring apologies, explanations or special instructions, although he, (like Mr. Petsinger), had never eaten an eggplant before, and certainly not in a lasagna. The sudden appearance of the food seemed effortless, as he had never observed his hostess leave her guests or any sign of help from the kitchen. Obviously there was a horde of such help, but they knew how to remain invisible and bring the food from the kitchen into the adjoining dining room without attracting anyone's notice. By the time the guests were encouraged to take a plate, whatever help there was had withdrawn.

But it wasn't food that made the difference, although a partially burned mystery meat casserole never helped matters. It was the storytelling he remembered. Once he'd realized that these Mountain Brook folks were not going to talk politics at the table, if ever, he had allowed himself to gear down and just enjoy the stories. There had been some great ones.

"So we get up there, to this place that is supposed to be the acme of education in America. So they tell me." Perry Elmore had already started this story by the time Daniel sat down. "And we're in Harvard Yard. And when we get to it, Caroline's freshman dorm is a red-brick building with ivy growing all over it just like in the brochures. Apparently it's one of the oldest buildings on the campus, it's behind the famous pump and the statue of John Harvard, and Emerson, Thoreau and George Santayana once lived there when they were students.

"We have had to tip the cab driver to park his taxi in Harvard Square and help us carry the luggage, because Caroline's mother has packed not one but two trunks along with two regular suitcases and various other bags containing winter clothes worth my annual salary. Caroline is now equipped for life at the North Pole. Of course the cab driver scampers off as soon as he gets a tip worth *his* annual salary from me, and it occurs to not one of the student geniuses on the Harvard campus that they could open the dorm room door for us and hold it open until we get the luggage in.

"They see us standing there, carrying bags and surrounded by trunks. They watch us eyeing the dorm room door. Not a one of them can connect the dots. I am forced to approach one of these high IQs and ask if he can open the door. Too bad I neglected to ask him to *Hold the door open, dammit!* because that bright idea did not enter his head, and the door slams on me before I can get even one of the trunks all the way through.

"Anyway, we finally get all the bags to the second floor, only to find that Caroline's dorm room is so filthy we can't possibly even bring in the luggage."

"Filthy!" affirmed Mrs. Elmore.

"Tumbleweeds under the bed, grit and grime on every surface, layers of dust in all the drawers. Trash everywhere. Old newspapers, notebooks, food wrappers, even Chinese food cartons. The room itself smells like sour milk, and there are plenty of obviously not quite empty milk jugs lying around. This room has not been cleaned all summer, and perhaps not in the last decade. For all I can tell, it hasn't been cleaned since Emerson, Thoreau and George Santayana lived there. It does *not* look like what's in the brochure, and I'm thinking I deserve a tuition reduction.

"If you think Caroline was taken aback, you should have seen the look on her mother's face. I'm beginning to wonder if I'm going to have to fight the battle all over again to convince Midge to let her daughter go to school at this place. So I'm racking my brains, trying to come up with some positive spin to put on this situation, and I point out that we are booked for an eight day stay at the Harvard Motor Lodge for exactly this purpose. We have plenty of time to get the dorm room in shape before Caroline starts classes.

"Midge wants to find a phone book and call a cleaning service, but I tell Midge she's looking at the cleaning service. It's the two of us. So we head back to the Square and buy a hundred dollars' worth of mops, brooms and cleaning supplies from a hardware store. Caroline stays with the luggage and holds down the fort by getting on the unmade bed and reading *The Magic Mountain* by Thomas Mann.

"We get back to the dorm room—I'm guessing it's about ten o'clock now. We work for two solid hours on just this one room, probably no bigger than eighteen by eighteen. We sweep, we mop, we use four rolls of paper towels wiping off dust and fill up twice that many garbage bags. At noon Caroline decides to make herself useful, goes out to the Square and brings back lunch.

We don't even leave the room and I don't even remember what we ate. We open the big windows facing out on the Yard and sit on the window seats looking at the famous pump where So-and-so used to rendezvous with So-and-so. Then it's right back to work, cleaning these windows next and tackling the closets, which are filled with even more trash and dust. I lost count of how many trips it took to get all the bags we filled up out to the garbage.

"So it's about four o'clock now, and we're beginning to think we've made progress. Midge is placing scented drawer liner in the chest of drawers and carefully stacking all of Caroline's brand-new, meticulously folded cashmere sweaters.

"It's about this time that Caroline's roommate arrives at the door. Her parents are behind her, and her father drops two green duffel bags on the threshold of the door. They look like big gym bags, printed on the side with 'Phillips Exeter Academy,' which, we learn, is where the girl went to high school. Her father, it turns out, is a nuclear physicist, and the mother looks like she could be a nuclear physicist too. We shake hands and introduce ourselves, and I'm wondering if it's too soon to invite everybody back to the Harvard Motor Lodge for a drink. God knows I need a drink, I deserve a drink, and I've been thinking of nothing but a drink for the last two hours, maybe three. And since this girl's parents have done absolutely nothing to help us clean up the room their daughter will be sharing with mine, I'd like to let them know just how much work we have done to make the room habitable for these two girls.

"Then the mother of this girl turns to her daughter and says, 'Well, let's go sit in the Yard and say good-bye. I've brought some yogurt.'"

Roars of laughter had followed that story demonstrating the superiority of Southern culture. The evening had been filled with laughter, stories and countless bottles of wine from the never-ending supply in Milton Albritton's cellar. Fresh bottles appeared and empty plates disappeared by some form of unobtrusive magic that never interrupted the flow of stories. His parents would never understand that this exchange of stories and conversation was the true essence of "sophistication," which was utterly unavailable to them although it had less to do with money than they would want to believe. Of course, the good food, the good wine and the good service had all played a part, but it was the art of storytelling that gave the evening its transcendence.

But his parents knew nothing of the art of storytelling. Silently they concentrated on the casserole, carefully avoiding the browned bottom layer. When they finally spoke, it was to bring up the most Serious topic of the evening.

"Your mother and I have been talking, Son," said his father, pushing away his plate.

"Yes, we have," concurred his mother. She nodded vigorously.

His father waited a suitable interval to let the gravity of the unstated topic descend upon his son. Then he continued carefully: "I'm not going to tell you what you can and cannot do with your life," he said. "You're a college graduate now, and you've earned the right to make your own decisions." He paused this time to look over at his wife for affirmation, which she gave by nodding again.

"But your mother and I are adamantly opposed to any postponement of law school."

"Dad—" he began, wondering how his parents had obtained knowledge of what was in his mind. Had Joab Tucker reported on their conversation? Or had his parents merely connected the dots?

"Hear me out, Son." His father's voice got even deeper.

"Listen to your father, Daniel," said his mother, as if she were talking to a five year-old child with attention deficit disorder.

Dr. Dobbs nodded in thanks to her support before addressing his son. "It is far from certain that this man you're working for will even win the primary, let alone the election."

"Dad—"

"I said, 'Hear me out, Son.'" He waited a moment for Daniel to submit. "Your place in the first year class has to be secured by the end of this month," he went on finally. "With a substantial deposit."

"I realize that. I'll pay it."

"You can pay it?" said his mother quickly.

She was never so happy as when a debt, a charge, a bill or an expense was unexpectedly expunged from her slate. In fact, this unhoped-for news of her son's financial resources was so gratifying that she settled back comfortably in her chair, as if all issues were now resolved.

"I'll pay it," he repeated firmly, hoping to curtail any further discussion.

"The main point, Son, is that we think you need to enroll and be in that first year class *this fall.*"

"Bobby, if he can pay the deposit out of what he's earning this summer, then he should do so."

"Shaye!" boomed her husband in his voice of God. "Of course he should pay for the deposit if he's able to! But that's not the main point here." He looked back at his son.

Recognizing her lapse, Shaye went back on the attack. "Explain to me how you're able to pay the deposit, Son. We've accounted for every penny of your paycheck and agreed on your summer budget. How can you pay this deposit and meet all your other expenses? There's no sense in robbing Peter in order to pay Paul. Because we're the Peter in this, Son."

His parents did not know that he and Will Hill were staying in Aaron Osgood's apartment in Montgomery, rent free with all utilities paid. Daniel had hoped to keep them in ignorance along with a little extra cash in his pocket. This way he could afford a few luxuries like paying for a deposit to secure a place in a law school class he didn't expect to be joining.

"We're not talking about the deposit or his summer budget!" thundered his father. "We're talking about the fact that politics is not a profession, Son. And it's not a very reliable job, either. **You need to go to law school.**"

Daniel tried to keep his sigh to himself and think of the best way out of this conversation, although he was aching to confront his parents with their hypocrisies and inconsistencies. Except for their neighbor Joab Tucker, a small-town lawyer who handled the wills and minor problems of everyone in town, white and black, his parents had never expressed anything but scorn for "the lawyers," whom they regarded as a contemptible breed of predators and profiteers. Yet this is what they most wanted their only son to become?

"Even if your man *is* elected and you *do* get a job with him, how long will that last?" his father was confronting him instead. "What will it lead to? How much will it pay? In general, Son, politics does not pay."

"And if you're not in school, all your student loans will start coming due," piped up his mother, who turned now to Caroline. "Daniel knows it will be up to him to re-pay his student loans. *We* certainly can't afford it. We'll do what we can to help with law school, but we cannot take on his student loans. That was made clear and agreed upon when he decided to go to Harvard."

"Mother," he interjected. "Caroline doesn't need to hear all this."

"This could well be every bit as much her business as it is yours, Son," said his mother righteously. "She deserves to know exactly what your debt load is so she can make an informed decision about her own life. She also deserves to know exactly what your plans are for the future."

The sense of her own rectitude straightened Shaye's spine even further: Caroline's parents, whoever they were, would thank her mightily for being so conscientious about their daughter's rights. Not for nothing was her four year-old niece, Bobby Shaye, named partly after her. Shaye had a reputation to maintain, a duty to perform for all those people still in rural Alabama who looked up to her and her husband as models of achievement and success. She had to uphold her half of Bobby Shaye.

"It comes down to this, Son." Dr. Dobbs picked up his dirty fork and pointed its soiled tines toward his son. "Sooner or later, you will have to get your law degree. Even if you decide you want to stay in politics. So you might as well get that degree sooner rather than later. It will only get harder to go back the longer you put it off."

"We're afraid Daniel *won't* go back if he puts it off," his mother helpfully informed Caroline. "And if he puts it off too long, he may not be *able* to go back. He owes it to himself not to squander his advantages. And that wouldn't be fair to us, either. We've worked hard and made many sacrifices to get him where he is in life today. He owes it to us as well as himself to capitalize on what we've done for him. Otherwise, our investment in his future won't pay off for anybody. And this concerns you, too," she pointed out to Caroline. "This is Caroline's life we're talking about as well, Son. Have you thought about that? And the future of your family. How are you planning to provide if you don't have a professional degree or professional credentials?"

"Education is the way out, Son," said Dr. Dobbs. "Education is the way up. The only way up."

"There's more than one kind of education," Daniel noted. "There's plenty of education to be gained on the campaign trail."

Dr. Dobbs pounded the table with his fist. "I'm talking about a piece of paper, Son! A degree! A diploma you can frame and hang on the wall for all to see! *That* is what you need to get. *That* is your ticket to the professional class. If your mother and I had not both gone back to school to get higher degrees, we wouldn't be sitting where we are today," he concluded. "And you wouldn't have even been able to dream of Harvard."

Daniel could have argued this point, since his parents had not paid one penny to send him to college, but thought it wiser to refrain.

"It wasn't fun, all those years—I can tell you that—but it was necessary and we did it," Shaye told him, as if this was supposed to be news to him. "When Bobby finally turned in his dissertation, we didn't even have time to celebrate. We were too busy moving to take the job here. It was contingent, of course, upon his dissertation being accepted, which thankfully it was because as you can imagine, the school we were leaving in Chunchula had already hired their new principal. There was so much stress involved, we never had time to be happy about any of it until it was all over."

His mother's last statement could have served as an epitaph on both the graves they were digging a little deeper every day.

He was determined not to live life or strive for success as defined by his parents. But he would have neither the reason nor the cash to defy their wishes, dreams, hopes, plans and arguments unless his candidate defeated George Wallace in the primary. Meanwhile, it was useless and always had been to try to convey to his parents what was in his own heart. He had always believed that he must have been chosen for a reason other than his own personal self-advancement. The Good Lord could not have bestowed what he had on one Daniel Dobbs for his own benefit alone. That would not make sense; the Lord didn't issue his most valuable gifts just so they could be used for one person's private advantage. With whatever God-given gifts he possessed, Daniel had a responsibility to use them for the benefit of others, especially those born in his same circumstances, but without his charmed fate. His parents would never understand this, Christians though they professed themselves to be. The time and place where they were raised had taught them only to hoard every scrap they had for their own individual use: they would need every bit of it, and it still wouldn't be enough to get them anywhere. Only by strictly conserving every last resource, they just might barely get by. If he had tried to express the substance of his own soul, they would have scoffed at him for a fool. The truest and best convictions of his heart would have been punctured like they amounted to nothing but a big balloon full of hot air. So how could he tell them he had always yearned to be part of something larger than himself? That he wanted more than anything to transcend the narrow, single-minded pursuit of personal self-advancement that had warped their own lives? How could they understand his need to find a grand common cause or noble purpose instead of securing his own "success"? None of this would "*pay.*" They wouldn't understand it, and they wouldn't agree with it either. Even when all of this had been translated into the most concrete terms, they had no use for it. Ridding the world of Wallace and making Alabama a better place: to them that was just meaningless chatter to fill up space between advertisements in the paper and on the radio. Or else it *was* an advertisement. When it came right down to it, his parents were as guilty as anyone else in the state for being so consumed by their own daily struggles and personal concerns that it blinded them to anything beyond the walls of their split-level house and the people who lived there.

He chanced a sideways glance at Caroline. What in the world could she think of the full-frontal assault his parents had launched on their son by way of dinner table conversation? How was she taking the news that he was even considering not attending law school?

To his extreme relief, she was suppressing a smile. She appeared to be amused by it all. Thank God for this girl, he thought, who was of the other Alabama than the one he came from! Probably she was imagining his parents wearing the "Life is hard and then you die" tee shirts she had seen in the hotel gift shop. A smile bubble popped out of his own mouth at the thought.

"This is *serious,* Son," said his father, deeply offended. He pushed back his soiled plate with a gesture of disgust, probably aimed at his son, but it had the effect of calling his wife's attention to the fact that it was time to clear the table and move on to the next phase of the evening. She hopped up with alacrity to start scraping and stacking the dishes. This meant that her husband was free to go outside and smoke his after-dinner cigarette. Shaye Dobbs assumed the look of martyrdom that took over her countenance every time she was privy to one of her husband's cigarettes. "I will be a widow one day, well before my time. I hope you know that," her face telegraphed her son. "And I hope you understand that I will need your help when that happens. And not just your emotional support, either, but your financial assistance. I'll have a mortgage, and bills I can't pay, expenses I can't meet. I'll have a young daughter bound for college. So you'll need to have that law degree as soon as you can get it because there may end up being two families you have to support with your income." He felt the hand of death clutch at his own heart and gladly accepted his father's invitation to join him outside.

There was a little strip of a landing outside the kitchen door leading to the back stairs down to the yard below. It could not be called a deck. There was no room for even one chair, and certainly not the festive grouping of patio furniture that Shaye Dobbs dreamed of. If ever they came into the least bit of money—through an unexpected legacy, or Bobby's long-anticipated promotion—then they would add a deck. Husband and wife were in agreement on that.

Meanwhile, Bobby Dobbs went out to the narrow landing every evening after dinner while his wife cleaned up. As he leaned on the railing and looked out at his yard, he sucked on his forbidden cigarette and blew smoke with all the vengeance and intensity of a factory worker or manual laborer taking a hard-earned break after a punishing shift. And that's exactly what the evening had seemed like, at least to his son. No doubt it had been the same for his father, who appeared to derive no joy or pleasure from his smoke. His lungs drew on the cigarette as if grasping for dear life. Mere survival was ever the goal; never happiness.

Father and son stood side by side in silence, until the cigarette was finished and had been flicked over the railing (in defiance of Shaye's objections to cigarette butts on the pavement in front of the carport.) As they turned to re-enter the house, his father clapped a hand on his son's shoulder. "You be careful with this girl. You hear?" Daniel nodded, though he wondered what that meant exactly. Don't get her pregnant? Or Don't break her heart? Probably both, he decided. Or rather, it meant: Don't do anything that will have that expensive Mountain Brook attorney coming after us with a lawsuit that would ruin our lives.

In the kitchen, his mother was scrubbing dishes at the sink with her big yellow latex gloves covered in soapsuds. Caroline was wincing from the steam of the hot water faucet as she stood by with a dishcloth to dry the many items deemed too good for the dishwasher. Shaye scrubbed with the same vengeance his father had smoked, and was in the middle of recounting to Caroline "the latest" on Cloyd Mullins. Instead of stopping to contribute to this story, Dr. Dobbs only raised his eyebrows at his son and moved on through the kitchen, snatching up the bourbon bottle from the counter directly behind the kitchen sink as well as his wife's back. When he reached the table in the dining room, a look of pure elation lit up his face when he saw that his (empty) bourbon glass was still there. He would not need to go back in the kitchen, open a cabinet, fetch a fresh glass and alert his wife to the alarming fact that he was planning to pour himself another drink. *Because his glass was still on the table.* It had not yet been cleared with all the other dirty dishes. Bobby Dobbs looked happier to see that glass than he had been to see his own son earlier in the evening. In fact, he looked happier than he had all evening. He pointed toward the living room, where he and his son went to sit back down.

"What's this about Cloyd Mullins?" Daniel thought it only polite to ask.

But his father just shook his head morosely. He wanted to drink, not talk about Cloyd Mullins. Besides, the story was always essentially the same. The plot never changed; it was just the details that varied. As the Superintendant of the Opelika City School system, Cloyd Mullins received a generous salary that was almost three times that of his assistant superintendant, Bobby Dobbs, who made only slightly more than his wife, a schoolteacher in this same system. To Dr. Dobbs and his wife, the injustice was not that Cloyd Mullins made so much more money, because they hoped one day that his salary would be theirs. The injustice was that Cloyd Mullins did not earn this salary. The work that supposedly justified his income was largely performed by the assistant superintendant, who was naturally expected to fulfill all the duties pertaining to his own "job description" as well. At first, it was just any new "initiatives" or "directives" that were handed over to Dr. Dobbs. But over time, Cloyd Mullins passed on more and more of his responsibilities to Bobby Dobbs, as if Bobby were some sort of personal assistant to the superintendant, instead of "assistant superintendant." Cloyd Mullins wasn't a bad man—just lazy and incompetent. But to make matters worse, over the past few years he had also begun suffering from chronic ill health. He had diabetes, recurrent kidney stones, bleeding ulcers and gallbladder surgery. Unfortunately, it was not enough either to kill him or force him into early retirement. But it was one thing after another. One reason after another that Cloyd Mullins wouldn't be in the office today, or this week, or for the next two weeks. More and more work for the assistant superintendant to execute in addition to everything else on his desk. The only duty Cloyd never failed to perform involved the scheduled appearances before the School Board to deliver the quarterly report. Somehow Cloyd's poor health managed to rally for each and every one of these appearances before the board, and neither kidney stones, gallbladder, ulcers nor diabetes flared up at these four important times of the year. Of course, it went without saying that the reports had been assembled and prepared by Bobby Dobbs, who had also done all of whatever work was referred to in the reports. So the Board had no way of knowing that Cloyd was useless, and besides, he was married to the daughter of the School Board's president.

So each day's burden of stress, injustice and overwork drove the stake that much deeper into Bobby Dobbs's heart. His wife thought she was helping when she treated each new outrage as a fresh assault; or when she pointed out that Cloyd's salary, which was rightfully Bobby's, would resolve many of their financial woes and might even enable them to add on that deck off the kitchen they'd both always wanted ever since they moved into the house. On Friday night after a long week, Bobby Dobbs wanted only to sit in silence and breathe in the bourbon fumes like earlier he'd inhaled so deeply of his cigarette smoke. Because there was nothing he knew to be said, just as there was nothing to do but endure.

WHAT WAS SO GOOD ABOUT THIS? Daniel's entire nervous system hollered in silent protest at the sight of his father's abject misery. Why was this middle-class life his parents had struggled to achieve so superior to the farm life they had struggled to get away from? It clearly wasn't making them happy. Whereas, he'd often noticed that his father never seemed happier than when they stayed at his in-laws in the country. Daniel himself loved going to visit his grandparents, and this was partly because his father was never more relaxed and peaceful than when sitting in the carport of his in-law's red brick house on folding lawn chairs gazing out at the county road. There wasn't any bourbon to be had, and what's more, his father didn't suffer from the lack. Instead, there was peach ice cream, made with the ancient crank his Mamaw turned so expertly. The peaches came from one of the half dozen peach trees at the edge of their property. Nothing he had ever put in his mouth, including the fancy food at the restaurants he'd been to in Boston, had ever tasted so good. Something about it was almost ambrosial. But it wasn't the taste so much as the feeling—the sensation of tranquility and serenity. No gourmet meal could ever equal that experience or evoke those emotions.

So what was wrong with it? Of course, Granny was impossible; Daniel conceded that. Determined that her seventh child, a son, would become a preacher and make her proud. Her husband had died before he could get out of cropping and get some land of his own. But his mother's parents, his Mamaw and Papaw, were wonderful people. Sweet, gentle, and above all, happy. This wasn't to say their lives were easy, though they were a lot better off than they ever had been. Still, his sixty year-old Mamaw rose before dawn, worked all day, cooked all week and prayed all Sunday. It would never occur to her to boast, complain or even make mention of what she did, because it was simply what had to be done, and besides, she mostly enjoyed it. She had a good life. A faithful, hardworking husband, a nice house, and good health. They were out of debt—for the most part—and had a savings account.

Although his Papaw did not really enjoy farming, he got satisfaction from it because he knew how to do it and did it well. He still fought with his tractor every day but Sunday, and usually came out ahead. What he loved was living in the country. He owned a field across the road down yonder, surrounded on all sides by dense woods. No matter how regularly he rotated the crops, fertilized and irrigated the soil, he couldn't get nothin' to grow there no more. For now he was letting the field go. Maybe he would plant it again in a year or two; maybe not. Meantime, he seeded it for the deer that lived in them woods around it. When he told his wife Ina that he was going to feed the deer, what he really meant was that he'd be spending a good hour or more settin' in them woods on a little campstool he had. Watching. After spreading the corn from one end of the field t'other, he'd tramp back into the woods and wait for them to come. He had a pair of binoculars Shaye and Bobby had given him for Christmas. The creatures that came out of the woods to eat his corn fascinated him with their grace and elegance. He loved watching them. Mostly does and fawns, though every so often he'd see a buck—once he'd even spotted a four-point on the edge of the field.

No New York arts patron ever enjoyed a performance more than his Papaw enjoyed watching the ballet those deer put on in his field. He gave them names, learned their habits and preferences, knew their personalities. There was Feisty, a male fawn who liked to try to get in ahead of the others. There was Lucky, a doe who had badly injured her leg somehow, but managed to survive, although she walked with a limp.

As a child on visits to his grandparents, he always insisted they arrive in time for him to go "feed the deer" with Papaw. He loved flinging the seed corn into the field, then sitting on his grandfather's lap as they observed the deer from their perch in the woods. Later he was given his own campstool, which he still used on these vigils with his grandfather. They could sit next to each other for an hour or more without saying a word, yet somehow they communicated better than he ever had with his parents. It wasn't just in spite of his silence, it was actually *with* his silence that his grandfather taught him lessons unknown to his mother and her barrage of language. From his grandfather he learned reverence for the spectacle they were privileged to witness: the miracle of life unfolding in front of them. To participate in this miracle, by feeding the deer and then bearing witness to their glory, was to achieve a transcendent state of grace on par with the grace of the deer themselves as they gamboled and frolicked in the open field. Meanwhile a bond knitted between himself and his grandfather tighter than any he had with either of his parents.

What was so wrong with this? He had never understood his mother's scorn and loathing for "the farm." The site of his happiest childhood memories was the site of her childhood nightmare. From an early age, he had suspected that the fault lay not with "the farm," but with his mother. To her, the deer his Papaw loved so much were nothing but "pests,"—officially so designated by the state of Alabama. Overpopulation was such a problem that it would be better—perhaps even kinder—to shoot them rather than feed them. She fussed that her father might even be charged or fined, issued a summons or citation. He would never forget that moment, coming back with the radiance of the woods and field still upon him, to hear his mother fret about "designated" pests and "possible misdemeanors." Not only did she fail to recognize the poetry of their experience, she damn near killed it. She thought she was so smart, but she knew nothing. His grandfather, on the other hand, understood beauty and had known joy, which was a lot more than his mother could say, for all she deplored life on "the farm."

But if she had wanted to leave that life on the farm as badly as he had wanted to leave his parents' house in Opelika, then he could understand and sympathize. Perhaps this was just the task of each generation; perhaps it was just human nature. But however much he wanted to put his own family behind him, he did not want to make the same mistake as his mother: of striving for "a better life" that he allowed someone else to define for him instead of figuring it out for himself. His mother may have thought she had a good life, simply because hers so exactly resembled that of everyone else "in town." But she didn't ask herself if she was happy. She didn't dare. He wished he could make this right for her—for both of them. But law school wasn't the answer.

Meanwhile, his father heaved a heavy sigh. His bourbon was gone, and they were being called to the table. Dessert was a chocolate mousse with Cool Whip topping served in the delicately etched fruit compote glasses his mother was so fond of. They had been a wedding present from her husband's oldest sister, who had done very well for herself, married a dentist and lived in Tennessee. Shaye loved this set of glasses and used any opportunity to show them off. The chocolate mousse recipe, clipped out of a Sunday *Parade* magazine, seemed to work the best and was used most often. Having made it into Shaye's pantheon of favorite recipes, it was secured on the refrigerator with a ladybug magnet.

Finally came the blessed release of his mother's announcement that she and her husband were exhausted and going to bed. But first his mother had to show Caroline all the important particulars of the guest room and bathroom, which were right next door to the master suite. Fortunately, his own bedroom as well as his sister's was on the bottom floor of their split-level house. "Don't stay up too late," was his mother's good night admonition, aimed directly at him. What she really meant was: Do Not Even Think of Screwing This Girl Anywhere in This House. Of course this was precisely what he wanted to do. His bed and his sister's were out of the question, he well knew, because his mother would have known immediately from the sheets if sexual intercourse had occurred in her house. Once he had even done a girl on the shag carpet of the rec room, but his mother had figured out it was dried jism that wouldn't come up with her vacuum cleaner. So she had clipped off the stubborn clump with her sewing scissors and brought it to him, asking if he had any idea what it could be. The look she'd given him indicated that she knew full well exactly what it was and didn't ever want to have to see it again on the rug in the rec room or more importantly, she did not want to have to pay for a carpet cleaning service. The family couldn't afford an expense like that.

But he really needed to get laid. It had been a most trying week, followed by an even more trying Friday night with his parents. Indeed, one of the disappointments was that he hadn't already gotten laid earlier in the afternoon, on the big king-sized mattress with black satin sheets and matching bedspread in the apartment he and Will Hill were sharing in Montgomery. Will Hill had offered to make himself scarce, and had even folded up the hide-a-bed sofa they'd agreed to take turns on throughout the summer. But Caroline had come down with yet another of the endless infections that had plagued her ever since he had finally persuaded her to yield her virginity to him in Cambridge. Little benefit that had brought him, and he wasn't sure what it had done for her either, other than to plunge her into the murky netherworld of female complaints. Virgins could be more trouble than they were worth. It was their third date, when he'd had the use of his absent roommate's much bigger room and much nicer bed, when she had finally acquiesced to his groping and pleading. But then she had looked positively shocked when he moved on top of her, as if she did not know what in the world getting on top of her had to do with making love to her. "Please let me make love to you," he had beseeched her, caressing her magnificent breasts. Finally she had agreed. But when he proceeded to mount her without further delay, she was stunned. Had she thought making love meant he would be reading poetry to her all night? Did the book her mama and daddy gave her about where babies came from fail to explain this part? Could it be true what they said of Mountain Brook girls: they didn't know where to put the tampon? To this day, at any rate, she did not seem to know what an orgasm was, which at least spared him the necessity of helping her have one. But he could certainly benefit from that experience right now.

Accordingly, he spread some towels down on the rug in front of the TV, and tried to pull her away from her inspection of the trophies lining the shelves in the rec room.

"I've never seen so many trophies in all my life," she said.

The wonder in her voice was not exactly that of admiration. So what was wrong with it? He looked around the room, which so precisely resembled most other rec rooms he'd seen in his life they all could have been carbon copies. The rec room where he had spent so much time with Ricky Jill in her house was almost exactly the same: Ricky Jill's cheerleading and gymnastics trophies on all the shelves, rows of school portraits or photographs of sports teams and extracurricular exploits on all the (fake) wood-paneled walls.

"Didn't you and your brothers get any trophies?" he asked, tugging on her hand.

"I guess we did," she said vaguely.

"All of you played sports," he said. "And there are four of you. What did you do with the trophies?"

"I guess we put them in a closet somewhere," she said, ignoring his attempts to pull her down on the rug. Instead, she crossed over to the other side of the room to examine the pictures from his track meets. There was a particularly dramatic shot of him crossing the finish line and breaking through the ribbon when he came in first in the fifty yard dash at the state competition. He had also broken a state record, and this picture had run on the front page of the Opelika *Sun.*

"I can remember my father saying something about not wanting to look at cheap pieces of fake wood and brass and being reminded that the cost for this junk was included in the registration fee he'd had to pay for us to participate in athletic activities."

"Sounds like something your father would say," he grinned, thinking of the difference between her family and his. The good thing about hers: they didn't take everything with such morose, morbid, godawful Seriousness, whether it was trophies from a track meet, a charge for pizza on the Master-Card or a child who might want to do something other than law school. They knew how to laugh, which came from knowing how to turn evil experiences into good stories. They had a certain amount of ironic distance that made room for a sense of humor, which made life bearable. His parents had no such distance from life's harsh realities. Born into a hardscrabble existence, they considered themselves fortunate, for now, that they had managed to achieve a slim margin of geographical and financial distance from their origins. But as they lived in dread that this could collapse into nothing at any moment, they would never gain any spiritual or emotional distance. In truth, they might have been happier back in the country if they could have opened their souls to that instead of becoming infected by middle-class aspirations. Something about their scratch and claw, tooth and nail climb upwards had permanently bruised their souls. As a result, they were incapable of laughter. Instead, his parents had fear. Fear of not doing the "right" thing, not being accepted, not being employed. Of being booted back where they came from, with egg on their faces. If not for their terror of losing the middle-class life they clung to, he was convinced his father would not be trapped in the middle-class grind which was killing him a little bit more each day. (Indeed, his dad could have used a strap-on tool for Father's Day.) A good lawyer, a formal complaint before the School Board, or a job application elsewhere, and Bobby Dobbs could have been delivered from his present misery. He would have said he could not "afford" to risk it. That was bullshit. "Healthwise," (as his mother would say), he couldn't afford not to. It wasn't all about money. And money wasn't all that separated her family from his, and gave her family that little bit of separation from brutal reality. After all, neither of her parents had come from the kind of money they now enjoyed. Of course, hard work was necessary, and so was intelligence. Luck, his parents would have said grimly, accounted for the difference in fate. He didn't agree. It wasn't luck; it was attitude. It was Libba Albritton sitting calmly on a floor cushion smoking her cigarette with almost erotic pleasure while one of her guests, who happened to be her daughter's father-in-law and a Big Mule of Birmingham, berated her hospitality and stormed out of her house. Already, he realized, he loved Caroline's family. He loved her. He needed her. And he wanted her. Badly. He pulled more urgently on her arm.

"Come on," he said.

"You know I can't."

"Maybe you're better."

"It takes several days! You know that."

"Let's just try."

But all he got out of it was a blow job, which would have to do. It was better than nothing, and anyway, at least he wouldn't have to wash the towels at midnight to eliminate any incriminating evidence.

"Why don't you stay?" he suggested sleepily. "Spend the night here with me."

"On the rug? You're crazy," she laughed.

But she continued to lie beside him on the towels. He really didn't want her to go, he thought as he drifted almost into sleep. Now that he was at home with his parents, she was even more necessary to his existence. She was *his* buffer, *his* barrier, *his* ironic distance from reality as experienced by his mother and father. At the moment, she felt like all he had in the world.

His first week of work for the campaign could hardly have been more of a letdown. He and Will had never even seen Aaron Osgood, who had been "detained" in Birmingham and had not come to Montgomery on Monday or any day that week. Of course, headquarters for the Osgood for Governor campaign was in Birmingham, but the two well-paid Ivy League recruits had expected to be charged with an important mission in Montgomery. Otherwise, what were the two of them doing there? Why had they been sent to the capital city? They still didn't know; they'd been at loose ends the whole week. When they visited the Capitol building where Will Hill had interned in the attorney general's office last summer, Aaron Osgood's chief aide looked downright displeased to see them as he stiffly conveyed the absolute need to maintain strict boundaries between official government duties and campaign operations. But at the campaign office, no one appeared prepared for their arrival, either. On the contrary, the two new people were greeted only with indifference, and when they inquired about a place in the office to settle themselves, they were answered with a shrug. Eventually someone indicated a space at the end of a row of phone banks where they could shove aside the piles of papers and station themselves temporarily. If they wanted. It didn't seem to matter to anyone in the office what Daniel and Will did with themselves. Quite different from the vision they'd had of being snatched up by Aaron Osgood and his campaign manager Gene Boshell and immediately charged with an important purpose. When they finally reached Aaron on the phone, he told them only to "hang on" until he could get to Montgomery.

"Something's wrong with this picture," Daniel had said to his friend on Monday night while they settled into the apartment where Aaron Osgood lived during his stays in Montgomery. "I've had a bad feeling since the other night. Do you think he's mad at us for not showing up together in Birmingham on Saturday?"

Will dismissed his concerns. "Don't be silly," he said. "Osgood's got a lot more on his mind than what did or didn't happen on Saturday night. Plans change all the time on the campaign trail. Things pop up constantly that have to be taken care of. Just be patient. When you really have a chance to get to know him like I do, you're going to be out of your mind with excitement. He is The Man, Daniel. He can do it. This is big, what's happening. And we're going to be a part of it."

Will speculated that he and Daniel were intended to take over the Montgomery office, or take charge of it in some way that would displace the current leadership. Of course this could not happen until Aaron Osgood arrived to instigate the changes. Meanwhile, he believed, it would behoove them not to behave like prima donnas, and demonstrate their dedication to the cause by performing whatever tasks they could help with until Aaron arrived to clarify their positions. Accordingly, they had spent their week making phone calls, running errands, and distributing campaign literature. Will Hill had even picked up some of Aaron Osgood's suits from the dry cleaners. Any high school volunteer could have done the same menial chores. Plenty already were, as the Montgomery office was staffed primarily with volunteers, many of them recent high school graduates. But unlike those campaign workers, Will and Daniel had both received generous paychecks at the end of the week, handed out with a sour look from the current office manager, who looked like he knew exactly what was in those pay envelopes, as well as exactly how little the recipients had done to earn them.

Caroline struggled to rouse herself from the floor.

"Don't leave," he said, eyes closed.

"I've got to," she whispered.

"We can go in my room. Sleep in my bed," he murmured drowsily.

"No, we can't."

I'll wake you up in time. You can sneak upstairs early in the morning. My parents will never know."

She responded by kissing him before rising to leave.

"Wait!" He grabbed hold of her arm.

"Sh!" She shook herself free. "It almost *is* early in the morning already. So I'm not going to take any chances."

Opening his eyes, he watched her tiptoe up the stairs and wave goodnight when she reached the top. With a sigh, he heaved himself up, pulled the towels with him and stumbled into his bedroom. His eyes were still so bleary that he almost overlooked the letter from Eleanor lying on his pillow as he pulled down his covers. Thank God Caroline had not come into his room after all! But what should he do about the letter? His impulse was to throw it away without reading it, or even better, tear it into pieces and flush it down the toilet so his mother wouldn't fish it out of the wastebasket and read it. But on further reflection, he remembered that knowledge was power, and knowing the contents of the letter might prove useful if Eleanor were to phone his parents' house, which she had been known to do. In fact, she had done so over the past Christmas holidays. Of course she'd had every right to do so, but as far as he knew, she didn't have the phone number. However, she had managed both to find it and use it, and might do so again. On the whole, he thought it best to read the letter first before tearing it into pieces and flushing it down toilet.

"Dear Daniel," it began,

"I'm back from Europe and miss you more than ever. And I'm more than ever sorry for the terrible misunderstandings that drove us apart at the end of our senior years. It should have been such a wonderful time for us to experience together, and I know I'm partly to blame for the fact that we didn't do so.

"Obviously I never began to understand how much Alabama means to you. It was stupid of me to assume that you would want to share my hometown simply because I'm so fond of it. I feel even more stupid it never occurred to me that you might want/need me to come to your native state instead. I take full responsibility for these mistakes and ask you to forgive me.

"It isn't that I'm totally blind to anyone's needs but my own. I trust you know that. It's just we spent so much time talking about what our life could be like in Greenwich I never realized how much Alabama was still on your mind. So when you returned from Christmas break talking about going back to Alabama, I'm afraid I was caught so completely off guard that I didn't respond well. Can you give me another chance to share in your dreams and vision for our future together? I'm perfectly willing to try to live in Alabama. I'm only sorry I never made that clear to you.

"As for your going to law school, I'm certainly in favor of that. My father says a law degree is as valuable as an MBA and would be just as much an asset if we ever decided to come back East. He also, by the way, has nothing but admiration for the way you've determined to strike out on your own. 'Eleanor,' he said to me in Paris, 'you can't help but respect a man who wants to prove himself and make his own way.' So there are no hard feelings or burned bridges there. He flat out told me he would welcome you into the firm if you ever wanted to learn his business, but totally understands if it isn't the path you want to take.

"What I regret most of all is that another girl got caught up in our misunderstandings. I don't mean to reproach you—I know I was being distant and ridiculous. Plus I was stressed with finals, thesis, etc. But this prevented us from being able to resolve our differences as we should have in time to enjoy graduation together and plan for the summer. Not to mention the rest of our lives!

"I am not going to rake you over the coals or make you pay penance for getting involved with another girl in the last month of senior year in order to prove your point to me. I was hurt—angry—shocked—bewildered beyond belief—and this only added to our estrangement. But I think the sooner we put this episode behind us, the better we'll be and the faster we'll heal from it. So as far as I'm concerned, if you can forgive me, I can forgive you, and we don't ever need to discuss it.

"Please call or write as soon as you get this. Preferably call. I'd like to join you in Alabama without delay so I can figure out my own next step. As you know, I'm planning to go to graduate school myself—still not sure in what— and will need to get an application in. I know state schools down South aren't as competitive as what we're used to up here, but I'd like to get this matter taken care of.

"Can't wait to see you again.

Love, El"

Toward the Future

Will Alabama cling to the past, or look to the future?

This is the question facing Alabama voters in the Democratic primary scheduled for September 7th.

Equally important: Who can best deliver a better future to the people of Alabama?

The answer might seem difficult to determine in an unusually crowded field of contestants. We believe the answer is obvious. To help clarify a potentially confusing picture in voters' minds, we are coming out with our endorsement now for the Democratic primary and the general election.

Of the 6 candidates currently seeking the gubernatorial nomination in the Democratic primary, two stand virtually no chance of winning, according to polls and veteran political observers.

One of these is 67 year-old Percy Atchison, a retired attorney from Mobile who has never held elective office. A highly regarded member of the bar, a man of sterling reputation and personal wealth who has dedicated himself to historic preservation in Mobile and many other civic causes, Mr. Atchison is undoubtedly a worthy individual. But he has released no platform, has no campaign office, and has made no statewide appearances. He is not a viable candidate.

The other marginal contender is former governor James E. Folsom, 73, who served two terms during the 40s and 50s. Legally blind, he does not possess the best of health and has not been an active campaigner.

Two other candidates are better positioned to be contenders but do not constitute the best choice voters could make.

One is Lieutenant Governor Kyle James, 45, a distant relative of the current governor, Fob James, who is not seeking re-election. Prior to becoming lieutenant governor, Kyle James was a high school football coach and had never held elective office. He was presumably voted in on the wave of enthusiasm that swept his second cousin into the governor's office four years ago. Although Kyle James has not been the disappointment or embarrassment that his cousin has proven to be, neither has he accomplished anything of note or substance indicating his fitness to take on the office he seeks.

In contrast, 65 year-old Billy F. Teasdale, known as "Big T," is a veteran with 40 years of service in the Alabama legislature. He is currently at the end of an unprecedented 3 consecutive terms as Speaker of the House. Admired by both Democrats and Republicans as a pragmatic compromiser who can muster the votes to get legislation passed, he has often been tainted by scandal or ethics complaints, although he has never been indicted or under investigation. As a master practitioner of "the backroom deal," Teasdale is entrenched in the politics of the past, in which special interests are invited to the table, and everyone gets a little of what they want, while the people of Alabama seem to get nothing and move no further toward a better future. He is not the man to lead Alabama where it needs to go.

The primary race really boils down to two main contenders: former governor George C. Wallace, whose last term concluded four years ago, and current Attorney General Aaron Osgood. Recent polls indicate that these two candidates will emerge with the most votes from the September 7th primary, and face each other in a run-off scheduled for September 28th.

The choice is stark, and it is clear.

George Wallace, 63, represents Alabama's past, which has given our state the negative image we are still struggling to overcome today. Industries and the jobs they create will not come to a state perceived as backward and regressive. But that will be just the impression we project once again if we re-elect the man most responsible for creating that impression in the first place.

Ironically, George Wallace is running primarily on his name recognition. Outside Alabama's borders, George Wallace's name recognition is not of the kind that will attract the businesses and opportunities our state desperately needs.

Despite three previous terms as governor, Wallace has few meaningful accomplishments to show for the many years he spent in office, including 16 months his wife Lurleen served as governor before she died of cancer. Alabama's very real problems and very real potential were never addressed by George Wallace. Instead, Wallace devoted himself to demagoguery in order to get himself elected and re-elected. He then tried to use his position as governor of Alabama as a platform to run for president. Wallace's entire political career has been about furthering Wallace's political career. It has not been about helping the citizens of Alabama.

Finally, Wallace's health problems alone make him a poor candidate. His physical condition has been steadily deteriorating since the assassination attempt in 1972 left him partially paralyzed. He is also partially deaf.

George Wallace is not the man to lead Alabama into the future.

By contrast, his strongest opponent is the 39 year-old Attorney General Aaron Osgood. In 10 years of elective office, Osgood has amassed an impressive record of achievement. As a member of the Alabama State Senate from 1972–1978, he is credited with introducing and winning passage of key legislation reforming state disbursement of federal highway funds. As attorney general he has become a champion for ethics reform, mounting three high-profile investigations of state contractors from the Wallace era of notorious cronyism and corruption. In the one case that has come to trial so far, Osgood proved to be a vigorous prosecutor and won a stunning conviction against Loman Brothers last year. Two other cases are still pending. Meanwhile, Osgood has also drafted ethics reform legislation that has already been brought before the House of Representatives. For these achievements, he was named one of the top five most important attorneys general in the nation.

Belton Collier, the unchallenged Republican contender, is a pistol-waving racist who makes George Wallace look like a bleeding heart liberal. As there has been no competitive two-party election and no Republican governor in Alabama since Reconstruction, a Collier victory is as unlikely as it is undesirable.

Aaron Osgood is the man to lead Alabama into the future. He can put a new face on Alabama politics, stand proudly beside other progressive, New South governors, and help our state claim its share of Sunbelt prosperity. He is the clear and obvious choice for all Alabama voters.

~ 7 ~

"Just wait till you see this!" A fat manila envelope landed with a smack on the floorboard as Will Hill twisted awkwardly around the passenger door and inserted himself into the car.

This particular door of the Chevette would only open so far and no farther; still, Will Hill had a surprising lack of grace for a guy every bit as short as Daniel. His movements were always cumbersome and slow. Those who knew him best (and had seen him in a locker room) joked that he couldn't move any faster because of all the weight he carried below his belt. His nickname was "Kong Dong."

"See what?" said Daniel, reaching over for the packet. As Will settled in his seat and tugged on the seatbelt, Daniel removed a sheaf of papers from the yellow folder. "Is this the fax that came in right before we left?"

Nodding, Will said, "That, my friend, is our sign from above, our herald of victory, our promise of a new day."

Rifling through the pages, Daniel couldn't make heads or tails of the charts, graphs and numbers, but it was too hot to remain sitting in the parking lot trying to make sense of it. He needed to crank up the car and get on the highway. "You'll have to translate this for me," he told his friend.

"Daniel," said Will in a voice so dramatic it arrested Daniel's hand as it moved to put keys in the ignition. His arm dropped to his lap. "What you are holding," Will went on, "is the latest poll commissioned by the Birmingham *News.*" The breathless reverence in his tone suggested it was a fifth holy gospel.

"And?"

"And," said Will, pausing for effect. "Let's just say that confidential sources have told us the *News* is going to release these poll results under the headline **Too Close to Call.**" A look of pure triumph spread across his face.

For a moment Daniel was speechless, as if unable to credit, or process, this startling development. Then he raised his palm to meet his friend's in a resounding high-five. Simultaneously the two young men exploded into cheering boisterous enough to rock the car.

Will punched the air in front of him. "This means he can do it, Daniel. With these new poll numbers, and the Birmingham *News* endorsement already in the bag, the momentum has definitely shifted our way. And it's only going to grow. Aaron Osgood is going to be our next governor."

Daniel cranked the ignition but kept the car in park to give himself a moment to absorb the heady impact of this news. Will resumed his tug-of-war with the seatbelt. "Does this thing work?" He yanked so hard on the belt that it finally came out of its locked position, but was now so loose as to be equally useless.

"Not really," Daniel admitted.

Will's own automobile was even worse, but he refused to give up the ancient Ford that was always breaking down and constantly in need of repairs. Although he could have afforded a newer vehicle, Will clung to the old one out of nostalgia for the days when his family struggled to make ends meet and could barely keep food on the table. Those days had shaped his character, he claimed, and he seemed to want to be reminded of them in every possible way, even if it meant his car wasn't fit to drive and was always in the shop, like it was today. Owning a reliable automobile that actually worked on a day to day basis would have been some kind of betrayal of his working-class origins in Gadsden, where his mother was a public school teacher and his father was a lifelong employee of Goodyear Tire & Rubber. So it was Daniel's car they were taking to Birmingham, where they both had girlfriends. Will's girlfriend, Rhea Mehta, was a medical student at UAB. The two young men would enjoy their female companionship on Friday night before heading the next day to Cullman, where they had been summoned for a meeting by campaign manager Gene Boshell.

"What else are all these poll numbers telling us?" Daniel handed the envelope over to his friend as he backed out of the parking space.

"Osgood stands to get more than 90% of the black vote."

"That's not news."

"No, but this is," Will thumbed through the papers until he found the page he wanted. "Aaron has 'strong white support,'" Will quoted, "in all the Black Belt counties and throughout South Alabama. It's considered 'too close to call,'" he quoted again, "which is the pollster's official conclusion that Aaron has pulled even with Wallace in the southern part of the state." He looked over at his friend. "That's why the *News* is going to use that phrase for its headline. It's actually in the summary here."

"Got it," Daniel grinned.

They go on to say this," Will read again from the paper. "'In South Alabama counties, the white support for Aaron Osgood is growing and should easily surpass support for Wallace by the time of the primary if current trends continue.'"

"Two weeks ago Osgood was four percentage points behind," Daniel commented. "Now it's neck and neck. And they project Osgood to pull ahead?" he shook his head, marveling at the turn of events. He'd always known Osgood could do it, but hadn't expected it to happen so soon.

"This is just South Alabama," Will cautioned him. "North Alabama is another story. It's like what Francis Miles used to tell us: That racism in the southern parts of Southern states was not nearly as bad as in the northern parts."

"How did he explain that? Remind me."

"Think about it, Daniel. Where most of the plantations were, there has always been a heavy black population. White folks have always lived around blacks and are used to working with them. Over time, whites learned they don't really have anything to fear from black people. So nowadays, the average white person from South Alabama is not nearly as racist as the hill farmers and factory workers in those mostly white counties in North Alabama."

"Like Cullman."

"Exactly," said Will. "Last time I was there, they still had that sign. You know which one I'm talking about?"

Daniel nodded. On one of the main roads leading into Cullman, there was a sign depicting a black man along with a stark warning: "Don't Let the Sun Go Down on You in This Town."

"What this means," continued Will, gesturing at the papers he replaced in the folder. "The battleground for this election is North Alabama. Today I was told Osgood isn't coming back to Montgomery until later in the summer, when Coretta King and Jesse Jackson are scheduled to make their tour."

"When will that be?"

"August, I think. Around the same time the Alabama Democratic Council is supposed to make their official endorsement of Osgood," said Will, referring to the state's organized black leadership. "I believe Aaron Osgood is pulling his troops up north, and we're going to be reassigned, if not to headquarters in Birmingham, then to Huntsville."

"That would explain a lot," said Daniel.

"It certainly would," Will agreed with satisfaction.

For the second week in a row, Aaron Osgood had failed to make an appearance in Montgomery, where his highly compensated Harvard talent had whiled away their time answering phones, stuffing envelopes and picking up bumper stickers.

Will nodded his head vigorously. "It would explain a lot indeed," he repeated. "And you know what else this means? By the time Coretta Scott King gets here to remind everybody what George Wallace did to the black people of this state, she'll have the ear of the white people as well. The candidacy of Wallace will seem like nothing more than the bad joke it is. A hopeless farce. Aaron Osgood is going to win this election."

As he navigated through Friday afternoon rush hour traffic out of Montgomery, Daniel gnawed on his cheek. It didn't seem right that a small, two-bit town like Montgomery in a down-trodden, no-account state like Alabama could generate as much traffic as a major metropolis. Considering there were few enough fringe benefits to being in Alabama, at least one of these should be the absence of gridlock.

"What's wrong?" said Will, turning to his friend.

"You know what's wrong."

"Eleanor?"

Daniel nodded, and fiddled with the knob of the air-conditioning, whose mildly cool air had turned humid now that they were on the interstate.

"I advised your mother how to handle the situation," said Will. "When Eleanor calls again, your mother promised me she would do exactly what I told her."

Eleanor had called his parents' house three times in the past week. The first was a polite call seeking Daniel's telephone number in Montgomery. Shaye Dobbs had dutifully passed on the phone number to the campaign office in Montgomery. Eleanor had then phoned the office numerous times to leave messages he had not returned. Next she had called Opelika a second time, to alert his mother that her son had not returned her calls and to find out why. Daniel could easily imagine the tone of voice Eleanor had used when speaking to his mother during this conversation. He had heard Eleanor use this tone with store clerks and waitresses. It was hectoring and demanding. It was outraged, arrogant and entitled. It was Yankee. And it was stupid, since even the dumbest Southern belles understood they could catch more flies with honey than vinegar. Above all, it made the person being treated as inferior and unintelligent want to respond with equal rudeness and put the rude b— in her place. So his mother had rared up and told Eleanor it was not her son who was behaving badly or dishonoring his commitments. It was Eleanor who was in the wrong for pursuing someone involved in another relationship.

"If my son thought it was appropriate to make contact or respond to your calls, I'm sure he would have done so. Obviously, he thinks it isn't right and wouldn't be fair to his girlfriend. Common sense or decency should tell you to stop calling him."

After which there had been a prolonged silence, followed by a strangled repetition of the phrase "His girlfriend!" and punctuated by the slamming of the phone in Shaye's ear.

The following night came phone call number three. Eleanor had tearfully apologized to Mrs. Dobbs for her outburst the previous evening, and explained that there were so many miscommunications and misunderstandings she simply had not been able to process them gracefully all at once. But it was she, Eleanor, who was her son's girlfriend. That freshman girl he might have mentioned had just been a distraction from the "issues" pertaining to his future with Eleanor. But so certain was she of this future that she had already picked out a wedding dress from a bridal shop on Newbury Street, and had her eye on an engagement ring she and Daniel had once glimpsed in a jeweler's window.

Shaye Dobbs was then flooded by the fear which ruled, and ruined, her existence. She realized at this point that she was dealing with "a scorned woman" who was rich enough to cultivate her wrath and translate it into revenge. And there was no telling what means her rich and powerful father had at his disposal to wreak havoc on the lives of those who had injured his daughter. Shaye thought the matter was serious enough to summon Bobby to the telephone to inform Eleanor in his voice of final and irrefutable authority that she must be mistaken: Daniel had brought someone else down to Opelika to visit the house *as his girlfriend.* Their neighbors across the street, Joab and Janet Tucker, had given a party to introduce this girl to family friends in Opelika. On Sunday, she had gone to worship with them at the First Baptist Church of Opelika, where she had met dozens more of Daniel's classmates from high school and their parents.

"Our understanding," concluded Dr. Dobbs, in his end-of-sermon rhythm, "is that this is the girl our son intends to marry. That is also the impression given to everyone she met in Opelika this past weekend."

At which Eleanor, who had never visited Opelika or met his parents, had burst into wracking sobs. Bobby Dobbs had passed the phone back to his wife and returned to his bourbon. Still sobbing, Eleanor had insisted that she and she alone was Daniel's *true* girlfriend. They had been together *three years,* whereas he had barely known this other girl *three months.* They had planned their whole future together. In addition to the wedding dress and engagement ring she had scoped out, they had already discussed *names for their children.*

The prospective names for these prospective grandchildren had caused Shaye Dobbs to begin crying, and the tears of her prospective mother-in-law gave Eleanor hope. Between her own sobs, Eleanor began to beg. She begged for Shaye's help. She begged for Shaye's intercession with her son. She begged for Shaye's understanding and support. She begged for Shaye to believe how much she loved her son, and how she never intended to give him up or give up on him, no matter how many unscrupulous girls tried to take him away from her. She begged Shaye to pass on these messages to her son, so he could expect to see her soon in Alabama, to resume the relationship that was rightfully hers and continue their planning for the future he had promised her. Lastly, she begged for Shaye to name a day that Eleanor could come to stay and try to work things out with her son.

Fortunately, it was Will Hill who had spoken with Daniel's hysterical mother when she first called the campaign office in Montgomery. Kong Dong had a voice not unlike that of Bobby Dobbs: strong and deep, it was soothing and reassuring to distraught females. Will was also an astute and quick-witted problem solver, who would undoubtedly make a brilliant attorney if he didn't go into politics instead. When Shaye had categorically declared that she wanted no more phone calls from Eleanor, no jilted woman staying in her house or outraged parents on a rampage after them, Will Hill had told her exactly what to say. The next time Eleanor called, (and there would be a next time, Will warned her,) Eleanor was to be told that both her phone number and her message had been given to Daniel. Anything further should be between the two of them. Shaye and Bobby did not want to be involved and were not involved. Shaye and Bobby wanted no further contact with the situation or with Eleanor. If Eleanor *did* choose to contact them again in spite of their expressed wishes, then that would be **harassment.** Shaye had gulped. **Harrassment.** Will was most emphatic that Shaye had to use that word. And if she wanted to do her son a favor, she could point out to Eleanor that if she continued to pursue contact with him that he didn't desire or reciprocate, that would constitute harassment as well.

"If Eleanor calls again, your mother is going to draw the line," Will said. "The 'Do Not Cross' line. I told her she must use the word 'harassment,' and I think she will. Often just using that word or invoking that concept can wake the person up. Confront them with the harsh reality, make them re-evaluate the situation, their actions, and then get them to withdraw. But your mother must use that word," Will insisted. "In the worst-case scenario, if the person doesn't go away, it's helpful from a legal standpoint if the victim has clearly drawn a line that the aggressor has crossed in complete cognizance of the victim's wishes."

Will's reference to victims, aggressors and worst-case scenarios was less than reassuring. What Daniel most wanted right now was some reassurance. For that, he really needed to talk with his minister Lewis Holditch, who at the moment was a thousand miles away in Cambridge, but would soon be en route to a summer vacation in Florida. When Daniel had called Lewis earlier in the week to discuss the situation with Eleanor, Lewis had suggested they do so in person. If Daniel were to name a specific time and place in Alabama, then Lewis could easily shape his travel itinerary accordingly.

The prospect was tempting: one of their long, satisfying discussions in which a problem, a question, an issue or a conflict that Daniel brought before the older, wiser man was carefully considered and thoughtfully addressed. He never left Lewis's company without feeling that a burden had been truly shared and then lifted from his mind. Lewis's advice was invariably sound and Daniel had invariably followed it without once regretting it. He missed their long talks as he missed the man himself. It would be good to see him again.

But after one of these long talks last February, when it was bone-cold and sleeting outside, Lewis had leaned over, kissed Daniel on the lips and suggested he spend the night at the rectory. At first, Daniel was taken aback, but after the initial shock passed, he wasn't all that surprised, since he had long understood that he had some kind of mysterious personal magnetism that made people want to kiss him. It had nothing to do with him, anything he did or said or in any way suggested. He couldn't see how it had much to do with his looks, either, which were nothing to speak of, although a college classmate once called him a Southern Bobby Kennedy. But for some strange reason outside his control or even his consciousness, people were drawn to him. He made no effort to draw people to him. They just came. Like Lewis just leaned over and kissed him, out of the blue, with no warning or preamble. But this was the first time he'd been kissed by a man, and it caught him so off guard he couldn't remember exactly how he'd responded. At any rate, the kiss had made no impact of the sort Lewis might have hoped and stirred no latent or repressed longings Lewis may have wanted to tap into. The invitation to stay had been politely declined, and a few weeks later, Daniel was talking of nothing but Caroline. Neither the kiss nor the invitation to stay the night had ever been repeated, or even mentioned. If Lewis had hoped or believed that Daniel had undergone a sexual as well as spiritual journey over sherry at the rectory, then surely Daniel's tactful silence on the subject had put an end to that fantasy in the kindest possible way. However, Daniel did not want to put this supposition to the test at this particular time in the state of Alabama, and had declined Lewis's offer to meet in person.

"What are you thinking?" Will was pressing him. "Talk to me Daniel. I know this is hard for you. I know how close you came to marrying Eleanor. I realize how much she meant to you."

In truth, Daniel's three year relationship with Eleanor May had all been a mistake. He had not intended to prolong it past the one night on which he'd met Eleanor at a Harvard-Wellesley mixer in the middle of his freshman year. At that time, he was still operating according to "the Sherman principle," which was the brainchild of a Brookie at Harvard named Prescott Lee, who had started the Alabama brunch tradition in the Eliot House dining hall, where he solemnly informed all incoming Alabama freshmen of the doctrine he had named after the dastardly Yankee general who had marched from Atlanta to the sea on an infamous path of destruction, which included the brutal deflowering of numerous Southern belles. According to Prescott, any Southern "gentleman" who found himself in the Northeast for any length of time, (and all Southern males in the Northeast were "gentlemen" by default), were duty and honor bound to exact payback for the burning, pillaging and raping of the South committed by Sherman's army. In practical terms, this meant that any Southern male at Harvard should at the very least "burn" as many New England women as possible.

Eleanor May was the girl who put a stop to the Sherman principle in Daniel's social life. After the mixer, she felt she warranted more of his attention, and demanded that he give her more of his time. He was not at all inclined to agree, because after all: Who did she think she was? Then one of his New England roommates informed him that she was the daughter of a very rich man who lived in one of the most exclusive neighborhoods in Greenwich, Connecticut. So that's who she thought she was. When she called again, he couldn't help himself: he had never before been the object of a rich girl's desire. He agreed to meet with her, to discuss what exactly had happened after the Harvard-Wellesley dance. Instead of discussing the experience, they had replicated it. Thus began his relationship with Eleanor May, which lasted almost three years.

Although it began and ended with his own disingenuous behavior, he honestly believed he had nothing to apologize for in the intervening three years. He gave no less than he got. He may not have been passionately in love, but he had been dutiful, if not completely faithful. And she had been demanding. He had spent every weekend with her, most holidays and two summers. At her suggestion, he had acquired a whole new wardrobe and changed his religion. What more could a man do for a woman who did not give him a hard-on whenever he thought about her? He had given her three good years, but was not prepared to lay his whole life at her feet.

However, he never wanted to actually break up with her. He'd always figured the relationship would die a natural death when he moved back to Alabama without her. Ending any kind of association with another person in a permanent way was extremely difficult for him. The last thing he ever wanted to do was wield an axe or deal a fatal blow to any connection that had sent love flowing in his direction. Plus, feelings would be hurt, tears would be shed, reproaches and recriminations would fly and fingernails might even dig into his arms clinging for dear life and begging for another chance to live. Above all, there were those who were bound to think ill of him after he'd let the hatchet fall, and he hated more than anything for people to think ill of him. So he had never really planned on breaking up with Eleanor after he became involved with Caroline Elmore. Instead, he had counted on circumstances bringing their union to its sensible conclusion. This is exactly what had happened with his first girlfriend, Ricky Jill. Just as going off to college meant leaving her behind, graduating from college meant leaving Eleanor behind. Of course, she would never move to Alabama. Why would she? Certainly his own attractions were not nearly enough to compensate for the deficiencies of life in Alabama, especially for someone who was used to the sophistications of Greenwich, Connecticut or Wellesley, Massachusetts. Truly, the only reason to live in Alabama was if you were born there.

But he had not reckoned on Caroline Elmore showing up at the Eliot House Garden Party. By then, they had had their second date, the one where he had kissed her as they walked along the Charles River. Afterwards, he had returned to his dorm room, entered the common area where his four roommates were enjoying their Sunday night keg, somersaulted over the sofa and announced that he'd just kissed the girl he was going to marry. And naturally, he would have preferred to take her to the Garden Party. But Eleanor had already bought her "frock" and her hat. However strained and distant their relations had become, she would never dream he wouldn't be taking her to the Eliot House Garden Party. Already they were like an older married couple who had never been right for each other but had stuck together through simple inertia and had learned not to question what they didn't have the courage to change. They might no longer be sleeping together, but they would certainly be going to the Eliot House Garden Party together. At least Eleanor was already filling the role of the estranged but entitled wife: she offered nothing but expected everything. However, it wouldn't hurt, he thought, for him to play his part this one last time. Afterwards, he could withdraw and disappear forever before she even realized he was gone. And her last memory of him would be of this lovely party.

But then, in the Eliot House courtyard on that Saturday afternoon of dazzling spring sunshine, one girl had stood out among the crowd in their capped sleeves and gaily be-decked hats purchased especially for this signature Eliot House occasion. Unlike the others, this girl was bare-headed and wore a simple, sleeveless sundress. Her hair glinted gold in the sun and her feet in their delicate flat sandals looked bare in the deep grass of the courtyard. In this dress that appeared to have seen many summers, her body looked like Elizabeth Taylor's in That Slip. In that movie. Whichever movie that was.

This was not just any girl. This was his girl. HIS GIRL. Inside he felt like a cargo elevator in free fall. The freight of his heavy heart landed with a thud at his feet. What was she doing here? Of course, she had a perfect right, but she was a freshman. She lived in Harvard Yard. The event was for Eliot House upperclassmen and their invited guests. Of course she could have been such a guest, but she had told him she wasn't dating anyone. And after their kiss, he didn't think she would ever date anyone else in her entire life. But here she was, standing next to a tall, handsome, Eliot House junior who was handing her a flute of champagne. He couldn't have been more outraged if this other man were making brazen advances toward his wife. He was all but oblivious to Eleanor tugging on the sleeve of his jacket as her gaze followed his.

At the moment he could not deal with Eleanor. There was his own inner turmoil to tend to. On the one hand, he wanted to leave the party altogether and immediately, so as to prevent Caroline from seeing him in Eleanor's company. Before his fateful kiss with Caroline, he had thoroughly described the demise of his relationship with Eleanor. It was a totally accurate description except in the particular of the relationship's actual demise. This being the most important particular, he did not want to be compelled to provide awkward explanations at what was supposed to be a graceful social ritual reminiscent of a more courtly era of strawberries and cream and pretty frocks and gay hats. So his first instinct was to flee.

But the stronger urge was to go claim what was HIS, and his alone. Accordingly, he had walked straight over, laid a hand on her arm and spoken her name softly but firmly. He hoped Eleanor wouldn't follow, but of course, she did. It couldn't be helped. Eleanor was out of his life, although she didn't yet know it and was in fact his date for the whole day, which had started that morning at eleven with Bloody Marys and would conclude later that evening with dinner at the restaurant in Boston where her parents were meeting them.

When Caroline turned around to face him, no words had been spoken. The eyes on both sides had said it all. His he knew were begging and pleading: for her to forgive, understand, and above all, be his. He would do whatever it took. If she had demanded that he leave with her immediately to go get married that instant, he would have done so gladly. On her side, the eyes had shown first a startled surprise and delight, followed by a dawning consternation as she quickly grasped the compromising situation for both of them.

"This is Tad Burnette," she said, introducing the junior he knew by sight. They nodded awkwardly at each other. "He's in my Shakespeare section and asked me on Friday if I would do him a big favor and come to this Eliot House 'thing' with him." She looked at Tad in mock reproach. "I had no idea this *thing* was such a formal affair. Look at me."

Look at her indeed. Along with her golden hair, she had a golden tan recently acquired from the spring break trip to Florida she'd taken with her family. It was the perfect match for her slip of a dress. And the other girls in the courtyard—every last one of them—were no match for her. Their expensive, elaborate outfits were to no avail, especially because they were all trying to look like Southern girls—like Mia Farrow playing Daisy Buchanan. Some of them actually looked quite nice. But no Yankee woman stood a chance next to a real Southern girl in a sundress.

Meanwhile, he was rapidly calculating. If Tad Burnette had asked her—*yesterday*—to a *thing* at Eliot House, then he most probably had been stood up by the date he'd secured a long time ago to the most important event on the Eliot House social calendar. Quite likely, he had a girlfriend who was either sick or called unexpectedly out of town for a family emergency. Not wanting to miss the prime social occasion of the year, he'd asked this beautiful freshman girl to do him a "big favor" and go with him.

"I'll see you next week," he had said to Caroline, before nodding again at Tad and walking away. After the date with The Kiss, he had already asked Caroline out for the upcoming Friday night, when there would be no Garden Party with Eleanor the following day, and no Eleanor ever again. Referring to their plans was the best he could do at that awkward moment to make sure she knew that she was his future, and he wanted to be hers. All other explanations would have to wait. The acknowledgement Caroline gave him indicated he was spared the worst, which would have been the loss of her trust, respect and the love he knew she already felt for him. (With Southern girls like her, when you kissed them as he had kissed her, they felt married or at least engaged afterwards.)

But this was his wake-up call. He had to get his act together and make sure that Eleanor never came between them again. So when Eleanor had picked the inevitable fight later in the evening, he let her do it. She had cried, accused, screamed and pummeled his chest with her fists. He denied nothing. Yes, he admitted, he had taken Caroline Elmore out for two dates during the past month, when Eleanor had been giving him the cold shoulder treatment.

"That's not how you're supposed to resolve our problems!" she had shouted. Fortunately, none of his roommates were back with their dates. "I do not want to see you again, Daniel, until you're ready to address the issues with me."

She had stayed the night, but turned her back on him in bed. Considering that he'd lost his chance for the seamless transition when Caroline Elmore turned up at the garden party, this argument was the next best resolution. Obviously she expected him to address "the issues" and make amends. Naturally he never even considered doing so.

"If it's any consolation," Will was telling him, "I think you did the right thing. In fact, you did a most heroic thing."

"I did?"

"You did," Will affirmed emphatically, inclining his head forward, as if bowing to Daniel's accomplishment.

"What exactly did I do?" said Daniel.

Will didn't reply immediately. "I've never told you this, Daniel," he began finally. "But when you started dating that woman from Connecticut, I thought I'd lost my best friend."

"What are you talking about? We never stopped being friends after I met Eleanor. You graduated is all. You've been in law school for the past two years in Tuscaloosa. We just haven't been able to see each other that much."

"I'm not talking about the physical distance between us after I left Massachusetts. I'm talking about what happened to you when you started dating that rich man's daughter."

"What happened?"

Will sighed. "Do you remember when we first met, Daniel? At the Key Club convention in Dothan, when I was president of the Alabama chapter?"

Daniel nodded.

"We stayed up all night in my hotel room, talking for hours, like we'd known each other all our lives. And in a way, we had."

Daniel grinned. "I remember," he said.

"Do you remember what we talked about?"

"We talked about what we would do if we ever became governor of Alabama." Daniel grinned again.

"Exactly!" said Will. "We spent hours and hours talking about Alabama politics. The problems of our state, the suffering of our people, and what needed to be done to address these issues. How we could make things better for folks like our parents. How it was our duty, in fact, to make things better, because our parents had sacrificed so much and worked so hard to put their children in a better position. We agreed that it would be the worst betrayal and the most selfish act imaginable if we simply took what our parents had done for us and ran away with it to our own cushy lives. It was incumbent on us, we said, to do for the folks of our state what our parents had done for us."

"I remember that too."

"When we both made it to Harvard, we talked about how we would get everything we could out of it, and then take it back to help make Alabama a better place."

Daniel nodded.

"Are you aware, Daniel, that after you met Eleanor, you stopped talking about coming back to Alabama? You stopped talking about dedicating your life to the betterment of your community? Whenever I saw you, all you ever talked about was the 'incredible business opportunities' Eleanor's father was offering you. I'm sorry to put it this way, Daniel, but it seemed to me that you'd become like all the other Ivy League assholes we went to school with. Making money was the only thing on your mind. All you ever talked about was all the money you were going to make when you'd graduated. After you started seeing Eleanor, that's what your Harvard degree meant to you. It was simply a ticket into the money-making universe; not an education that was going to help make the world a better place. I thought you had turned into the worst kind of sell-out—much worse than the typical Ivy Leaguer we met up there—because at least you had some ideals before you got there. Some noble purpose other than the best way to enrich yourself for the rest of your life."

"You never told me any of this."

"I thought I'd lost you! I considered you a lost cause!" Will pounded the dashboard. "I'm still not sure what made me mention your name to Aaron Osgood. But last summer? When I interned in the Attorney General's office? When he pulled me aside and told me he was going to enter the governor's race? He told me he wanted me in it with him. He told me something else: he wanted a corps of young people enlisted to the cause. He didn't want the usual team of political hacks or campaign veterans. Experience wasn't what he was looking for. It was passion. Optimism. The energy of youth. A cadre of young people who believed wholeheartedly in their candidate. *That* was going to be the lifeblood of his campaign, he said. 'What about your friends?' he asked me. 'Surely you know some other young men who share our vision of Alabama's future.' That's when I thought of the Daniel Dobbs I used to know. But honestly, I never dreamed when I gave him your name that it would turn out like this. Even when you called me after the interview to tell me how well it went, I still didn't get my hopes up. And when you'd called to say you'd taken his offer, I couldn't believe it. And buddy—forgive me—but I figured that once you got back to Harvard after Christmas, and Eleanor started working on you, I'd be hearing that you weren't going to be coming down for the campaign this summer after all. It was only when you told me that you'd started dating an Alabama girl that I knew I still had my best friend. Trust me: Eleanor was the worst thing that could have happened to you. I know it didn't look like that. I know how tempting it all was. I was around it myself for four years. I know how much it took for you to turn your back on it and walk away. That's why I say I'm proud of what you've done. Proud to be your friend. Proud to have you with me here in Alabama, on this historic campaign."

"Will, I got to admit something to you."

"What's that, buddy?"

"Eleanor just didn't get my dick hard anymore."

Will pounded the dashboard again before leaning back and roaring with laughter.

"Thank God you figured this out in time!" said Will. "Just look at the way she's treating your mother! Like some sort of incompetent secretary who keeps failing to perform her duties! And, she's behaving as if she owns you! As if you are *her* property! And believe me, that's exactly what you would have been if you'd married her!" Now he pounded the passenger door with his fist.

"I just hope my mother can follow your advice and keep her from coming down here."

"Whether she does or doesn't, if Eleanor calls again after that, then I myself will be glad to call Eleanor's parents and inform them of the nature of their daughter's conduct."

"You would do that?"

Will nodded fiercely. "I'd be glad to."

Daniel hadn't counted on this, and it was an enormous relief.

"I would actually love nothing better than the opportunity to tell Eleanor's father that neither he nor his daughter have any claim on you, and that his daughter is actually committing acts of harassment. It will be my pleasure, to inform him of the fact!" He pounded the car door again. "And if I have to point out that his daughter's behavior is legally actionable, psychologically unstable and possibly even criminal, I will be happy to do so! And I'll tell you what else! It would make my day to go to the police, file a complaint and take out a restraining order on that woman! What I wouldn't give to take out a restraining order on even one member of the class of people she belongs to!"

Daniel grinned: He should have known. Although Will looked like an Ivy League preppy, with his yellow-blond hair, his tortoise shell glasses and somewhat lockjaw manner of speaking, he was a committed class-warrior who remained fiercely wedded to the lower class from which he came. His father, A.J. Hill, was a union leader who had been passed over for promotion many times in his 30 years at Goodyear by much less experienced men. Only when he finally allowed a labor lawyer to file suit on his behalf was he instantly promoted to supervisor and given years of back pay. Although this startling turn of events had transformed the family's prospects, it would never alter Will Hill's outlook on life. To him, the very wealth of Eleanor's family made her guilty in Will's eyes. Wealth could never be anything but ill-gotten gains, and Eleanor's pursuit of Daniel was nothing more than the acquisitive drive to seize what was not hers. Will had been so relieved to hear that Daniel had found "a good Alabama girl," that he had not yet summoned the courage to say the words "Mountain Brook." Daniel had always been careful just to say "Birmingham." Since neither Birmingham nor Alabama were synonymous with wealth, Daniel hoped that Will's good opinion was being formed and had a chance to crystallize before he saw Caroline's house or learned of her family.

The thought of Caroline caused another weight to crash down on his consciousness. Apparently she had not been able to start on those birth control pills she had gone to such trouble to acquire because her period was three weeks late. "You said you were not going to play Russian roulette with my life!" She had tearfully accused him on the phone earlier in the day. This was in reference to what he'd said when trying to convince her not to make him wear a rubber. Well, it had been true. He had not intended to play Russian roulette with her life; he had just intended to make love to her without a rubber. He'd had a hard-on. He wasn't totally responsible for everything he might have done, and for nothing he might have said. Hard-ons had a way of

From "Tee-Time" in the Anniston Star, *June 28, 1982*

Will the "Real" George Wallace Please Stand Up?
by T. Tom McGinnis, political columnist

George Wallace, they say, has mellowed. He has changed. He has accepted
Jesus Christ as his savior and become a born-again Christian. He has even
been down to the Dexter Avenue Baptist Church in Montgomery to tell the
black people of our state that he loves them, and explain that his reputation as
a racist is all a misunderstanding. There was never a race question, the misun-
derstood segregationist told them. "It was a question of big government." As
Wallace seeks this true understanding from black Alabamians, he is also, not
coincidentally, seeking their votes.

What I would really like to say about all that in response is not printable in
this newspaper. But a common four-letter word, preceded by the four letter
word for a male cow, would sum it up nicely. Instead, I'll have to respond at
greater length.

If George Wallace has "mellowed," it's because he is paralyzed from the waist
down and survives on painkillers to blunt the agony caused by three bullets
that severed his spine in the assassination attempt 10 years ago.

Don't get me wrong. I don't want to beat up on a broken-down 63 year-old
body in a wheelchair. That would turn him into a martyr and help him get
re-elected, which is what happened in '74 when he got a big sympathy vote.
Since he was all shot up and couldn't run for president anymore, folks felt
sorry for him and let him be governor of Alabama again. But I cannot allow
the implication to stand that George Wallace has undergone some political
transformation or spiritual awakening.

George Wallace is simply doing what George Wallace has always done. Which
is: whatever it takes to get elected.

There are many Alabamians, both white and black, who would agree that Wallace has not changed fundamentally. However, they argue, the Wallace of today—who speaks of compassion and racial harmony—is actually the "real" Wallace.

I find this argument most disturbing of all.

By now we should all know the story of Wallace's first run for governor in 1958, when he campaigned as a racial moderate but was defeated by the segregationist John Patterson, who was backed by the KKK. "I'll never be out-segged again!" Wallace vowed.

Some say that Wallace used a racial epithet and actually cried "I'll never be out-n---d again!" Wallace claims he never made either statement.

Although there is no reason ever to trust anything Wallace says, it doesn't matter whether he uttered the infamous phrase or not. And I would also argue that it doesn't matter whether he was a man of ideals and principles to begin with. If he was, he betrayed them and destroyed them, and that's what matters. His actions are what's important, and he carried out those infamous words whether he said them or not. No one has ever out-segged George Wallace.

As governor, he spent his time proving what a good segregationist he could be, most notoriously in 1963, when he stood before the schoolhouse door in Tuscaloosa, trying to bar two black students from entering the University of Alabama. But this was really just a photo opportunity engineered by federal Attorney General Bobby Kennedy, who promised Wallace his dramatic moment in front of the cameras if integration could proceed quietly the next day. And it did.

Fortunately, Wallace failed at maintaining segregation, but unfortunately, he also failed at being governor. His philosophy of governing can be summed up in his famous remark: It's not your enemies who get state contracts and business deals. Who does? Your friends and family, of course. For years and years, Wallace's friends and family members got state contracts and business deals. (Exhibit A and A1: Gerald Wallace and Oscar Harper.) The Alabama Legislature spent its time drafting bills that could be killed by a "fee" given to the "bagman."

By electing George Wallace again and again, the people of Alabama have paid the bagman to kill their own state.

Almost every other Southern state has elected a New South governor with a progressive agenda to lead the state out of its economic and cultural doldrums. Alabama now has a chance to do the same. In this election, we really are at the crossroads we thought we had reached four years ago, after Wallace's last term. But our current governor, Fob James, has been nothing but a disappointment to everyone.

Agreed.

This does not mean the people of Alabama should give up hope for progress and take George Wallace back on like some comfortable old bathrobe that fits us better than anything new.

Just because Fob has had a dreadful term and declined to live in the Governor's mansion does not mean we need to invite Wallace back into it as if he owns the place, though he clearly thinks he does, since he even had the Mansion worked over to accommodate his wheelchair.

And just because Wallace thinks he owns *us,* does not mean we have to elect him to a fourth term. Five, if you count the time he propped up his cancer-stricken wife as a candidate when he couldn't get around the state constitution to seek a consecutive term.

Yes, George Wallace is our past. But he does not in any way deserve to be our future, no matter how much he may now want to distance himself from that shameful past of his own making. I don't doubt that he's sorry for what he did. In fact, I'm sure he is sorry about it. Of course he is, because what he did back then in order to get elected could prevent him from getting elected now. My point is: it *should* prevent him from getting elected now, especially because that's all Wallace cares about—getting elected. He'll do and say whatever it takes to get there, but once he's there, his agenda can be summed up by the bumper sticker we've all come to know so well over the years: WALLACE.

It is high time the state of Alabama showed the rest of the world that George Wallace is not us. We are better than that. We are better than him. Let's prove it by getting ourselves one of those New South governors.

~ 8 ~

The following night, Daniel and Will had been asked to join Aaron Osgood and a few other key campaign staffers at the Bug Tussle Steakhouse, which they were familiar with from their days in Key Club, when Manley Hellman, aka "Grosspapa," used to lead his troops there after a state Key Club meeting. Mr. Hellman was the beloved bachelor principal of Cullman High School, and the overseer of Alabama's Key Club chapter. Like many in Cullman, Mr. Hellman was of direct German descent, and had a house full of relics, heirlooms and sepia-tinged photographs left him by "Grossmama" and "Grosspapa," whom he remembered vividly and fondly. He spoke so often of his grandparents who had immigrated to America, and so closely resembled the "Grosspapa" in the photographs, that he soon acquired the nickname of "Grosspapa" to all the students at Cullman High and to the boys in Key Club. With no immediate family of his own, he was more or less the papa to these young people, and he was endearingly "gross" with his red face, his double chin and protruding belly. Although nowhere near as obese as Norman Laney, he had been to Daniel what Mr. Laney was to Caroline.

Good German that he was, Mr. Hellman never missed a meal, and did not consider these complete unless they contained a copious amount of red meat. His favorite restaurant in town was the All-Steak. His next favorite was the Bug Tussle Steakhouse, located about twenty miles outside Cullman in the middle of nowhere, or Bug Tussle, Alabama. According to legend, the town derived its name from the fact that nothing ever happened there except once in a while you might see two bugs tussling in the dirt.

The Bug Tussle Steakhouse was in a big barn-like building that may in fact have been a converted barn; Daniel wasn't sure. But that was certainly the effect. It was surrounded on all sides by a huge gravel parking lot, which was itself surrounded by open fields bordered by woods in the far distance. Rumor said there was another barn-like structure somewhere in those woods, where people came from all over North Alabama to watch the cockfights and win or lose considerable sums of money, though cockfighting was technically illegal in Alabama. Mr. Hellman claimed to know nothing about any cockfighting, and no one at the Bug Tussle would tell you or answer any questions about it. If you had to ask, then you were probably an unfriendly form of law enforcement, and nobody was going to tell you nuthin.' But especially on Saturday nights, the parking lot of the Bug Tussle Steakhouse was filled at an early hour with license plates from Alabama, Tennessee and Georgia. The rear fenders on most of these vehicles were punctuated by bumper stickers like: "Proud Descendant of a Confederate Soldier," "American by Birth; Southern by the Grace of God," "UnReconstructed Southerner," or "Jeff Davis for President." Whatever the slogan, they all sported an image of the rebel flag.

When Daniel and Will arrived there as instructed late Saturday afternoon, their job was to secure a table that would be ready when Aaron Osgood arrived from his campaign stop in Cullman. If you weren't there by five-thirty on a Saturday night, you might as well wait till eight, when the Bug Tussle Steakhouse mysteriously emptied of at least half its crowd. At five-thirty sharp, there was already a line forming just inside the door. Near the head of this line stood Ray Haynes, head of the Osgood campaign headquarters in Birmingham. A junior associate at Oliver, Osgood, he had taken a leave of absence from the firm to work on the campaign and manage the Birmingham office. Will had met him a few times, and said he was a nice guy. Obviously, he had been issued the same instructions they had; when they caught his eye, he waved them over to where he stood further up in line. The punctilious Will felt obliged to ask whether anyone in the line ahead of them minded if they joined their friend.

"Naw, g'on [gawn] ahead," was the friendly reply.

"Even if they *are* here to watch chickens tear themselves to bloody pieces, folks are still nice," Will observed under his breath.

"Maybe that's because we're not chickens," said Daniel. "Or black people."

"True enough. True enough," acknowledged Will, with appropriate seriousness. He shook hands with Ray and introduced Daniel.

They secured a large round table in a far corner of the cavernous room. It was not as strategically located as they might have wished, but it would have to do. In addition to Aaron Osgood and Gene Boshell, the campaign manager, a reporter from the Atlanta bureau of the New York *Times* was tagging along in order to gather material for a New York *Times* profile. Ray Haynes rehearsed the details with considerable satisfaction as they took their seats and waited for the others. Aaron Osgood was now universally considered to be George Wallace's main opposition. He had already been endorsed by the Birmingham *News*. Reliable polls indicated that he was neck and neck with Wallace in South Alabama, and catching up to him in the northern part of the state. Of course he would get the black vote everywhere in the state. All signs indicated that he could actually beat George Wallace. If he did so, he would turn the tide in the history of Alabama and change the face of Alabama politics. The only defeat Wallace had ever suffered in an Alabama election was when John Patterson had out-niggered him in 1958. When Fob James had become governor four years ago, it was because Wallace had retired, not because Wallace had been defeated. If Aaron Osgood actually beat George Wallace, it would signal a new day in Alabama. The New York *Times* was duly taking notice. It was even being said that Powell Gaines himself, the Birmingham native who now worked out of the Washington bureau of the New York *Times,* might author the profile on Aaron Osgood. Gaines had contacted the campaign already to see if he could meet with the candidate over the Fourth of July, when he would be coming back to Birmingham for a family visit. Meanwhile, a reporter from the Atlanta bureau had been dispatched to cover the speech in Cullman, and would travel up to Scottsboro tomorrow with the Osgood campaign.

"Far as I know, this is why y'all been dragged up here," Ray told them as he unrolled his paper napkin. "Aaron wanted to show off his Harvard boys to the New York *Times* reporter."

As they waited for the others, the restaurant was filling up quickly with patrons, cigarette smoke and voices that had to shout to be heard even by the person right next to you. Acoustics weren't great in an old barn. So the din got louder and louder, especially as the clock edged toward six and people began to figure it wouldn't look too bad if they took a drink now and then. Although Cullman County was dry, you could bring your own liquor to the Bug Tussle, which many of the men did, in little flasks stashed in their hip pocket. They might have iced tea on the table, but they had whiskey under the table, and they took discreet swigs at regular intervals, wiping their mouths with the back of their hands. Often people drank homemade stuff that was much more potent. This is the way the people were, in this part of Alabama—sweet tea on the surface, and gut-rottin' whiskey underneath.

"I was given strict instructions not to bring any wine," complained Ray jokingly.

"Wouldn't want our candidate called a pseudo-intellectual," said Daniel, mispronouncing it the way Wallace had made famous: "sway-doe intellectual."

By the time Aaron arrived with the rest of his entourage, every table was filled with diners and a large crowd waiting to be seated milled contentedly inside the door, smoking and drinking whatever they'd brought. Everyone seemed to know each other, or acted like they did. It looked rather like a party. A jukebox somewhere had started up, playing George Jones and Tammy Wynette. The arrival of a gubernatorial candidate who was not in a wheelchair went completely unnoticed.

The campaign manager Gene Boshell gripped their hands, thanked them for coming, and without further ado sat down at the table, took out his own flask and swigged heavily from it. His eyes bulged fiercely out of their sockets, as if some inner intensity were thrusting them forward. His shirt was soiled with cigarette ash, and a row of cheap ballpoint pens lined the front pocket, which was blotched with blue ink spots.

Although Will had met Gene Boshell, on several occasions in the past, Daniel never had. Of course he already knew about the legendary Gene, as did anyone who knew the slightest thing about Alabama politics. Gene Boshell had been the veteran political reporter for the Montgomery *Advertiser* until he retired a dozen years ago after covering a notoriously nasty and brutish campaign conducted—and won—by George Wallace. It had cost him his health and his second marriage. That was too high a price to pay, especially as none of his fine reporting had any bearing on the outcome of the race, although it later won a Pulitzer Prize.

Born in Michigan, he had spent the first ten years of his life in Detroit, and still had the accent to prove it. His father had been on the assembly line for G.M. until he lost his thumb. The payout enabled him to experiment with life in Prattville, Alabama, a few miles north of Montgomery, where his wife had cousins. One of these thought he could find some work for a guy missing a thumb. He did find work, so his family had remained in Prattville.

Gene's background gave him a special vantage point on the culture in which he came of age. Having spent crucial formative years "up north," he never lost his outsider's perspective. But this was combined with inside knowledge and experience of the Deep South. Smack dab in the middle of Alabama, Prattville was like the heart of the heart of Dixie. From the moment he arrived there as a ten year-old boy, Gene could see the things that had become invisible to those whose eyes could not see what had always been around them. Many of these things were wrong in the human as well as the legal sense. The regular folks from Prattville couldn't see it because it was just the way things had always been, and they didn't know no differnt. But Gene had seen a different way. With the enthusiasm, optimism and idealism of youth, he didn't see why things couldn't be different—and better—in Alabama.

This vision is what drove him, even as he became a cynical, jaded and world-weary political reporter for the Montgomery *Advertiser.* After covering his last election, he was a human wreck. He had an alcohol problem and a two-pack-a-day habit. Although this was not an unusual profile for a newspaperman, with Gene it was all too personal. Of course, as a reporter, Gene was supposed to be objective and impartial, a mere conduit for verifiable facts and quotations. And as a reporter, he succeeded in being objective and impartial. But he was also a human being, and that human being hated George Wallace. However, he did not need to betray his duty or his mission as a reporter in order to "get" Wallace. The mere facts ought to be enough. Gene kept thinking that if people just knew the truth, *the truth,* THE TRUTH about George Wallace, then they would do the right thing at the voting booth. Gene thought the truth led people to do the right thing. He thought that the truth was enough. In that sense, he had never lost the core of his idealism. When Wallace won the election, he defeated Gene Boshell as well as his opponent.

People said Gene was a heart attack waiting to happen. His wife left him. He quit the paper. He tried to quit drinking, smoking and politics. He couldn't. But he managed to cut back enough to keep himself alive. Nowadays, he was more like a nervous breakdown waiting to happen. As a political consultant, he had never wanted for clients, and had worked on many campaigns. But he had never before agreed to manage one, although he had been asked many times.

Aaron Osgood was different. Gene had seen that immediately. He had the right background. He had the right reputation. The right record. He had done the right things. He had a chance to beat George Wallace. Gene could not stop himself. He was in. This election would either redeem his whole career, and his broken life, with two ex-wives and three estranged children; or it would break him for good. Gene was going for total redemption; he was going for broke.

Aaron winked at the table as he tugged off his tie and introduced the New York *Times* reporter, who turned out to be a girl. A woman, Daniel corrected himself silently, named Helen Mendelssohn, who had loads of dark unruly hair and a large canvas tote bag slung across her shoulder. A Jewish girl— woman—he realized. She sat down next to him in the place that had been carefully allotted her between the two "Harvard boys."

"Is it true what I heard?" Helen muttered in his ear. "There's a cockfighting operation around here? Or were they bullshitting me?"

Not a Southern Jewish girl—woman. Probably from New York. He was intrigued. He shrugged and grinned at her. "That's what I've always heard," he said. "Nobody knows for sure except those who go there."

She could not control an involuntary shudder and looked around the room, as if it could provide the necessary clues to what lay beyond its walls.

"What do you think?" he asked her.

She drew a blank and gave him an uncomprehending stare.

"These people," he explained. "Do they or do they not go to cockfights after they eat here?"

"What do you think?" She was all seriousness, and had to check a movement to get something out of her bag, like a notepad she could record his answers on.

"Well," he reflected. "They're listening to George Jones and Tammy Wynette. That's a cockfight right there."

She drew another blank, but looked at him suspiciously this time, as if afraid of being "bullshitted." These were clearly her two biggest fears: 1) being bullshitted and 2) not realizing it.

"That's a joke," he assured her. "Just a joke."

The waitress arrived to take their order.

"I haven't even seen a menu," said Helen.

Everybody at the table laughed, except for the humorless Gene, who might be able to afford a chuckle after Aaron Osgood was sworn in as governor of Alabama next January.

Helen was trying to be a good sport, but she really didn't understand. As there was only one thing to get at the Bug Tussle, there was no menu except for a distant chalkboard somewhere covered in smudged, faded and illegible chalk. The only choice you really needed to make was between the one, two, three, four or five pound steak. The enormous grill in the kitchen would be full of all sizes, plucked off when ready to fill orders. Theoretically, you could get a T-bone, but most folks ordered the rib-eye. "Two-pound rib-eye" was the most commonplace order, although some ordered the three pound. Nobody could eat the five pound in under an hour and get it for free, plus it and the four pound were too tough. They weren't worth the leftovers you gave to the dog. The two or three pound made for the best eatin,' and even the one pound lapped over the plate. All steaks came with baked potato and side salad or slaw, plastic red baskets filled with cornbread and biscuits. Caddies filled with tubs of whipped butter, sour cream, shredded cheese and bacon bits were brought to each table with the meal so you could dress your own potato.

Helen Mendelssohn, it turned out, was a vegetarian. And the waitress at the Bug Tussle had never heard of soy burgers.

"Just bring her a baked potato and a house salad," said Daniel. He caught Aaron Osgood's eye, and the older man winked at him. He knew that his "assignment" right now was to make sure the New York *Times* reporter had a positive experience with the Osgood campaign. Accordingly, he began asking her all about herself. In his rise to International Key Club president, one of the first things he'd learned is that if you want to get people to like you, then all you really had to do was ask them about themselves.

Helen Mendelssohn, he learned, was a thirty-two year old native of Brooklyn who had attended Barnard and then the Columbia School of Journalism. After first landing a job with the Atlanta *Constitution* right out of J-School, she had later been hired by the Atlanta bureau of the *Times,* where she had been for the past two years. She appeared to believe that because she had lived in Atlanta for five years that she now "knew the South." Of course, if she had at all "known the South," she would have known that Atlanta was not it. However, it could have been worse. She could have thought she knew the South because she had read books about it. She could have turned out to be a guy that he needed to converse with all night.

Growing up in Opelika, Alabama, Daniel had met not one single Jewish girl in his entire childhood. At Harvard, he was suddenly surrounded by dozens. They were fascinating to him, like a special female species he had never met before. Whereas Southern girls grew up learning to be coy and subtle, these Jewish girls crackled with open energy, both intellectual and sexual. They didn't seem to care who they offended or appealed to with either their opinions or their bodies. They were who they were, and that was that. If you were insulted or disgusted, too bad for you. (Fuck you.) Plenty others would be impressed and attracted. Daniel definitely counted himself among these.

He loved the way they often went bra-less in an old tee shirt and piled their hair on top of their head as they dashed off to breakfast before the dining hall closed. Inevitably, loose tendrils or curls escaped immediately and framed their face in a way that Southern girls might spend hours trying to duplicate without coming close to the same effect. Often they wore no makeup except for a dab of lipstick or a few brushstrokes of mascara that somehow achieved the most brilliant results. Most of all, he loved the way they could go from zero to one hundred in less than sixty seconds, from bed to the dining hall, where they were soon pounding the table in a heated discussion as they consumed eggs and coffee. The passion with which they argued a point was enormously exciting to him; he couldn't help but imagine they would bring the same passion to bed. They also had the ability to read his mind. Some just suppressed a smile, but others raised their eyebrows at him and he followed them from the dining hall back to their unmade beds right after breakfast.

They were straightforward, business-like, and insistent upon the worst kind of contraceptives, but they always had plenty of these readily available. They could be even more wild and imaginative than he had hoped. They had even less use for subtlety in the bedroom than they did in public. And really—when it came to sex, what was the use of subtlety? Once your own body was naked and in close proximity to another naked body, the time for subtlety was over, especially because there was nothing subtle about putting one of your most intimate body parts into an intimate body part belonging to someone else. You just needed to go for it, and that's what these Harvard girls knew exactly how to do. They had indeed expanded his horizons a great deal. Afterward, there was no expectation that he need ever so much as say hello or even make eye contact again, especially as the campus on the whole was not given to friendly hellos or eye contact. In two weeks they might have forgotten who he was.

Helen Mendelssohn reminded him exactly of these particular Harvard women. All of her reactions were extreme and intense. She was intensely interested in this campaign. She was extremely repulsed by the notion of cockfighting. She was extremely curious as to why those four state troopers over there—she nudged him and nodded in their direction—did not just walk immediately into the woods, investigate the situation and bust up any cockfighting organization if they found one.

"Oh, they'll be going there tonight," growled Gene. "That's why they're eating here now."

Her eyes had widened with excitement. "Is this a raid, then? Will they be making arrests?"

"No, darlin'," Gene drawled, in the pseudo-Southern accent he liked to affect with Northerners. (With Southerners, his leftover Michigan accent became more pronounced, but with Northeasterners, he put on a Southern drawl.) "Those four troopers over there will not be making arrests. They'll be making bets, just like everybody else."

All laughed, except Helen, who didn't get it. But she wanted to get it; she desperately wanted to get it. She wanted to know all there was to know about Alabama, the election, George Wallace and the Bug Tussle Steakhouse. These were the most fascinating subjects in the world to her, and she wanted to master them in five minutes at the most. (For the purposes of her job, she needed to master these subjects in the next five minutes, and she would.) The zeal with which she quizzed him could not help but be flattering. This was his state, his culture, his steakhouse. He was the object of attention and desire, which had not yet climaxed. Until then, he did not need to remember that she

146

was intellectually promiscuous, and would be pursuing a story on a peanut butter plant in Georgia next week with similar passion.

"I have some friends who went to Harvard," she told him, as the waitress began unloading huge platters of steaks.

He did not find this information at all surprising. She rattled off names while he cut into his enormous slab of meat. None of the names meant anything to him, but he politely refrained from pointing out their age difference. He was twenty-one to her thirty-two.

"Whenever I went to visit," she said, "I used to love to go hear the lectures by Francis Miles. Did you ever take any of his courses?"

"Francis Miles was my thesis adviser."

Her pupils dilated in disbelief. "Francis MILES? Your THESIS ADVISER?"

He nodded modestly, though he might as well have told her his thesis adviser was God, as this was the way so many people thought of Dr. Miles, who inspired a cult-like devotion even among those who had only heard of him.

"Oh, my God," she said. "No shit. That is unbelievable. What was it like?"

What was it like being the protégé of one of the most famous, sought-after professors on campus? Not what she would have thought. If she wanted the truth, he should tell her that Miles rarely showed up at his office for the weekly tutorials when they were supposed to discuss the progress on his thesis. When Daniel arrived at the appointed time each week, he usually found only a closed and locked office door. Once there was a note saying: "Meet me in the Coop, History section, 11:15." Although Daniel had raced across campus and then the square, he had not made it in time. He and his thesis advisor had passed each other on the escalator, Miles coming down with an armload of books, Daniel going up with his pile of thesis pages. When they got level with one another, Miles had reached out his hand and Daniel had passed over the pages. Apparently Miles lost them before he got back to his office. But in return for the missed appointments and lost pages, Dr. Miles had approved the final draft of Daniel's senior thesis, although it was never clear to Daniel how much of it, if any, he had actually read. In the end, the relationship had worked out just fine. However, this wasn't the story Helen Mendelssohn wanted to hear.

"Francis Miles was—unbelievable," he assured her.

"Oh, I'm sure. I'm sure." She began tucking strands of hair behind her ears in agitated, staccato movements. "What was your subject? Of your thesis?" She even seemed a bit nervous, which was not like her. But to be so close to one who had been so close to Dr. Francis Miles. . . !

"The Role of Religion in Alabama Politics." He proudly quoted the title of his thesis, which had been the best and most fully realized thing about it.

"Oh, my God," she said. "Do you know how much I admire that man? Do you know how lucky you are? You know, his book. The one called *Telling Stories, Changing Hearts and Minds in the South* is what inspired me to get a job at the Atlanta *Constitution*."

What Daniel knew is that he could have sex with this woman later that evening if he were so inclined.

"Who is Francis Miles?" grumbled Gene irritably, interrupting his conversation with Will Hill, who sat beside him.

"Francis Miles is a cultural historian at Harvard," Will told him. "Daniel and I both had courses with him there."

"He's a writer, too," said Aaron. "Written many fine books about Southern society. You've never heard of him."

Everyone laughed. Helen looked from one face to another trying to figure out the joke. But it was an inside joke, referring to the fact that Gene Boshell, a writer, was also illiterate, as he never read the words of anyone but himself.

"Okay, okay," said Gene, like a cantankerous schoolteacher trying to get his students re-focused on their lesson. Shoving aside his plate, utensils and water glass, he lowered his head until his chin nearly rested on the surface of the table. Instinctively, everyone else did the same. The plate Helen shoved away contained her uneaten, untouched salad and baked potato. Whether she had been too caught up in her passion for Francis Miles, or too concerned about her food containing animal products, Daniel did not know.

"Look around you," Gene said, almost under his breath.

They could barely hear him above the din and had to lower their own heads even further to catch what he was saying.

"This is what we're up against," said Gene. "We're in the heart of George Wallace country. This is the crowd we've got to win over in order to win this election. So take a good long look."

Obeying his command, they all glanced surreptitiously around the room, as Helen had done when she first arrived. But the people they saw seemed nothing more than average, ordinary American citizens, unremarkable in any tangible way. They did not look like the kind of people who would thrill at the sight of one animal tearing another to pieces. They looked like the kind of people who enjoyed going to Shoney's on Sunday mornings before church for the all-you-can-eat breakfast buffet. Given the bulges in their figures, no doubt they did this on a regular basis. The complacency on their faces suggested that one of their happiest experiences in life was the anticipation of a good meal such as the one that awaited them in this here steakhouse. The very happiest experience, of course, was the actual consumption of that meal. They did not in any way look like the kind of people who harbored hatred or prejudice or who would hurl spittle and ugly epithets at strangers of different skin color or religion. Was this just the sweet-tea South, or was the gut-rot underneath? Impossible to tell. The worst you could guess about these people just by looking at them was that they had not gone to college and may not have graduated from high school. Perhaps this simple lack of education was the problem, if their minds were imprinted with only a few fixed ideas, one of which was **WALLACE,** all of which were instilled by the cultural traditions of their birthplace. It was hard to know, and even harder to find out, since these were the kind of people who would become even more blank in protective posture when accosted by a stranger's prying eyes or questions. And even if they had wanted to, these were not the kind of people who could articulate themselves even to themselves. Some of them would go to the cockfights, because that's what people did on Saturday nights around here. Most of them would vote "Wallace" because that's what folks had always done around here. How did an outsider make headway with these people?

The reporter from the New York *Times* didn't get this, or else she was simulating ignorance and fishing for quotable remarks.

"The polls have you almost even now," she addressed Aaron, while fumbling behind her for the contents of her bag. "There's double-digit unemployment in this state. Inflation—stagflation—the recession, have hit this region as hard as any other place in the country. Why would even those who have some—sentimental attachment—vote for a man who's . . . past his . . . prime? Who's . . . not all there? How can they afford to? I just don't see how he can win."

Either someone had instructed her on the drive, or she had managed to pick up on the necessity of avoiding any mention of the name of George Wallace. The very name was already myth, and gave power to the decrepit old body which was its still-living vessel.

"You can *never ever* count him out," said Gene Boshell emphatically, thumping the table with a fist containing an unlit cigarette.

"Never," agreed Aaron, just as emphatically.

"When he gets desperate, that's when he gets dirty," said Gene. "And when he gets dirty, that's when you'll know you're gettin' to him. And it ain't got dirty yet." He scratched his graying, grizzled, unwashed curls as if he were picking at a scab underneath.

"But it will," said Aaron, momentarily losing his good cheer. "Before it's over, it will get dirty."

"And he'll deny all responsibility," said Will, with disgust. "Claim that 'supporters' and 'sympathizers' did this dirty work and he knew nothing about it."

"I've said it before, and I'll say it again," said Gene, thumping the table with his still unlit cigarette. "This election is going to be a re-play of the race in '70 with Brewer. "That's why I'm in this."

Aaron exchanged conspiratorial glances with his fellow Alabamians as Gene finally lit the cigarette he had been trying to deny himself. Everyone in Alabama knew that the '70 race had been Gene Boshell's personal Waterloo.

"Dear God, Gene," said Aaron. "I've told you never to mention that other election. Especially not where Mary Winston can get wind of it." He indicated Helen Mendelssohn with a quick glance in her direction. "You'd lose your client. Mary Winston would make me drop out of the race."

"Why?" said Helen quickly, pen now uncapped and ready. "What happened in '70? Who is Brewer?"

"Albert Brewer," said Gene, drawing heavily on his cigarette. "Is one of the finest men ever to jump in the cesspool of Alabama politics. I covered him when he took over the Mansion in '68. And I covered him when he ran for his own term. It could easily be called the dirtiest race ever to take place in politics *in this country*. Not just in Alabama." He exhaled a huge cloud of smoke almost regretfully, as if he hadn't wanted to give it up.

"Brewer was Lieutenant Governor when Lurleen died of cancer," explained Will.

"Lurleen?" said Helen, bent over her notepad.

"Lurleen Wallace," said Daniel, leaning over to whisper the forbidden name of "Wallace" in her ear. "His wife. She was the governor and her husband was her 'chief adviser.' But she had cancer."

"Albert Brewer got more done in the three years he served out her term than any other governor in the history of Alabama," said Gene. "If he had defeated Wallace in '70, he would have been our first New South governor. Not you," he looked affectionately over at Aaron Osgood.

"So what happened?" said Helen.

"Brewer won the primary," said Daniel.

"He won the primary?" She was confused.

"But unfortunately failed to get a clear majority," said Gene, tapping ash fiercely onto his half-eaten steak. "So he got himself in a run-off."

"That's when it got dirty," said Will.

"Exactly," said Gene.

"But he can't do that again," noted Daniel. "The times have changed. Now *Wallace* is playing the white nigger."

"The white nigger?" Helen whispered the word she would not be able to put in her newspaper and couldn't bring herself to say out loud.

"That's what he called Brewer. For being a 'racial moderate.'" This last was the phrase Daniel whispered. Among the crowd at the Bug Tussle, the word "nigger" need not be whispered, but the phrase "racial moderate" might raise eyebrows.

"When Brewer won the primary," said Gene, stubbing out his cigarette. "George's brother Gerald said they all knew what they needed to do." Gene looked dramatically around the table. "'Holler nigger as loud as they could.'"

The shock on the face of the Jewish girl reporter for the New York *Times* was a sight to behold.

"Gerald said 'We'll just throw the niggers around his neck,'" continued Gene. "'Promise them the moon, and holler nigger.' That's an exact quote. You can probably look it up. It's on the record now."

"I can still remember the ads from that campaign," said Will. "I must have been about twelve then. There was one radio spot that started with sirens blaring louder and louder, like a police car arriving on the scene. Then this deep voice came on and said: 'Suppose your wife is driving home at eleven o'clock at night. She is stopped by a highway patrolman. He turns out to be black. How would you like for your wife to get stopped on a dark night on a lonely road by a black state trooper? Think about it. Elect G.[eorge]C.[orley] W.[allace]'"

"The worst was the print ad of the blonde girl on the beach surrounded by smiling black boys," said Gene, leaning back in his chair. "The caption ran: 'This could be Alabama four years from now. Do you want it?'"

"This was in 1970?" Helen demanded. "After the Civil Rights Movement?"

Everyone at the table nodded solemnly in acknowledgement of the rather terrible truth.

"Some folks is slow in these parts," drawled Gene. "Slow to catch on. Slow to catch up."

Nevertheless, Daniel experienced that peculiar pride he would never have admitted but couldn't help feeling whenever an outsider was amazed by Alabama. Even if the amazement was horror or disgust, it was somehow better than nothing. Better than not being noticed at all. He was sure this was the same kind of pride that had enabled Aaron's infamous opponent to win election after election.

"But isn't Daniel right?" she wanted to know. "About those days being over? He can't play the race card in this election? Because he's trying to win the black vote. He's apologizing. He's repenting. He's not race-baiting. Right?"

"Ohhhhhh," said Gene. "He had more than the race card in his black bag, even then."

"Don't I vaguely remember something about Brewer's wife being called an alcoholic?" said Will.

"Please, please, please do not remind my wife of this," begged Aaron. "She does not need to hear this."

"There was that." Gene acknowledged Will and ignored Aaron completely. "That and lots more. After the primary," he fixed Helen with a ferocious gaze. "Thousands of leaflets went into the rural parts of the state. The small towns, the working class districts." Gene took a pen out of his pocket and pulled a paper napkin in front of him, where he wrote 'KKK' in big letters. He shoved it across the table at Helen. "The circulars were stuffed in mailboxes and plastered on windshields in church parking lots. And they were vile. Mrs. Brewer was an alcoholic. Her two daughters, who may or may not have been fathered by Mr. Brewer, were both pregnant by black males. And Mr. Brewer was a homosexual."

Helen erupted with laughter. "But that's so over the top!" she said. "How did anyone take this seriously?"

Gene's mouth turned down at the corners. He did not take it kindly when anyone did not take what had been a very serious business very seriously. "Gals from 'Women for Wallace' used to show up right after Mrs. Brewer had made an appearance at a Garden Club or something. Posing as her aides. 'She wasn't slurring her words, now, was she?' they would ask. All nervous and anxious-like. They booked appearances for her at nursing homes, and the old ladies got all dolled up, and of course Mrs. Brewer never showed, because she knew nothing about it."

"Mrs. Brewer fainted in a department store when she heard one of the rumors being spread about her family," said Aaron. "I told Mary Winston she would not be part of this campaign. And she told me, she would not be part of this campaign. And she better not be."

"Was there any truth at all, to any of these . . ." Helen searched for the right phrase.

"Scurrilous accusations," Gene suggested.

"Scurrilous accusations. Was there any truth to them?"

"Not one iota," said Gene.

"Then why did all the rumors have an effect on people?"

"Because, darlin', they appealed to the sordid imagination. Mrs. Brewer was a drunk because she'd had to use a stud—possibly black—to father her two daughters, because her husband was a homosexual."

"But these just sound like stupid schoolboy taunts that no one ever takes seriously," Helen persisted.

"Well, Brandy Ayers was worried about 'the wimp issue,'" said Aaron.

"Who's Brandy Ayers?" asked Helen, pen poised.

"J. Brandt Ayers," said Gene, lighting another cigarette. "Is the publisher and owner of the Anniston *Star*. The most liberal newspaper in the state of Alabama. He's as close as we get to a Hodding Carter. Don't tell me you haven't heard of Hodding Carter. And I'm surprised you haven't heard of Brandy. He writes op-eds sometimes in your newspaper."

"That might be before her time," Aaron pointed out.

"Maybe so," said Gene. "Anyway, he's our liberal conscience. Our lone liberal voice crying out in the Alabama wilderness. (Gene admired Brandy because he'd offered him a job—a columnist's spot on the Anniston *Star* after Gene quit the *Advertiser*. But Gene had said he was through.)

"Brandy had me for dinner at his home last month, when I was in Anniston," said Aaron. "He wanted to warn me. He said: 'Albert Brewer was too much a gentleman to win. He was too nice a guy—that was his biggest problem. He came across as a wimp. He acted like a mama's boy and a teacher's pet. The kid in the front row with his hand in the air. His shirt never had a wrinkle, he never stubbed his toe, never scraped his elbow, and his britches never got dirty.'"

"Wallace called Brewer a 'sissy,'" Gene spat out the word, and forgot, in his disgust, not to utter the forbidden name. "Said if Brewer was elected, the state would be ruled by 'a spotted alliance'—that was the phrase they used—'a spotted alliance' of black people and 'sissy-britches from Harvard who drink tea in country clubs with their pinkie finger stuck in the air.'"

Helen clapped a hand over her mouth—to stifle laughter or horror—it wasn't clear. Perhaps it was a mixture of both.

"Do y'all drink tea with your pinkie finger stuck in the air?" Ray Haynes addressed Will and Daniel with amusement.

"I thought that's what he said about the 'rich folks from Mountain Brook,'" said Daniel, affecting a Wallace-like demagoguery. "'They live up on the mountain, those rich folks in Mountain Brook, and go downtown in their chauffeured limousines, then go back to their big old houses or the Mountain

Brook Country Club, sip on martinis with their fingers stuck in the air.'" Now he mimicked Wallace mimicking the Mountain Brook "sissies." "'And they say: Oh, we must have progress.'"

Fleetingly he thought of his future father-in-law, Perry Elmore, who did, in fact, drink martinis, but not with his pinkie stuck up in the air. Indeed, the image Daniel retained was of Perry spreading sacks of manure on his beloved vegetables. Or the blustering, red-faced Julian Petsinger dragging his beleaguered wife off to the Mountain Brook Country Club so he could eat "good American food" instead of "fancy French glop" like eggplant lasagna. Neither man had appeared to care about "progress"; the status quo was just fine for them. It wasn't the first thing or the worst thing Wallace had deliberately gotten all wrong.

Gene picked up the thread, mimicking Wallace. "'And guess where *their* children go to school? These rich folks in Mountain Brook who want *progress*? Their children go to a lily-white private school. Or a lily-white public school, because they live in a lily-white suburb on the mountain across from Birmingham. *Progress* is fine for them, because they've bought their way above it all!'"

"Bottom line," said Aaron. "If you ran against him, you were either a white nigger or a sissy-britches."

"Which amounts to the same thing," noted Gene.

"But surely a man in a wheelchair, who needs two state troopers to lift him out or get him in, surely he won't be calling anybody a sissy this time around," Helen argued.

"Don't be so sure," Gene's lip curled. "He has a way of making people look 'sissified' next to him. That's why Albert Brewer lost. He took the high road. He stayed Mr. Clean. He didn't get down in the dirt. He ran those stupid ads that said 'Good grief, Mr. Wallace.' He wouldn't fight, and that's why he lost. Because people in Alabama despise a man who won't fight. They always respect a man who will."

"Stands to reason," muttered Helen. "They like chickens who fight."

"But as Brewer himself said, you can't go on television and say: 'I am not a drunk,'" said Will.

Ray Haynes let out a whoop. "But with all those painkillers, now Wallace is the one more likely to be slurring his words."

Gene banged on the table with his fist. "Albert Brewer could have won that election. He should have won it. But all he could say was 'Good grief, Mr. Wallace.' He started reminding people of Charlie Brown. A loser. A pitiful loser who wouldn't stand up to the schoolyard bully. So the bully won. By default. More than a million ballots were cast, and a mere 32,000 votes was the difference. Brewer could have won if he'd fought back. That's why I'm in this. It ain't g'on happen again. That sombitch ain't gonna do it again. The right man is going to win this time. When he pulls his dirty tricks out of the bag, whatever they are, we'll be ready. *And we will fight back*." His fist banged again on the table after each emphatic word. "Bring it on!"

"You know he's going to call Aaron a 'pointy-headed intellectual,'" observed Daniel.

"I don't know 'bout that intellectual part," drawled Aaron. "But I cain't argue 'bout bein' called a pointy-head."

"Let him," said Gene. "We're ready for that one. Bring it on. A state with 14.5% unemployment could use a pointy-head to get us out of it. We're ready for that one. We're ready."

There was a respectful and reverential silence as everyone contemplated Gene's state of readiness. He looked ready to fight George Wallace with his fists that very minute.

"Okay, here's what I want you two to do," Gene pointed with his cigarette at Will and Daniel in turn.

Electrified, they nodded vigorously. Had their moment finally arrived?

"Gadsden," said Gene.

Gadsden? They blinked.

"Gadsden," Gene repeated. "We need to open us an office there. Here's why. You probably know the union vote usually goes to our opponent. But one in five people in Gadsden are *out of work. Out of work.* One in five. So we're going to challenge him on the union front. The economy gives us a chance with these people we don't normally get. Aaron tells me he's got two Harvard boys doing nothing in Montgomery, so I say let's put 'em on to Gadsden. That's your hometown? Am I right?" He looked fixedly at Will.

"Yes, sir," Will nodded.

"Your dad's with Goodyear?"

"A supervisor now."

"And still a union leader?"

"Yes, sir," said Will.

"All right, then. You're going to open a Gadsden office. You're going to open it, you're going to staff it, and you're going to run it. That's your assignment. I've got a budget for you, and a campaign credit card. But the office is mainly for cover, you understand. Your real job is: you go with your dad to the union meetings, if you can, wearing your Osgood button. Any time you can get into the union hall, you go there. You sit with these people, these *out of work* people in the coffee shops near the automobile plants *where they used to be employed.* You offer to take 'em to Denny's for dinner. See if any of 'em is interested in volunteering their time. Answering phones. Making calls. Going door to door. Don't matter if they do or don't. Give 'em the idea that Aaron Osgood is the man who can put food on the table in front of them and offer them honest work."

Will Hill was sitting stiffly upright in his chair, trying to camouflage the erection this assignment was giving him.

Daniel was thinking: Gadsden? He and Will had guessed Huntsville, where they might spearhead the campaign's push in North Alabama. Not that he'd been too thrilled about the prospect of Huntsville. Daniel's personal opinion was: If he was going to be in Alabama, he might as well go the whole hog and be in the *real* Alabama. With its space center and its community of rocket scientists and intelligent, educated people from other places, Huntsville was not the *real* Alabama. But it was not enough of anything else to compensate for being that far below the Mason-Dixon line. However, it was better than Gadsden.

"Now," said Gene, slapping the table. "Anybody know how we can work this room?"

Daniel had always been good at this sort of thing, although he never thought of it in quite those terms. Perhaps that was why he was so good at it. And a way had magically presented itself, as it tended to do for him. The assistant principal at Cullman High was seated a few tables away, with his back to Daniel, who had recognized him instantly. Daniel wished it had been Mr. Hellman, whom he longed to see, but Irwin Dyce would have to do. He popped up from his chair and went over to the other table.

"Mr. Dyce?" he said, putting a hand on the man's back. Mr. Dyce looked around and soon broke out into smiles of pure delight.

"Daniel Dobbs!" he exclaimed. "I am not believing what I am seeing here tonight! I was just talking about you the other day, and here you are, right in front of my eyes! How long has it been?"

It had been four years. Daniel had seen Manley Hellman, but not Irwin Dyce since he left for college. Mr. Dyce had four years' worth of greetings, good wishes and questions, and three other people at the table to introduce.

Mr. Dyce was a Southern "bachelor" in a way that Manley Hellman was not. While both men were unmarried, Mr. Dyce was the one who might have experienced a personal revelation if he'd ever found himself in Istanbul or Amsterdam in certain parts of those towns where young and naked boys were put on display. He wore a cloying cologne that was nauseating and overpowering. His longish fingernails were manicured and slightly pointed at the tips. His accent was super-Southern, and something about his manner made you think of a Southern lady instead of a man.

But if you had told anyone in Cullman you thought Irwin Dyce was an old queer, they would have said: "Oh, no. He's Wilma Jean's boy, you know." He was not a queer, because he was one of them. And as long as Irwin Dyce behaved as one of them, nobody would know or even think he was at all "different" or "off." The fingernails, the cologne, the fussy, over-sprayed hair and the mincing Southern speech with a hint of a lisp would never even be noticed. That was how it worked in the South. That was the contract, and Irwin Dyce had honored it so completely he had never realized that there was a contract or that he was a homosexual. And he would never set foot in Istanbul or Amsterdam.

Miss Wilma Jean, his 83 year-old mother, was seated at the table. "You remember Daniel Dobbs, Mama. He was our International Key Club President."

Miss Wilma Jean nodded enthusiastically and fiddled with her hearing aid. Her sister was the other lady at the table, and that was her son, visiting from Memphis. His visit home was the occasion for their trip to the Bug Tussle.

"And what brings you here? Mr. Hellman will be furious—few-ree-us— when he finds out you came so close without calling us. In fact, he would have come with us tonight if he'd-a known you'd be here. You should-a called."

Daniel should have. (And he would.) But he was here now because he was working for Aaron Osgood.

"Aaron Osgood? The one running for governor? Is that so?" Irwin Dyce turned around to look at the table Daniel had come from.

Aaron Osgood knew his cue and rose at once. Just as he did so, someone at another table shouted "Dickhead!" and Daniel feared for a moment that it might have been directed at Osgood, whose mostly bald, pointed head with its fringe of hair looked exactly like—well—a dick. But whoever it was must have been addressing a companion, or perhaps Daniel hadn't heard correctly. At any rate, somebody had shouted something and penetrated the din, which had the effect of startling everyone else out of their conversations at exactly the right moment to notice Aaron Osgood as he rose gracefully from the table and reached his impressive height.

He beamed over at Irwin Dyce as if he were a long lost friend, and strode over to the table as if there wasn't a moment to lose in renewing their acquaintance. Irwin Dyce was beside himself, and became as flustered as an old maid preparing hastily for the attention of an unexpected suitor. After checking with both hands to make sure his pompadour was still in place, he tugged at his shirt to make sure it was covering his belly. Daniel observed the whole scene with fascination, and sensed that everyone in the restaurant was equally enthralled. At least, all conversations had ceased and the juke box was miraculously silent. When Aaron Osgood reached out for his hand, Irwin Dyce was as flattered and delighted as if a Hollywood celebrity had strayed from the red carpet to come seek him out.

"Aaron Osgood!" he exclaimed in fervent gratitude.

Was it Daniel's imagination, or was a chorus murmuring "Aaron Osgood" throughout the restaurant?

Aaron shook Irwin's hand with enthusiasm and clasped him briefly on the shoulder.

"Mama!" he called over loudly to the old woman at the other end of the table. "This is Aaron Osgood!"

"Who?" she said, reaching up for her hearing aid. "Who did you say?"

"Aaron Osgood!" Irwin shouted. "The one running for governor!"

The Osgood campaign could not have scripted a better opening. Given the acoustics of the former barn, and Mrs. Dyce's deafness along with her total ignorance of the gubernatorial campaign or any of its candidates, the name of "Aaron Osgood" had to be shouted repeatedly.

Now there was clearly and unmistakably a chorus of "Aaron Osgood, Aaron Osgood" throughout the room, as people turned to one another to explain who that big tall man was over there. Then a hush descended as everyone else, along with Irwin Dyce, began to feel as if they too had been favored by a visit from a celebrity. The truly great thing about Aaron Osgood, Daniel realized suddenly, was that he looked every inch like a man who had done serious, important things, and would do them again in the future.

"I saw him today at the park in Cullman!" a woman explained excitedly to the table directly behind Irwin Dyce's. "I was there for the Girl Scout meeting with my daughter, and there he was, big as life, right up there on stage, giving a speech!"

Aaron whipped around and thrilled her by grabbing both shoulders, pulling her up and "hugging her neck" in the Southern way.

"Who else do we have here?" Aaron asked her. She took great pride in introducing everyone at the table.

"I've seen that man on TV!" shouted an excited voice from the far corner. "He's in commercials!"

Naturally Aaron had to make a beeline for this table. As he passed by, diners looked up at him with something like awe on their faces. One little old lady even tugged on Aaron's shirt sleeve. As he leaned down, she whispered something in his ear. No one could hear what it was, but Aaron proclaimed loudly enough for all: "Thank you very much indeed, ma'am! My wife doesn't even tell me that anymore!"

Laughter broke out everywhere and someone clapped. Somebody else gave a whistle—one of those serious, dog-calling whistles often necessary in rural Alabama.

It was then Daniel understood the genius of Aaron Osgood's ill-fitting suit, which looked like something his mama or his wife had insisted he wear, as if he were going to church, or a wedding or funeral. He looked like a good Southern boy, raw around the edges like everyone else in the room, who had submitted himself to the will of his womenfolk. It was a look and a feeling they could all relate to and respect. And it was flattering. Aaron Osgood hadn't done this for God or Jesus or even his wife. He was wearing a suit on a hot summer night for *them*. He wanted to be their governor, and he was dressing for the part.

Aaron visited every table, met every person, and shook every hand. To those back at Aaron's own table, exchanging glances of satisfaction and congratulations, it was a thrilling indication of Aaron Osgood's potential for victory. Clearly, this man was a winner. He had come straight into the heart of Wallace country and charmed everyone he met just by being there and being who he was, all six feet four inches of himself. Gene left a hundred dollars' worth of twenty dollar bills in tip, which would buy as good a kind of publicity as could be had in these parts. All in all, it seemed a good night's work all around.

"Where are you guys staying the night?" said Helen, looking only at Daniel as they reached the gravel parking lot.

"We're headed back to Birmingham," Will told her, though she hadn't even glanced at him.

"I'm spending the night in Cullman," she told Daniel.

They stared at each other for a meaningful moment. Given the cold shoulder he was getting from Caroline at the moment, he had half a mind to spend the night in Cullman himself.

"We've got to re-group in Birmingham and prepare for our assignment in Gadsden," Will informed her.

"Oh," she said, not even looking Will's way. "Do you have a card?" she asked Daniel. "I'd like to call you if I need more details. And some other time, I'd love to hear more about Francis Miles."

"We'll have a phone line in the Gadsden office by the end of the week," Will declared proudly.

"Here's my card." Helen thrust it toward Daniel. "Atlanta's really not so far," she pointed out. "I can come over any time. I always get better material in person than over the phone."

"Well, Gadsden is a ways from here," said Will. "And it's an hour and a half from Atlanta. It's really kind of in the middle of nowhere."

The middle of nowhere, Daniel thought. Hell of a place to be headed.

What the Governor's Race Means to the People of Alabama: One Big Yawn
Entering the final stretch before the Democratic primary, the six contestants seeking their party's nomination for governor are trying to reach voters who could hardly care less. This is the conclusion that emerges from dozens of interviews conducted across the state by Huntsville *Times* reporters and correspondents. The general electorate is uninterested, unexcited, and undecided.

"People are confused," said Glenn Bannon, owner of an auto repair shop in Jasper. "There's too many candidates."

Political observers are already predicting a less than average turnout for the primary, and are calling for a scheduling change for future elections.

"The election process cannot withstand the heat of an Alabama summer," said Frank Robbins, a political science professor at UAB. "It's too hot to get fired up about anything. No one wants to go to rallies in this weather."

Jake Littlejohn, a barber in the L&L Barbershop in Fort Payne for 25 years, said, "There's been less talk about this race than any other I can remember." When asked who he was supporting, he said, "Nobody."

Retired Auburn history professor Marlin Staples attributed the apathy partly to "Fob fatigue," referring to the statewide disillusionment with the current governor, who is not seeking re-election.

"Fob promised a 'new beginning' after Wallace's last two terms," noted Staples. "Fob was the Auburn football hero and millionaire businessman who had never been in politics and was going to run government like a successful business, tackle all our problems and lead the state to victory. But what did we get out of his four years? An unconstitutional constitutional amendment instituting prayer in public schools. Meanwhile, inflation and unemployment keep rising. If that's what 'a new beginning' is, it's hard to blame folks for not being too excited about the chance for another 'new beginning.'"

Several voters admitted they didn't even know who was running for governor. Of four students approached on the campus of UAH, not one was able to name any of the candidates in the race, including George Wallace.

"There was a guy who gave a talk here. Bald-headed fellow," said one student. "I don't remember his name."

Attorney General Aaron Osgood delivered a speech on the campus last week. . . .

~ 9 ~

In Gadsden, Will Hill was in his element. After two blank and empty weeks of petty labors far beneath his abilities, he finally had his important mission, and on top of that, it was in Gadsden. He was the native son who had gone on to glory in the wider world, but had returned home to help slay the dragon, fight the good fight and defeat George Wallace once and for all. For Will, every moment was now charged with significance and drama, because this was *his* campaign office in *his* hometown. He had to set it up, get it going, keep it running and harness it to the noble cause of eliminating the evildoer and establishing the rightful leader for the people of Alabama.

But just as Will Hill was starting to swell with the importance of his job, Daniel found himself struggling against inner collapse. The two idle weeks in Montgomery had deflated his initial enthusiasm, and the transfer to Gadsden hadn't really helped *him* any, although it had fired up his friend. For Daniel, however, all it amounted to was a carpeted office space in a half-empty strip mall much like the one they'd occupied in Montgomery. Although Will bustled with the urgency of his duties, what these consisted of at the moment was not much more than the kind of mundane tasks that had bored them in Montgomery: manning phone lines, stuffing envelopes, running to and from the printers. It was not what he'd imagined when he'd met with Aaron Osgood last December and was promised "the experience of a lifetime." In fact, the day-to-day reality was exactly like the kind of humdrum office job Daniel had hoped to avoid by entering a life of politics.

He was unable to shake the conviction that he and Will had been meant for far greater things, but forces he couldn't yet identify had conspired to keep the two young men tethered to ordinary tasks. At the very least, he had imagined his summer would be like something out of his favorite Southern novel: *All the King's Men,* only better. Like Jack Burden, he would be sent on an individual quest of supreme importance, but instead of the moral ambiguity of

Burden's assignment, there would be absolute moral clarity. Instead of digging up dirt on the not-so-bad guy in order to get the not-so-good guy re-elected, Daniel would be digging up dirt on the bad guy and ensuring the victory of the good guy, who in turn would install him at his right hand, where he would prove indispensable and in due time become the new leader himself. Daniel had looked forward to his role as one of the good guys, the Jack Burden, the Atticus Finch.

Truth be told, Daniel had also imagined being on the campaign trail himself this summer, going from town to town meeting people and shaking hands like he had when he was International Key Club President. To him, that's what "politics" meant. It did not mean being in one place in one town all the time. It did not mean being in an office. It meant being on the road and meeting new people, which to him was one of the most rewarding experiences in life, perhaps the next best thing besides sex. (Often it could lead to sex.)

But Daniel wasn't the candidate; he was only a measly campaign worker. Why was he surprised? Once again, a banal and commonplace reality was crushing his childish and farfetched fantasies. The road to victory, it appeared, would be traversed in his piece-of-shit Chevette as it accomplished a daily round of housekeeping errands. Not only was there was no glory in this, no excitement, no adventure, no heroism, the best part of himself was not being put to use.

But the given situation did not require the best part of himself, so there was no way to be a Jack Burden-like hero or an Atticus Finch. Circumstances didn't call for heroism, only for drudges and drones. For one thing, George Wallace had already been shot, but unlike Willie Stark in *All the King's Men,* he had survived to run another day, even if in a wheelchair. For another thing, there was no dirt to dig up on George Wallace, because the dirt was there for all to see. It was part of the historical record. It was already in the books. Anybody who wanted could read it for themselves, if anyone in Alabama were at all inclined to read, that is. And Wallace was even worse than the bad guy— he was an old guy. Slumped over in his wheelchair, he looked like he was on the brink of death, not poised for another triumphant victory. Supposedly he still had a very slight edge in the statewide polls, but some were now saying the race was too close to call *anywhere* in the state. As far as Daniel could see, the main thing the Osgood campaign needed to do at this point was simply not fuck up. There would be a runoff, of course, but once it was Wallace v. Osgood and the stark, clear choice was put before the voters of Alabama, many of them black, the outcome was beginning to seem inevitable, provided the Osgood campaign did not fuck up. But how could it? Aaron Osgood had been in politics for over a decade. Any dirt on him would have surfaced by now. The victory Daniel thought he would be helping to fight for seemed already won by forces he had not been a part of or contributed to. Before he could even partake, the climactic battle between good and evil had been quietly won already, and all he had to do battle with was the crushing sense of anticlimax.

Perhaps it was just the heat of mid-July, but Daniel Dobbs felt as if he'd lost his bearings, his sense of purpose and even the ideals that had landed him in Gadsden, Alabama, instead of Greenwich, Connecticut. For him the election had become little more than an office space rented by H&R Block every March and April. Bea's Diner for breakfast, Piccadilly Cafeteria for lunch, Denny's or Shoney's for supper, and one of the twin beds in Will's old room back at his parents' house.

Then there was his girlfriend, now 60 miles and an hour away, who still hadn't got her period yet. If this were not a false alarm, then what? How would she react? What would she want to do? Until now, he felt like he'd known her all his life—this was part of what it meant to fall in love—but he realized he'd really only known her for four short months. He had no idea what she'd want to do if she were actually pregnant. Perhaps she wouldn't want to get an abortion. Perhaps it was just as well if he lost his sense of political commitment: even if Osgood won the election, Daniel might have to go to law school anyway. The irony of this was too much. He had this sense that the bottom was dropping out, not just from his summer, but from his life.

The phone rang.

"Osgood for governor."

"Daniel?" His mother. Keeping the phone to his ear, he killed the connection and waited till Will went over to the filing cabinets before calling his mother back on the campaign WATS line.

"Did you get the package?" she wanted to know.

"Yes, thanks."

"Books and notebooks are expensive to send first-class," she said. "I hadn't realized how heavy they are. How quickly the postage adds up."

"The campaign will reimburse you. I told you that."

"I hope so, Son. I sent the receipt along with an envelope you got from the law school. I think they're asking for your deposit. You remember you said you could pay for that."

"I remember, Mother," he said wearily, stifling another yawn.

"Have you decided what you're going to do, Son?"

"What do you mean? About what?"

"About your life, Daniel. I don't appreciate your tone, Son. Your father and I worked hard and made a lot of sacrifices to send you to Harvard. We made an investment in your career, and we have a right to know what you plan to do about it."

"I wasn't being flippant. It's just that it's ten o'clock on Wednesday morning and it's not a great time to talk about my life right now."

"When would be a good time? Your father and I think you should come home this weekend so we can discuss the matter as a family. The last time you were here, you brought company, and there was no chance for a private discussion. You owe this to your parents. Can we expect you this weekend?"

"Mother, I don't know. I have no idea where I will need to be this weekend. The campaign is heating up, you know."

"I'm only asking you to make a commitment for the weekend, Son. Can you not do that? It seems little enough for your parents to ask. Surely Aaron Osgood can spare you for one weekend. Surely he'll understand the need for you to discuss your future with your family. Your father had a long talk with Joab, too, and Joab is anxious to talk to you as well. You know Joab loves you like the son he never had. He feels the same way we do about you getting your law degree. The best way to get ahead in politics, Joab said, is to come back home. You know he's always wanted to make you his partner and turn his practice over to you. Being a small town lawyer is a tried and true way to become a state representative. But if you didn't make it, or it wasn't for you, there'd always be a law practice to fall back on."

"Why did you involve Joab in this?"

His mother sniffed in self-righteousness. "Your father was upset, Son. As you well know, his life is full of stress, and he doesn't need one more worry on top of everything else. He has a right to ease his own mind and seek advice from someone like Joab."

"Well, I wish he'd let Joab represent him before the School Board. *That's* what he needs to be talking to Joab about. Joab has always said he'd do it for free."

"Don't change the subject, Daniel. We're not talking about your father's job. We're talking about *your* job and *your* future."

"I'm not changing the subject. I think the real subject *is* Dad's job. Dad's job and Dad's lousy life and his poor health because of his lousy boss and his lousy job. But he'd rather focus his worries on me than do something about his own. And I can tell you right now: nothing I ever do in my life—whatever it is—can make up for Dad's unhappiness with his own life if he doesn't have the guts to make it better for himself."

(What he wanted to say was: "Get Dad a strap-on tool!!!!!")

"That's not fair, Daniel. With the economy the way it is, your father can't afford to lose the job he has for another one that may not exist out there. Mamaw was just telling me the other day that things have never been so bad in Alabama since she went through the Depression."

Daniel groaned audibly. When his mother played the Depression card, the argument was over.

"Joab believes that a law degree is absolutely essential for you to establish yourself as a politician or anything else. And if politics doesn't pan out, you'll always have your law degree."

Was it coincidence that the words attributed to his neighbor Joab Tucker bore an uncanny and exact resemblance to the words his parents had been repeating ad nauseam for the last month?

"Can I tell Joab and Janet they can expect to see you this weekend?"

"No, Mother. Not yet."

"It's already the middle of the week, Son. It's Wednesday. By now you ought to be able to plan for your weekend. If not now, then when will you know?"

"Mother, I am in the middle of a political campaign. Things pop up unexpectedly every minute for us to deal with. You need to understand that. This is the way campaigns are. It's a fluid, developing situation that's very hard to predict or plan for."

"Well, I do not understand. It's not like you're on the campaign trail yourself."

This was a low blow.

"I may not be on the campaign trail, Mother, but I'm in Gadsden, and my girlfriend is in Birmingham. I need to see her too, you know."

"Why? Is something wrong?"

"Why would you think anything is wrong?"

"If something happens and she gets hurt, Son. . . . Or, God forbid, she turns up pregnant. . . . Do I need to remind you how disastrous the consequences could be for your entire family? We don't have the resources to fight a lawsuit. And on your father's career ladder, he needs to demonstrate exemplary moral character. Any cloud hanging over him would wreck his chances when Cloyd retires as well as wreck the family finances. Think of your little sister, Son. She deserves her chances in life too."

"Mother," he groaned. "Why must you be so negative? Why do you always harp on the worst case scenario? Caroline is not pregnant. Whatever gave you that idea?"

"It's just that you worry me, Son. The careless way you conduct your private life. If not for Will Hill, Eleanor and her father might be down here right now, going after everything we've worked for."

"That's highly unlikely. Eleanor does not want what's in your bank account. She just wants a boyfriend. You and Dad have nothing to worry about. This is not about you."

"Well it sure felt like it was about me when she was calling me all the time. You didn't talk to her; I did. And she was in some state, let me tell you. Your father and I started going out the back door when we left the house. In the grocery store I was looking over my shoulder every five minutes, afraid she would pounce on me out of nowhere and tear me to pieces like a wildcat. Because that's exactly what she sounded like on the phone."

"So just be glad she's not in my life anymore."

"I'm trying to tell you, Son: as far as she's concerned, she's still in your life. She even said you never broke up with her. There was a fight, she said, but no breakup. I'm not saying she's right, or that she's telling the truth. I'm just trying to explain to you how she sees it. I'm trying to warn you. I think she's determined to come down here and hash this out with you."

He sighed. "Mother, I can handle this."

"Well what about Caroline? Can she handle this? What if Eleanor decides to confront Caroline and drag her into the middle of all this? Because that's who she blames, you know. This is all Caroline's fault. You she's still in love with. But Caroline—I don't even want to repeat the words she used about Caroline. What if she goes to the Elmore's house in Birmingham while you're in Gadsden? Accuses Caroline of stealing her fiancé—that's what she calls you—and calls her all those names? To her face? And we could be talking about more than just a verbal attack here. I have no doubt she's capable of physical abuse on top of everything else. How do you suppose the Elmores would react to all that? And don't think Eleanor would be the only one they'd blame. They'd come after you, too, Son. And the Elmores are not a thousand miles away. They are right here in Alabama, and they could ruin our family name forever."

"Mother, look. I know you didn't get to teach a course in summer school this session. But I have a job that's paying my salary right now. And I'm very busy at the moment. I'll call you when I can, but in the meantime, please don't make any plans for this weekend that involve me. I've got to go."

He hung up abruptly as if he were too busy for formal farewells. In truth, the office contained just himself and Will Hill, along with a couple of desks and a row of filing cabinets. The rest of the office furniture would be delivered on Friday, and the phone company had promised that all the phone lines would be installed by Thursday at the latest. Not till next week would the office be staffed with the volunteers recruited from among the teaching colleagues of Will's mother.

"Your parents," Will stated, perusing a stack of papers he'd retrieved from the filing cabinets.

"My mother, yes," Daniel sighed.

"Wanting you to get your law degree and start making the big money." Will looked up at him.

"How did you guess?"

"It's our society, Daniel. Our culture. Making the big money is now officially the American dream. I honestly believe that most people these days don't even realize there ever was another definition of the American dream. One that didn't equate with money. So many of the people we went to school with at Harvard, even: they were unaware of the original ideals behind the American dream. And they should know better. They've studied American history and literature. They've read *The Great Gatsby*. Supposedly. Yet even they define the American dream as the pot of gold. But you know it's infiltrated our values as a country when people who grew up poor on farms in Alabama start thinking dollar signs instead of damn-Yankees when their boy goes to college up North. You're doing the right thing, Daniel."

"I am? What am I doing, exactly?" Instinctively he looked around the empty room, whose one working telephone was not ringing.

"Aaron Osgood is going to win this election, Daniel. It's really going to happen. Wallace is going to be put down like a mad dog. If the people of Alabama can pull together and do that, it's going to change all of us. It's going to change Alabama, and maybe even the rest of the South. Who knows? It might even change the political landscape for the whole country. But at the very least, we'll be able to see ourselves in a new light. And we're going to put ourselves in a new light. Folks are going to look at us differently. And I want to be a part of all that. I want to be there in Montgomery when the new day begins. I've made up my mind."

"So you're going to defer."

"I am."

This announcement should not have struck Daniel like a thunderbolt, and would not have had that effect if Daniel had not had a possibly pregnant girlfriend in the state of Alabama. Without that complication, he would have welcomed Will's decision. And he wouldn't need to delay making his own.

"Have you told the law school?" he asked his friend. "Sent in the paper-work?"

"It's different for third years, apparently. I can apply for deferral as late as August, I'm told."

Daniel was silent as he absorbed the unpleasant sensation that Will was moving beyond him and without him. Will had no doubts in his mind, no complications in his private life, no harassment from parents.

"I've looked into it for you, too," said Will. "You're going to have to finesse it. Pay your deposit, join the first year class, and then petition in August for deferral on emergency grounds. But this will work out perfectly for you. This way you can tell your parents you're signed up, paid up and set to enter law school. It will be the truth. Then in August, submit your petition."

"How can you know for sure it's the right thing to do?"

"Daniel," said Will. "Of course there's no way we can know for sure. I agree it certainly would be great if we had knowledge and guarantees about how everything would work out before we had to make our decisions about what to do. But unfortunately, life isn't like that. I hope this is not a news flash, but most things in life worth doing require a leap into the unknown. There comes a point when you have to make a commitment in your heart, take a leap of faith and plant your flag. I've reached that point, and I think you have too. When you came down here this summer, the main thing on your mind was how to get around your parents about law school. Don't tell me you're getting cold feet now that our candidate looks like he could actually win. You would not be here right now if you didn't know it's the right thing to do. The only thing."

Actually, Daniel wasn't sure what he was doing in a half-empty strip mall, in the once and future office of H&R Block, sandwiched between a beauty supply shop and a Christian bookstore. All he could really think about was that he would need Will's help, or specifically, the help of Will's girlfriend Rhea, who would be the logical one to accompany Caroline. But would Will agree to it? Even more troubling, would he insist that Daniel resign from the campaign so as not to risk tarring Aaron Osgood with the brush of abortion? Would it taint him anyway? Would Daniel Dobbs go down in history as the one who had sabotaged the white knight in his bid to rescue the state of Alabama from the evil old dragon? And what if Caroline, unlike Ricky Jill, didn't want an abortion? What if she insisted on immediate marriage? Either of these scenarios meant that Daniel Dobbs better not think about deferring law school at the moment.

"Here's the speech," said Will, handing over the papers he'd been reading.

"Speech?"

"The one he gave in Scottsboro on Sunday. Pretty much the same one he's been giving all over North Alabama. I agree that we can do better. When do you expect that package with your notes to arrive from your mother?"

"It came this morning. While you were out at the copy shop."

"Great! Why don't you see what you can do while I start delivering the yard signs? Next week there won't be this kind of peace and quiet."

Daniel sighed and took the pages from Will. It was his own fault. In the parking lot of the Bug Tussle Steakhouse in Gene Boshell's car, he had for some reason unknown to him now informed Gene that he, Daniel Dobbs, had delivered the Class Day speech at his Harvard graduation. No doubt he'd had one too many sips from the flask Gene had offered around in celebration. It had not tasted like any commercially produced liquor Daniel had sampled during his college years when he had liberally sampled them all. The burning substance contained in the flask suggested that Gene had procured some of the local brew. At any rate, after just a few sips, Daniel was able to see in his own mind a simple, straight line between telling Gene of the Class Day speech and then having his speechmaking abilities immediately put to use, first on the stump for Aaron Osgood, and then in short order, in support of his own candidacy.

Instead, he had succeeded merely in insulting the legendary Gene Boshell. "If you think you can write a better speech than me, have at it," Gene had grumbled. "Why don't you use some of that stuff from your professor? The famous one who writes about the South? Only don't let the word Harvard come anywhere near anything you say."

In the abstract, it was the kind of work Daniel had been eager to perform, and it wasn't such a bad idea: Francis Miles' most acclaimed book, *The Southern Culture of Poverty*, had drawn on his research conducted almost exclusively in Alabama and had focused on both the psychological and social effects of poverty on school-age children. It was a brilliant fusion of his expertise in child psychiatry and his work as a cultural historian. One entire chapter had been devoted to the children of factory workers who manned the auto plants in North Alabama. And now many of those workers were out of work.

But in actuality, Daniel was much better at giving speeches than at writing them. Still, when Will left the office, he dutifully thumbed through the pages of notes he'd attempted to take in Francis Miles's classes. The trouble was, these notes, like Miles's lectures, were an impressionistic blur comprised of key words or phrases that often did not add up to coherent sentences or paragraphs. At least, they hadn't ended up that way on the pages of Daniel's notebooks. When it came to Miles's lectures, you kind of just had to be there, which is why so many people often were, many of them not even registered for the class but just dropping in to hear him speak.

Although Dr. Francis Miles was a god among professors, physically he was a small, wiry man who usually wore scuffed jeans and a wrinkled shirt. He had very dark eyes, mostly dark hair, big bushy eyebrows and a five o'clock shadow by the time he gave his eleven o'clock lecture every Monday, Wednesday and Friday for the famous Soc/Sci 33 course he taught in the spring. Although his last name was Miles and he was a devout Catholic, he had been called a "dirty little Jew" when he found himself in certain parts of Georgia, Alabama and Mississippi conducting field research. And in all truth, his family name had once been Milstein. Daniel was not quite clear about when and why the conversion to Catholicism had occurred. He didn't care; he was one of the many who worshipped Francis Miles.

The man did not really lecture, although he had an M.D. as well as a Ph.D. in sociology. What he did was *emote.* Three times a week, right before lunch, he ripped his heart out in front of a crowded lecture hall crammed with hundreds of students, far beyond capacity. He put his bleeding heart right out there on the lectern for all to witness during the fifty minute class period. Meanwhile he would wrap his head in his arms and moan.

"Agee! Agee! Agee!" was a frequent topic of his moaning, often accompanied by a pounding fist on the lectern for emphasis. "So Agee goes *down there!* *To Alabama!* (Pounding fist) *Alabama!* (Pounding fist) He's supposed to do a quickie, for a *fancy, glossy* magazine and earn some much needed cash. But he sees the *suffering.* He sees the *poverty.* He sees the *people.* And he knows he can't do it, this assignment. He knows he can't stay there, for a mere two weeks, and write a mere few hundred words about these *people,* and their *suffering,* and their *poverty,* for a posh New York magazine that will sell ads aimed at rich people—ads placed next to an article about *poor people* that will make these rich people feel richer than they already *are.*

"And Agee *knows,* because Agee is *tortured* and *tormented* by the way *capitalistic, corporate* America keeps the money machine running on the elbow grease supplied by the impoverished *working class*—Agee knows that he will only be contributing to the *exploitation* of this working class if he writes an article about them for his fancy magazine."

At this point, Miles might be interrupted with applause, or even a standing ovation, from students who were now working on Wall Street for *capitalistic, corporate* America. Or in Manhattan at *fancy, glossy* magazines. Daniel didn't know the exact statistics, but his impression was that most of his classmates—the ones he'd been with in Eliot House—were either already working on Wall Street or working on MBA degrees so they could land a job on Wall Street. Daniel could easily have been one of them if he'd been so inclined. Why hadn't he jumped at the chance to do what most Harvard graduates actually did? Partly it was because of Dr. Francis Miles. He'd had some romantic, glamorous notion of being *in Alabama,* like Francis Miles had been for his research, or like Agee himself, who had come back to the South to *pay his debt to his origins.* Francis Miles had made it sound so exciting, like playing the lead in a Hollywood movie.

"Agee does not want to exploit these people! Agee does not want to enable a glossy magazine to exploit *these people! These poor people. Sharecroppers!* Tenant farmers! In *Alabama!* During the *Depression!* The lowest of the low! The poorest of the poor! But Agee needs the money. My God, he needs the money. If he does this article, the money he stands to make is a small fortune.

"And he wants to help these people. No one else is helping these people. It is human misery such as he has never seen, such as he never dreamed existed anywhere in America, even in *Alabama.* Maybe, he thinks, if he completes this article, he will do more than just supply copy to fill the pages of a ritzy magazine and give it a reason for being other than to sell ads that will try to convince rich people to purchase luxury goods whose price tags alone could transform the lives of an entire generation of *poor people in Alabama.* Maybe, just maybe, if he does it right, this article can call attention to the unbelievable *suffering* and *poverty* of these *poor people in Alabama.* But it will take him longer than two weeks. It will take him longer than a few hundred words.

"So he stays in Alabama, amidst the fields of cotton and sharecropper shacks. He needs a drink. He needs a woman. He goes to Birmingham, less than a hundred miles away. He gets drunk. He gets laid. But he goes back, to the cotton crops and the sharecropper shacks. He's racked with guilt, doubt, uncertainty. He is *tormented* and *tortured* by his conscience. Is he doing the right thing? For the right reasons? Is he going about it the right way? Is he just going to end up exploiting these poor people, just like their landlords? Just like his magazine? Will whatever he writes be just another betrayal of these people and their *humanity,* their *decency,* their *dignity*? But he stays. And he writes."

Then Miles might pause to mop his brow and catch his breath as the audience held its own breath, knowing there was more to come, that Miles was gearing down one part of his lecture and trying to gear up for another. They didn't want to make the slightest sound that would interrupt his concentration or the train of his thought, the flow of his powerful words.

"Then there's Walker Evans," Miles would begin again quietly. "A photographer. Hired by this same fancy magazine to take pictures of the sharecroppers Agee is supposed to write about. He's gay. My God! And he's being sent to Alabama on assignment! *A homosexual in Alabama!* My God! This is the *1930's!* This is *Alabama!* Evans is a *refined, sensitive* man. He has *struggled* and *struggled* with his homosexuality. He has had a hard time dealing with it in New York City, for Christ's sake. And now he is being sent to Alabama to take photographs of *poor people.*

"The last place on earth he wants to go is Alabama. And the last thing he wants to do is turn these *poor people* into zoo animals for *rich New Yorkers* to stare at in self-congratulatory fascination! He knows what it's like to be one of the despised. To feel like a leper. To worry if people would as soon spit on him as look at him *if they knew what he was.* He feels an odd kinship, this homosexual living in New York City, with these poor people of Alabama. They both belong to the despised of the world. The last thing he wants to do is betray them to those who would point and laugh or look down on them, or just not *understand.* The last thing he wants to do is serve them up like naked primitives in a *National Geographic* so wealthy people can feel even more cultured and superior than they already think they are.

"So just like Agee, he is *tortured* and *tormented.* By his own private sorrows and struggles, and by the same guilt, the same doubt and uncertainty that sends Agee back to the Petsinger Hotel in Birmingham every few weeks to get drunk and get laid with some prostitute he picks up."

Just the way Miles moaned the word Alabama in his Kennedy-of-Boston accent and smote the lectern with his fist to emphasize the name of Daniel's native state made him a god in Daniel's eyes. And the mere fact that Daniel was a native of Alabama seemed to endow him with genius in the eyes of Francis Miles. It was the one time in Daniel's life that just being from Alabama was more than enough. He got A's in Miles's classes just by being from Alabama. It certainly wasn't on the basis of his work, some of which he never turned in, none of it on time. But he spent many emotional hours in Miles's office talking about *Alabama* and what it meant just *to be from Alabama.* Although the section leaders who graded his midterms and final exams usually gave him C's, his final grade, determined by Miles, was never less than an A. Naturally he wanted Francis Miles as his thesis adviser and senior tutor. And by extension, he had wanted to return to Alabama as if to the source of what made him so special.

But now, in a rented office space in a failing strip mall in Gadsden, Alabama, he didn't feel so special. He certainly didn't feel like the lead in a

Hollywood movie. There was nothing overtly glamorous, exciting or romantic about fighting the good fight or trying to defeat George Wallace. As usual, the sophisticates who'd been his classmates at Harvard were way ahead of him. Fighting the good fight was something they could applaud in a movie or a lecture hall, but they knew better than to think it would get them anywhere if they were to try it themselves. Noble and heroic causes had entertainment value which his college classmates had appreciated during the four years they'd had to wait before entering the real world where they could start making money. Once they were in this real world, however, they had to put aside diversions like noble causes which simply did not pay, as his parents would say.

He was beginning to feel not only that he'd lost his ideals, but that he never had any real ideals to begin with. It wasn't ideals he'd had, but a pitiful vision of personal glory. He had assumed this would be easier to achieve in Alabama, where there wasn't as much competition and he'd have the playing field pretty much to himself. So after his parents had fought their way off the farm, and he'd fought his way up North to the Ivy League, he had casually thrown it all away on the basis of a B movie playing in his head in which he had the starring role. It wasn't even a Hollywood production, but a cheesy historical docudrama for a lesser cable channel. Although he'd had a chance at the likes of Wall Street, Manhattan, or D.C., he had thought that chance would always be available for him while he tried the state of Alabama back on like a costume that might show him off to better advantage. But only now did he realize he couldn't just cast it off and re-claim what he'd once had within his grasp. What a chump he'd been. And as a result, he might very well find himself right back at the bottom where he started, in Opelika, Alabama, working as a small town lawyer in a small time firm.

It wouldn't be such a bad fate, either, he mused, to become the protégé of a stellar soul such as Joab Tucker, who could perhaps show him how to get where he wanted to go better than anyone else he knew. Joab and Janet both had been better parents, advisors and mentors to him than anyone, including his own parents and his world-famous Harvard advisor. The trouble was, going back to Opelika meant being too near his own parents. And honestly, how did you go back to a place like Opelika after you'd gone to Harvard? The whole point of Harvard seemed to be to get away from places like Opelika and never having to go back. Once you'd scaled the heights of Harvard, you were supposed to make the leap to the next mountain top. Then the next, and the next, and the next. Going back would be a failure he didn't think he could stomach, as well as an open admission of defeat. Why would anyone go back to a place like that unless they had absolutely no other option? And why would he even want to work his way up from the bottom of a place like that, not once, but twice? After all, his Harvard degree should mean that he didn't have to. Harvard was supposed to open every door, make anything possible.

And yet, he couldn't even put his finger on anything he'd gleaned from his years at Harvard that would help him fight the good fight or defeat George Wallace. Flipping through the pages of his notebooks, filled with words and phrases like "*Agee!*" and "*poor people of Alabama!*" he wasn't sure that he had anything he could really work with or make use of. It was hardly possible to address a group of unemployed factory workers in North Alabama with repeated references to *poor people of Alabama,* although that's exactly what they were. If only Aaron Osgood could wrap his head in his hands while moaning "*Wallace! Wallace! Wallace!*" and pounding his fist on a lectern to punctuate his distress. It would have worked in Massachusetts. Unfortunately, in Alabama, the incantatory repetition of George Wallace's name would only help get the man re-elected. In despair Daniel dropped the entire stack of notebooks in an empty desk drawer and kicked it vehemently shut, as if his entire Harvard education was useless—at least in the state of Alabama.

With relief he heard Will return and glanced at his watch: eleven-thirty. A bit too soon to go to lunch, but he was anxious to get out of the office anyway. When he looked up, though, it wasn't Will Hill he saw standing in front of his desk. It was Lewis Holditch. Surprised and delighted to see his old friend, he leaped up to greet him without even wondering how or why Lewis had got there.

"Lewis!" he cried in disbelief.

"Take you to lunch?" Lewis grinned, offering his hand across the desk.

Daniel shook it enthusiastically. Lewis held onto both Daniel's hand and his gaze a beat longer than he needed, as had always been his custom. It was part of his priestly manner toward everyone, as if to say: This is not just a social occasion and I am not being merely polite. I care about you. I am here for you. This is my calling.

"How in the world did you find me here?"

"It wasn't easy," Lewis grinned again. "But not for nothing did God give me a brain. Care for some lunch?"

"Absolutely. Let me just leave a note."

In the process of writing this, he realized that Will had taken the Chevette they now proudly shared as the perfect run-down, second-hand American-made automobile like everyone drove in North Alabama. Although it wasn't a pickup truck, at least it wasn't a foreign car like that Honda Civic would have been.

"How do you think I got here?" Lewis chuckled. "My rental car is right out front. We're good to go."

Daniel pressed a Post-It note to the front door before locking it and getting into a shiny red Malibu Lewis had rented early that morning at Hartsfield International Airport in Atlanta.

"So you're on your way to Florida?" Daniel said, as Lewis nodded. "I envy you."

He was still so pleased to see Lewis that he did not stop to think what it meant that Gadsden was an hour and a half in the opposite direction to Florida from Atlanta. Lewis was simply there like Lewis was always there when Daniel needed help sorting out the complications of his life. Lewis had materialized as if he had heard Daniel calling out for help. At the moment, the only thing that struck him as strange was Lewis's everyday attire. Previously, he had encountered Lewis only in his collar and priestly vestments.

"Where to?" said Lewis, cranking up the car.

"Good question. This isn't my town. Let me think."

Ultimately he directed Lewis to a Red Lobster on the outskirts of town which catered mainly to those passing through or on their way back out after a morning or afternoon of business. Locals might go there for a special occasion, but these weren't likely to be happening on a Wednesday morning in the middle of July. Daniel really wanted to get Gadsden and the campaign out of his mind for a while, and the Red Lobster near the interstate was the best he could do. His instincts proved correct. The hostess showed them to a booth in a mostly empty restaurant. At the moment, the only other diners were at the other end of the large room, at a big table of about twelve decorated with helium balloons heralding someone's 70th birthday.

"So, my friend," Lewis slapped at the table after the waitress had taken their order. "How goes it with you?"

Then it all came pouring out. The campaign. His girlfriend. Will Hill. His parents, who expected and demanded so much, as if it were his duty to fulfill the dreams they had worked and sacrificed for but would never enjoy themselves, except vicariously, through him. The overwhelming burden of trying to satisfy everyone. He was failing everyone, including himself. It was as if he'd woken up one morning this summer inhabiting a different life in a different body. He couldn't even pinpoint the day, or the moment, it had occurred. But it was as if everything he'd known about life and every conviction he'd possessed about it had just evaporated. His girlfriend, the love of his life, had become a stranger to him. She might even be pregnant. He might be called upon to marry this person he didn't even know, and begin a life of ceaseless toil and unstinting drudgery, such as his parents had always had mapped out for him. He did not want to be a mule. But where was the way out? His work for the campaign, for example, had proven to be a lot more like drudgery than the thrilling, heroic activity he had imagined. Aaron Osgood was still more of an abstract idea than a person he'd come to know. He'd only seen the man twice so far in the course of the summer. What was he to think? What was he to do? Where was he to turn?

Lewis listened like Lewis always listened. He didn't interrupt or interject. He asked no questions, made no comments. He never fidgeted or fiddled with his fork. He never lost his concentration on what was being imparted, just as he never lost eye contact with the person speaking to him. He sat straight and still in the booth as he carefully took in the whole burden being laid before him.

"You're at a crossroads in your life," Lewis observed finally, eyes still on Daniel even as the waitress delivered their food.

Daniel nodded in agreement as he tested the steaming glazed shrimp placed in front of him. It looked exactly like the shrimp pictured in the Red Lobster commercials on television; however, he wasn't sure if this was a good thing or a bad thing.

"There are any number of different directions you could take from this point," Lewis continued, still ignoring his food completely. "It's important that you make the right choice—the choice that's best for who you are—and not simply submit to demands placed upon you by others."

Daniel nodded again as he submitted to the demands of his stomach. A mouth full of glazed shrimp made it hard for him to speak.

"The best way to make such an important decision is to remove yourself temporarily from all the circumstances and people surrounding you and pulling you in so many different directions. You need a vacation, my friend."

"That I do," Daniel agreed, digging back into his food.

Lewis's plate remained untouched, with the napkin rolled up tightly beside it. Lewis gave no indication that he even noticed the meal in front of him. He sat still and straight in his booth, arms locked by his side, as if now tense with the burden Daniel had transferred onto him. His gaze had never left Daniel's face.

"Why don't you come with me to Florida?" he said quietly.

"What's that?" Daniel looked up from his plate.

"Come with me to Florida," Lewis repeated softly.

Daniel stared at him. Go to Florida with Lewis? If only he could. The vision of Florida was definitely tempting. The prospect of talking to Lewis for hours and hours was even more tempting, as he felt the older man would put him on the right path for his future. Lewis could afford to pay for the trip as well, he knew. Still, he couldn't figure the logistics. Will Hill wanted him in Gadsden. His parents wanted him in Opelika. His girlfriend wanted him in Birmingham. It would have been wonderful to do none of these things, and just go to Florida. But what would he tell the others? If he could think of a way to manage it, he would.

Lewis reached out across the table to clasp Daniel's free hand.

"Come with me," he said.

Then Daniel understood. Hastily withdrawing his hand, he looked around nervously to see if there were any witnesses to the scene that had just occurred. Unfortunately, an entire row of idle wait staff was standing close by ready to offer any assistance to one of the two tables of diners currently patronizing the Red Lobster. Their waitress hurried over as soon as Daniel glanced in her direction.

"Just the check, please," Daniel told her.

"Come with me, Daniel," Lewis repeated.

"I wish I could," Daniel said. "But I've got too many responsibilities here. In fact, I'm overdue back at the office as it is."

The waitress arrived with their tab. "Would you like me to box that up for you, sir?"

Lewis shook his head without removing his gaze from Daniel. "No, thank you," he said, not looking at her.

"Was everything all right with your meal?" She stared pointedly at the congealed and untouched food, some of the most expensive in the town of Gadsden.

"Fine. Fine. I just wasn't hungry." Lewis looked over at her finally and issued a fleeting smile of reassurance.

When she left, Daniel wasn't sure what to do. He was ready to bolt for the door, but Lewis did not even budge. There was nothing for him to do but reach for the check. If this was the only way out, he would have to make use of it. Fortunately, as soon as he did so, Lewis placed three bills on the table that more than paid for the meal and a generous tip. In fact, one of those bills would have fit nicely in Daniel's wallet. But he knew he should keep his focus and get out of the restaurant as soon as he could.

He welcomed the silence in the car on the ride back and prayed only that it would continue. It did not. As they pulled up in an empty parking slot in front of the Osgood for Governor campaign office, Lewis looked over at him and made no movement to get out of the car.

"I think we missed a moment back there, Daniel," he said.

"At the Red Lobster?"

Lewis winced. "Not at the restaurant," he said. "But back in Cambridge."

"I'm not sure I know what you're talking about." Daniel looked around to see if there were anything or anyone in sight to provide an excuse for exiting the vehicle. Unfortunately, the parking lot was mostly deserted at this end. No one was buying beauty supplies, Christian books, or getting an *Osgood for Governor* bumper sticker. There was no sign that Will was in the campaign office either.

"There was an important moment back in Cambridge," Lewis continued. "After you became estranged from a woman you had never loved but had been involved with for three years. I think you plunged headlong into a relationship with a woman you had just met because you were afraid of what was happening between us. You were scared by the powerful connection we formed instantly. You were in flight from an attraction you didn't know what to do about. So you threw yourself into a relationship with the first woman you came across. Daniel, you're running away. You're trying to avoid the inevitable. You're frightened of who you really are and what it means. This won't work forever. It's not even working now. I think this is why you're in such turmoil. I think there are parts of yourself—essential parts—that you are trying to suppress. That's not healthy and it's not the path to happiness. I think you should give yourself a chance to discover all the aspects of your nature. You should come with me to Florida. Let me help you explore and discover who you really are. I believe it will be an epiphany for you. The kind of transcendence you've been seeking since I met you."

Deliverance if not transcendence arrived as the Chevette pulled up beside them. Daniel almost hurled himself out of the car as if afraid of being caught derelict in his duties. At any rate, there was definitely some dereliction he was eager to avoid.

Lewis got out of the car more deliberately but shook hands enthusiastically with Will as Daniel introduced them. There was a moment of extreme awkwardness as the three stood there baking in the hot, empty parking lot, as if stuck in glue. If Will Hill had moved toward the office, Daniel could have made his farewells to Lewis and followed suit. But out of either perversity or some sixth sense, Will seemed reluctant to leave the two of them alone together. Daniel didn't know whether to be grateful or exasperated. And he didn't know what else to do besides invite Lewis back into the office. Will shot him a fierce look as Lewis admitted he might just make use of their facilities before leaving.

"What is he doing here?" Will hissed when the bathroom door closed behind Lewis.

Daniel shrugged. He didn't understand what Will was so uptight about—it wasn't as if *he* knew what he and Lewis had been discussing.

"He's on his way to Florida, and just stopped off to have lunch. He's the one I've told you so much about. He's my minister. My friend."

"Daniel, that man is a homosexual!" Will whispered ferociously.

Daniel was caught off guard: How did Will know that? He shrugged. "Yes," he concurred. "I guess he is. So what?"

"*So what?!* We can't afford to have a man like that in here!"

Daniel stared at him. "What are you talking about? What do you mean: *a man like that?*"

"You know what I mean! Any minute the guy who's setting up our computers is going to walk through that door! We cannot have that—your friend!—here when this guy arrives! That would send the wrong signal about the Osgood campaign!"

"Will, I think you're over-reacting." Daniel was tempted to laugh. Unfortunately, his suppressed smile served not to dispel the tension but escalate it.

"Not in the state of Alabama, I'm not over-reacting!" said Will through gritted teeth. "I've been back here longer than you have. You're still looking at this with a Massachusetts mentality. It's different, here, remember?"

"Yes, but even in Alabama, having a—someone like Lewis—visit a campaign office is not going to torpedo a candidate's campaign. Don't be ridiculous."

"Don't be naïve!"

"I'm not! But think about it. Last Saturday night! At the Bug Tussle Steakhouse! Aaron Osgood marched right up to Mr. Dyce—shook his hand and nobody thought a thing about it."

"Dyce is different."

"Different? Dyce is as queer as a three dollar bill! How can you say that's different?"

"Of course it's different. You know that as well as I do!"

"No. I don't get it. How is Dyce different?"

Will sighed and glanced toward the bathroom to make sure Lewis was not in earshot. "Dyce is one of us, Daniel. That's the difference. Folks are going to politely pretend they don't notice a thing wrong with one of their own. But Southern politeness does not extend to *flagrant homosexual men with Yankee accents and tight jeans!*"

At that moment, Lewis emerged from the restroom and appeared surprised to find the two young men simply standing in the middle of the office as if there were nothing better to do.

"Hope I haven't kept you," he said, extending his hand to Will. "I'm so glad to meet you finally. Daniel has told me so much about you—I feel as if I know you already. I wish there were a way we three could spend more time together."

Will was momentarily at a loss. "Likewise," he said finally, in a strangled voice. Clearing his throat, he repeated, "Likewise. Daniel has told me so much about you too." Will could not restrain himself from looking nervously toward the door.

Lewis turned and handed a card to Daniel. "Here's where I'm staying tonight," he said. "It's the same Holiday Inn we could see from the restaurant where we had lunch. I'd love to get together with you—and Will too—for dinner or a drink or even a late nightcap if you have time."

Daniel didn't know what to say.

"I'm afraid tonight we're going to a bingo game with my dad and some of his buddies," said Will. "We do anything to spread the word. Even Wednesday night bingo."

"Bingo?" said Lewis. "My grandparents used to take me to Wednesday night bingo at their church in St. Louis. I loved it as a boy."

There was a bit of an awkward silence until Will said emphatically, "I don't think you'd love it here, with my dad and his buddies from Goodyear."

"I'm willing to take my chances on bingo or anything else," said Lewis. "Or maybe Daniel could skip the game just this once and have dinner with me." He turned back to Will. "Though I'd love the chance to get to know you better."

For a moment no one spoke. "Just give me a call," said Lewis, locking his eyes with Daniel's. "Hope to see you both," he waved as he left the office.

Will waited until the red Malibu had exited the parking lot altogether before he turned toward Daniel, whose first instinct was to run for the cover of his desk, but thought it more strategic to stand his ground.

"What was he doing here?" Will asked accusingly, menace creeping into his voice.

Daniel tried for nonchalance. "I told you."

"Gadsden, Alabama is not on the direct route from Massachusetts to Florida," said Will in a steely voice Daniel had never heard before.

Nor was Gadsden on the direct route from Atlanta to Florida. So Daniel thought it best not to contest Will's point.

"So what was he doing here?" Will persisted.

"Why is it such a big deal if he wanted to visit me?" said Daniel crossly.

"Because the man is a homosexual, Daniel!"

"Does that mean he's disqualified from humanity?" Daniel summoned justifiable indignation. "It's true I haven't been back here long, but I think the real problem is that you've been back here *too* long. What exactly is wrong with homosexuals? Are you telling me the man is contaminated? That he can't be a good minister? Or a good friend?"

Will was visibly devastated, as if he'd just suffered a blow to the head. It wasn't just that he had transgressed his own values. It was also as if he'd betrayed his education. According to one of his own favorite stories, his liberal education had crystallized for him one afternoon during his senior year. On the way to get a paper from the newsstand in Harvard Square, he had walked past an obviously crazy and totally nude male singing one of the songs from *The Sound of Music.* What was interesting, Will remarked later, was not the public nudity but the fact that four years in Cambridge, Massachusetts had so altered his definition of normalcy that he noticed nothing out of the ordinary about a nude male singing in a public place in the middle of the afternoon. He also marveled at the way everyone else walked right on by without appearing to notice either the deranged mind or the naked body. Tolerance was the moral of that story for Will. The man was bothering no one, so no one bothered him. Will admired the charity of the live-and-let-live response to human variation, even in the rather extreme form he'd witnessed that afternoon.

But a mere two years later it seemed as if Will had lost sight of his principles and his core beliefs. He shook his head and groped for a chair. Wearily he sat down and closed his eyes against the damning evidence of his own perfidy.

"I'm sorry, Daniel," he said. "Please forgive me and let's try to forget what I said. The campaign is getting to me. Aaron Osgood seems to have victory in his grasp. Instead of making me happy, it makes me scared."

"I know," said Daniel, pulling out his own chair. "Me too," he sighed. "After what Gene said about Wallace getting dirty when the race gets close, it's like I'm sitting here waiting for a bomb to drop. The main thing we all need to do is just not fuck up and provide the ammunition ourselves."

"Exactly!" Will pounded the hollow desk with his fist. "Thank you for understanding! I guess I had visions of this computer tech walking into an empty office space in a deserted strip mall and thinking the worst when he found the two of us in here with a flaming queer."

"Flaming queer?" chuckled Daniel, whose own fears had nothing to do with Lewis and everything to do with the status of his girlfriend's womb, which might or might not be harboring a potential campaign-wrecking bomb. "What's flaming about Lewis?"

"Oh, come on, Daniel. His shirt unbuttoned practically to the navel so he can show off his abs? His jeans so tight at the crotch he's practically advertising his package?"

His "abs?" His "package?" These words were not in Daniel's everyday vocabulary, nor had he paid any attention to the body parts they referred to. He had noticed only that Lewis was wearing street clothes he didn't usually wear. How had Will made such close observations in such a short period of time when Daniel had gone all through lunch and not once noticed Lewis's "package" or his "abs?" What exactly *was* Will afraid of? Was it something more than Wallace and his crooked henchmen? Daniel was tempted to crack these jokes, but thought the better of it. He didn't want to jeopardize the high moral ground he had somehow managed to seize.

"Wallace campaigns have always used spies," Will went on. "For all we know, the next guy who comes in here asking for a yard sign could be working for Wallace. If he had seen your friend in here . . . who knows what he would have done with that information? The whole idea of Wallace supporters spying and posing as something they're not has made me paranoid. I'm sorry. Everything I said was unworthy of me, unworthy of you, and unworthy of your friend. Forgive me."

"Forget it," said Daniel.

Will tapped his chin musingly with a pencil. "I do think it's strange, though, that your friend seemed almost like he was trying to put us in a bind."

Daniel yawned. "What do you mean?"

"Oh, nothing, probably. Just he seemed to be suggesting that either he comes with us to bingo or you have dinner with him."

"Well, I guess he was suggesting that." Daniel yawned again.

"But Daniel!" Will exploded, forgetting himself. "That can't happen! He can't come to the bingo game! And you *cannot* be seen with him *anywhere* in Gadsden tonight, most especially *NOT AT THE HOLIDAY INN!*"

"No, of course not," said Daniel reasonably. "I'll just let him know that nothing's going to work out and leave it at that. Why are you so upset?"

Will calmed instantly. "I'm sorry. I just get the sense that something's wrong with this picture. Like he was trying to . . . well . . . not exactly force— that's not the word—or threaten. Like he was trying to . . . manipulate us. Either you, or we, have dinner with him, or he's coming to the bingo game whether we like it or not."

Daniel gave Will a look of pity and scorn. "Honestly."

Will held up his hands. "Okay. Okay. I'm sorry. I'm willing to take your word for it. If you tell me this guy came to see you out of pure friendship, out of his concern for you as a minister, I believe you. We'll say no more about it."

At this point Daniel thought it best to tell Will the whole story, beginning with Lewis's unexpected kiss in Cambridge and ending with the hand-holding in the Red Lobster along with the invitation to accompany Lewis to Florida.

Afterwards Will just stared at him, unable to speak, his face frozen and unable to move. He could have been a wax figure. Daniel had never seen him like this, and didn't know what to do or say to break the glacial silence.

"Daniel," Will said finally. "Let me ask you this. Are you gay?"

Daniel laughed. "No."

"Did you tell the man this in no uncertain terms? Back in Cambridge?"

"Well," Daniel considered. "Not verbally, but . . ."

Will slammed his hand down on the desk and shook his head ominously.

"I didn't think it was necessary to spell it out," Daniel said defensively. "He may be gay, but he's not obtuse. He's not without feelings. And he's also a very good minister. I thought my actions were enough to tell him what he needed to know without getting into an awkward discussion."

"And just what were your actions?"

Daniel shrugged. "What do you think they were? Let me put it this way: None of my actions were at all homosexual."

Will snorted. "But you went back!"

"What do you mean?"

"You went back to his church after he kissed you! Back to the confirmation sessions!"

"Why shouldn't I?"

Will shook his head again and gave Daniel a look of disgust.

"What?" Daniel demanded. "What's wrong with that?"

"Did you stay *after* the supper? After the others had left? Like you did before?"

"I guess so," said Daniel, losing his confidence as he saw where Will was headed.

Will slammed his hand down again.

"Dammit, Daniel! Can't you see? Can't you see how stupid that was? If those were your *actions*, then you were telling that man the opposite of what he needed to hear!"

"That's crazy! It was about two weeks later that I met Caroline, and all I could talk about was this beautiful girl I'd fallen head over heels for! I even brought her to church on Easter Sunday. That was our first date. He met her. He knew the score. The other—matter—was completely dropped! It never came up again. So why drag the issue out in the open if it's not necessary? Why shouldn't I allow the man to keep his dignity?"

Will heaved a big sigh. "Obviously it *was* necessary, Daniel, or the man wouldn't be pursuing you like this."

Pursuing? Was that what was happening? Daniel was taken aback at the thought and at Will's stark use of such brutal terminology. Nevertheless, he had to concede that Lewis had not driven an hour and a half out of his way to sample the pleasures of the Red Lobster and the Holiday Inn in Gadsden, Alabama.

"Daniel, you have to make things crystal clear for people! You have to draw absolute, definitive lines and let people know where you stand! Where *they* stand! Anything less is unwise! It's also *unkind,* for God's sake! To send mixed signals! To allow people to nurse false hopes!"

"That's not what I was doing!" Daniel said hotly.

"We could argue that point. But you cannot tell me that you drew clear lines for this man! Because *you did not draw clear lines!* Otherwise, he would not be in the Holiday Inn right now waiting for your phone call!"

Clear lines? What was so great about clear lines? Daniel wanted to ask. Will was all about clear lines. That's how he saw the world. You were either a Democrat (good), or a Republican (bad). You were either a working-class wage earner producing something of value, or a greedy corporate capitalist living off other people's labor. You were either committed to making the world a better place for others less fortunate, or you were a selfish, mindless bourgeois who thought only of himself. You were either a liberal (full of generosity, compassion and altruism) or you were a conservative, dedicated to preserving the power of the wealthy white male elite.

Daniel had never seen the world, either himself or others, in these definitive terms. Try as he might in Will's company, he could never see where the lines were drawn. He just didn't see or feel clear lines anywhere with anyone. He himself felt like a hopeless jumble of values and motives—of right and wrong, good and bad, greed and compassion, selfishness and generosity, nobility and immaturity. Sometimes he wished he had Will's clarity of self and purpose. But most times he didn't, because he wasn't sure he believed in clear lines he couldn't see or feel. What he needed was someone who could help him bring out the best stuff in himself, and tell him what to do with or how to handle all the other stuff in himself that wasn't so great but wasn't going away either. But it was all hopelessly mixed up and entangled inside of him, and no one, not even the Good Lord, had shown him the way yet.

For example: Of course he wasn't gay, but he had come to love Lewis Holditch in an entirely different way. And it was encouraging that the man loved him in return. Although Lewis's kiss had not aroused him, it had certainly gratified him. Daniel saw no need to terminate any love aimed in his direction. All he needed to do was make sure the love was channeled appropriately. Otherwise, he didn't see the point in turning his back on any love the universe saw fit to shower upon him. To him, that would be the act of unkindness, or brutality—to kill someone's love. And surely he could use all the love he could get.

"Okay," Will was saying. "Here's what you do."

"What?"

"Nothing," said Will emphatically. "Take that card he gave you, and tear it up. Do not call the Holiday Inn. MAKE NO FURTHER CONTACT WHATSOEVER. Write him a letter that will be waiting for him when he gets back from Florida. If he even *goes* to Florida. Make it short and simple. Thank him for his counsel and friendship. Apologize for giving him the wrong impression, and ask that he MAKE NO FURTHER CONTACT WITH YOU. Period. If he tries to call you before he gets back, tell him you sent, or are sending, a letter to his address in Cambridge, and that you'd rather not have any communication with him. Period. Understood?"

"Understood." Daniel sighed.

"Whatever you do, do not let him find out where the bingo game is tonight."

* * *

The computer tech never arrived. At five o'clock, Will went to the bathroom before leaving and Daniel made a surreptitious call to the Holiday Inn before tearing the card into bits. Instead of asking for Lewis Holditch, he left a message for him at the reception desk: "Sorry we won't be able to get together. See you some other time."

When the telephone rang just as they were leaving the office, Will and Daniel stopped in their tracks and stared at one another, stock still.

"I'd better get it," Will declared, though it was clear he'd just as soon ignore it. However, his sense of duty was too great. What if it wasn't Lewis

Holditch, but the computer guy? Or a potential campaign donor? Someone wanting a bumper sticker? Will hurried over to the phone.

"That was Helen Mendelssohn," said Will, taking out his keys as he joined Daniel on the sidewalk outside the office.

"Who is Helen Mendelssohn?"

"The New York *Times* reporter. You remember."

"Oh, yes." He did remember. "What did she want?"

"She wants to come over from Atlanta."

Letter to the Editor from Augusta Upchurch, President,
Mobile Preservation Society
In the Mobile Press-Register, *July 22, 1982*

A newspaper article the other day outrageously described Mr. Percy Atchison as one of the "eccentric" candidates running for governor. Percy Atchison is the least eccentric, most upstanding gentleman I know! And I have known him and his wife of 40 years all my life. I have worked for many years with Percy on historic preservation, just one of the many good causes he has promoted in our town. I firmly believe that he would make the best governor of any man in the race. He was a prominent attorney, a president of the Alabama Bar, and has been a civic leader in Mobile. He is a man of principle, integrity, intelligence and experience. Not an eccentric! Unless possessing a strong mind and moral character makes someone eccentric. It's too bad that what it takes to win elections is state-wide name recognition or a lifetime in politics which teaches nothing but how to navigate corruption or become corrupt yourself. We would all be better off if a man like Mr. Percy Atchison could become our next governor.

~ 10 ~

Three days later on Saturday night, Daniel's work for the campaign took him to a cocktail party for Aaron Osgood in Mountain Brook. Democrats were scarce in the Tiny Kingdom, and those you did find tended to be almost exactly like the Republicans. Had he not known beforehand, Daniel would never have been able to tell that this party was hosted by Democrats in support of a Democratic candidate. For starters, the house itself where the party took place was located across the street from the country club. Inside the house, with all the men wearing jackets and ties, all the women in churchy dress pumps and hose, there was a starched formality he would normally have associated with conservatives.

His hostess seemed the most Republican of all, as she stood before the hearth in the living room in exact imitation of the pose she had struck for the oil portrait hanging above the mantel. She neither mingled with her guests nor assisted the small army of black servants who passed hors d'oeuvres on silver trays and tended bars in two corners of the room. Instead, she scrutinized the room with the gimlet eye of a headmistress on the watch for the slightest sign of misbehavior. Her lips were frozen in a permanent pucker, as if from the distaste and displeasure of sucking on a sour lemon. Likewise, her whole personality suggested a sour lemon. Instead of enjoying themselves, the partygoers standing in front of her seemed to be paying their respects at a funeral they were obligated to attend. Taking careful sips of their drinks, they stood stiffly and conversed in hushed, subdued voices. Occasionally the weird laughter of one of the men rose above the low murmur of voices in a kind of yuck-yuck-yuck that traveled into his sinus cavity, where it was transformed into the snorting sound of a hog. Daniel observed his hostess wince at the sound, whether from this particular laugh or from laughter in general, it was hard to say.

The candidate himself had yet to arrive at his own meet-and-greet. Daniel stood waiting awkwardly with a room full of strangers who didn't appear to know each other much better than they knew him. Clearly those few Democrats living in Mountain Brook were a sad collection of oddballs and misfits who didn't really know how to have any fun. In truth, Daniel felt more akin to his girlfriend's Republican family, who had thrown a far superior party with less obvious expenditure and fewer servants, none in evidence. Here there were almost more servants than there were people. Caroline's aunt Libba had a much more liberal spirit than the Democratic hostess before him sucking on the sour lemon of her life. She had even tried to tell him she wasn't a Republican.

"I don't have a political philosophy," Libba Albritton had told him that night. "Unless it's God bless the child who's got his own."

"That means you're a Republican," he'd said.

"Does it?" she seemed surprised.

"That's the best one-line definition of Republicanism I've ever heard," he told her.

She had shrugged and sipped her wine. "Maybe so," she conceded. "I guess that's usually the way I end up voting. Whenever I get around to voting, that is. But it isn't because I was born with any of *my* own."

"No?" It was his turn to be surprised.

"Not at all," she said, almost proudly. "I always knew, whatever I wanted, I'd have to get for myself."

He had glanced inadvertently in the direction of her husband, the heir of Dixie Pies & Pastries.

"I'm not saying I married for money," she told him, having followed his gaze. "I'm not that dumb. The stupidest thing a person can do is to think they can share a life or a house, or a bed, a bathroom, or vacation, with someone they don't love. You can get away with it for a weekend, maybe, but not your whole life. Women who marry for money work very hard for their living. I see the evidence of that every day of my life. There was evidence of that here earlier this evening."

He had supposed she was referring to Lula Petsinger, whose marriage did indeed look like it was working her to the bone and literally killing her.

"So I would never marry just for money," Libba had continued. "But I sure as hell never saw the point in marrying somebody who didn't have money. If the most stupid thing is to marry for money, the second most stupid thing is to marry without it."

He understood her completely. What's more, he agreed with her. Otherwise, he would have married Ricky Jill a long time ago. In other words, there was no reason to get married at all unless the marriage brought some benefit other than sex, which he'd never had any trouble getting without marrying the girl first. So he had felt this unexpected kinship with a woman connected to a Big Mule family which had donated so much money to the Republican Party that one of the daughters now worked for Ronald Reagan's vice-president.

"You look more pensive than usual!"

The booming voice appeared to emanate from the enormous stomach suddenly crowding in upon him. It was Norman Laney, the schoolmaster who better resembled a jovial party host than their dour hostess with her schoolmarm prune face. He was carrying a large plastic cup emblazoned with BCC and filled with a substance as effervescent as his mood.

"And you look like you're at a different party from the one I'm attending." Daniel held out his hand.

The laughter that erupted from Norman Laney's vast depths threatened to transform the muted gathering into a real party at last. The wine and food on his breath corroborated what Mr. Laney admitted when he leaned over to seize Daniel's hand and mutter in his ear: He had just come from the fabulous debut party for Elise Partington across the way at the country club, and was simply sneaking in to meet Aaron Osgood so he could be back on his merry way.

"Where is he?" said Mr. Laney, turning his head sharply and looking around the room. "I don't see him."

"He's not here yet," said Daniel.

"Not here yet?" cried Mr. Laney. "Doesn't he realize that he should never ever be late for Adelaide Whitmire? Surely his wife could tell him that? They're in the Garden Club together."

"Aaron was in Florence this afternoon. I'm sure he'll be here shortly."

"He better be," said Mr. Laney. "Because at least half these people here are dying to get over to the country club, and the other half are wishing they'd been invited."

"So that's what's wrong with this party."

"Well . . . partly. Not entirely." Mr. Laney glanced surreptitiously at Adelaide Whitmire, who had been staring fixedly at him so she could summon him to her side.

"It's hard to believe she's a Democrat," said Daniel.

"Ohhh, Adelaide is no Democrat," said Mr. Laney, taking a large, last swallow from his cup before looking for a place to stash it.

Daniel was confused. "If she's not a Democrat, then what is she?"

"She's a pain in the ass. That's what she is," muttered Mr. Laney. Abruptly he crumpled the hard plastic cup and thrust it into his jacket pocket. "I better go see what she wants before the pain is in *my* ass." Mr. Laney raised his voice as he began making his way over to Mrs. Whitmire. "And your man better show up in the next five minutes, or he'll be history in a way he never dreamed of. I mean, beating George Wallace is all very well and good, and I'm all for it, but—" here Mr. Laney leaned over to whisper in someone's ear—"but not if I'm going to miss out on Elise Partington's debut party!" Raising his voice again, he continued in the direction of his hostess. "After all, it *is* Saturday night, and I have one less Saturday night in my life span than I did a week ago. I'm not going to waste this one waiting for Godot!"

His movement through the crowd left laughter in his wake. Daniel looked around for Caroline, who had gone some time ago to fetch drinks and never returned. Although he was perfectly capable of fending for himself, he'd been counting on her to introduce him around. Eventually he caught sight of her at one of the bar tables, deep in conversation with the only other young person besides themselves. This was a guy who looked exactly Daniel's age, maybe a bit older. If possible, he was also a bit shorter than Daniel, and Daniel was short. Furthermore, whatever looks Daniel had were far better than the looks of this guy Caroline was talking to. And it wasn't that the guy was so bad-looking, either. It was more his body language, made up of hesitant, halting, tentative gestures and awkward, jerky movements. He had LOSER stamped all over him like a disfiguring birthmark. Still, Caroline was deep in animated conversation with him while she had hardly spoken to Daniel all evening.

He knew he ought to join them. And yet he hung back because he found himself enjoying the interest Caroline and this other guy took in each other. He was not threatened in the least. Instead, the little scene reminded him of Caroline's beauty and the desirability that had—only temporarily, he hoped— lost its hold on him. If pregnancy changed a woman, then fear of pregnancy changed a woman even more, and not in any good way. So as he gazed at her from across the room, it was nice to feel her desirability come rushing back all over him. It was like falling in love all over again. She was unquestionably the most beautiful female in the room, although she was wearing the least expensive dress. But it didn't matter what the dress was. When a woman was beautiful, what she wore was her beauty. Her clothes were irrelevant. The more irrelevant they were, the more beautiful she appeared, as the clothes did not detract from her beauty but reflected it, like a second skin. Pleasantly dazed with desire, he walked over to join them.

Ham Whitmire was the name of the guy, who extended his hand half-way toward Daniel, tentatively pulled it back as if afraid it would be rejected, and then finally reached out to shake Daniel's own forthrightly offered hand. His movements suggested the same sort of stammer as the voice which eventually managed to utter a greeting. Poor guy, Daniel thought; apparently he was the son of the woman giving the party, which explained a lot. He had attended the same private high school as Caroline, though she was still in the lower school when he had graduated. From there he had gone to Williams, and had recently returned from a Rotary Fellowship to Germany. In the fall he would begin classes at Harvard Law School.

Harvard Law School! Daniel was dumbstruck. This pitiful little shrimp who could barely string a few words together in a coherent sentence? Harvard Law School?! He hadn't even been able to string the syllables of one *word* together to form a coherent sound! "Hello" had come out a hesitant "hell," followed by another hesitant "hell," followed by a tentative "o." If this guy was Harvard Law School material, then no wonder Daniel was rejected.

"If he's any later, this house will be the scene of another famous gunshot!"

It was Norman Laney, playing to the crowd who had finally become glad to be right where they were on this Saturday night. (Wherever Norman Laney was, that was always the place to be.) Laughter broke out all over the room, especially the yuck-yuck-yuck from the man in the blue and white striped seersucker suit and the red bow tie. But "another famous gunshot?"

"What did he mean by that?" Daniel stared pointedly at Ham, who deferred apologetically to Caroline, as if he couldn't trust himself to speak.

"I told you," she said crossly. "On the way over here. This is the house where Walker Percy grew up."

He didn't see how this explained the reference to the gunshot. And he wished she wasn't so obviously exasperated with him.

"I don't get it. What's the connection between Walker Percy and a gunshot in this house?" Afraid to meet Caroline's withering gaze, he looked at Ham, who deferred, once more, to Caroline.

Meanwhile, the look she gave Ham suggested that he, Daniel, was the pitiful creature. Fine! he wanted to tell her. If that's what you want! Fine! Go for it! He seems like a great guy! He'll call his mother to ask her permission to take his dick out and use it! And he might even need her to come over and hold it up for him! If that's what you want, you can have it!

"Walker Percy's father shot himself in the attic of this house," Caroline explained, in the voice of a third grade teacher.

Ham gave a conscience-stricken nod, as if this suicide were somehow his fault.

Just then a woman with long dark hair and Gloria Steinem glasses came up to greet him.

"Daniel Dobbs," she said, in a monotone that could have come from a robot. She didn't crack a smile either, or make so much as one body movement

195

in his direction. Obviously not a Southern woman, who would have cried out "Daniel Dobbs!" and rushed up all smiles to "hug his neck" as if he were the one person on earth she most wanted to see. But this was the woman who had gotten him into Harvard, so he owed her.

"Mrs. Ritchie!" he said, moving swiftly to hug *her* neck. It was a bit like embracing a broomstick, but she seemed pleased nonetheless.

"Susan," she told him sternly. "Call me Susan." She turned to introduce him to her husband, who was proudly attired in a navy blue three-piece business suit and beaming as if he'd just won the lottery. He was flanked on both sides by tall boys who were clearly his sons, with the same dark, lank hair as their mother. This was the much-maligned Warren Ritchie he had heard about at Libba Albritton's party. The older one of his sons had recently been accepted into Harvard Law School, and Warren Ritchie's opportunity to announce this fact in a very loud voice while congratulating Ham on his own acceptance appeared to account for his elation.

"We were so happy when we heard you two had gotten together," Susan told Caroline when she greeted her. "Weren't we, Warren?"

Actually, Susan Ritchie looked like she'd never been happy in her life, and her husband's countenance darkened ominously.

"I've always thought Stephen was going to marry Caroline," he informed Daniel, referring to his younger son, who had also just finished his first year as a Harvard undergraduate. "They make a perfect couple. And they dated in high school."

"They went steady in sixth grade," his wife corrected him.

Warren's face darkened further and threatened to explode like a storm cloud while Stephen lurked in the background with an arrogant smirk on his face. Stephen had never once responded to Daniel's invitations to the Alabama brunches at Eliot House, and obviously never once considered attending. Daniel had heard through the Southern grapevine that Stephen had fallen in with the wrong crowd, a group of would-be hippies trying to re-create the Harvard-in-the-sixties experience.

"Why aren't *you* going to Harvard Law School?" Warren asked him abruptly.

"I couldn't get in," Daniel told him. "Harvard Law School obviously knew better than Harvard College."

"Ha!" Warren shouted triumphantly, as a gleam came into his eye. Daniel knew he'd said the right thing.

Warren turned his back on Daniel to address his wife, who was now in conversation with Caroline. "See, Susan!" he declared. "I told you this boy was a mistake. He didn't get into Harvard Law School!"

Susan looked first at Daniel, then at her husband, in extreme consternation. "Nonsense," she replied.

"He told me so himself!" Warren insisted, spewing spittle for emphasis. "*He did not get into Harvard Law School!*"

"I'm sure he didn't even apply," said Susan, looking nervously around to see whether her husband was creating a scene. Indeed, heads were turning in their direction.

"Why would anyone who wants to be an attorney not apply to the best law school in the country? That makes no sense. Besides, *he told me he couldn't get in!* That means he *did* apply! That means he was *rejected,* Susan!"

"Don't forget, this fine young man has political aspirations in his native state," said Susan. "Alabama Law School is where he belongs, so that's why he's going there."

Daniel pitied the poor woman. She didn't need to take care of him; she needed to take care of herself. Daniel would be fine—much better than anyone who had her husband for a husband.

He half winked at Warren as if to say, "Let's not shatter your sweet wife's illusions," and moved quickly to introduce himself to Stephen, who displayed all the manners of a sulky adolescent. Which is exactly what he was, Daniel realized, Harvard or no Harvard.

All at once Norman Laney was upon them, having been dispatched by Mrs. Whitmire, Daniel surmised, to handle the problem of Warren Ritchie. No doubt Warren had *had* to be invited, as one of the very few registered Democrats in Mountain Brook. Mr. Laney was trailed by the man in the seersucker suit with the yuck-yuck-yuck laugh, who proved to be a law partner of Warren's. A native of Chicago and a graduate of Northwestern, he had fallen in love with an Alabama girl he'd happened to meet when she was visiting his city. She, (the second most beautiful woman in the room), had refused to live anywhere but "home," so he had found himself wedded to Alabama when he married her. The seersucker suit was either his attempt to fit in or else gently mock his adopted Southern state. Daniel couldn't yet figure which; perhaps it was a bit of both. At any rate, the two most over-dressed men in the room were, ironically, not Southerners. Just taking a wild guess that Warren Ritchie was not, strictly speaking, a Southerner. And the two non-Southerners had overdone it and missed their mark.

"Where in the hell is Aaron Osgood?" hissed Norman Laney. "At this point, I'd rather kill him than vote for him! I am officially missing Elise Partington's debut!"

Daniel commiserated. "I'm beginning to think my buddy got the better assignment for the weekend," he said.

"What was that?"

"Driving back to Montgomery with his girlfriend to pick up a car he left in the shop."

But instead of laughing, Norman Laney only narrowed his eyes. Obviously the champagne which had improved his opinion of Daniel earlier had worn off.

"Is she *satisfactorily* on the pill?" Mr. Laney muttered, à propos of nothing.

Before Daniel could formulate a lie or a reply of any kind, Mr. Laney continued, his voice dropping lower.

"She better be. And there better be no *untoward* repercussions, or you'll find your political career to be extremely short-lived."

"There's nothing to worry about," Daniel assured him.

"If she doesn't get her Harvard degree, I'll kill you," said Mr. Laney cheerfully.

"What's this?" said Warren, literally pushing away his law partner Ed Blankenship. "Are he and Caroline already *engaged*?"

"Mind your own business, Warren," snapped Mr. Laney irritably. "Of course they're not engaged. I am simply reminding this young man that Caroline's education must come *before anything else happens.* That's all." He turned his back on Warren.

"I think Caroline would sooner drop me than drop out of Harvard," Daniel murmured, hoping this was true.

Norman Laney was supremely happy to hear this, and said so in those exact terms. His mood lightened considerably and Daniel thought it wise to change the subject while he had the chance.

"I am mystified by Mrs. Whitmire," he said, nodding in the direction of their hostess. "How does a woman like that come to be hosting a party for a Democrat?"

Mr. Laney sighed. "I've spent half my adult life either trying to avoid her or trying to stay on her good side. I've never attempted to explain her. This calls for a drink." He headed in the direction of one of the bar tables.

For the first time Daniel noticed that he'd never received even that first drink Caroline had offered to procure. And Caroline hadn't seemed to care whether he got that drink or not, whether he was introduced to people or not, whether he had a good time or not. He joined Mr. Laney at the table and selected a cold beer from a large silver tub sweating water drops from its load of ice.

Mr. Laney stood at the bar and downed half a glass of white wine in one gulp. Silently he held out the half-empty cup toward a grinning bartender, who obligingly filled it to the brim.

"Thank you, Clarence," said Mr. Laney primly.

"For some reason," the bartender grinned again, "your glass always *do* spring a leak!"

Mr. Laney sipped his wine and observed Daniel with his narrowed eyes. Was it an extra-dry white wine? Or was Mr. Laney going to start in on Daniel again?

"You were going to tell me about Mrs. Whitmire," Daniel reminded him.

"Was I?" said Mr. Laney. "Well, I'll have to make it quick, because I don't intend to stay here all night. If Aaron Osgood is not here in five minutes, I'm going back to the country club to attend a real party, Adelaide or no Adelaide." He slurped his wine defiantly but showed no sign of starting to tell his tale.

"Now I'm really curious," Daniel prodded.

"I don't know any story," said Mr. Laney ungraciously. (Daniel was certain he did.) "As best I can gather, Adelaide Whitmire suffered several years of primal fear in her youth. That's all."

"Primal fear?"

"She was mortally afraid she would die an old maid."

Daniel burst out laughing for the first time that evening.

But Norman Laney's eyes narrowed again. "You laugh," he said accusingly. "But it's deadly serious. This is why it is *so* important for Caroline to go to Harvard and *graduate*."

Daniel nodded, afraid to say anything lest it encourage Mr. Laney to dwell on the topic he most wanted to avoid. However, he did not understand the connection between Mrs. Whitmire's primal fear and Caroline's education.

"If there had been any other future besides marriage available to Adelaide when she was a young woman, she might not be standing there today in a position to torment the rest of us," declared Mr. Laney, confident that whoever overheard him would only agree with his statement. "She might have discovered something she's actually good at, because I'm convinced it's not marriage, and I know for a fact it's not motherhood. If she were doing something she truly enjoyed, she might not suffer from the chronic disgruntlement of an ill-tempered soul. She might be barking orders to employees who actually get paid to put up with her. Instead, there was Adelaide at age twenty-five, all her friends married and having children, while Adelaide is mortally humiliated and terrified that she will never "get a husband," as they still say in the South.

Then along comes *the* most eligible bachelor from one of *the* wealthiest families in Mountain Brook, and he proposes marriage to Adelaide within three months. To this day, no one is quite sure why."

Daniel tried to absorb this information as he and Mr. Laney both took long sips from their drinks. Mr. Laney reached out suddenly to grab a handful of homemade benne bits from a tray passing somewhere in his general vicinity. Daniel glanced in the direction of Mrs. Whitmire.

"Didn't look any better back then than she does now," stated Mr. Laney flatly with his mouth full. "Or so I'm told. Anyway, in a six-month time span, Adelaide went from the primitive animal terror of the unmated female to the imperial sense of entitlement of a crowned head of Europe or a Saudi Arabian princess. I don't think her personality has ever recovered from the shock of going from one extreme to the other. Of course there are hundreds of Southern women like this, but Adelaide is the most extreme example I know of. She is a most trying combination of abject terror and unbridled self-importance. A terrible, terrible combination."

"But how does this make her a Democrat?"

"I told you," said Mr. Laney impatiently. "Adelaide is no Democrat. She's just doing her queenly duty. Her mother-in-law—bless her beautiful heart—was a famous Democrat. Now Bella Whitmire is another story, but I don't, I really don't have time to tell it tonight. So Adelaide believes she must carry the mantle of the pre-eminent family she married into. She must be the most Whitmire of all the Whitmires. It's that simple. Adelaide knows nothing of politics, I assure you, and couldn't care less."

"What about her husband?" Daniel looked around in hopes that Mr. Laney would point him out.

Instead, Mr. Laney leaned over to whisper in his ear.

"Her husband is one of *the* nicest, sweetest, kindest, most gentle and generous souls ever to walk this earth. He gives *thousands* every year to support our school. I mean *thousands* upon *thousands*. And no one even knows because he insists on being an anonymous donor."

Daniel blinked. He had a hard time imagining that kind of money. "What does he do for a living?"

"Oh," Mr. Laney waved his hand. "Real estate. Holdings. I don't know. All I know is: he owns property. Lots of it. Everywhere. All over downtown Birmingham. All over the state of Alabama. What he does with it all, I can't quite tell you."

From his experience with Eleanor's family, Daniel had learned that the richest people who made the most money did so in ways that were often hard to fathom or explain. It only stood to reason, he supposed, that the wealthiest men made their money in the most opaque ways. Otherwise, if it was obvious, why wouldn't everyone be doing it? But he found himself as bored as Mr. Laney by the topic of money. It didn't interest him in the least. Neither having it nor making it were that important to him. What was? He looked over at Caroline, engrossed in conversation with Ham Whitmire and the older Ritchie son who was also going to Harvard Law School. What did he want? It wasn't Harvard Law School or the practice of law. He still really didn't know what it was he wanted, except he just wanted to put himself *out there* in the world, in some form of heroic endeavor or enterprise. Politics was the best way he knew to do what it was he wanted to do with himself. He wished he could put himself out there right now. In fact, if Aaron didn't show up soon, perhaps he even ought to.

He said as much to Mr. Laney.

"Brilliant!" said Mr. Laney, seizing his arm. "Let's do it!"

Before he could think twice, Mr. Laney had pulled him into the center of the living room, installed him in front of the crowd in place of Mrs. Whitmire, and introduced him. Daniel had no choice but to speak. However, he had done no public speaking in a while, and on the last occasion, he'd had a highly polished and much rehearsed speech in typed pages on a lectern in front of him. But this was a small collection of bored and half-inebriated people desperate for a reason to be where they were this Saturday night instead of anywhere else. He should be able to give that to them. This should be easy.

And it was. For one thing, unlike many others in the state of Alabama, these people did not need to be told why George Wallace should be defeated.

"I won't insult your intelligence," he began, "by telling you why our state needs to get rid of Wallace and elect a New South governor. You know that already. Instead, I'll answer the question that has been uppermost on your minds all evening: Where is Aaron Osgood?"

There was a ripple of appreciative laughter.

"I know you're also wondering what could possibly take precedence over a party in Mountain Brook. I'll tell you: Aaron Osgood has spent all afternoon in the high school gymnasium in Florence, Alabama judging the annual square dancing competition."

There were shouts of laughter. Out of the corner of his eye he noticed Caroline smiling at him. Mrs. Whitmire was seated in a chair to his right, staring blankly beyond him. He supposed it was all the same to her, whoever spoke, as long as someone did and she could say she'd done her duty. Mr. Laney was pacing to and fro behind the assembled guests as if he were now responsible for the evening's entertainment and wanted Daniel to succeed. As he paused, Mr. Laney stopped his pacing and looked up at him sharply to see what the matter was. It wasn't just concern for himself, Daniel saw. There was concern for the young man he had put so unexpectedly on the spot, as if Daniel were more than just the boyfriend of a special protégé, but was just such a protégé himself. Mr. Laney wished him well! Mr. Laney wanted him to succeed!

"I only wish I were joking about the square dancing," he went on. "But in fact, it gets worse. Not only was Aaron Osgood supposed to judge the competition; he told them he might just show the crowd a thing or two about square dancing himself."

There was more laughter. Mr. Laney resumed his pacing, his eyes on the floor.

"I feel obligated to warn you that you might just wake up tomorrow to see a picture of your future governor square dancing on the front page of your Sunday paper."

Yet more laughter, as Ed Blankenship called out: "Who would he be dancing with? Surely not his wife!" This generated another round of cackles.

"No," agreed Daniel. "It's hard to imagine Mary Winston doing a square dance."

"Mary Winston wouldn't know how to!" declared Ed.

"Luckily Mary Winston doesn't need to know how to," Daniel continued. "But Aaron Osgood does. Unfortunately, this is the kind of thing it takes to get elected, and this is why Aaron Osgood is late."

The buzz of laughter was instantly stilled. It was a sobering, but strategic and necessary reminder.

"However," he said, "let me point out that this is progress. Aaron Osgood is running against an opponent who gained his power by appealing to the basest instincts of the Alabama population—its racism, bigotry and prejudice. I'll take square-dancing over a KKK rally any day of the week."

There was now not a sound. He'd made his point and he'd turned Aaron Osgood's tardiness into a virtue. He'd more than made his point; he'd done his job. Now he needed to lighten up again.

"If you think square dancing is bad, let me tell you what it's like at Bea's Diner for breakfast in Gadsden, Alabama, where I've been stuck for the past week. I think I'd rather be square dancing."

An undercurrent of muted laughter rose up again.

He believed he struck just the right balance between entertaining his audience while informing them of the suffering taking place only an hour away in

Gadsden, which was filled with the laid-off and the unemployed. This is why he would always be a Democrat—there was much better material to work with, and it required no effort to deliver it with conviction. Quite simply, it was the better script.

It seemed to be working with his audience, who were encouraged by this reminder of how well off they actually were, although they obviously had not been able to go to Europe this summer, or they would not be standing around Adelaide Whitmire's living room in the middle of July. At least they weren't hanging around the Goodyear plant after breakfast at Bea's Diner, hoping to land a day's odd labor from the factory that had laid them off last month.

At any rate, when Aaron Osgood finally walked in, he was greeted by sustained and hearty applause. Without further ado, Daniel heralded the arrival of the candidate, and immediately ceded his spot in front of the mantel. As they crossed paths, the two men exchanged a vigorous handshake. Aaron gave him a playful thump on the shoulder, as if to suggest they were the best of friends and the closest of allies, when in truth, they knew each other hardly at all. Still, it was such a seamless performance it could have been rehearsed.

Aaron found an unusually receptive and enthusiastic response to his apology for being late.

"Show us your moves, Aaron!" from Ed Blankenship, of course.

As Aaron square danced with an imaginary partner, the portrait of Adelaide Whitmire frowned down upon him from above. Everyone else, however, convulsed with laughter. So for the second time that day, Aaron Osgood was advancing his candidacy by square dancing. Of course, the Mountain Brook socialites would have protested that their enjoyment of the spectacle was from a sophisticated remove: They were really laughing at the spectacle of Aaron square-dancing in the Florence high school gym, which he conjured by square dancing in Adelaide Whitmire's living room. They were not being entertained by Aaron's square dancing as the people in Florence had been entertained; they were laughing at the lack of sophistication of the people in Florence who could be entertained by Aaron's square dancing. But laughing they were. At first Daniel assumed that Caroline had doubled over in laughter as well, but soon enough he realized she was cramped in pain, as if she might throw up any second. Putting his arm around her, he led her away from the gathering and steered her to the bathroom pointed out by a scowling Mr. Laney.

She was in there a long time, although he heard no sounds of vomiting or other gastric eruptions he'd rather not think about. Finally he knocked softly on the bathroom door.

"Are you all right?"

He believed he understood the muffled voice to say she was fine.

"Do you need anything?"

"No," came the voice. "But I'll be in here a while. Go on back to the living room."

Gladly he turned to do so, only to find Mary Winston Osgood charging toward him.

"I'm sorry, but the bathroom is occupied," he told her politely.

At first he was afraid he hadn't spoken loudly enough, because she continued to bear down until she reached him, and then, to his astonishment, she leaned over to put her face level with his.

"Don't think I don't know exactly what you're up to!" Her voice was a deadly snarl. She must have confused him with someone else. He held out his hand.

"Daniel Dobbs, Mrs. Osgood. We met once last December."

"I know exactly who you are," she snapped, ignoring his outstretched hand. "And I know exactly what you're here for. And believe me, you are going right back where you came from as soon as I get around to it."

For a second he experienced the terrible reality of what it must be to live like his parents, whose sad existence he had been in flight from all his life. He knew what he was fleeing from, but he hadn't yet identified what he was running toward, and here he was caught in mid-flight. He was a hopeless country boy, a stupid redneck trying to transcend his origins, but he had been found out and would be sent back.

Then it occurred to him that she must be angry at the way he had seized the floor and held the audience until her husband arrived. Perhaps she thought he had attempted to overshadow her husband, or steal his limelight.

"I'm only trying to help, Mrs. Osgood," he assured her. "I was only trying to do my job."

"If my husband is elected, I don't want you anywhere near him. Is that understood?" Her voice had become an ugly hiss, and her eyes were like slits to match it.

At that moment, Caroline emerged from the bathroom, beaming triumphantly. Mary Winston Osgood gave her a curt not, turned on her heels, and walked away. Caroline squeezed his hand.

"You better take me home," she said happily.

"Why? What's wrong?" he said abstractedly, his mind still trying to make sense of Mrs. Osgood's inexplicable outburst.

"I just got my period."

"That's great." He squeezed her hand to convey an enthusiasm his voice couldn't muster. "*I know exactly who you are and exactly what you're here for,*" she had said. Well, if so, she knew a lot more than he did, and he wished she'd enlighten him.

"What's the matter?"

"Oh, nothing," he said, still lost in thought.

"Well, you better take me home," she whispered urgently. "For some reason, I'm already running rapidly through my supplies."

Then it occurred to him she was probably having a miscarriage, which had happened once with Eleanor: the acute cramping and the copious bleeding.

"What's going on here?" demanded Mr. Laney, rounding the corner. "What's wrong?"

"Caroline isn't feeling well," Daniel explained. "I've got to take her home."

Unfortunately, Caroline looked like she'd never been happier and never felt better. The joyful relief shining from her eyes was palpable. He was sure Mr. Laney could feel it, and he was certain to see it as he peered closely at Caroline's face as if to divine its every secret. For a second his eyes darted over to the bathroom, then back again to Caroline. Daniel knew he must be connecting the dots.

"Go on and make your good-byes to Adelaide and get out of here," Mr. Laney ordered Caroline, who gladly complied after blowing Daniel a kiss behind Mr. Laney's back.

For a moment the two of them just stood there looking at each other. Daniel desperately wished he could ask Mr. Laney about Mary Winston Osgood and what she had said to him. If anyone could explain what had transpired, it would be Mr. Laney. But Mr. Laney, he knew, was intent on Caroline.

"Is everything all right," said Mr. Laney. It was less a question than a menacing statement suggesting that everything better be all right.

"Everything's fine," Daniel said.

"You were pretty good in there," Mr. Laney said. "Much better than what's-his-name, although I suppose he'll have to do."

Daniel nodded his thanks.

"Make no mistake," the older man said, eyes narrowing. "You have a future that can be ruined just like hers can. And once you lose your future, it's hard to get it back." Mr. Laney turned around abruptly and stomped off.

Alone in the narrow corridor outside the powder room, Daniel realized he had every reason to be as relieved and jubilant as his girlfriend. Now he could really forget about law school. Nothing stood between him and a job with the next governor of Alabama except the increasingly unlikely prospect of a George Wallace victory. He grinned as the image came to mind of an old man slumped over in a wheelchair.

From the Birmingham News, *July 29, 1982*

Osgood Won't Press Charges

Attorney General Aaron Osgood has decided not to press charges against a man arrested Saturday night after attempting to use a credit card issued in Osgood's name at a downtown motel.

Dominic Peruzzi, 32, gave the credit card bearing Osgood's name to the night clerk at the Shadytime Lodge on 39th Street North, near the airport.

"Normally I don't pay that much attention or ask for i.d.," said Dwayne Wilson, the clerk. "But this time the name on the card leaped out at me because it sounded like one of those guys running for governor. So after I gave this fella the room key, I called the police."

When Birmingham police verified that Osgood was missing a credit card, two officers went to the Shadytime Lodge and arrested Peruzzi without incident.

Peruzzi, a convicted sex offender, is wanted in New York City for attempted robbery and assault as well as numerous parole violations. He is being held at Jefferson County Jail pending extradition to New York.

Osgood says he has no idea how a convicted criminal came into possession of his credit card, but believes it was stolen from his campaign headquarters, located on 16th Avenue South, where a steady stream of visitors comes through every day to collect yard signs, bumper stickers and campaign literature.

"Campaigning in the summer heat has many disadvantages," explained Osgood. "Usually I go through three or four suits in one day. My credit card apparently got lost in transition. I'm just thrilled to learn I had some name recognition with the motel clerk."

Brad Hunter, a full-time volunteer answering phones at the campaign headquarters, believes the card must have been stolen somewhere else. According to Hunter, Osgood was campaigning out of town all week, and spent

Friday evening at his law office. He did not visit the headquarters at any time on Saturday, so Hunter is not sure why Osgood thinks his credit card was stolen there.

Osgood decided not to press charges when he learned of the outstanding warrants for Peruzzi in New York.

~ 11 ~

Later, Daniel Dobbs realized "it" had happened when he'd chatted with the Elmore's maid.

"Who are you voting for in the governor's race, Pearl?" he had asked her.

He was just making conversation in the kitchen after he'd finished his breakfast and was waiting for Caroline to come downstairs. He knew without asking who Pearl would be voting for. Aaron Osgood stood to get at least 90% of the black vote.

So he was barely paying attention when she said: "George Wallace."

George Wallace? He checked to see if she was joking. She stood at the sink scrubbing fried egg off breakfast plates before loading them in the dishwasher. There was no trace of a smile on her face. She wasn't joking. She had work to do, and that work had just begun.

"You're not serious?" he chuckled, hoping to force a bad joke out in the open. "You're not really planning to vote for George Wallace?"

"Well, that's what they're telling us."

"What do you mean: 'That's what they're telling you'?" he said sharply. "Who's telling you what?"

She looked over at him from the sink. The stare she gave him suggested he was an idiot. "The church," she said, in a tone that added "of course."

"Oh," he said, uncomfortable enlightenment dawning. "What church do you belong to?"

"Mount Zion Baptist," she said, with such pride it could have been the Vatican. She resumed her work at the sink with increased vigor.

"And all the folks who go to your church? They're voting for Wallace?"

"Well, sure. That's what Reverend Peters say for us to do."

"Your minister is telling you who to vote for?"

"Of course," she said. "Who else going to tell us?"

"Everyone in your church is going to vote for whoever the minister tells you to vote for?"

The dish she was rinsing dropped with a clatter into the sink. Pearl turned all the way around to face him. Now she *was* amused. His abject ignorance was downright comical.

"Of course we do what the minister tell us to do," she said. "Why would we go to church if we wasn't going to listen to what our minister say? You go to church, you do what your minister tell you to do. That what it means to be Christian. That's how you get right with the Lord." Shaking her head at white folks, she turned back around to the dishes.

"But why George Wallace, Pearl?" he persisted, incredulous. "Why Wallace?"

"Now that I couldn't tell you," she said, shaking her head again, but for a different reason. "Reverend Peters preached a big sermon about it last week, and the Lord's truth is I don't know most of what he was talking about. Just that we should vote Wallace. But that's all I really need to know, so I just didn't worry about the rest of it."

He wasn't sure how to go up against this, or even if he should. After a moment's pause, he picked up his own dirty breakfast plate and carried it over to the sink.

"But what about George Wallace's—" He stopped in his tracks, unsure what word he could use to convey racial atrocities without upsetting a member of the victimized race. There wasn't such a word, he realized. "What about Wallace's past?" he said. "What about everything Wallace has done?"

"I know George Wallace has been a sinner," said Pearl, reaching for a dish towel to dry the skillet. "He hasn't always been a man of God. But the Lord worked on him and brought him around. George Wallace has accepted Jesus and prayed for forgiveness. Now, if the Lord can forgive, then so can I. I can't hold the sins of the past against a man who has come to the church for forgiveness and salvation just like every last one of us."

Daniel couldn't restrain himself. "But what about everything Wallace did to black people?"

"That's just it," she said, laying down her dish towel and placing the skillet in the drying rack. "Time was when George Wallace meant nothing but misery for black people. I know that. Everybody know that. But all that's turned around, too, now. See? Reverend Peters say, if Wallace wins, it's gonna be our turn at the trough. It's gonna be payback time. George Wallace is going to pay for his sins. He want to pay for his sins. Now, when a man want to pay for his sins, I got to give him a chance."

Daniel had heard these rumors, the whispered promises put out there by the Wallace campaign, that if Wallace were "forgiven" by the black people of Alabama, he would re-pay the debt he owed and pay for his sins by hiring more black people as state employees and contractors than Alabama had ever known. He still couldn't give it up. "How do you know George Wallace has truly repented?" he asked. "How do you know he's not still a sinner?"

"No man is ever washed clean," said Pearl. "We all sinners. It's a constant struggle for all us here on earth. Now what about this? That man you working for? He a sinner. And to my knowledge, he ain't going around repenting or asking for redemption. And he the worst kind of sinner there is. What he done is much much worse in the eyes of the Lord than anything George Wallace ever done."

"What has he done? What are you talking about, Pearl?"

Pursing her lips tightly, Pearl would only shake her head.

"I have no idea what you're referring to, Pearl," he persisted. "What in the world could possibly be worse than anything George Wallace has ever done?"

Again Pearl just shook her head vehemently, as if mere mention of it would stain her lips.

"If what he's done is so bad, how come I've never heard about it?"

Try as he might, Daniel could not get Pearl to reveal any particulars of Aaron Osgood's supposed sins. She just kept her mouth tightly shut, shook her head, and commenced sweeping the kitchen floor with vigorous broom strokes that seemed largely intended to shoo him away.

* * *

Back in Gadsden on Sunday night, Daniel had recounted this conversation to Will Hill as they sat on the back porch of his parents' house drinking beer. Will had been troubled enough to put in a phone call to Gene Boshell on Monday morning.

"Yeah, there's some of that going on," Gene had growled, referring to black ministers endorsing Wallace. "Still, we're pretty sure we got the black vote."

Yet Gene Boshell had been troubled enough in turn to put in some phone calls of his own. Late Monday afternoon, he called Will back to report that the Alabama Democratic Council, the black political machine, was still planning to endorse Osgood at their August convention, and was confident that the vast majority of the black vote was his.

But then on Friday afternoon, just as Daniel and Will got back to the office in Gadsden after lunch, one of the volunteers waved frantically for Will to come over to the telephone. It was Ray Haynes from the office in Birmingham. At that time, given the lack of privacy in either office, Ray imparted no details. He simply issued the summons for an emergency meeting to take place in Montgomery the following evening. He asked Will to call him back when his office cleared out, and hung up abruptly.

Will's first wish was to close down for the day right then and there so he could call Ray back immediately. He looked at his watch. It was one-fifteen. He made himself wait until four. Meanwhile, he surreptitiously re-set the thermostat so the crowded little office gradually became seven degrees warmer. At five after four, Will started yawning. Then he picked up a yard sign and started fanning himself with it. Two of the women did the same.

"It's not just me, then?" said Will. "I'm burning up."

"I thought it was just me," admitted one of the women. "I was scared to say anything."

Will made a show of looking at his watch. "It's ten after four," he said. "I think we've done a good week's work here and deserve to knock off a little early. What do you say, Daniel?"

Daniel agreed.

But the volunteers had suddenly become so lethargic there was no immediate rush for the door. Happy enough to quit making phone calls, the women seemed just as happy to stay right where they were for a while and enjoy a moment's camaraderie with their fellow campaign workers. Daniel and Will were forced to gather their own belongings and make for the exit in order to prod the women into doing the same.

As they said their good-byes on the sidewalk, Will realized he must have left his keys to the office inside his desk. He went back to retrieve them while Daniel waited on the sidewalk, waving as the volunteers got in their cars and left the parking lot. When the last car was two blocks away, Daniel turned and went back inside. Will Hill had not been able to wait a second longer and was already on the phone, the receiver clamped to his ear like a vicious barnacle causing him to wince with pain.

"That's outrageous!" he exploded, every so often.

When he hung up the phone, he just stared at his friend.

"What is it?" said Daniel.

Will's eyes bugged out ferociously.

"What is it?" Daniel repeated impatiently.

"All over South Alabama," said Will, shaking his head in disgust, "in the truck stops, the coffee shops, the diners, the corner drugstores and the ice cream parlors." He stopped, unable to continue.

"What? What is it? Tell me!"

Will's voice dropped to a whisper, although there was no one to overhear. "They're passing out three-dollar bills featuring Aaron Osgood's face."

* * *

At first Daniel didn't get it. But when he did, he was unperturbed.

"Actually, I think it's a good sign," he argued to Will as they drove in the Chevette to Montgomery on Saturday afternoon. "The Wallace crowd tried this with Albert Brewer back in '70," he pointed out.

"There were no three-dollar bills that I heard of," said Will.

"No, but it's the same dirty rumor. The same stupid whisper campaign."

"Well, it worked," Will noted grimly. "You take a decent guy, an intelligent candidate who wants to run on the issues, doesn't want to get in the mud, and you call him a sissy. A sissy-britches with his pinkie stuck in the air. Then the KKK puts out leaflets calling sissy-britches a homosexual who can't even father his own children. It worked."

"Who knows if that's what worked? That was a dozen years ago. Alabama was still raw from the beating it took in the Civil Rights Movement. And Wallace was still a vigorous contender with presidential ambitions. He made the state feel better about itself. Made folks feel like he was gonna whip up on those Yankees who had humiliated us all over again. Today there's a totally different climate. Civil rights are on the law books. Alabama's in the dust. And George Wallace is in a wheelchair. The stunt he's trying to pull stinks more of desperation to me than anything else. It's just a tired old campaign trick that's being used one too many times. I'd be real surprised if it's got any juice left in it. Frankly, I'm surprised this is the best they could do. The best they could come up with. Because it could backfire in a big way. I mean, George Wallace ain't the feisty little bantam rooster he was when he first started out. He ain't the fighting cock he used to be. Wallace can't even get his own cock up anymore. He's just an old peahen. And this move they've made just goes to prove it. I was expecting far worse than this. I really was."

Unconvinced, Will just shook his head and stared fixedly at the road ahead.

"Remember that New York *Times* reporter?" Daniel continued. "At the Bug Tussle?"

"What about her?"

"Remember when we told her what the Wallace crowd had pulled against Albert Brewer? How she just laughed? They called Brewer's wife an alcoholic. His daughters were sluts impregnated by black males. And Brewer himself was a homosexual. She just burst out laughing. Remember? She said it was so over the top. Like silly schoolyard taunts from a stupid bully. Your mom's a drunk, your sister's a whore, your dad's a faggot. It's a joke."

"Why am I not laughing? Could it be because a Jewish woman from New York with several Ivy League degrees and a job at the *Times* doesn't exactly represent the average Alabama voter?"

"But *I* wanted to laugh," said Daniel, exasperated. "When you first told me about the three dollar bills. That was my gut reaction. Honest to God."

"Honestly, Daniel?"

"Honestly," he affirmed. "This whole thing is like the last pitiful gasp from a pathetic old man. I just can't believe that people are going to fall for it. If this is the worst Wallace can do, I think we should count ourselves lucky."

Over the course of the ninety minute drive, Daniel's insistent optimism gradually penetrated Will's gloom. By the time they arrived at the restaurant in Montgomery, Will was actually cheerful. And Aaron Osgood was downright jubilant when he welcomed them into the private dining room at Longhorn Steaks. He was the only one there and appeared to be several drinks ahead of them.

"Where are the others?" said Will, staring at Aaron's stocking feet.

"Oh, Gene's off on some wild goose chase," said Aaron, swatting drunkenly at the air. "He got a tip from a buddy—some reporter from the *Press-Register* in Mobile—thinks he knows the whereabouts of a certain printing press turning out funny money." Aaron winked hugely until a hiccup high-jacked his face. "He grabbed poor old Ray and tore off. Don't know when they'll be back, but probably not tonight. Still, no reason we can't have ourselves some fun for a change. Take off your jackets, why don't you? Get comfortable. We're all alone in this nice big private room. We could take off all our clothes and run around naked if we wanted to."

As Aaron pulled out his own chair, the two young men stood motionless, staring at him in dismay.

"Okay. Okay," said Aaron. "I apologize. Bad joke. But do take off your jackets and go get a drink." He nodded to indicate a side table stocked with bourbon and Scotch.

Daniel began to wonder if Aaron had ingested something more than liquor. His mood was so odd; his eyes glittered strangely and he was downright giddy with inexplicable elation. Then it occurred to him that the stress of the campaign must have taken its toll. Perhaps Aaron was more concerned by recent developments than he wanted to let them know. Perhaps he was even scared shitless. He had sat alone in the private dining room at Longhorn Steaks and drank bourbon until he came unglued. On purpose. Will and

Daniel exchanged uneasy glances as they poured themselves drinks and sat down at the table.

"Drink up, boys!" Aaron urged them. "Lighten up, too, while you're at it! Please loosen up. What I need to do most of all right now is relax. But how can I do that around two glum-faced Harvard boys who don't know how to party? Let me tell you something. You want to know what the worst thing is about being on the campaign trail? I'll tell you. It's not dealing with a silly mess like this. It's the fact that I can't really let my hair down and just be myself. I have to be "the candidate" all the time! This is impossible! It's like I can't be human. Between what Mary Winston tells me to do, and what Gene tells me to do, I don't have a second I can call my own. I'm too busy doing whatever I'm told. And I do what I'm told to do. A damn good job I do of it too. Don't you think that earns me something? Don't you think every once in a blue moon when the wife's not here and Gene isn't around I deserve to do whatever the hell I want to do? Let me tell you boys something else: The most important thing you can do for me right now is to help me unwind. I mean it! Gene and Ray are off doing crisis management. They're doing whatever they think they can do. So in the meantime, let me take a break from being the candidate. Let me be a human being. For once I'd like to have a normal Saturday night like other people. I'd like to have a few drinks and a good dinner and forget about work. I'd like to enjoy myself. Okay? Haven't I earned that? Don't you think I'm entitled to a little fun? So let's have no talk about the campaign. No campaign talk at all. Let's try to behave like normal people and just have a good time on a Saturday night. That's all I want. All I'm asking for right now. Okay?"

Will and Daniel exchanged more uneasy glances. This was not what they had expected, but: Okay. They all three drank up. And drank and drank and drank. As stipulated, no one mentioned the campaign. Instead, Aaron Osgood began planning his administration. The more they all drank, the more grandiose these plans became. Will Hill, he said, had first choice because Gene Boshell was going back to consulting. Gene wanted no part in any government. A good horse race was what Gene liked, but when that was over, Gene was out. He might stay on the payroll, but he wouldn't be on the governor's staff. Gene had pointed out that he could do a much better job of telling them everything they were doing wrong if he wasn't one of them himself. So Will Hill would be Chief of Staff if that's what he wanted. However, Aaron understood if Will wanted something with more intellectual heft, like Policy Director. In that event, Daniel would be Chief of Staff and would be a good one at that. He had such incredible people skills. But those could be put to equally good use as Deputy Chief of Staff, or assistant to the Chief of Staff, if Will didn't want Policy Director, which, in Aaron's humble opinion, was where Will would shine most brilliantly. But it was Will's call.

"And eventually," Aaron said, "we're going to run you boys. Will's going to be attorney general, and Daniel's going to be lieutenant governor. Whether this starts during my second term, or sometime later, we'll just have to see."

It was heady talk. Ever since Daniel had taken his fourth grade tour of the Capitol building in Montgomery, he had wondered what it would be like to work there, to call that big, beautiful building his office. It was like a palace, especially compared to the glorified cubicle his father occupied as assistant principal of Chunchula High. After that momentous field trip, it was Daniel's ambition to work in that palace. Nothing really had ever replaced this initial schoolboy ambition. Even when he later saw the federal capitol in Washington, D.C., it had not dazzled him the way his state capitol had. He was older then, and not as susceptible. That first impression made on him at an earlier age proved to have the deepest impact. It had worked within him far longer, and its influence was unshakeable. It was the same way the Mountain Brook girl represented for him the pinnacle of female attraction and desirability. A mere heiress from Greenwich, Connecticut was nothing compared to that. He had been made to understand that a Mountain Brook girl would never have anything to do with the likes of him far longer than he'd even known there was such a place as Greenwich, Connecticut. He would always be a provincial at heart. Four years of Harvard had not changed that and he would be the first to admit it: he was still a redneck. This redneck wanted to marry a Mountain Brook girl and become governor of Alabama. And now both of these dreams were on the road to reality.

But did Will want Policy Director or Chief of Staff? The two young men debated the choice before Will as they drove to the apartment they had shared for two weeks earlier that summer. Daniel tended to agree with Aaron Osgood, that Will was a natural for Policy, and Daniel was better suited to Chief of Staff. But it was for Will to say. Daniel didn't much care what the job was. Whatever it was, it was only the first necessary step toward his ultimate goal.

When they reached the apartment, Aaron Osgood was waiting for them with three glasses of brandy. As he yanked at his tie, he handed them each a glass. Then he turned the stereo on much louder than was probably normal for an attorney general or gubernatorial candidate. He clinked glasses with the two young men. "To our administration!" he proclaimed before proceeding to drain his glass.

"Cheers!" they said, and tried their best to follow suit. It was very strong brandy.

After setting his empty glass down on the living room coffee table, Aaron began dancing alone to the music. His movements belonged to no form of dancing known to either of his companions. It was what you might expect of a country boy from Andalusia, Alabama who had come to Montgomery to party. What he lacked in skill or grace, he made up for with energy and enthusiasm. This had always been his winning combination. The gung-ho hick whose open-hearted eagerness was so endearing you forgave him for being a rube. To Daniel, Aaron seemed to be performing his own peculiar mixture of square dancing, disco, and calisthenics. He and Will couldn't help laughing.

"Let's see you do better!" Aaron dared them, grinning. "Come on, Harvard boys! Let's see your moves, then!"

But neither of the young men could be enticed. It was too much fun to watch the antics of Aaron Osgood.

"Have another brandy if you need to! But get out here on the dance floor!" Aaron commanded.

As the song ended, he went over to the stereo to scan the radio channels until he hit on a station playing Saturday night disco. Then he switched off the two lamps and the overhead lights, making the room totally dark until he placed a disco ball on the coffee table and turned it on. Grabbing Daniel's hand, he pulled him out to the open space in front of the entertainment center.

"And now!" said Aaron. "The Chief of Staff for the Governor of Alabama will provide an excellent example of disco dancing and lead our state to heights never dreamed of!"

It was all too funny. The pulsing music, the rotating rainbow of disco lights, the flapping of Aaron's ridiculously long arms as he did the funky chicken. Will laughed his head off until Daniel pulled *him* out on the makeshift dance floor. If ever there was a stiff who did not know how to move his body, it was Will Hill from Gadsden, Alabama. His dorky dance movements were the funniest of all. Fortunately, Will had had enough to drink that he reveled in the laughter and tried all the harder.

Breathless after half a dozen disco tunes, Aaron excused himself and went to the bathroom.

"There's a pick-me-up for you boys in there!" Aaron called out.

Curious, they filed in to the bathroom, where Aaron had laid out two lines of cocaine on the black marble counter. Fresh from Harvard, Daniel knew exactly what it was. Furthermore, he had never been one to deny himself opportunities right there for the taking. On the other hand, Will didn't appear to understand what he was looking at. Cocaine had come along after his years in college.

"Just do what I do," Daniel told him. Will did so probably without realizing exactly what he was doing. The quantities of bourbon and brandy he had consumed, along with his Eagle Scout existence, had made him blind to the stupidity and folly of putting his nostril down on the bathroom counter and sniffing what might have looked to him like talcum powder.

"If you think that's good, you ought to see what I got in here!" Aaron called from the adjoining bedroom.

When they peered into the room, they could see Aaron lying buck naked on his black satin sheets sporting a huge erection.

"Look at my pointy head, boys!" he crowed.

The cocaine had already kicked in to the point that the young men did not do what they should have done or think what they should have thought. Indeed, they thought Aaron's joke was hysterical, and they just stood there, gaping at their gubernatorial candidate. And he sure was a sight to behold, lying stark naked, all six feet four inches of him, with a fully engorged cock to match.

"I've got me a problem, here, boys," he grinned from the bed. "I need one or both you boys to take care of a little problem for me. Actually, it's a big problem. Who's going to handle it for me? My Chief of Staff? Or my Policy Director? But don't worry. I got plenty of work for everybody. Lots of jobs to go around."

Without warning, Aaron shot up from the bed, leaned over, grabbed Will's hand and pulled him down on the satin-sheeted mattress. Daniel stumbled out of the room and shut the door. Unfortunately, he couldn't flee the apartment because the car keys were in Will's pants' pocket. At least he could turn off the rotating disco ball. However, he thought it best to keep the disco music itself playing on the stereo at the same loud volume.

With a tall glass of iced water, he sat down in the living room and tried to clear his head. It wasn't easy. In addition to the bourbon, brandy and cocaine running riot inside him, his brain was reeling from a violent shock, as if he'd just suffered a concussion and was too dazed and dizzy to think clearly. Instead of coherent thoughts, random images exploded into his consciousness like fireworks, except none of these were pretty. As soon as one image faded, another took its place with a loud bang causing his head to throb. There was Wallace in his wheelchair; Osgood's bald head, which turned into Osgood's erection; Mary Winston bearing down on him with snake eyes. The three-dollar bill with Osgood's bald head; Aaron in his sock feet; Mary Winston bearing down on him with snake eyes. White lines of cocaine on a black marble counter; the swirling rainbow from the disco ball; Mary Winston bearing down on him with snake eyes. "I know exactly who you are," the snake eyes hissed at him. "And I know exactly what you're here for." Osgood's bald head replaced by Osgood's engorged cock. "I know exactly what you're here for."

Again the swirling rainbow from the disco ball burst into his brain, but when the colors faded, the whirling movement continued and even traveled to his stomach, whose contents were thrown into immediate upheaval. Bourbon and brandy-flavored bile rose in his gullet. For a panic-stricken second, he couldn't breathe, as if something was being stuffed in his throat while a hissing voice snarled, "I know exactly what you're here for." With a shaky hand he brought the iced water to his lips, and the choking sensation went away. But when he leaned back in his chair, the pictures began flashing across his brain all over again. He knew he needed to exert some control, because if the rainbow lights came back, there would be no stopping the upchuck this time. But when he concentrated on banishing the disco ball, what popped into place was Osgood's bald head, looking like an erect penis on which a face had been drawn. "I know exactly what you're here for."

It was the most monstrous erection he'd ever seen in his life. Of course, it was the only erection he'd ever seen in his life, not counting his own.

Is that what he was there for? Is that who he was?

And he thought he'd been helping to defeat George Wallace. Helping to bring a new day to the state of Alabama.

He thought he'd been hired for his brains, his skills, his ideals.

But he'd been trying to live in the wrong Southern novel. Hoping for *All the King's Men,* he found the world he lived in was more *A Confederacy of Dunces.*

He'd been the biggest dunce of them all, with his dream of belonging to a band of brothers, a team of heroes who would slay the dragon Wallace and free the people. There were no heroes here. Just a bunch of fools snorting cocaine, flapping their arms to a disco ball and getting entangled in black satin sheets.

* * *

Kong Dong remained in the bedroom with Aaron Osgood a lot longer than Daniel would have. When he emerged, he threw up in the bathroom and then stumbled into the living room, where he passed out in an arm chair. He had no clothes on.

Will's nakedness had a number of implications, one of which was that Daniel still could not retrieve his car keys. There was no way he was going back in that bedroom, although he could hear Aaron snoring. Soon enough, Will was snoring also. The clock on the microwave in the kitchen glowed a green 2:30 in the darkness. There was nothing to do but get some blankets from the hall closet and stay the night. He threw one over Will and spread the other on the sofa where he stretched out.

By the time Daniel woke up the next morning, Will was in the shower and there was no sign of Aaron Osgood. The Sunday serenity of the quiet little apartment made Daniel question his entire recollection of the previous evening. The bed had been made so expertly it looked as if no one had even disturbed the air in that room for weeks. The brandy bottle, the three glasses and the disco ball were nowhere in evidence. Indeed, there was no evidence Aaron Osgood had ever been in the apartment at all last night and no trace of a bacchanal of any kind. Their gubernatorial candidate had not even left a note for his two loyal campaign workers, the linchpins of his future administration.

They learned later that Aaron Osgood had driven to Birmingham that Sunday morning to accompany his wife and daughters to the ten o'clock services at the First Baptist Church of Birmingham.

* * *

As Daniel and Will left the parking lot of the apartment complex, a black custodial worker got out of a decrepit pick-up truck whose rear fender had a brand-new bumper sticker proclaiming **WALLACE.**

"WMBL Radio in Mobile has just learned that Eugene Boshell, former po-litical reporter for the Montgomery *Advertiser* and currently the campaign manager for gubernatorial candidate Aaron Osgood, suffered a massive heart attack early this morning and is in critical condition at South Alabama Medi-cal Center in Mobile. Boshell was in Mobile on official campaign business, according to another campaign associate who accompanied him but declined to specify the reason for the visit. Gubernatorial candidate Aaron Osgood is scheduled to make his next appearance in Mobile on August 21st, and spent Saturday evening in Montgomery in private consultation with two other cam-paign aides. He has not yet been reached for comment. Stay tuned to WMBL Radio, Mobile, Alabama, for up-to-the-minute breaking news."

~ 12 ~

Daniel and Will drove straight from Montgomery to Gadsden without stopping in Birmingham. The last thing they needed were any questions from their girlfriends about the "meeting" with Aaron Osgood. Groggy, hung-over and nursing splitting heads, they didn't even want to face their own questions about the cocaine-fueled romp they had stumbled into. But over the course of the drive, they found themselves talking around the subject neither of them could bring themselves to confront directly.

After a pause in the discussion, Will declared emphatically, "If a man cannot govern himself, then he has no right to try to govern anything else."

Daniel readily agreed.

Privately, however, Daniel believed that the hardest thing to govern was yourself, and that anything else—even a state or a nation—was easier to govern than your own unruly self. If you thought maybe you could keep a lid on it by getting married and going to church, you might end up just like Aaron Osgood, who obviously thought he deserved to let his cock out of the box every once in a while precisely because he was married and went to church and did everything else he was told to do. If there were any easy answers to the human condition, then folks in Alabama would have had it made. But even in Alabama, small town country boys like Aaron Osgood knew what it was to be something other than what they were supposed to be, and found a way to be what they really were, at least on certain occasions. No doubt there were plenty more even in the state of Alabama who engaged in something other than straitjacketed Baptist sex for the purpose of procreation.

It was an irony and a damn shame—the man who had failed as governor of Alabama three times already was the one who had best governed himself, at least in terms of suppressing any personal needs or private beliefs while devoting the entirety of his being to the sole cause of his own eternal candidacy. On the other hand, the man who would make the best governor of the state was not going to get that chance, because he couldn't even supervise himself. When it came down to it, he couldn't help but be more than just a candidate. He had to be a human being too. And as a human being, naturally he was flawed. Did good men often lose, Daniel wondered, simply because of their own humanity?

He felt sorry for Aaron Osgood. But he was mad at him too. The man had put himself out there on the battlefield as a leader and mustered his troops in a righteous cause. It was a historic moment; the stakes were high. Aaron owed it to his cause, the people who were fighting for it and those who would benefit from it to be something more than an ordinary human being. The times had called on him to be a hero. It was a chance that many dreamed of and few were given—a chance to be a hero. A chance to go up against George Wallace and beat him. How many people were given such a moment to show what they were made of? How many ever had such a golden opportunity to lead a noble cause and go face to face with evil? How many times in your life would folks be willing to plaster their cars with bumper stickers of your name? Daniel himself would have given anything to be in Aaron Osgood's position, but the world today didn't allow many occasions for those kind of heroics. Aaron had been blessed to be called on by history to be the man of the hour, and he'd blown it. Not only was he not going to win, he wasn't even going to lose to Wallace. He was going to be defeated by himself.

The sheer folly of it was mindboggling. Aaron Osgood had *known* that Wallace could play the queer card as well as the race card. They had all sat there and talked about it at the Bug Tussle Steakhouse. Even before then, Brandy Ayers had taken Aaron aside to give him a word to the wise about the "wimp" factor Wallace had used against Albert Brewer. Was this really a coded warning to Osgood? Of course it was, Daniel realized now. But Aaron Osgood should not have needed a warning. The handwriting was on the wall for all to see. How had Osgood failed to heed it? Why had he failed to keep himself in check? Why was he *still* failing to keep himself in check?

Daniel looked over at his friend. "Do you remember what they've always said about what it's like to watch George Wallace eat?"

"Eat? No. What are you talking about? Remind me."

"Just that Wallace doesn't care what he eats, or even notices it. He just puts ketchup all over everything and eats whatever's on his plate. It could be meatloaf, it could be steak, it could be the end of his tie. It's all the same to him, covered with ketchup."

"That's from Marshall Frady's book," said Will. "I remember. But what's that got to do with what we're talking about?"

Daniel bit his lip. "Well, obviously, a man who can live off the taste of ketchup alone has an advantage over the rest of us."

"I don't follow you."

"What it means is that he hasn't got the same—appetites—as the rest of us. He doesn't care what he eats. Or who he fucks. He'll eat whatever rubber chicken's put in front of him, fuck whoever he's supposed to fuck and never want for anything else. He may not even need to eat anything or fuck anyone."

Will nodded slowly. "Wallace just wants power. Center stage."

"Everything else is just ketchup."

"You're right, Daniel," said Will with dawning enlightenment. "I see what you're getting at. These are the people most likely to get elected, because that's all they care about. And these are probably the most dangerous people there are. The most capable of evil. Because there's so much missing inside. The parts that make a person human. Ethical. And vulnerable too," he added after a pause.

This was what Daniel had been thinking. It was Aaron Osgood's humanity that made him qualified to be a hero in the first place, but it was that same humanity that must be set aside in order for him actually to become a hero. How did a person do that? he wondered. Also: What exactly had Will Hill done in that bedroom with Aaron Osgood? Why had he stayed in there for so long, and come out of there so completely naked? Although Daniel was dying to know, he thought it best not to ask.

"What do you think we should do?" he asked instead.

Will took his time to answer.

"Let's give the man a chance," he said finally. "To explain. Apologize. He deserves at least that much. After all, he is still our best hope in this election. Based on what I saw when I worked with him in the Attorney General's office, he would make a damn fine governor."

"He didn't—" Daniel paused. "Fool around, I take it?"

"He most certainly did not," Will stated firmly, as if he'd read Daniel's mind and knew the more explicit question lurking there. "Daniel, I swear to you," he continued. "The man I knew as the Attorney General was nothing but a workhorse. Dedicated to an obsessive degree to the task at hand. Which was, if you'll recall, the Loman Brothers trial."

"Winning that's what got him in the governor's race," Daniel mused, almost to himself.

"But last summer," said Will, "the trial was in its final stage. Aaron Osgood was a man who had no time for anything other than getting ready for the next day in court. If you left before ten P.M., you were a no-good, lazy son-of-a-bitch. If you left at midnight, he'd grunt at you on your way out. That was 'thank you.' And the bourbon we drank last night? The brandy?" Will shook his head. "All we knew last summer was Mr. Coffee."

"He could hardly have liquor in the Capitol building," Daniel noted. "Not in Montgomery."

"You're not getting my point, Daniel," said Will with impatience. "I'm talking about a man who didn't want a drink. Who didn't have the urge to 'fool around,' as you put it. This was a man utterly devoted to his cause, with no time for anything else. He rarely even cracked a smile, let alone a joke. I want you to know—I admired the hell out of this man. I—" Will stopped abruptly in mid-sentence.

Daniel looked over, afraid Will had choked up. "What was he like in—court?" he said quickly.

"Brilliant. Absolutely brilliant. I thought I told you that already."

Will had indeed told him that numerous times, but Daniel had thought it wise to change the subject, and this was the first one that occurred to him.

"I wish you could have seen him in action in the courtroom," Will sighed. "He was a firecracker, and at the same time, a consummate professional. Impeccable delivery, lightning bolt responses to anything thrown at him from the other side. All on three or four hours of sleep a night. If that. After all day in court, it was all afternoon and all evening in the office, getting prepared for the next day in court. And we won. We did it. We beat George Wallace's corrupt cronies. We felt like we'd beaten Wallace himself."

Will was silent for a long minute.

"I was hoping to be able to say the same thing about this governor's race," he continued finally. "We won. We did it. We actually *did* beat George Wallace himself." He looked over at Daniel. "But this summer has not been like last summer. And the man I saw last night was like a different person from the one I knew a year ago." Will slammed the steering wheel in fury. "I just don't get it!" he shouted. "All that drinking! The cocaine! Flapping around like a jackass to a disco ball! A disco ball! When there was so much we needed to discuss! An election hangs in the balance! And we broke the law, Daniel! Do you realize that?" Will whipped his head back around. "We ingested an illegal substance! With the Attorney General of Alabama!"

Daniel did not know what to say, especially since he could not say what was on his mind. Namely, on the list of last night's trespasses and indiscretions, Will had left off the most problematical one of all, at least in the state of Alabama. This one involved Aaron Osgood's erect penis, and—in one way or another—Will Hill's naked body. Was there some part of last evening Will

Hill was blocking from his memory? Was there some part of *himself* Will Hill was blocking from his mind?

Of course, it was more than likely that Will literally did not remember what had happened before he passed out, and had been merely an easy victim, all liquored and coked up like he was. Will had never been much of a drinker, and judging by the look on his face last night, had not even recognized the cocaine for what it was. The fact that he had snorted it anyway was proof of just how smashed he already was from all that alcohol. Obviously he wasn't thinking straight; at any rate, he wasn't thinking like Will Hill. Daniel himself had been so high that all he'd done was laugh like a hyena when he saw Aaron Osgood lying naked on the bed. They had both been so far out of their right minds that it seemed only natural to enter the bedroom.

They had stood at the foot of the bed together like loyal and devoted staffers obeying an urgent summons from their Governor. At that drug-addled moment, the eager-to-please young Chief of Staff and the equally dedicated Policy Director did not question why their orders came from Aaron Osgood's dick. Before they could formulate a challenge to this particular authority, Osgood had seized his Policy Director, aka Kong Dong, by the hand.

This was the first time in his life Daniel was glad not to be the chosen one. Thinking back to the kiss he'd once received from Lewis Holditch, Daniel recalled how this had prompted him only to rise from the dinner table and take his leave. But then there had been no drugs and much less drinking involved. Just a few glasses of sherry. Daniel could not be absolutely certain that if Aaron Osgood had grabbed his Chief of Staff instead of his Policy Director, his Chief of Staff would have sobered up instantly and gotten the hell out of the room with every stitch of clothing still on his body. Not only had Osgood served a heady brew, he had also slipped them a mickey: bourbon, brandy and cocaine laced with visions of personal glory and grandeur. This was the kind of cocktail that could turn a man into Silly Putty.

He didn't even want to think about who had done what to whom in that bedroom, and was fairly sure Will Hill wouldn't know what to tell him. Because Will remembered the bourbon, the brandy, the cocaine and the disco ball. What he had never mentioned—not even once—was the two nude male bodies that had shared a bedroom for at least an hour.

Many miles went by in silence. They passed several campaign billboards, including one for Aaron Osgood that said: "Elect a man who really will stand up for Alabama." It had seemed like a good idea at the time, turning that slogan around on Wallace. But Daniel was figuring now that the good folks of Alabama would rather elect a cripple in a wheelchair than a man whose dick had done whatever Aaron Osgood's had done last night. Those three-dollar bills featuring Aaron Osgood's face would probably prove to have enormous value as hard currency in the campaign, and buy George Wallace his fourth term as governor.

"Talk to me, Daniel," said Will. "What are you thinking?"

"I'm thinking of what you said about last summer," Daniel lied. "How hard Osgood worked. You know what they say about all work. I'm wondering if the man worked himself to a frazzle—as my Mamaw would say—and then just busted loose."

Will nodded solemnly.

"There's only so long that a man can deny his—humanity," said Daniel. "Only so long you can keep yourself under lock and key. No doubt he has had to work his ass off his entire life to get where he is, and now that he's on the last lap, he's losing his grip. That tight grip he must have had on himself all his life up to now."

"Either that, or he's celebrating a little too early," Will said grimly.

"Like he's spent a long time sacrificing his true self so he can earn his rewards, and can't wait one more minute till he gets them," Daniel added. "Except if he rewards himself too much, he won't be celebrating for long. Not in Baptist country."

"What is the lesson here, Daniel?"

"Hell if I know, buddy."

"Bullshit. Cut that dumbass crap. You were onto something a second ago."

"I was?"

"When you said the man had been keeping himself under lock and key. The lesson is: You can't do that. It doesn't work. Sooner or later, that part you've been keeping in the dungeon is going to escape. And when it does— look out. There's an ex-con on the loose who's coming after the guy who put him in jail. Just like you can never get away with ignoring the elephant in the room. The elephant who isn't dealt with will eventually stomp all over you."

"The state of Alabama makes it very hard to deal with the kind of elephants who wouldn't be good mascots for the Crimson Tide."

"Yes," Will agreed, inclining his head. "But there's a difference between self-control and self-denial. I think the lesson is: Know who you are and deal with it in a responsible way that's true to yourself. Don't deny who you are and think that's the way to deal with it. Whatever you suppress will ultimately break out and run wild. That's the only explanation I can come up with for the kind of reckless, self-destructive behavior we witnessed last night."

This was a fine speech. Will was a wise man. But did he know who *he* was? And by the way, did he really know what they needed to do?

"So you still think we ought to cut the guy some slack?" Daniel said.

"I do," Will sighed. "Aaron Osgood has been in politics a dozen years. The man has a sterling record of achievement and an unblemished reputation. As far as we're aware, this is his first misstep. Fortunately, we are the only witnesses. No one else ever has to know."

Daniel gnawed the inside of his cheek. It was now clear to him, if not to his friend, that someone else already did know. Hence the three-dollar bills, which he'd originally dismissed as nothing more than a variation of the same old stunt Wallace had pulled on poor old Albert Brewer. But that stunt had worked before on a man who was straight as an arrow, and it was going to work now on a man who was queer as a three-dollar bill. Because whatever else Aaron Osgood was—husband, father, country boy—he was no first-timer at last night's fun and games. Similar sprees with other young men must have happened before along the campaign trail. And they would happen again. In fact, if Aaron had spent more time in Montgomery, as originally planned, last night would not have been the first the three of them spent together in the attorney general's apartment. Mary Winston's words echoed in his head. "I know exactly what you're here for. . . ."

"My guess is Aaron Osgood comes to see us," said Will. "Tells us he doesn't know what came over him in Montgomery. You know: the stress of campaigning, the long hours, life on the road. How could it not take its toll?"

"The temporary insanity plea," said Daniel. "The temporary infidelity plea. The temporary adultery plea. The temporary homosexuality plea. Forgive me: I was temporarily gay there for a minute. Forgive me: I temporarily went to a hooker before I went back home to my wife."

"I hear you, Daniel," said Will, sighing heavily. "But we owe it to ourselves as well as him to hear what he has to say for himself."

"Remorse. Contrition. It'll never happen again."

"We've got to allow the man to make some mistakes," Will argued. "After all, he *is* a man, and not just a politician. We cannot demand that a candidate be a perfect human being."

Daniel was pretty sure the voters in Alabama would demand that a candidate be a *heterosexual* human being.

"And when a man stumbles as all men do occasionally, we should allow him the opportunity to regain his footing," said Will, warming to his subject. "He deserves a chance to redeem himself."

In other words, thought Daniel, Aaron Osgood deserved the chance to be a hypocrite. To be one thing, and pretend to be another. Just like George Wallace. He thought it best not to share his thoughts with Will, however. Some people had major blind spots and simply could not connect the dots.

* * *

Daniel Dobbs and Will Hill returned to Gadsden and resumed their duties. Coretta Scott King and other luminaries of the Civil Rights Movement arrived for the promised tour of South Alabama with the Osgood campaign. As expected, the Alabama Democratic Council, the state's black political organization, officially endorsed Aaron Osgood for governor.

However, Gene Boshell never left the ICU and died of complications following his massive heart attack. Through Ray Haynes, manager of the Birmingham headquarters, Aaron Osgood summoned Will Hill and Daniel Dobbs to the funeral in Montgomery. Instead of attending, the two young men decided not to defer their law school careers after all, and resigned their positions from the campaign.

~ 13 ~

Although he had never intended to enter law school, and certainly did not plan to practice law, Daniel saw no good reason not to go along with the idea of law school until he figured out what he really wanted to do with his life. There was nothing so terrible about hedging his bets, either. In the event Osgood did beat Wallace and offered Daniel a job in the new administration, he could always take it. But without that solid job proposition, it made more sense to continue with his education. It also made his parents very happy.

A week after the start of law school, over the Labor Day holiday, Will Hill got engaged to his girlfriend Rhea Mehta. They planned to marry the following summer, after her graduation from medical school and Will's from law school. Rhea would seek her pediatric residency in the state of Alabama, and Will would go wherever she was "matched," be that Huntsville, Birmingham, or Mobile. There, he planned to study for the bar exam and pursue a career as a labor lawyer. His summer stint on a political campaign had pointed out the path he needed to take. It wasn't politics.

The Tuesday after Labor Day, when Will shared the news of his engagement with Daniel, the Democratic primary took place in Alabama. As predicted, Aaron Osgood and George Wallace won the most votes among the six candidates, and would face each other in a run-off at the end of the month.

* * *

A few weeks later, as Daniel made his farewells before Caroline headed back to college, he suggested they simply "see what happened" during the remaining three years of her undergraduate education. He was caught off guard by the vehemence of her reaction to an insult he had not intended to deliver.

"What do you mean: 'See what happens?'" she had demanded. "That's not what a commitment means! A commitment means you decide what you *want* to happen, and then you *make* it happen! Are you trying to tell me you're not committed to me?"

He assured her at great length that he was not. Not trying to tell her any such thing, that is. Of course he was committed to her. All he meant was that she was just eighteen, with many more years of college ahead of her, and he did not want to limit her opportunities. He had only her best interests in mind.

The day following Caroline's departure, when he returned from his classes and entered the house he shared with Will Hill, the phone was ringing. He assumed it would be Caroline, sobbing over how cold it was already in Cambridge. Much as she claimed to hate the South, she hated the Northeast even more. But it wasn't Caroline on the phone. It was Ricky Jill McNeese calling from the hospital in Brewton, where she had just given birth the day before to a baby boy.

"Congratulations," he told her.

"He looks just like you," she said.

He wasn't sure what that was supposed to mean.

"He's olive-complected, just like you are," she added.

True, Daniel was rather olive-toned, whereas Kirk McNeese had very fair skin and red hair. Ricky Jill wasn't nearly so pale, but you wouldn't call her olive skinned either. Still, he hoped she wasn't trying to read too much into the color of a newborn's skin tone.

"He's our baby," said Ricky Jill happily.

He wasn't sure who "our" referred to, and didn't want to ask. Also, he didn't want to know.

"I just thought you'd want to know," she said. "You got yourself a baby boy now."

"Ricky Jill," he said. "How in the world can you say he's *mine* and not your husband's? Just because of his complexion. . . ."

"Oh, that's not all," she said. "He's got the same long dark eyelashes that stick out a million miles like yours do. I'm looking at 'em right now. Kirk's got stubby little albino lashes, and mine are hopeless without mascara."

"Still," he said. "That's not a lot to go on."

"Oh, that's not the main reason I know he's your baby," she said, lowering her voice to a whisper. "The main thing is," she paused and lowered her voice even further. "The main thing is—two years ago? I don't know if you heard. But Kirk had this cancer of the testicles? And those treatments they gave him? Well, the doctors said he wouldn't be able to give me any more babies."

Daniel was silent. "How did you explain your pregnancy, then?" he said finally.

"Oh, I didn't have to explain it," she said.

"No?"

"Well, our church had formed this prayer circle, see? You know what a prayer circle is? The purpose was to send all these prayers for Kirk to be healed. Not just so he could survive the cancer, but so's he and I could have a bigger family. He always wanted a son."

"So now he thinks his prayers have been answered?"

"Everybody at First Baptist in Brewton thinks their prayers have been answered," she replied. "This little boy is everybody's miracle baby. But I just know in my heart he's yours. I think the Lord always did want for us to have a child together. You know what I mean?"

He did. "But Ricky Jill, don't you think it's best if Kirk and—everybody in Brewton—goes on believing in their miracle?"

"Oh, nothing can shake Kirk's faith," she said. "When Kirk told the doctor his wife was pregnant, the doctor tried to tell him it was impossible. But Kirk just turned around and told the doctor that the power of prayer was stronger than the power of medicine."

"I think it is," said Daniel hopefully.

"Well, we all got what we prayed for," said Ricky Jill. "Kirk and me got a son like we both always wanted. You should see him with this baby. He's already the best daddy in the world. I just didn't want to leave you out. In case *you* always wanted a son. Now you know you have one. We'll take the best care of him we know how."

No sooner had he hung up the phone than Will charged into the house and made straight for the TV without even saying hello. Will never watched television.

"What happened?" said Daniel. "Did a plane crash somewhere?"

"Don't tell me you forgot," said Will, turning sharply around toward him.

"Forgot what?"

"The run-off, dummy. I reminded you last night when you got in from Birmingham. Please tell me you remembered to vote."

"Of course I remembered to vote," said Daniel indignantly, though he had not, in fact, actually cast his ballot. It wasn't entirely his fault, either. After leaving the campaign, he had barely had time to get his act together for law school, let alone go register to vote in Tuscaloosa.

They watched as the numbers came in all night long. But at midnight, the race was still too close to call. It was the next day the winner emerged. George Wallace won by little more than a percentage point.

Later analysis revealed that George Wallace eked out this victory over Aaron Osgood by winning one third of the black vote.

All in all, Daniel considered he had done the right thing by entering law school. It wasn't nearly as bad as he'd feared it would be. The campus at the University of Alabama in Tuscaloosa was gorgeous, especially during the early fall, which was really nothing more than Indian summer. Many of the school buildings looked like antebellum plantation manors, and most of the girls looked like Southern belles from an equally bygone era. Indeed, the undergraduate 'coeds'—as they were still called—were the most beautiful girls he had ever laid eyes on. Only very rarely did he catch a glimpse of a poor homely girl whose looks reminded him of Eleanor. Once or twice he thought he even saw Eleanor herself, but he knew it had to be his mind playing tricks on him. Eleanor had never called his parents again since that last time, when his mother had slammed the phone down after crying, "You're harassing me!" Daniel had begun to wonder what had happened to her.

As luck would have it, the most beautiful girl he'd met so far was actually in his law school class. She was not only beautiful; she was a former cheerleader for the Crimson Tide. He'd always been fascinated by the Bama cheerleaders—every single one of them could have contended for the Miss America crown. He'd always wanted to meet one, but never thought he'd even come close to one except on a television set. Now he had a date with one on Saturday afternoon.

They were going to the first home game of the season. This game was a big deal for everybody: the team, the student body, the fans all over the state, as well as for himself, since he was escorting a former Bama cheerleader who had cried when she expressed her own personal belief that this was Bear Bryant's final year. She wasn't sure she could handle the prospect, especially as a mere spectator instead of as a cheerleader. He had offered to see it through with her, and had a lot to do to get ready because folks dressed for a football game like they were going to church. No tie, but he would need a jacket over a starched and pressed buttoned-down oxford shirt. His khaki pants should have a knife crease, and his penny loafers should be gleaming. He didn't even own a pair of penny loafers. He needed to go to the dry cleaners as well as the shoe store.

Any Alabama game, but especially the first, was a momentous occasion. There was a palpable amount of drama in the air, much more so than there had been with the governor's race, especially now that Wallace was bound to win the general election. Daniel was glad he'd gotten politics out of his system. After all, politics really *was* just a fool's game; whereas football, especially Alabama football, was serious business.

EPILOGUE

Three years later, when he graduated from law school, Daniel Dobbs got another car. This one was not only brand-new, it was also a BMW. Of course, it was not a gift from his parents: they could never have afforded such an extravagance. And of course they were worried that he couldn't afford such an extravagance either. But he had saved quite a bit of money from his lucrative summer clerkships in Birmingham law firms. He had been able to put down a sizable amount up front at the dealership, and his monthly payments should not present a problem, considering what his monthly income was going to be at the law firm he would be joining as soon as he passed the Alabama bar exam.

It went without saying that he needed a new car. Even his parents could not object to a new car, especially since he was paying for it. But they could and did object to a BMW. "You can't say you *need* a BMW," his mother sniffed. There were others, however, who said that a BMW was exactly what he needed. Actually, she had not said so in those precise words, but in so many words, which continued to echo in his mind.

"Imagine what it's going to be like at the going away," she had said. "When you walk out of the country club with everybody clapping, waving and throwing rose petals. Your car will be waiting under the porte cochere, and the valets will be standing by ready to open the doors for the bride and groom. Everybody will be watching as you get in your car and drive off. Think to yourself what car you want that to be parked under the porte cochere at the country club. Whatever image pops into your mind—*that's* the car you should get for yourself."

She had not exactly said "BMW," but since that was the automobile that popped into his mental picture, that was the one he decided to get. And she was right. He had known as soon as he met his future mother-in-law that she was a natural ally, and he had learned to pay attention to what she said. Now that he was about to become an attorney at a top-tier Birmingham law firm, he needed to present himself in the best possible way at all times and in all situations. There could hardly be a more important such occasion than his wedding to Caroline Elmore.

And since she deserved a far better man than he could ever be, at the very least he could bring to the marriage a far better vehicle than the Chevette. In the three years he had spent at the University of Alabama, he had never yet met her equal, and he had met plenty of dazzling girls who had turned his head. Many of them had more beauty; a few even had her brains. One or two possessed that rare combination of both. However, none of the ones he'd gotten to know better had been from Mountain Brook. Without exception, the Mountain Brook girls on the Bama campus had not wanted to get to know him better. They were perfectly polite; they just weren't interested in a South Alabama boy like him. His Harvard degree counted for nothing with them; what mattered most, apparently, was that he had not been a KA or an SAE at the University of Alabama. By the end of his third year of law school, it was clear that he could not do better than Caroline Elmore. And his heart was set on marrying a Mountain Brook girl.

AUTHOR'S NOTE AND
ACKNOWLEDGMENTS

The plot of this novel is faithful to the broad outlines and essential details of George Wallace's last run for governor of Alabama in 1982. In that campaign, Wallace's main rival for the Democratic nomination was a young, progressive, New South candidate who lost in the run-off to Wallace by a little more than one percentage point. Wallace eked out this victory by winning one-third of the black vote in Alabama. Many political commentators observed that this unexpected turnout of black voters in favor of Wallace won him the election. It was also noted that while Alabama's black political organization endorsed Wallace's opponent, the Wallace campaign succeeded in co-opting many of the state's black preachers. Wallace went on to win easily in the general election, garnering 76% of the black vote.

However, the main characters in the novel, especially the candidate Aaron Osgood, are fictional creations. There was no attorney general running in the 1982 race for governor of Alabama. Although the then lieutenant governor and speaker of the house were candidates, those real people bear no resemblance to the fictional substitutes I've invented for the purposes of this novel. The newspaper articles, profiles, columns, editorials and letters to the editor preceding the various chapters were all written by the author of this novel, who tried to recreate the flavor of what was written about the campaign during the time it was taking place.

Former Alabama governors Fob James and Albert Brewer, along with George Wallace, are historical figures as well as off-stage characters in this novel. Concerning all three of these real people, my narrative hews to the facts of the historical record as I know it. Brandt Ayers, publisher of the Anniston *Star,* is also a historical figure, but the meeting the novel refers to between him and the fictional Aaron Osgood is likewise fictional. The family the novel

237

places in Walker Percy's former Birmingham home is a complete product of my imagination.

For any readers interested in knowing where I obtained my facts, I will list a few key sources. Besides Marshall Frady's fascinating unauthorized biography *Wallace,* there is Dan Carter's excellent book *The Politics of Rage: George Wallace, the Origins of the New Conservatism, and the Transformation of American Politics.* George Wallace's rant against Mountain Brook, Gerald Wallace's racist campaign strategy and the racist campaign ads that my characters quote from or allude to have all been collected and documented in Carter's book. In *Mudslingers: The Twenty-Five Dirtiest Political Campaigns of All Time,* Kerwin Swint portrays the 1970 gubernatorial race in Alabama between George Wallace and Albert Brewer as the nastiest campaign ever to take place in this country. To capture the tone of the 1982 gubernatorial race, Wallace's final campaign, I relied on articles primarily from the Birmingham *News.*

Two former reporters for the Birmingham *News* were of great assistance to me. One is my sister, Anna Velasco, who tracked down in the dusty archives all the articles published in that newspaper on the 1982 gubernatorial campaign. The other is Tom Gordon, who wrote about politics for the Birmingham *News* and interviewed George Wallace many times in the course of his career as a journalist. He now works as a freelance writer, and kindly consulted with me on this fictional rendering of the '82 campaign. My knowledge of what Wallace said at the Dexter Avenue Baptist Church comes from an article he wrote for the *News* entitled "Dexter Apology: Fact or Figment?" published August 31, 1997.

Once again I am indebted to Tom Uskali and Sean Smith for their numerous careful readings of this novel as it evolved. Their extensive and intelligent comments were crucial in helping me refine my work. Pat Conroy offered two brilliant suggestions, but I was only able to implement one of these because I'm not as good a writer as he is. Still, I am beholden to him for much more than the one brilliant suggestion I could actually execute. Without him and his Story River Books imprint, this novel would not be in print. Jonathan Haupt is a visionary publisher and editor, and I am grateful that his vision includes the publication of my Mountain Brook novel series. These novels have benefited greatly from the peer reviewers he has assigned to my novels, John Sledge and Lanier Scott Isom. All of these readers have been both the enthusiastic cheerleaders and the astute critics that every writer needs.

I also want to thank Kathe Telingator for her faithful and vigilant representation, and Brandon Dorion for the support which makes it all possible.

ABOUT THE AUTHOR

KATHERINE CLARK holds an A.B. degree in English from Harvard and a Ph.D. in English from Emory. She is the coauthor of the oral biographies *Motherwit: An Alabama Midwife's Story*, with Onnie Lee Logan, and with Eugene Walter for *Milking the Moon: A Southerner's Story of Life on This Planet*, a finalist for a National Book Critics Circle award. *All the Governor's Men*, the second in her series of novels featuring Laney and his students, is preceded by *The Headmaster's Darlings* and will be followed by *The Harvard Bride* and *The Ex-Suicide*, forthcoming from the University of South Carolina Press's Story River Books. Clark is currently collaborating with Pat Conroy on his oral biography, also forthcoming from the University of South Carolina Press. She lives on the Gulf Coast.